SACRIFICE

While studying for a degree in IT, Will Jordan worked a number of part-time jobs, one of which was as an extra in television and feature films. Cast as a World War Two soldier, he was put through military bootcamp and taught to handle and fire weapons in preparation for the role. The experience piqued his interest in military history, and encouraged him to learn more about conflicts past and present. Having always enjoyed writing, he used this research as the basis for his first thriller, *Redemption*, supplementing it with visits to weapon ranges in America and Eastern Europe to gain first-hand knowledge of modern weaponry. He lives in Fife with his wife and son, and is currently writing the third novel in the Ryan Drake series, *Betrayal*.

www.willjordanbooks.com

Also by Will Jordan

Redemption

WILL JORDAN
SACRIFICE

arrow books

Published by Arrow Books 2013

4 6 8 10 9 7 5 3

First published in Great Britain in 2013 by Century

Arrow Books
Random House, 20 Vauxhall Bridge Road,
London SW1V 2SA

www.randomhouse.co.uk

Addresses for companies within The Penguin Random House Group
can be found at global.penguinrandomhouse.com

The Random House Group Limited Reg. No. 954009

A CIP catalogue record for this book
is available from the British Library

ISBN 9780099574477

Typeset by Palimpsest Book Production Ltd, Falkirk, Stirlingshire

Penguin Random House is committed to a sustainable future for
our business, our readers and our planet. This book is made from
Forest Stewardship Council® certified paper.

Printed and bound in Great Britain by Clays Ltd, Elcograf S.p.A.

For Margaret, my rock

SACRIFICE

Part One

Recollection

In 1839, British troops based in India invade Afghanistan, beginning the First Anglo-Afghan War. Despite their capturing key cities, a growing tide of rebellion forces the army to withdraw two years later. Subjected to constant ambushes, the entire force is annihilated.

It is considered one of the worst disasters in British military history.

Total Casualties:
16,500 British and Indian soldiers and civilians killed
Total number of Afghan deaths unknown

Chapter 1

Parwan Province, Afghanistan, 8 August 2008

Dust.

Dust and sand and rock, stretching from horizon to horizon.

Sitting perched by the open crew door on the side of the UH-60 Black Hawk chopper, Private Lawrence 'Law' Carter watched as the arid, wasted landscape of eastern Afghanistan slid by beneath them at 120 knots.

Everywhere he looked he saw withered fields, wind-scoured outcroppings of rock, endless stretches of open dusty ground and winding, tortuous valleys that led nowhere. All of it stretched out beneath him, fading away to a hazy yellow-grey horizon that masked details and defied any estimation of distance.

The whole country looked the way he imagined the Dust Bowl of the 1930s Midwest had been – all the life and colour bleached out of everything, scoured away by the relentless wind and dust.

What a hell of a place to be fighting a war over.

He tracked the six barrels of his door-mounted M134 Minigun slowly from left to right, not really expecting to see anything, but feeling the need to do something to ease the boredom. Cruising at 2,000 feet, they were too high for him to make out much on the ground anyway.

'I heard they're sending us out tomorrow night,' a thin, nasal Texan voice remarked. Carter could almost picture the mischievous grin behind that voice. It belonged to Eric Myers; a pinched, red-headed San Antonio native who hadn't even left his home state until he joined the army. 'Night patrol, along the edge of the green zone. Captain's got us specially picked out.'

'Yeah? Who'd you blow to get that intel, Myers?' another man asked, his voice deep and gruff. Dino Hernandez, a wiry Hispanic man from Fresno, California, who had enlisted to join his two older brothers.

'It's God's honest truth, I swear,' Myers promised, as if that meant anything. Roughly 50 per cent of whatever he said was pure bullshit. 'Heard one of them tactical planning REMFs talking about it. We're on the company HQ shit list, you mark my words, brother.'

REMF, or Rear Echelon Mother Fucker, was a colloquial and obviously none too flattering term for anyone involved in the planning, but not the execution, of front-line ops.

'You mean *you're* on the shit list,' Carter replied, turning away from the Dust Bowl terrain to speak to Myers. 'Your number's been up ever since that fuck-up with the 203.'

During a firefight with Taliban insurgents several months previously, Myers, fancying himself the hero, had crouched on the flat roof of a building, taken aim at his elusive target and triggered off his M203 grenade launcher, only for the high-explosive round to slam into the stone parapet right in front of him. Fortunately for him, the projectile was designed not to arm itself until it had travelled around 20 metres.

'I guess they really are retard-proof after all,' Hernandez concluded, laughing at the memory of

Myers' panic-stricken leap from the roof, his former bravado gone.

Carter couldn't help laughing as well, and after a few moments of stubborn silence, even Myers joined in.

But one man who wasn't laughing was the fourth occupant of the crew cabin. A real gloomy customer sitting at the aft bench on the port side, directly behind Carter.

The young private couldn't help but look at him again.

He was easily in his fifties, he guessed, with a tanned, deeply lined face hidden by a greying beard that made him look a lot older. Clearly he'd been in-country a while. His eyes were staring out at the Dust Bowl through the grimy window beside him, dark and pensive.

There was a tension, a nervousness about the guy that put Carter on edge. The fact that he hadn't spoken a word to any of the men on board the chopper since they'd lifted off from Firebase Hammer thirty minutes ago only added to his disquiet. He had been bundled aboard at the last minute; a hitcher, a foreign and not altogether welcome presence.

He wasn't military – that much was obvious. There was no name tag on his body armour, no unit badge or rank insignia on his clothing. Nothing to identify him at all, in fact.

None of them had said it out loud, but they were all thinking the same thing. The guy was a spook, either CIA or NSA or some other clandestine group that was way above their pay grade. Part of another world that neither Carter nor the others had any desire to join.

But what was he doing on their chopper?

Unknown to Carter, a pair of binoculars was trained on the lumbering chopper as it beat a path through the dusty sky, exhaust fumes shimmering from the engine outlets. The thud of the main rotors from two miles away was just faintly audible in the warm air, but getting louder as the chopper approached.

The hands clutching the binoculars were big, square and strong, the digits – all eight of them – thick and powerful, hardened and calloused by years of manual labour. The last two fingers on the left hand were missing, terminating in lopsided stumps just before the first knuckle.

The field glasses were lowered, revealing a lean, gaunt face, prematurely lined and marked by a lifetime of conflict and hardship. A man, middle-aged, halfway through a life that had been neither short nor easy.

Dark eyes surrounded by deep crow's feet surveyed the rapidly approaching target, the keen mind behind them imagining the sequence of events that was about to play out.

The men inside the chopper were confident and complacent, oblivious to what was coming. They thought themselves safe, protected by altitude and armour and technology.

They thought wrong.

Myers was about to launch into another story when suddenly high-pitched threat warnings started blaring from the cockpit, the aircraft's on-board computers screaming a warning that they were being targeted by something.

Instantly Carter felt himself tense up, his heart rate soaring as his body prepared itself for a danger it didn't understand. He was a gazelle on the African plains that had just spotted a lion stalking him in the long grass. Death coming for him.

In his mind he begged for it to be a false alarm. An instrument malfunction, a blip from a nearby radar array, even some asshole on the ground with a radar gun who was curious to know how fast military choppers really travelled.

'We're being lit up,' the pilot warned.

A moment later, the bleeping alarms changed to a constant, high-pitched tone.

'Shit! We're locked up. We're locked up.'

'Anybody see anything?' the co-pilot called out.

Leaning out further, Carter looked down towards a range of low hills off to the east, saw an innocuous little puff of white smoke and felt his blood run cold.

The missile was about 1.5 miles from its target when the operator depressed the trigger. Just shy of 2,500 metres. It left its launch tube an instant later, propelled by a small disposable ejector unit that fell harmlessly away after serving its purpose. The main rocket motors kicked in a second later, and with a tearing roar the missile accelerated up to Mach 2.2 – more than twice the speed of sound.

'Missile inbound!' he yelled, more through instinct than intent.

The pilot's reaction was immediate. 'Hang on.'

Jinking the stick left and jamming the throttles wide open, he put them in a hard turn to port under full power, raising the collective to claw for more altitude. He was no nervous rookie on his first flight, but a seasoned veteran of the Afghan theatre who had been shot at by rocket-propelled grenades and small arms fire more times than he could count. He knew all the tricks, and how best to exploit them.

Turn, increase speed, gain altitude.

The Black Hawk was no Apache gunship. Its turns

were slow and lazy by comparison, like a luxury sedan set against an F1 racing car, but even then the sudden violence of the turn was enough to push Carter forcefully down into his seat.

'Deploy flares.'

An instant later, the chopper ejected a stream of bright incandescent flares from both sides, designed to confuse and disorient incoming warheads that might be homing in on the heat from their engines.

All of it was futile, because the missile stalking them had been designed to defeat such things. Ignoring the flares, it came straight at them: 1,000 feet, 500 feet, 200 feet.

The bright flash as 3 kilograms of high explosive detonated against the port engine housing was followed a moment later by an expanding cloud of superheated gas that rippled outwards, peeling back armour plates, buckling internal support struts, shattering highly stressed machinery, tearing apart hydraulic lines and electrical cables, and turning all of it into a deadly hail of shrapnel that ripped through the chopper's body, causing yet more damage.

The aircraft appeared to flinch, knocked sideways in mid-air by the force of the blast, one side crumpled, one engine reduced to a burning ruin while the other faltered and belched oily black smoke.

Hernandez, unlucky enough to be sitting next to the point of impact, didn't stand a chance. His soft and fragile body presented no resistance whatsoever as the bulkhead behind him disintegrated, fist-sized chunks of shrapnel scything right through him.

'Oh, Christ! Oh, Christ!' Myers yelled, his cries almost drowned out by the scream of overloaded machinery and the groan of rending metal as the airframe started to give way around him.

'This is Kilo Six Niner, we're going down,' the pilot managed to say, having to shout to be heard over the din of his stricken aircraft. 'I repeat, we're hit and going down.'

Further forward, Carter could do nothing but cling to his safety harness as the chopper lurched and spun towards the ground in its death throes. He had no idea how fast they were descending, whether the pilots still had any control or whether they were falling out of the sky like a stone.

The world outside was a blur of movement and lurching horizon and dusty orange sky and dirt and rocks and winding valleys that led nowhere.

The Dust Bowl.

Not far away, the silent observer watched the aircraft spiral down towards the ground, trailing smoke and flames. Its rotors were still turning, probably because the engine's freewheeling unit had automatically disengaged from the crippled drive train, but there was no purpose to its movements. If the pilots were still alive, they would be wrestling with ruptured hydraulic lines and control surfaces that were no longer connected.

He almost felt pity for them.

The missile had done its work well. There had been no spectacular explosion, no thunderous fireball like in the movies; there had just been a small, efficient flash and a jet of flame that soon died down, giving way to a pall of smoke from the crippled engines.

It had taken a good second or two for the concussive boom of the explosion to reach him, but when it did, he spread his arms as if to embrace it, revelling in the sound of the blast as it echoed off the rock walls around him.

Now he watched as the nose tilted down, the stricken craft yawed violently left as the last semblance of control vanished, and it ploughed into the ground in a spray of dust and soil and smoke.

He smiled, thinking about the reaction this attack would provoke, the fear and panic it would instil in his enemies. The game had changed today, changed for ever.

And soon, very soon, he would have the one thing he desired most – retribution.

He was alive.

For several seconds, Carter's mind could process nothing beyond that one remarkable realisation. He was alive. He could feel the blood pounding in his ears, could hear the ragged sigh of his breathing.

Somehow he had survived the crash.

As his mind snapped back into awareness, the first waves of pain rushed in against it, all struggling to reach him at once.

His world was pain. His chest felt as though it was being crushed in a vice, squeezing his lungs, every feeble attempt to draw breath bringing a fresh stab of agony. Broken ribs pressing against his lungs.

He opened his eyes with difficulty and looked around. The inside of the crew compartment was a mess of deformed metal, broken instrument panels and human bodies that had been thrown around like rag dolls in the crash.

One was dead for sure, lying sprawled against the rotor column, his head virtually severed from his shoulders by a chunk of rotor blade that had sheared off. It took Carter a moment to realise it was the pilot. Perhaps he'd been thrown from his seat on impact.

He could smell fuel. He had to get up. The shock of the crash was fading now, survival instinct taking over.

He made to get up, then instantly regretted it. Agony exploded outwards from his right leg as shattered bones grated against each other, and he let out an involuntary scream as his vision blurred.

Suddenly Carter spotted movement outside. And a moment later, two men ducked into the cabin. Silhouetted as they were against the blinding light streaming in through the open doorway, it was impossible to make out their features, though he did see the distinctive weapons they both held. AK-47 assault rifles.

Further back in the cabin, another man was dragging the limp body of the spook who had hitched a ride with them, pulling him towards the open hatch to take him outside. Carter couldn't tell if he was dead or alive.

His thoughts were disturbed when he heard Myers pleading with the armed men. 'W-we're Americans,' he stammered, crawling into view with his hands up. 'We ain't armed, man. Don't—'

With casual ease, the first man to make entry raised his weapon up to his shoulder, took aim and squeezed off a single round. There was a deafening crack that reverberated around the cabin, and suddenly the back of Myers' head exploded, blood and brain matter coating the wall behind him. Carter could feel some of it on his own face, still warm with recently extinguished life.

Too shocked to move, he could only watch as the barrel of the assault rifle swung around towards him. He should have felt fear, terror, grief at knowing his life was about to end, but none of those emotions stirred in him. There wasn't time to feel them.

He glanced outside, seeing the dust and sand and wind-scoured rocks.

What a hell of a place to die, he thought as a second sharp crack echoed through the cabin.

Chapter 2

It was a warm, humid Friday evening in the nation's capital, the sky glowing vibrant orange in the west as the sun set, with the first stars starting to appear in the deep azure expanse to the east.

It was the tail end of the rush hour, but traffic was still heavy as the last government employees filtered home after a long week. Row after row of bland, efficient saloons, SUVs and the occasional limousine rumbled along the main drags, looking as tired as their drivers.

And amongst the weary procession, a silver sports car weaved in and out, changing lanes, accelerating and braking hard, jostling for position like a racehorse in the midst of a pack.

'Come on, come on,' Ryan Drake said under his breath, gunning the accelerator to get in front of a GMC Yukon that was trying to block him out. The stressed-looking office worker at the wheel gave him a look of pure disgust.

Drake ignored such censure, took an off-ramp to escape the crowded freeway and hit the gas, pushing the Audi TT hard. The powerful German sports car wasn't great on corners, but with 250 horses under the hood, it more than made up for it on the open road. The 3.2-litre VR6

13

engine roared as he accelerated through a set of lights that had just changed to red.

He glanced at his watch and swore under his breath. He was going to be late for his rendezvous. And this was one meeting at which tardiness would not be tolerated.

'She's going to kill me. I know it.'

Seeking to divert his thoughts from this unpleasant prospect, he switched the radio on. It was the financial round-up.

'The Dow Jones fell in afternoon trading again today, closing two hundred and fifteen points down, with analysts predicting another major slump in prices amidst growing concerns of insolvency in major investment banks. Overall the Jones has fallen over twenty per cent since this time last year, with further turmoil in European markets . . .'

There were a lot of reports like this nowadays, all using terms like 'sub-prime mortgage crisis' and 'unsustainable debt burden'. The truth was obvious even to those who didn't understand the finer details – the economy was rapidly going from bad to shit to worse, and nobody knew how to fix it.

It was funny how much things could change in a year, Drake thought as he turned left at an intersection.

He soon found himself in a world of plush suburban houses, vibrant green lawns and immaculate SUVs. The whole place had the feel of a planned community, as if Walt Disney had designed it all.

Every block or two he'd pass fashionable coffee houses with tinted-glass windows and stainless-steel tables; regular hangouts for people with thick-framed glasses and hair they'd spent half an hour styling for the just-out-of-bed look, pretending to be doing something important with their laptops as they sipped their moccaccinos.

But not now. Now the tables stood empty, with scarcely a laptop or pair of designer glasses in sight. One place even had its shutters pulled down, as if the world were bracing itself for a gathering storm.

Pushing those thoughts aside, he made a hard right turn at the next junction, changed down into second gear and stamped on the pedal.

He arrived at his destination an hour and fifteen minutes late. Not bad by his standards, but unacceptable for the people he was meeting.

Killing the engine, Drake stepped out into the warm evening, the chirp of crickets and other night insects plainly audible. Tiny flies buzzed and flitted back and forth around him, circling each other in lazy arcs like ancient biplanes locked in an endless fight for supremacy. A house on the opposite side of the road had the stars and stripes flying above their porch – it was that kind of neighbourhood – but the flag barely moved in the still air.

He inhaled, tasting the scent of fresh-cut grass, the fragrant bloom of flowers, the sharp tang of newly sawn wood and above all, the smoky aroma of meat cooking on a nearby grill.

Or perhaps burning was the more accurate definition.

Hoping his olfactory senses were mistaken, Drake jogged up the brick driveway to the front door and knocked. There was no reply.

He knocked again, louder this time, only to meet with the same result.

'Oi, John! Anyone alive in there?' he called out,

backing up a little so his voice could be heard in the backyard.

At last he was rewarded with a reply.

'Round back, buddy! Gate's open.'

Vaulting over a shrub at the edge of the porch, Drake headed for the side gate and let himself in.

John Keegan's home, in stark contrast to his often dishevelled personal appearance, was a neat, well-ordered suburban house in Brookeville, a small town about 15 miles west of central DC. Indeed, 'small town' was the perfect description of this place. It was the sort of area where people left their cars unlocked overnight, where everyone knew each other and stopped to shoot the breeze when they passed in the street.

Drake doubted he'd spoken to his own neighbours more than a dozen times in all the years he'd lived there.

As he'd smugly admitted on more than one occasion, Keegan had picked up this place for a song, buying it at auction when the previous owner died. The fact that the roof had leaked, the electrics had been shot and it hadn't been redecorated in twenty years hadn't fazed him for a second.

Keegan was an eternally practical man, throwing himself into the renovation with the kind of patient confidence that somehow reminded Drake of his grandfather. Guys like that belonged to a different generation; one that just seemed to know how such things were done.

But the house was a mere side-show tonight. Keegan's pride and joy was the solid brick grill he'd built for himself in the backyard. True to his Southern roots, it was a genuine mesquite wood-burner rather than gas or propane.

In his own words, gas was for pussies – real men cooked with wood.

16

It made little difference in Drake's opinion, but then he supposed his palate had been ruined by his days as an SAS operative. Their barbecues had consisted of an oil drum cut in half lengthwise and filled with just about anything that would burn. And if they'd been struggling on that score, there was usually a jerrycan of gasoline on hand to help things along.

Keegan grinned like a lunatic as he worked the barbecue, beer in one hand and spatula in the other. His scruffy mane of blond hair was hidden beneath a frayed baseball cap emblazoned with the Carolina Panthers team logo. Even his bushy moustache looked like it needed trimming.

His DIY abilities were unfortunately not matched by his cooking skills, and he seemed to have an innate desire to cremate everything that had once been alive.

'Nice of you to join us, mate,' he remarked. For some reason, he seemed to find it amusing to say the word 'mate' in his distinctive Southern drawl.

Keira Frost, standing a safe distance from the billowing smoke, wasn't quite so subtle.

'Where the hell have you been, Ryan? You stop for dinner on the way?'

Drake forced a smile and nodded at the grill. 'Can you blame me?'

Of course, there was another reason he'd been late tonight. It was the same reason he was late for almost everything outside of work, even if he wasn't prepared to admit it. Burying himself in work helped him forget what had happened last year.

And it helped him forget the woman behind it all.

Frost didn't look convinced, and seemed on the verge of saying something else when Keegan, perceptive enough not to push the issue, nodded to the steel bucket off to his left. Beers of various brands floated in the icy water. 'Well, you're here now. Grab yourself a beer, man. I'm almost done.'

Drake smiled and grabbed a Corona, wiping most of the water off before popping the lid open. He was more of a Peroni man, but when his throat was dry and the beer was plentiful, he wasn't complaining.

'So what's the deal, John?' Frost asked, taking a pull from her own bottle. 'Were you taking a shit when they taught us all how to cook or what?'

The older man grinned. 'Damn. You're on fire tonight, Frost.'

'So are those burgers if you leave them any longer.'

Drake smiled at the banter between the two specialists. They had served together on a dozen operations over the past couple of years, and despite their differences, a certain grudging affection had developed between them.

That was part of the reason Keegan had taken to hosting occasional barbecue evenings, particularly when the team had just finished their debriefings and wrapped up another operation. It was like a wrap party; something to bring an op to a definitive end.

Or in Keegan's case, it was an excuse to open the tequila and put the world to rights.

A slow smile spread across Keegan's face as he turned to look at Frost. 'Hey, I meant to ask you – how's that car of yours?'

Even in the dim evening light, Drake could see the colour rise to Frost's face. The young woman had bought an old, beat-up Ford Mustang at the start of the year, hoping to turn it into a restoration project. The last time Drake had had the heart to ask about it, the entire engine block had been lying in pieces in her garage.

'Doing just fine,' she replied, but there was no conviction in her voice.

Keegan paused in his work, his expression pensive. 'You know, my daddy once said never let women near guns, cars or VCRs. Sometimes I think he was wiser than he knew.'

Frost wasn't rising to the bait. 'Yeah, well, I suppose that kind of attitude was common in the 1930s. You know, when you were a kid.'

Seated at the edge of the garden's decking area – another flawless creation built from scratch by Keegan – Drake took a pull on his beer, closed his eyes and exhaled slowly.

After a day of flickering computer screens, ringing phones and whirring printers, it was a relief to be outside in the fresh air, just listening to the sounds of the world around him.

'Hey.'

Drake opened his eyes as Frost sat down beside him.

He winced, already bracing himself for another verbal assault. 'Listen, Keira. About tonight –'

To his surprise, she shook her head. 'Don't worry about it. You're here now, at least – that's the important thing.'

Drake raised an eyebrow. It wasn't like her to be so forgiving.

Her unexpected conciliatory attitude had caught him off guard. He felt awkward, unsure of what to say, but he didn't want to let the conversation falter.

He recalled something about her moving house, yet the details remained elusive, like a half-formed idea long since discarded. His mind was a jumble of reports and classified documents and deadlines and a dozen other work-related problems that seemed to swallow up everything else.

'So how are you doing with the new apartment?' he asked, deciding to chance his hand. 'Moved your stuff in?'

The flicker in her eyes told him he'd made a big mistake. 'Ryan, that was three months ago. And it was my sister who was moving.'

Drake's heart sank. He worked with these people almost every day, spent far more time with them than his own family, yet at times like this he felt he barely knew them. The only reason he was even here tonight was because Frost had parked herself in his office and refused to leave until he agreed to come.

Her excuse had been that she didn't intend to suffer Keegan's food alone, but even then he'd sensed a deeper motivation. She'd wanted to keep him involved, to make him focus on something outside work.

It was a valiant but futile effort.

'I'm sorry, Keira,' he said, taking a pull on the beer to hide his embarrassment. 'My mind's been all over the place lately.'

In truth, his mind had been in one place, and one place only – Iraq, last year. After being hunted as a fugitive by his own people and travelling halfway across the world, he had uncovered conspiracies and corruption that went almost to the very top of the Agency.

Then it had all unravelled. The one man who could help them had been executed, while those behind the entire thing had not only survived, but prospered. Drake himself was only alive because of a deal struck by his friend Dan Franklin, buying his security in exchange for silence.

Drake's life was now in limbo; he was unable to leave the Agency, yet knew that one day his luck would run out. He understood now how Damocles must have felt at that banquet table, trying to enjoy his roast beef with a bloody great sword hanging over him.

'Easy mistake to make.' Frost was silent for a few moments, contemplating something. Or maybe weighing up whether the time was right to say what she wanted to. 'Mind if I ask you something?'

He looked at her, wondering what was coming. 'You've never let it stop you before.'

'Why do you push yourself so hard?' she asked, dead serious.

Drake hesitated. Keira Frost was a straight talker who wasn't afraid to voice her opinions, but it wasn't like her to get into this deep and meaningful stuff.

'You're in that office working until Christ knows when,' she went on. 'You barely do anything in the real world. I mean, shit, I had to practically hold a gun to your head to get you here tonight. My company that bad?'

'I'll take the Fifth on that one,' he said, hoping to lighten the mood but soon realising it was a wasted effort. She wasn't about to let this one go. 'Look, it's just the way things are with work . . .'

'Ryan, there's always going to be too much work if you want there to be.'

Drake was careful to avoid her gaze. 'I imagine you're going somewhere with this,' he prompted, wishing he didn't sound so defensive.

'You're burning yourself out,' she said simply. 'It's like you're trying to punish yourself, or prove something. Either way, it's not good.'

'For who?'

'For anyone,' she answered. 'If you're exhausted and strung out, you're not thinking straight, which means you put all our lives at risk next time we're in the field.'

21

She fixed him with a searching look. 'And as much as I'll hate myself for saying this, I'm worried about you. I don't want to see you burn out. You don't deserve it.'

At last Drake turned to look at her, his vivid green eyes shimmering in the glow of electric lights nearby.

But before he could reply, he felt his phone buzz in his pocket. Out of habit he fished it out and checked the caller ID.

It was George Breckenridge – the officer in charge of the CIA's Shepherd programme, and Drake's immediate superior. The man who'd previously held that post, Dan Franklin, had been promoted to director of Special Activities Division last year, leaving a power vacuum that had to be filled.

Drake had little contact with his former friend now.

There was little choice but to take the call. In the Agency, if one's boss called outside work hours on a Friday night, chances were the news wasn't good.

And yet, for once, he welcomed the distraction.

'Yeah, George?' Drake said.

Breckenridge was, as always, brisk and to the point. He had little time for grunts like Drake, and made no attempt to hide that fact. 'We need you to come in. Where are you?'

'Brookeville. Keegan's place. Why, what's going on?'

'We've got a situation here. We want your input.'

Which told him nothing at all. Not that he was surprised – this was an open line, and while Drake doubted the Russians or Chinese were listening in on his every phone call, there were still rules. More than one op had been compromised in the CIA's history by casual conversations on unsecured lines.

'How urgent is it?'

'I'm sorry, did I give the impression this was a dinner

invitation?' Breckenridge asked, employing his most patronising tone. 'We want you and your team here five minutes ago. Exactly what part of this is unclear?'

Not for the first time, Drake found himself seriously questioning Franklin's choice of successor. Whatever the vetting process for that position, it clearly wasn't designed to filter out arseholes. 'Abundantly.'

'Good. I'll see you in Conference Room One in thirty minutes.' He hung up without saying anything further.

'Prick,' Drake said under his breath as he closed down his phone.

Frost regarded him suspiciously. 'Trouble in paradise?'

'SNAFU, as your Marine cousins are fond of saying.'

She nodded sagely. SNAFU – Situation Normal: All Fucked Up.

'What does he want?'

Drake tipped back his beer and downed it in one gulp.

'Well, the good news is you've escaped Keegan's food tonight.'

Chapter 3

One thing Drake had to commend the Agency on was their sense of irony. The George Bush Center for Intelligence (itself a contradiction in terms) was where some of the most important decisions in the world of espionage, counter-terrorism, clandestine operations and global politics were made, yet the place reminded him more of a garden centre than an intelligence-gathering hub.

Set within acres of well-maintained parkland, there were trees and flower beds and neatly trimmed lawns everywhere. The main entrance was even a long glass-covered archway with plants and expensive decor. All they needed to complete the look was a coy pond and a café selling overpriced coffee and pastries.

There were two main elements to the CIA's headquarters – the Old Headquarters Building (OHB) and the imaginatively named New Headquarters Building (NHB). The OHB was a double H-block arrangement that dated back to the Agency's beginnings in the 1950s, while the NHB consisted of a pair of six-storey office towers that dominated the landscape like a pair of modern-day castles.

Drake and his two companions were headed for the

24

northernmost of the two towers. After passing through the main security checkpoint and traversing the length of the glass tunnel, they took a left at the T-junction.

'This had better be fucking good,' Frost hissed, striding along beside her two companions with a look in her eye that would give most guard dogs pause for thought. 'I'm talking alien invasion or Presidential kidnapping here.'

'That how you define good, huh?' Keegan quipped.

'Big words, John,' she bit back. 'Thought you rednecks were still learning how to read and write.'

The older man flashed a grin. 'Must've been a child prodigy.'

Their route took them past an outdoor seating area overlooking the infamous *Kryptos* sculpture. Appearing as four large metal plates engraved with a seemingly meaningless stream of letters, *Kryptos* had been an object of fascination for code breakers and conspiracy theorists since it was unveiled nearly twenty years earlier. The code on three of the plates had since been broken, but the fourth remained stubbornly unsolved.

Even today, Drake knew that people within the Agency liked to hang out around it, particularly the intelligence analysts who made a living breaking codes and sought to test their mental prowess. He had never understood the fascination himself. Breaking codes for bragging rights made about as much sense to him as jumping into an empty swimming pool. Still, each to their own.

Passing through the automatic doors that led to the north tower, he and his companions found the nearest elevator and rode it up to the fifth floor, Drake ignoring the curious glance from the young man in a sharp business suit who got in at the second floor. Langley was a shirt-and-tie kind of place, but unfortunately Drake wasn't a shirt-and-tie kind of man, especially not tonight.

If Breckenridge wanted him here so urgently, he would have to take him as he came – in this case clad in cargo pants, a casual shirt and trainers that had seen better days.

Frost didn't take kindly to the disapproving look either. She had been in a foul mood since finding out that her planned evening of drinking and relaxation had been whisked away and replaced with a high-priority briefing with a man nobody liked.

'Something wrong, pal?' she challenged, staring right at him.

She was spoiling for a fight, and the young man sensed it. Saying nothing, he glanced away and suddenly became very interested in checking his cufflinks.

Smart guy, Drake thought.

Conference room 1 was first in line as they stepped out on the fifth floor. It was a big, plush room reserved for top brass and high-level briefings, partly because it looked impressive but mostly because it was totally secure from any form of surveillance. The fact that the meeting was being held there told Drake a lot more than Breckenridge's ambiguous phone call.

It was in this very room, over a year ago, that he had first been handed the mission to break into a Siberian prison and rescue a woman identified only by her code name Maras. It had seemed like a simple objective at the time; only later had he discovered how wrong he'd been.

Drake hadn't been back here since. Normally his orders and debriefings were handled in one of the many smaller, more utilitarian rooms downstairs which were more suited to the unobtrusive nature of his work.

Access to the room was controlled by a swipe-card terminal next to the door. Drake's personal access card would have been cleared in advance, so all he had to do was swipe it through the reader, punch in his PIN, and he was good to go.

There was a single beep and a crisp click as the lock disengaged. As always, everything worked flawlessly here. Here we go, he thought.

As the door swung open, he couldn't help comparing the room before him to the one vividly imprinted on his memory.

The place hadn't changed much in the past year. Same long conference table topped with a single unbroken length of polished mahogany that probably cost more than he made in a year. Same high-backed leather chairs, same expensive silver coffee set. Same majestic view over Langley's garden-centre grounds, the dense woodland beyond and the muddy sweep of the Potomac about half a mile away.

In fact, the only thing different about the room was the occupant. Instead of Dan Franklin and Marcus Cain, the former director of Special Activities Division, this time he was greeted by the fleshy, unsmiling face of George Breckenridge.

In his early fifties, greying and overweight in a way that suggested he'd never really been in shape, Breckenridge looked exactly like what he was – a guy who'd been shining seats with his not-inconsiderable arse since leaving college. God only knew what strip-lighted back-room office Franklin had dug this guy up from, but it wasn't a place Drake was keen to visit.

He knew little about Breckenridge, because theirs was not the kind of relationship that encouraged the exchange of personal information, but he knew one thing – his volume of admin and paperwork had more than doubled since Breckenridge took over the Shepherd programme.

It was hard to say how much Breckenridge knew of

Drake's past exploits, or indeed whether he'd been brought in specifically to keep an eye on him and ensure he didn't cause further trouble. Either way, Drake had resolved to keep him at arm's length and tell him as little as possible.

'Drake. Good of you to join us.' There was no thought of calling Drake by his first name; Breckenridge wasn't that sort of man. He barely even acknowledged Keegan and Frost.

He eyed Drake's casual clothes with unveiled disdain. His own dark blue business suit looked as though it had been pressed that very morning.

In response, Drake gave a dismissive shrug. 'You wanted me here as soon as, George. Well, you've got me.' He always called his boss George because he knew it pissed him off, and that made Drake feel just a little better. 'So what's this about?'

Breckenridge said nothing to that. Instead, he reached for the speaker phone in the centre of the table and punched in a couple of buttons. The dial tone sounded three times before it was answered.

'Yeah?' a familiar voice asked, sounding tired and strung out.

'It's Breckenridge, sir.' He sounded like a schoolboy talking to the headmaster. 'They're here.'

In a moment, the voice changed, becoming more focused and authoritative. 'Good. I'll be right along.'

The phone clicked off, leaving the two men standing on opposite sides of the table in an awkward silence. Neither was willing to sit down, as if it would be seen as a sign of weakness.

Frost had no such compunction, and immediately helped herself to a chair, tilting it back as far as it would go. Keegan followed suit a moment later.

Drake occupied himself staring over Breckenridge's shoulder, watching a red sports car cruising along the road on the far side of the Potomac. He hoped the driver was having a better evening than him.

At last the doors buzzed and clicked open, and Drake turned to greet his old friend.

Dan Franklin had been an infantryman once upon a time. He and Drake had served in the same composite task force in Afghanistan, until a roadside bomb put an end to his military career and very nearly his life. The old shrapnel wounds had left him with ongoing back pain that worsened after long periods of inactivity.

But as the director strode into the room, Drake paused a beat, taken aback by the change in his friend. Franklin had just turned forty, yet he looked many years older. His forehead was etched with deep worry lines, and there was a visible tension in his posture, as if he carried a heavy weight on his shoulders. The burden of responsibility was, it seemed, not an easy one to bear.

Franklin glanced at Drake, and for a moment he saw a glimmer of warmth in the older man's eyes. Franklin's right arm moved a little as if to shake hands, but he quickly thought better of it and turned away, making for the far end of the conference table. He was almost able to make it seem as if the gesture had never happened. Almost, but not quite.

'Good to see you again, Ryan,' he said, though his words were as stiff and formal as his posture. 'How have you been?'

'Can't complain,' Drake replied, wondering how long it had been since they'd last spoken. He certainly hadn't seen much of the man since his promotion last year, which he supposed wasn't surprising. The Shepherd teams were just a small gear in the complex machine that was Special Activities Division.

That seemed to satisfy Franklin. He gestured to the chairs running the length of the table. 'Please, have a seat.' He glanced at Frost and Keegan with a raised eyebrow. 'I see your team's ahead of you.'

'We don't stand on ceremony in this unit, sir,' Frost replied innocently. 'That's the way Ryan trained us.'

Drake shot her a sharp glance as he helped himself to a chair, but said nothing. Now wasn't the time for petty reprimands.

'I was just bringing Mr Drake up to speed, sir,' Breckenridge said.

Franklin gave a curt nod that made him look exactly like what he was – a senior executive impatient with trivialities. 'Then don't let me stop you.'

Breckenridge coughed, clearing his throat, and turned his attention to the wireless keyboard in front of him. A few keystrokes and mouse clicks were enough to bring up an image on the big flat-screen television at the far end of the room.

The image was a personnel photograph of a man in his mid-fifties. With a greying beard, dishevelled hair, strong and severe features, and a nose that looked as if it had been broken at least once before, he was a serious-looking customer. The hard, penetrating look in his eyes told Drake that the man was a field operative.

'This is Hal Mitchell, one of our case officers based in Afghanistan,' Breckenridge began. 'He's been with the Agency nearly twenty-five years now, and he's an expert in that theatre. A good man.'

Drake would take his word on that one. 'Smashing. So what's the problem?'

Breckenridge shot him an impatient glance, as if he

was a magician whose trick had been spoiled at the crucial moment. 'About twelve hours ago, Mitchell boarded a Black Hawk chopper heading for one of our firebases about fifty miles east of Kabul. He never made it back.'

He brought up another image, this one showing the charred and blackened remains of what might once have been a helicopter airframe. Drake could only assume the fuel tanks had gone up, because the entire thing looked as if it had been blasted apart from the inside. The metal skeleton was warped and twisted by the extreme heat.

'His chopper was brought down by some kind of surface-to-air missile while en route to Bagram,' Breckenridge went on. 'By the time a search-and-rescue team arrived on site, well, there wasn't much left to recover. Five men were killed in the attack – the pilots, plus three army passengers.'

'What about Mitchell, sir?' Frost asked. Something about the way she said 'sir' held a note of contempt – a fact that was not lost on Breckenridge.

He looked at her for a few moments, seemingly on the verge of rebuking her, then thought better of it. 'About an hour ago, we received this.'

A couple of mouse clicks, and the display changed as a video file started to play. Drake once again found himself looking at Hal Mitchell, only this time he was looking very different from his file photo.

This time the man was duct-taped to a crude wooden chair, his mouth gagged, his clothes ripped and torn and stained with blood, from injuries sustained either in the crash or afterwards. His head lolled to one side, his eyes barely open, one of them blackened and swelling shut.

Drake felt his stomach churn. He had seen videos like this before, and could guess where this one was heading.

The camera, shaky and clearly manipulated by an amateur, zoomed out a little to show Mitchell's surroundings. He was in a room of some kind. There was a bare brick wall behind him, the mortar crumbling, the stones cracked and stained in places by yellow mould. Electric light was coming from an off-camera source, though it flickered from time to time as if the bulb was about to give out.

Another man walked into view. Dressed in loose flowing trousers, a heavy, worn-looking camouflage jacket and ancient webbing that looked as if it had been pilfered from a dead Russian twenty years earlier, it didn't take a genius to work out that he was an insurgent. He was tall and lean, and even the thick jacket couldn't mask his spare frame.

He was an older man, his skin leathery and lined from years of sun and wind, his heavy brows and thick beard greying. Drake could have sworn he recognised him but immediately discounted the possibility. There was no way the man he was thinking of could be on this video.

'You know now what we can do,' he began, his voice deep and heavily accented. 'None of your men are safe from us. Not on the ground, not in the cities, and not in the air. We can strike anywhere we wish, at any time. Nothing can stop us, because we are Allah's holy warriors. Everywhere we go, we will root out traitors, unbelievers and spies.'

At this, he gestured to Mitchell.

'You send men like this to *our* country to turn *our own people* against us, to ask the faithful to betray their brothers. And you dare to call *us* terrorists?'

Reaching into his heavy camouflage jacket, he withdrew an automatic pistol. Drake couldn't be sure, but it looked like a Browning 9mm; a reliable old semi-automatic that had been around since the 1930s.

But there was another thing Drake noticed as he pulled the jacket aside to draw the weapon. The last two fingers of the man's hand were missing. In that instant, he felt as though a knife had been driven into his stomach.

He knew this man.

Without hesitation, the insurgent aimed the gun downwards and calmly squeezed the trigger. There was a flash, a sharp crack, and suddenly Mitchell was no longer semi-conscious. His body went rigid and he strained against his bonds, screaming into his gag, his eyes wide with agony. A crimson stain was now spreading out across the left leg of his trousers.

'Fuck . . .' Frost said under her breath, shaking her head.

Drake ignored her, concentrating instead on the video.

The gag muffled Mitchell's cries, but the gunman was forced to raise his voice to be heard when he spoke again.

'You are illegally holding dozens of our brothers captive inside the Parwan Detention Facility. You will release these prisoners, make a public statement condemning the illegal torture and interrogation of innocent men, and shut down the facility for ever. If you do this, your man will be returned to you unharmed. Well, more or less.' With malicious glee, he pressed the barrel of his pistol into the bullet wound on Mitchell's leg, prompting another agonised groan. 'If you do not comply by midday on August 14th, we will execute this spy and shoot down more of your aircraft. And believe me when I say our next target will be . . . bigger.'

A moment later, the screen was replaced by a blur of movement as the camera operator turned the device on its side to power it down, then at last the feed went blank.

Silence reigned for several seconds as each of them digested what they had seen and heard, though Drake was quick to break it.

'Tell me that isn't who I think it is, Dan.' The initial shock of his discovery was rapidly giving way to anger.

Franklin shook his head. 'Facial recognition confirmed it. It's him, Ryan.'

Frost glanced at the two men. 'What's the deal here? Who is this asshole?'

'His name's Kourash Anwari. We believe he's former Mujahideen,' Franklin explained. 'He fought against the Soviets back in the eighties, then formed his own militia group during the civil war that followed. Mercenaries, basically. They pretty much dropped off our radar once the Taliban came to power. It was only after we invaded in 2001 that he appeared again, this time working for the insurgents.'

'The Taliban hiring mercs now?' Keegan asked.

'We do. Why shouldn't they?' Franklin shrugged. 'It's a case of supply and demand, really. Now that al-Qaeda's on the ropes, there's a big market for trained men ready to fight.'

The CIA, along with various other military and intelligence agencies, had been quietly eliminating many of al-Qaeda's senior leaders over the past seven years, more or less crippling their higher command structure. As a result, al-Qaeda had to all intents and purposes ceased to exist as a coherent organisation. These days it was a fictitious blanket term used only by the news media.

The reality was far more complex, and ever changing. Factions and splinter groups were on the rise, made up either of lower-level al-Qaeda commanders, former

Mujahideen who had once fought alongside the West against the Soviets, or new groups eager to join the global jihad. Freed from any form of centralised command or control, and able to indulge their wildest excesses, these groups were rapidly becoming a nightmare for Western intelligence agencies.

'We eventually caught up with him near the Pakistan border. We sent in a strike team to take him down.' Franklin glanced over at Drake, who had remained silent throughout this discussion. 'Ryan led the team. He's also the reason the guy's missing a couple of fingers.'

Finally Drake looked up. 'And now he's free and shooting down helicopters,' he said, his tone faintly accusing. 'Care to explain why, Dan?'

Franklin cleared his throat and looked down at the folder in front of him. 'Anwari was being held in one of our . . . facilities in the east of the country.'

He was referring to a Black Site, Drake knew. Such facilities were scattered all across Afghanistan, and usually served as secure locations where terrorist suspects could be held without trial, interrogated and tortured without official accountability. Since nobody knew they existed, human rights laws could be effectively disregarded there.

'Apparently the facility was attacked in a coordinated night raid. In the confusion, Anwari and several others managed to get out.'

Drake shook his head, hardly believing what he was hearing. He had risked his life to take that piece of shit out of the game for ever, and now here he was, back to his winning ways.

'That was last year. Since then, Anwari has reconstituted his militia group and started a guerrilla war against us. They've staged at least a dozen bombings in and around Kabul, plus sniper and RPG attacks. Now it seems they're moving up in the world, literally. Shooting down aircraft is a whole new ball game.'

Air superiority was one of the few advantages that ISAF (International Security Assistance Force) enjoyed over the insurgents. If they lost control of the air, the war in Afghanistan was quickly going to turn into the second Vietnam that everyone had always feared it would.

'They've got us by the balls on this one, and we need to respond. Mitchell's too valuable to lose.'

'Why? What was he working on out there?' Drake asked.

Breckenridge cut in. 'Drake, I'm sure I don't need to remind you about operational security. It's not necessary—'

Franklin silenced him with a raised hand, which was good for all concerned. Drake had been seconds away from telling him to go fuck himself.

'He was part of a programme to establish an intelligence network amongst the civilian population out there,' Franklin explained. 'Most of them know something about Taliban activity, but they're too scared to tell anyone. They certainly won't approach ISAF with intel because they know the Taliban will be watching. Mitchell was there to try to change that, and by all accounts he was making progress. He knows a lot of names and addresses, if you catch my drift.'

Drake was starting to see the implications. 'So if they get him to talk . . .'

'He could compromise the entire network,' Franklin finished for him. 'As you can see, their methods aren't exactly sophisticated, but they're effective. Mitchell might crack, in which case we've lost a year's worth of intel. Needless to say, we can't let that happen.'

Drake knew what was coming, but he wanted to hear Franklin say it.

'You know what I'm going to ask of you, Ryan. I need you to take your team out there, find out what happened to Mitchell and bring him home. And you need to work fast. As our friend on the video made clear, time is of the essence.' He paused a few moments, leaning forward a little, his hands resting on the polished table. 'That's all I've got. The rest is up to you.'

Frost wasted no time voicing her thoughts. 'Sir, we just spent the last three weeks hunting pirates in Somalia. Don't you have another Shepherd team who can handle this?'

'None with Ryan's experience and knowledge of the target,' Franklin admitted. 'Anyone else I sent would be at an immediate disadvantage.'

There could be no more stalling, Drake knew. Franklin needed a decision now. He wouldn't order Drake and his team to go, wouldn't order anyone in fact, because he needed to know that whoever took this operation on was totally committed to its success.

You can walk away if you want.

'All right. I'm in.'

No, you can't. You never could.

He glanced at Frost. 'It's your call, Keira. I won't force you to go.'

He knew what she was going to say, but he had to ask anyway, had to give her the chance to back out.

The young specialist returned his searching look for a long moment before rolling her eyes. 'Shit, Ryan. You know I've never left you hanging,' she said irritably. 'Despite my better judgement.'

He would take that as a yes. It was about as close to a caring sentiment as she was likely to get.

Last of all he turned his eyes to Keegan. 'John, what about you?'

With wide open spaces, scant cover and plenty of high ground, Afghanistan was a sniper's paradise. Keegan's skills might well prove invaluable.

The veteran sniper raised his bushy eyebrows. 'Somebody's got to keep you two under control. Of course I'm in.'

Drake nodded. As Frost had reminded him, neither of them had let him down before, and he hadn't expected them to start today. Still, he had to know for sure.

'We're going to need some kind of forensics expert to go over the chopper wreck,' he said, already compiling a mental list of requirements. 'Preferably someone who knows about surface-to-air missiles. Anything we can learn from the crash site might help us track down Mitchell.'

He couldn't think of anyone off the top of his head who would fit that particular bill. They had weapons specialists and forensics experts, but no one with an intimate knowledge of missile systems.

'Already covered,' Franklin assured him, sliding a personnel folder across the table to him. 'We've got an explosives expert named McKnight seconded to your team for the duration of this op. She's not part of the Shepherd programme, but what she doesn't know about modern infantry weapons, isn't worth knowing.'

Drake glanced down at the folder, studying the file picture. The face staring back at him was early thirties, evenly proportioned, with pale skin, dark shoulder-length hair and hazel-coloured eyes. He wouldn't have called her beautiful, but there was a certain gleam in those eyes that caught his attention. Her lips were upturned a little at the corners, as if something amusing had just come to mind as the picture was taken.

'She's been in-country defusing IEDs for the past few months, but she's been briefed on the situation. She'll rendezvous with you when you arrive.'

Drake regarded him with a raised eyebrow. 'You told her we were coming?'

He saw a glimmer of a smile. 'Anticipation, Ryan. I knew you wouldn't turn this down.'

Drake said nothing to that. Just as he'd known Frost and Keegan wouldn't refuse the mission, Franklin no doubt expected the same of him.

'That still leaves us light on firepower,' he pointed out, switching back to more practical matters. 'If we find Mitchell, we'll need a heavy assault team to get him out.'

'It's Afghanistan, Drake. There are Special Forces units on station who can handle assault and rescue ops,' Breckenridge reminded him. 'And I'm sure they'd be spoiling for some payback on the guys who shot down one of their choppers.'

'Agreed,' Franklin said, which prompted a smile from his subordinate. 'Your goal is to track down Mitchell. Let the military do the rest.'

Drake rubbed his jaw. His mandate as a Shepherd team leader allowed him to requisition military resources if the situation demanded it, though it was far from an ideal working arrangement for either party.

'Fine, as long as we have overall control. I don't want a turf war.'

'It won't be,' Franklin promised him, arching his back a little to relieve the stiff muscles. 'Now I suggest you grab your gear and whatever else you need. We've got you a spot on the next flight out from Andrews, which leaves in . . .' He checked his watch – an expensive Breitling model, Drake noted. 'Just over four hours. Briefings and intel will have to be handled en route.'

That was fine as far as Drake was concerned. The sooner they got out there, the sooner he could begin his hunt for Kourash.

Franklin saw the look in his eyes and guessed his thoughts well enough.

'Remember, this isn't a search-and-destroy mission, Ryan. Your goal is to find Mitchell and bring him home. Don't make this personal.'

Too late, Drake thought.

Part Two

Accession

In 1878, British troops once again invade Afghanistan. Again they succeed in capturing Kabul, but rebellions and casualties continue. The war concludes with the Treaty of Gandamak, signalling the withdrawal of British forces from the country.

Total Casualties:
10,000 British soldiers killed
5,000 Afghan soldiers killed
Number of civilian deaths unknown

Chapter 4

Drake gritted his teeth as the aircraft rocked and shuddered like an ancient sailing ship caught in a gale, jarring his spine against the exposed aluminium airframe. Outside, the engines whined and roared as the pilots adjusted their power output, trying to compensate for the vicious high-altitude winds which hammered them without remorse.

The C-17 Globemaster that had been their home for the past fourteen hours was one of the biggest aircraft in the USAF's inventory. Each was capable of carrying nearly 80,000 kilos of equipment, and by the looks of things, this one was filled to capacity.

Boxes, crates of all shapes and sizes, steel drums and machinery he couldn't begin to identify were all crammed in there, all shrink-wrapped, painstakingly labelled and catalogued, fitted on rolling pallets and lashed to the deck. It reminded him more of a warehouse than a plane.

The flight across the Atlantic had taken a good eight hours, with a refuelling layover at Ramstein in Germany followed by another hop to Turkey. He had no idea what time zone they were in, or indeed what time of day or night it was out there.

All he knew was that he was cold, tired, uncomfortable, and by now thoroughly sick of air travel. He was almost looking forward to disembarking into a war zone.

Still, his enforced inactivity had at least afforded him some time to review Mitchell's personnel file.

Harrison Mitchell, born 6 June 1952, enlisted US Marine Corps in 1970 before mustering out ten years later. He'd joined the Agency shortly thereafter, working first as a paramilitary operative and then as a case officer in the Middle East. As far as Drake could make out, his service record was impeccable, and he'd been recommended for promotion several times, finally retiring from field ops in 2001.

Then, six months ago he'd requested a transfer to the Afghan field office. Drake couldn't help but wonder why a man in his late fifties would throw in a comfortable job at Langley to get his hands dirty once more. Was it simply itchy feet, or a desire to prove he could still cut it against the younger crop of operatives? Or was it something else?

His thoughts were interrupted when the plane's loadmaster wandered over to join him. The tag on his flight suit identified him as Walcott. 'Hey, man. How you holding up?'

Drake stifled a groan. A stocky young man of perhaps twenty-five years, with a beaming grin and a never-ending supply of stories, Walcott approached life with the kind of manic enthusiasm that made Born Again Christians look positively subdued. There was just no shutting the guy up.

'Looking forward to being on the ground again,' Drake said, pasting on a weary smile. 'No offence.'

Walcott threw back his head and laughed. 'Fuck, man, that's all part of the service! Doesn't matter how nervous guys are about going to Afghanistan – by the end of a sixteen-hour flight, they're fucking desperate to get on the ground!'

'How much longer do you think it'll be?' Drake couldn't help asking. What he really meant was, 'How much longer do I have to put up with you?'

Walcott checked his watch. 'We're almost there, my man. Should be on the ground in twenty minutes, tops.'

Drake frowned. 'We haven't started descending.'

'We don't until the last minute – standard precaution right now. Some poor bastards got their Black Hawk shot out from under them the other day,' he added, looking serious for perhaps the first time. 'When it's time to go in, trust me, you'll know about it. Gets a little bumpy but it's a hell of a fucking ride. Better than a roller coaster, that's for damn sure.'

Perhaps so, but at least on roller coasters you don't have to worry about people launching surface-to-air missiles at you, Drake thought. As if sensing his disquiet, the aircraft lurched upward, followed by a sickening drop that left his stomach several feet higher than his body.

Seeing his unhappy expression, Walcott grinned. 'Hey, you think this is rough? Trust me, this is nothing! Couple of months back, we were hauling a Marine Corps rifle platoon and we hit a big motherfucker ice storm over Turkmenistan. Or was it Tajikistan? Fuck it, all the Stans are the same to me. All shitholes. Anyway, the pilots were damn near breaking their arms trying to keep us in the air, and even I was starting to shit myself, then all of a sudden one of the jarheads blows chunks everywhere. Straight away the two guys next to him started throwing up too. Before I knew what was happening, we had a whole cargo hold full of puking Marines.'

Despite himself, Drake couldn't help smiling. 'So what did you do?'

'I bailed the fuck out of there and let them get on with it – no use messin' with stuff like that. Poor bastards had to spend the rest of the flight ankle-deep in puke. Most of 'em looked like the living dead by the time they got off. Made for a fuckin' awesome YouTube video though.'

Before Drake could reply, Walcott cocked his head as his radio headset sparked up. Hitting the transmit button at his throat, he said, 'Roger that, flight.'

Glancing at Drake, he pointed to the cockpit and gave an apologetic shrug. 'Gotta go, dude. Keep it real.'

With that, he departed, making for the ladder leading to the deck above. The aircraft's wild lurches didn't seem to bother him one bit.

Alone once more, Drake surveyed the other two members of his team.

Keegan was lying stretched out on a bench on the opposite side of the cavernous hold, hands behind his head, his tatty Carolina Panthers cap pulled down low over his face. He hadn't stirred for some time, and the slow rise and fall of his chest suggested he was fast asleep despite the uncomfortable situation.

The man had the uncanny ability to fall asleep anywhere, any time he wanted. He'd explained it once by saying that while soldiers learned to eat whenever food was available, snipers learned to sleep whenever the opportunity presented itself because they never knew when they'd find themselves on another 48-hour stint with nothing but a rifle for company.

Frost was sitting cross-legged by the forward bulkhead, listening to music as she worked away on her laptop.

Drake had tolerated Walcott with a degree of patience, but Frost was of another sort. The first and only time

Walcott had tried to hit on her, she had put a friendly arm around his shoulder and told him in no uncertain terms that if he wanted to reach Afghanistan with his balls intact, he should leave her well alone.

That had been about the only time Drake had seen him lost for words.

Sensing his eyes on her, she glanced up and flashed an impudent grin that could have been seen as friendly or mocking – knowing her, it was probably a little of both – before resuming her work.

Wishing to stretch his legs, he rose from his bench and crossed the cargo hold to join her, having to brace himself against a stack of packing boxes as the plane took another lurch.

'How's it going, Keira?'

She glanced up from her laptop. 'Huh?'

Reaching out, he yanked her headphones off. 'I said the plane's about to crash and I hope you've got your insurance forms filled out.'

'Very funny.' He saw a flash of annoyance in her eyes at being disturbed from what had clearly been an absorbing task. 'I'll be better when I'm off this thing.'

'I know the feeling.' He looked down at her computer screen. It was Mitchell's hostage tape. 'Not much of an in-flight movie.'

She gave him a disapproving look. 'I'm not doing this for pleasure. I'm trying to learn more about Anwari.'

'Anything so far?'

'Maybe.' She removed her headphones from the laptop and hit the play button.

The video came to life, right after Kourash had put a round through Mitchell's leg. Once more Drake found himself listening to the man's deep, accented voice.

'If you do not comply . . . we will execute this spy and—'

Frost hit the pause button and looked up at him. 'He called Mitchell a spy. How did he know Mitchell works for the Agency?'

Drake shrugged. 'He was on a military flight. He was too old to be a soldier and he wasn't in uniform. It wouldn't be hard to work out.'

The young woman shook her head. 'He could have been a journalist, an engineer, a politician or a reality TV star for all they knew. Instead they called him a spy.'

'You think Kourash got him to talk.'

'Maybe.' She stared at the screen for a long moment. 'Or maybe he knew what Mitchell was before he shot down that chopper.'

Drake said nothing to that. It was a valid assumption, but an unsettling one.

'Mind if I ask you something?' she said, breaking the silence.

'Sure.'

Her gaze was direct and searching when she looked at him. 'What happened when you took Anwari down?'

Drake felt himself tense up. 'What do you mean?'

'I saw how you reacted when Franklin mentioned it.' She shrugged. 'Thought there might be more to it than he was letting on.'

What she really meant was, why hadn't he killed the man when he'd had the chance? He could have done it, and many times he'd caught himself wishing he had. But the thing that separated Drake and Frost was that he knew the real reason he hadn't done it. It wasn't mercy or compassion that had stayed his hand. Quite the opposite in fact.

He had been a very different man back then. A man he wasn't proud of.

But before Drake could reply, the pilot's voice crackled

over the intercom. 'Crew compartment, we're about to begin our descent. It's gonna be a rough one – you'll want to strap in.'

'Ah, shit. Here we go,' the young woman groaned.

'Don't worry,' Keegan said, having awoken as suddenly as if a switch had been flicked inside his head. 'There's parachutes in the back.'

Frost shot him an angry look. 'Bite me.'

After being forced to jump from an aircraft at 30,000 feet and parachute onto the roof of a Russian prison, she had vowed never to engage in any such activity again. Drake couldn't blame her – he certainly wasn't eager to repeat the experience.

Quickly packing away her laptop and documents, she took a seat along the outside edge of the cargo area. Drake sat down beside her, strapped himself in and waited for the roller-coaster ride to start.

A few moments later, the aircraft dropped like a stone as the pilot put them into a hard spiralling descent. Crosswinds buffeted them, making the big cargo plane lurch sickeningly from side to side. There was nothing the passengers could do except hold on and hope nobody on the ground decided to ruin their day by putting an AA round through the fuselage.

'I love this part!' Walcott called, having just descended the ladder from the flight deck to strap himself in.

There were no windows in the cargo hold. A low shuddering hum as the landing gear extended was the only indication they were approaching the runway. Waiting in strained silence, they braced themselves for touchdown.

The plane came down hard, the impact jarring them through their seats despite the landing gear's hydraulic dampers. The pilot applied full brakes a moment later, the aircraft shuddering and bumping its way across the rough tarmac before slowing to a more manageable speed.

After sixteen hours of flying, they were at last back on solid ground.

Drake turned sideways to glance at Frost, vaguely aware that he'd been holding his breath. 'Look on the bright side. We're still alive.'

She gave him a faint smile. 'The night is young.'

Chapter 5

The Globemaster bumped to a halt, and a few moments later the engines began to cycle down. Walcott, grinning like a lunatic – which he quite possibly was – unstrapped himself and strode over to a control box to activate the rear cargo ramp.

'Welcome to paradise.'

With a harsh buzz and a faint hydraulic hiss, the rear ramp opened up like the jaws of some immense beast, allowing them to finally glimpse the world outside.

Their first impression was of light; blindingly intense sunlight. Next to the dingy interior of the plane, looking at the world beyond the cargo doors was like staring into a camera flash, colours and details burned and bleached away. All they could see was cracked grey concrete at the foot of the ramp and further away, the hazy shapes of other aircraft in the distance.

Their second impression was of burning, stifling heat. The very air around them was scorching hot. Dry gritty sand, kicked up by the wind, blew unobstructed across the concrete runway and into the open cargo bay.

'Jesus,' Frost gasped, daunted by what she was seeing and feeling.

'Come on, let's go,' Drake said, shouldering his backpack. Every second they wasted here was a second lost for Mitchell.

As he descended the ramp, he couldn't help but remember the first time he'd stepped off a similar plane as a young SAS trooper, eager to be in the action after months of training and preparation. It seemed like a lifetime ago.

Sweat droplets began to form on their skin within moments as they moved away from the shadow of the aircraft, each donning sunglasses, and surveyed their surroundings.

Bagram Air Base was a serious facility, home not only to the entire 82nd Airborne Division and its support elements, but also to Marine and Air Force companies, and even contingents of the British and German armies. The base also served as the headquarters of ISAF's Regional Command East, making it a vital element of the Coalition's presence in the country.

It had been laid down by the Soviets back in the 1980s, and had been a fiercely contested prize in the bitter civil war following their withdrawal. Now it had new owners and was a hive of activity once more. With cavernous hangars, refuelling depots, administrative buildings and workshops laid out all along the aircraft dispersal area, Bagram was a veritable city in its own right.

Glancing up at the distinctive thump of rotor blades, the small group of weary travellers watched as a Chinook came in to land, nose flaring upward to slow its forward momentum before touching down a few hundred yards away.

Frost and Keegan were still taking it all in when Drake spotted a vehicle heading their way – a big sleek Ford Explorer with darkened windows, its once black and gleaming paintwork faded by wind-blown sand and dust.

The vehicle came to a halt in a small cloud of dust, its

massive 4.6-litre V8 engine rumbling away. The sun glinting off the windshield made it hard to see the driver or even to tell how many were aboard, but Drake didn't think there were many bodies inside judging by the way the vehicle was riding on its axles.

Shutting down the engine, the driver threw the door open and stepped out.

He barely recognised Samantha McKnight from her file photo. Her once pale skin had darkened, her hair lightened by constant exposure to the harsh sunlight. The slightly girlish face had changed as well; ageing, maturing, hardening. Her lean physique only added to the impression that Afghanistan had toughened her up.

Like them, she was wearing aviator sunglasses, though she removed them to survey the small group standing before her.

'I'm looking for Ryan Drake.'

She made it seem like a question, but Drake felt her gaze linger on him a little longer than the others. She knew who he was.

'You've found him,' he confirmed. 'You're Samantha McKnight, I assume.'

She nodded, offering a smile that was both friendly and disarming, and only then did he see a hint of the woman in that photograph. Smiling came easily to her, it seemed.

'And you're late,' she added, shaking his hand. Her grip was firm, her hand warm.

'We were delayed at Andrews.' They had been due to arrive here four hours ago, but slow loading of their plane had lost them their departure slot and forced an unwelcome delay. 'Anyway, it's good to meet you, Specialist McKnight.'

'Call me Sam. If we're going to be working together

out here, I'd prefer not to have to address everyone by their job titles.'

Drake wasn't about to argue with that. He'd never been one for formalities.

'Fair enough, Sam.' He gestured to his companions. 'This is my team. Keira Frost and John Keegan.'

Shepherd teams weren't spies, so anonymity amongst their own people wasn't necessary. Anyway, McKnight had already been briefed on the team's arrival. She knew who they were, and what they had come to do.

'Good to meet you all. Now I guess you'll want to get out of this heat,' she remarked, her hazel eyes flashing with a hint of humour. She could see the sweat beading on their foreheads already. 'You want to grab your gear and follow me?'

With that, she turned on her heel and started walking towards the Explorer.

Frost hurried to catch up with her. 'Is it always this goddamn hot?'

'Of course not,' McKnight replied over her shoulder. 'You should have been here last month. We were averaging ninety degrees in the shade then. Takes a few weeks to get acclimatised, then you're good to go. You'll want to drink plenty of water until then, otherwise you'll start to dehydrate after a couple of hours. But don't let the daytime heat fool you – it can get cold as hell at night.'

Drake said nothing to this. He'd experienced his share of Afghan nights up in the mountains, and hadn't come away with pleasant memories.

'By the way, the local time is 09:20,' McKnight added as she pulled open the Explorer's trunk. 'Time difference is a bitch, huh?'

'Roger that,' Keegan said, grinning.

After dumping their gear in the back, McKnight fired up the engine once more and eased them away. There was a strict speed limit in the aircraft dispersal areas that even the Agency wasn't allowed to break.

They hadn't gone far before they encountered a security checkpoint at the perimeter of the airfield. A quick flash of McKnight's ID card, along with an official document signed by the office of Bagram's commanding officer, was enough to get them through.

Leaning back in her seat with the air conditioners blasting cold air in her face, McKnight drove with the casual ease born from familiarity through the bustling military base.

Around them, soldiers, engineers, civilian contractors and technicians hurried back and forth, all with places to go and things to do. The roads were busy with vehicles of all kinds, from big M35 military cargo trucks down to Chevrolet Tahoes and other civilian 4x4s.

Beyond the airfield's maintenance facilities and admin buildings lay a vast swathe of wooden huts the size of a small town. Known as B-huts, they served as accommodation for more than 7,000 military and civilian personnel living and working on base.

Their guide pointed to a large steel-and-concrete air-raid shelter half buried in the ground as they cruised past. A layer of dirt had been piled on top to add to the protection. 'Keep those shelters in mind. If the air-raid warnings go off, you drop whatever you're doing and double-time it to the nearest one. No exceptions.'

That didn't inspire confidence. 'What's the security situation here?' Keegan asked, echoing all their thoughts.

'They hit us with rockets once or twice a month, usually at night.' She pointed to the nearby mountains. 'That's where most of them come from – only takes a couple of minutes to set up, fire their birds and bug out before we can target them. The Taliban have started bribing the locals to launch rockets and mortars on their behalf. Most of them are so dirt poor they'll do anything to make a few bucks.'

'What about outside the base?' Frost chipped in.

'Not so good,' she admitted. 'We've established green zones around strategic towns and along most of the major highways, but anything outside that is fair game. Taliban, al-Qaeda, Iranians, Uzbeks, anti-Coalition militias – you name it. They cross over from Pakistan, set up an ambush and plant trip mines in ditches and culverts. Our guys get blasted apart when they try to take cover. Then they bounce back across the border before we can nail them.'

Frost raised an eyebrow. 'Sounds like the goddamn Wild West.'

'You get used to it.' She turned to Drake, a flicker of amusement in her eyes. 'So what's the plan, sheriff?'

'Is Mitchell's office near here?'

'He'd have been based at the Agency's HQ,' she judged, pointing off to the right. 'It's about half a klick that way. It looks like a fortress – you can't miss it.'

'Good.' Drake twisted around in his seat to speak to Frost. 'Keira, double-time it over there. I want you to find Mitchell's office and go through everything he was working on. Computer files, documents, Post-it notes . . . whatever.'

'What am I looking for?'

'Anything out of the ordinary,' Drake replied. 'Any sign that he was involved in something he shouldn't have been.'

It was a pretty broad remit, but in situations like this he trusted her judgement implicitly. Frost was nothing if not thorough in her work.

The young woman made a face. Such a task was likely to be both difficult and laborious, and certainly wasn't something she relished after a sixteen-hour flight.

Drake, however, was in no mood to discuss it. 'No arguments. Just get it done,' he said, cutting her off before she could protest. 'Oh, and find us somewhere to work from. An office or a briefing room. I don't care.'

'Anything else? Want a masseuse on standby?'

Drake gave her the thousand-yard stare.

'Okay, okay. I'll get it done,' she conceded unhappily, pulling her door open. 'What about you? Where the hell are you going?'

'The crash site.' There was no question in his mind. He wanted to understand what had happened out there. 'I want to see it for myself.'

Rounding the vehicle, Frost retrieved her bag from the back. 'Sure. Leave me with the shitty job.'

'That's what you get paid for,' he reminded her. 'Call us if you find anything.'

Giving him the finger, the young woman turned and strode off down the road.

'She's . . . colourful,' McKnight remarked.

'You have no idea,' Drake assured her, checking his watch. They still had most of the day ahead of them, and he intended to use it. 'We need to get to that crash site now.'

She flashed a grin and threw the big 4x4 into gear. 'I was hoping you'd say that.'

Chapter 6

Drake fired up his cellphone as soon as they were clear of the airfield. He was greeted by two messages: one from Etisalat Communications welcoming him to Afghanistan, and another from Breckenridge back at Langley advising him to check in as soon as he'd landed.

One advantage of working with the Agency was that they were actually allowed their own cellphones out here. Regular soldiers had to leave them at their embarkation area back home. Of course, the door swung both ways. The obvious downside to always being in touch with one's superiors was dealing with constant requests for updates and information.

Steeling himself, Drake dialled Breckenridge's number. Afghanistan was about nine and a half hours ahead of Langley, making it just after midnight on that side of the world.

It rang only once before it was answered. The man must have been hovering over the damn thing. Drake was beginning to wonder if he ever slept.

'Talk to me, Drake,' was the curt greeting.

Drake's reply was equally brief. 'We're on the ground. We're en route to the crash site now.'

'Good. Keep me updated. I want a written summary of your findings by the end of the day.'

Drake frowned. 'I'll update you when I can.'

It wasn't as if he was going to be sitting in an air-conditioned office while he was out here. Finding Mitchell was the priority. Writing up reports could come later.

'No, you'll update me when I say so,' Breckenridge corrected him. 'I have to report in just like you, and I can't do that if I'm in the dark. Is this in any way unclear?'

Drake's grip on the phone tightened. 'No, George. As always you've made yourself very clear.'

His tone was lost on the older man. 'Good. I'll expect to hear from you after you've surveyed the crash site. Out.'

Shutting down the phone, Drake shook his head. 'Prick.'

'Christ, and I thought Dietrich was hard to work with,' Keegan remarked. 'This guy makes being an asshole a full-time job.'

Dietrich had been a specialist drafted into their team for the ill-fated prison break operation last year. Though he had ultimately proven his worth in the tumultuous events that followed, he had been a nightmare for Drake during the planning stage, clashing constantly with him over important decisions.

Still, Drake would rather have dealt with a dozen Dietrichs over one Breckenridge at that moment.

'Well, he's halfway around the planet,' he reasoned. 'Be grateful for that.'

'Not far enough for me, buddy. I can't believe Franklin picked a dumb REMF like him to run the Shepherd teams. I guess shit rolls downhill, huh?'

'Dan's not a bad guy.'

'He makes deals with bad people,' Keegan reminded him. 'Same thing in my book.'

At this, McKnight frowned and glanced over at Drake. 'Something I should know about?'

'Long story with a not particularly happy ending,' he evaded.

This prompted an amused smile. 'We've all been there.'

McKnight turned off the main road shortly after clearing the base's outer security perimeter, and wasted no time putting her foot down. Soon they were careening at breakneck speed down a dusty, cracked, barely paved road that snaked through the network of small villages clustered around Bagram.

The woman drove like a lunatic, churning through the gears, keeping the engine revs high and flooring it around corners, leaving clouds of dust and burned rubber in their wake.

Leaning forward, Keegan tapped her on the shoulder.

'You got yourself a death wish, Sam?' he asked, having to brace himself against the seat as they bounced through a pothole. The suspension groaned under the strain.

'Standard precaution,' McKnight called over her shoulder. 'We move fast so the Taliban don't have time to set up IEDs on the road ahead.'

IED stood for Improvised Explosive Device – basically anything the insurgents could slap together that would go boom and put chunks of metal in Coalition soldiers. They could be anything from coffee cans filled with plastic explosive and nuts and bolts, to 105mm artillery shells buried underground.

'That's them, over there,' she added, nodding casually towards a group of men standing on the second-floor balcony of a dilapidated-looking house off to their left, perhaps 50 yards distant. There were three or four of them, all sporting long beards and civilian clothes, just standing there watching the vehicle speed by.

'That's who?'

'The Taliban,' McKnight explained, perfectly nonchalant.

'You're fucking kidding me.'

She shrugged. 'They're spotters, reporting our movements. One of their buddies in the back is probably calling his superiors right now. We know they're Taliban, and they know that we know, but they also know we won't detain them without evidence,' she said, giving Drake a significant look. 'So, we watch them, and they watch us, and most of the time that's all that happens. It's just the way things are out here.'

As if on cue, they passed a couple of burned-out vehicles abandoned by the side of the road, their blackened chassis so twisted and warped by the extreme heat that it was impossible to tell what they had once been.

Keegan leaned back in his seat and stared at them, saying nothing.

Unknown to the three occupants of the Explorer, another pair of eyes was watching them through a high-powered telescopic lens. The single observer was protected from the intense sun, and any aircraft that might be circling overhead, by camouflage netting strung over the low depression in which he was crouched. Flies buzzed around him, and the oppressive heat caused droplets of sweat to form at his brow, but he didn't care. He was used to such things.

Situated on a low hill about half a mile north of the road, the man who had become known as Kourash Anwari watched as the big vehicle bounced and jolted across the uneven surface. Even through the haze of dust, he was able to make out the driver and passengers.

Two men and a woman, all dressed in civilian clothes.

He didn't recognise the other two, but the man in the passenger seat up front was very familiar to him. His was a face that Kourash would never forget as long as he lived. After all, how could one forget the man who had cost him everything he'd ever cared about?

Ryan Drake.

It had taken no small amount of time and effort to learn what had become of the man who ruined his life, who took everything from him in a single day. But patience was a virtue he had learned a long time ago.

Half a world had separated the two men until yesterday. And now here they were, barely 300 yards apart. Drake had arrived just as Kourash had known he would, ignorant of the work and planning and calculations that had brought him here.

As the Explorer roared past on the dusty road below, Kourash reached for the cellphone resting in the depression beside him. It was a specialised encrypted unit, firing off its transmissions in a randomly cycling burst of data that was next to impossible to lock down.

Shielding the screen from the bright shafts of sunlight peeking through the camouflage netting, he powered the phone up. No numbers were stored in its digital memory – they all had to be learned and held within one's mind. It wasn't easy, but Kourash prided himself on his mental discipline.

Discipline was the core of a man's being, a source of strength more potent than the strongest arm or the stoutest heart. Kourash had learned this truth from a young age.

His father had been a common labourer who flattered himself with dreams of success and wealth, lacking both the intelligence and the motivation to succeed. As his fledgling business failed and his money vanished, he had turned his anger and frustration on his own family.

His mother by contrast had been a quiet, melancholy woman who endured the beatings he doled out without complaint, who would not even say a word against him when those same fists were turned against her own children. She would just get up and silently leave the room, her eyes blank, seeing nothing.

Both of them had been weak and deserving of their miserable lives. Kourash would despise them to his dying day.

Dredging up the familiar number from memory, he punched it in and waited for the call to be answered.

As always, it didn't take long.

'Yes?' came the curt greeting.

'The CIA are here. They are on their way to the crash site.'

Chapter 7

'This is it. The chopper's on the other side of that ridge,' McKnight said, slowing the Explorer as they approached a couple of armed men up ahead, part of the security detail charged with protecting the crash site.

One look at them was enough to confirm they weren't US Army, or any branch of the armed forces for that matter.

For a start they were much older than twenty-five, the average age for a US infantryman. Neither had seen less than forty years by Drake's estimate. Still, they were serious-looking men. Both tall, both bulked up from heavy weight training, both with thick necks and grim, unsmiling faces. Neither man had shaved for several days judging by the thick growth along their jaws.

Instead of the standard MultiCam patterned Army Combat Uniform, they were clad in black T-shirts, with sand-coloured combat trousers and body armour that was some kind of hybrid design Drake had never seen before. There were no identification marks anywhere on their clothing. No unit badge, no rank marks, not even name tags.

Both were armed with M4A1 carbines; a modern replacement for the old M16. Designed around the modular weapons system concept, they were very much the military equivalent of Lego blocks allowing the user to add all kinds of attachments, from silencers to grenade launchers. In this case, both weapons were fitted with M68 close combat optic sights, and foregrips for easier carrying.

'Who the hell are these guys?' Keegan asked, eyeing the nearest man as he approached the Explorer, weapon at the ready.

'Mercenaries,' Drake said, an edge of disdain in his voice.

'Private military contractors,' McKnight corrected him. 'They work for Horizon Defence. One of our biggest security companies these days.'

'Creators of all things bright and beautiful, huh?' Keegan prodded.

She shrugged. 'Supply and demand, I guess. We supply the war, they supply the soldiers.'

The Explorer came to a halt, its engine ticking over. McKnight rolled down her window to speak to the perimeter guard. Both he and his companion were wearing mirrored shades, and neither man seemed inclined to remove them.

'ID please, ma'am,' the man said, sounding bored and wary at the same time.

His gloved hand was resting on the windowsill, and as he moved a little, Drake spotted a tattoo on his forearm. A sword intersected by three lightning bolts.

Drake recognised the tattoo well enough; it was the unit symbol for US Army Special Forces.

McKnight handed over her ID card. 'We're here to inspect the crash site.'

The guard's head swivelled to stare at Drake and Keegan.

'And your passengers? I'll need IDs for them too.'

'No, you don't,' Drake informed him.

The man's head snapped back towards Drake in an instant. 'Yeah, I do. This site is locked down. Nobody gets in or out without authorisation.'

'How about the Director of National Intelligence?' Drake challenged him, irritated by the delay. 'Is that good enough? Or should we take it up with your CO?'

The guard stared at him a moment longer, saying nothing. Drake was quite certain the man was glaring at him behind those mirrored sunglasses, though he returned the stare with equal intensity.

Without saying a word, he turned away, retreated several paces and spoke into his radio, keeping his back to them. His companion stood in front of the vehicle, barring their way and making sure his assault rifle was plainly visible.

Several seconds passed, during which no words were spoken. Drake glanced at McKnight but said nothing. Now wasn't the time for voicing his thoughts.

Then, just like that, the guard turned to face them, marched over to the driver's side window and handed McKnight her ID back.

'Go on through, ma'am,' he said, practically spitting the words at them.

'Appreciate it,' McKnight returned as she revved the engine and hit the gas, forcing the other perimeter guard to dodge aside as the big vehicle lurched forwards.

'What an asshole,' Keegan remarked, glancing back at the two men from his window seat.

Drake had been thinking along similar lines. 'Is it always like this, dealing with PMCs?'

McKnight shook her head. 'This is frontier territory. You can't blame them for being cautious.' She gave him a sidelong smirk. 'Anyway, I thought you Brits were all about politeness and fair play.'

'Only in cricket. And I don't play.'

Cresting the ridge at low revs to keep from skidding on the loose dirt, the Explorer's nose dipped and they began their descent of the reverse slope.

At last they saw the crash site.

The Black Hawk, or what was left of it, lay about 50 yards from the base of the slope, having come down in flat open ground that had once been a broad floodplain in wetter times. These days it was a barren expanse of rocks, dirt and dry scrub, all of it blending to the same washed-out brown as everything else.

All of it, except a wide swathe around the wreckage. There the stones had been blackened, the brush incinerated, the dusty ground itself charred by the intense heat. Bits of twisted wreckage lay everywhere, most so badly burned and deformed in the explosion that it was impossible to tell what they had once been.

The airframe itself was still recognisable, barely. Two of the massive rotor blades had sheared off, probably during the crash, but the other two remained attached to the engine assembly.

Clustered around the wreck were half a dozen men in similar attire to the two guards they'd just encountered, all armed with a mixture of assault rifles and submachine guns. The protection detail was backed up by a couple of armoured 4x4s that Drake recognised as RG-33s.

Made in South Africa, they were popular with the UN and other peacekeeping forces because of the excellent protection they offered, and it seemed Horizon felt the same way. These ones both had 50-calibre remote weapons stations mounted on their roofs, allowing operators inside the vehicles to track and engage targets without ever having to leave their seats.

These weapon mounts were much sought after by US Army vehicle crews, though the cost per unit made them as rare as gold dust.

McKnight brought them to a halt at the edge of the debris field and killed the engine. Hauling his door open, Drake stepped out, his boots crunching on the dry rocky ground.

The heat seemed to have grown more intense as the sun rose towards its zenith, the feeling amplified by their sudden exit from the air-conditioned vehicle. Drake checked his watch – 10:46.

His thoughts were interrupted when he noticed one of the Horizon security men coming their way, presumably the leader of the protection detail.

He was a big guy, not so much tall as broad. He couldn't have been more than 5 foot 10, yet Drake guessed his weight at perhaps 220, maybe 230 pounds of solid muscle. He had the look of a rugby player: short and stocky, rugged and powerful.

His head was covered with a sweat-stained bandanna, his deeply lined face darkened by several days' growth. He looked to be in his late forties, and judging by the confidence in his stride, he was no stranger to places like Afghanistan.

'My name's Vermaak,' he began. 'I'm in charge here.'

Drake was surprised by his heavy South African accent, though perhaps he shouldn't have been. A lot of their operatives had drifted into mercenary work after the end of apartheid. Vermaak looked as if he belonged to that generation.

'Ryan Drake, CIA,' he replied, shaking hands with him. The man's grip was strong enough to crush boulders.

Drake's accent prompted a raised eyebrow. 'I didn't know the boys at Langley employed foreigners.'

'They're an equal opportunities sort of place. Just like Horizon, I imagine,' Drake added with a pointed look at the South African.

The older man grinned. 'Fair enough. So what can I do for you, Mr Drake?'

'We're here to survey the crash site.'

Vermaak glanced at the rest of the group and frowned. 'The army forensics guys already surveyed the whole site. I know, because I spent four hours sat on my arse waiting for them to get it done.'

'I understand that. But we have to make our own assessment.'

'We have orders to destroy the wreck and pull out before nightfall.' To emphasise his point, Vermaak pointed towards the ruined chopper.

Fixed to the crumpled forward bulkhead was a cylindrical steel container the size of a small beer keg. The distinctive yellow wires trailing from the top made its purpose obvious. No doubt it was filled with high explosive – enough to vaporise the chopper and prevent anything valuable falling into the wrong hands.

'Our orders come from the Director of National Intelligence, and they supersede yours.' Drake glanced up at the sky. 'Anyway, you've got at least eight hours until sunset. That's more than enough time for us to finish up here.'

Vermaak said nothing for a few moments. Clearly he didn't like what he was hearing, but neither could he ignore Drake's authority. It was rather like poker, and Drake held all the aces in this case.

Finally he shrugged. 'Fine. Do what you have to. But come sundown, my men and I pull out. Do we understand each other, Mr Drake?'

Drake nodded, unperturbed by his hostile tone. He

hadn't come here looking for a new best friend; he had come to get results.

'Perfectly.'

As Vermaak strode away to confer with two of his men, Drake turned to his own two teammates. 'John, I want you to take a look around. See if you can find any evidence of the people who did this. Boot prints, vehicle tracks . . . whatever.'

In addition to his skills as a sniper, the man was an outstanding tracker, able to discern meaning from something as insignificant as a scuff mark on the ground or a few bent blades of grass. If there was anything in the vicinity worth finding, Drake felt certain he would find it.

'On it, buddy,' Keegan replied, already moving.

'Sam, you're with me. Let's get to work.'

Chapter 8

'Wow, real garden spot,' Frost remarked to herself as she surveyed Mitchell's office.

His place of work was a modest, unremarkable little office, perhaps 10 feet square, with a small window overlooking a parking lot. One desk, metal framed, with a wood laminate coating marked by coffee rings, faced the window. On it sat a dusty computer with an old-fashioned CRT monitor and a cheap inkjet printer.

Scattered across the desk was the usual office paraphernalia, none of which sparked much interest, while a couple of filing cabinets were set against the wall.

And that was it. All things considered, it was a bland, clinical working space that looked barely used. The only hint of personality was a framed photograph sitting on the edge of the desk. Mitchell, several years younger and with more hair, plus what Frost assumed to be Mrs Mitchell. They were standing together at a beach somewhere, his arm around her shoulder, smiling and relaxed.

Frost glanced away, thinking it best not to get too involved. Settling herself at the desk, she fired up the computer and waited for it to start up, drumming her fingers impatiently on the cheap wood-veneer desk as the seconds dragged on.

'Jesus, their IT people should be shot,' she said.

Realising the computer would take a while to boot up, she crossed the room to the nearest of the two filing cabinets. At least she could make a start on Mitchell's paper trail, she thought, reaching for the first drawer.

The drawer moved half an inch, then came to a halt, jammed on its runner. She pulled again, to little effect.

'You picked the wrong day, and the wrong girl,' the young woman said, gripping the drawer tighter and gritting her teeth, just allowing the frustration to build. 'Come on, you son of a bitch.'

One hard yank was enough to free up the jammed runner, and the drawer shot open with a grating rasp.

Peering inside, she frowned in confusion. 'What the fuck?'

With Vermaak and his security team standing a short distance away, Drake and McKnight picked their way through the mangled remains of the Black Hawk chopper. Both had donned surgical gloves for handling any wreckage they came across, partly to avoid disturbing the scene further but mostly for their own protection. Choppers were filled with all kinds of toxic fuels and chemicals.

'That's where the missile impacted,' McKnight said, indicating the mangled engine pod overhead.

'That's what the army forensics team concluded,' Drake agreed. He had read their preliminary report on the flight out. 'An RPG impact against the outer armour.'

The RPG-7, or rocket-propelled grenade, was a Soviet-made anti-armour rocket dating back to the early 1960s. Simple, reliable and capable of punching through 12 inches of high-density armour, they had been the bane of tank crews for nearly half a century. Close to 10 million of the things had been made, with tens of thousands ending up in the hands of militias, terrorists and insurgents.

It was easy to see why the army forensics team saw the RPG as the most likely culprit. However, it seemed McKnight didn't agree. 'It wasn't an RPG round. It was a guided missile.'

That was a bold claim to make, considering she had been here all of five minutes. 'What makes you so sure?'

She glanced at him, a faint smile on her lips. He was testing her, and she knew it. 'The RPG is an anti-tank weapon. It's designed to take out slow-moving targets from close range, not fast aircraft hundreds of feet in the air. A Black Hawk's standard cruising speed is a hundred and fifty knots. It's about twenty metres long and five metres high, right?'

Drake shrugged. He wasn't exactly an aircraft buff. 'If you say so.'

'I do. The US Army did a hit evaluation of the RPG-7 a few years back. The chances of hitting a slow-moving target from two hundred metres were less than fifty per cent. Factor in the relative velocity and the increased range, and you're talking about a hit probability of less than one per cent. Bad odds by anyone's standards.'

'Maybe they were lucky,' he suggested. Just because the odds were against something, didn't mean it couldn't happen.

Turning her attention back to the wrecked chopper, McKnight pointed at the engine pod again. 'Look at it. The blast pattern's all wrong. RPGs are designed to penetrate armour with a high-pressure jet of gas and liquid metal. In the demolitions trade, we call it brisance. But whatever the name, it should have crumpled the engine pod like a giant fist and burned a hole right through it. That didn't happen here. It's been shredded, as if some kind of fragmentation device exploded nearby. Like a missile with a proximity fuse.'

'RPGs come with frag rounds,' Drake reminded her. Though intended as an anti-tank weapon, they had been adapted over the years to a number of different purposes, from laying smokescreens to anti-personnel strikes.

McKnight said nothing to this. Moving closer, she knelt down beside the chopper, reached out and pulled open a small hatch. The mechanism was stiff, having been either damaged in the crash or deformed by the resultant fireball, but with some effort she was able to free it up.

The small compartment within held an empty metal rack, clearly designed to hold a number of small objects. 'Flares,' she explained. 'Standard countermeasure against guided missiles. They've been used up. The pilot must have deployed them to try to lose whatever warhead was tracking him.' She glanced up at him. 'Still don't believe me?'

'All right. If it wasn't an RPG, what do you think did this?' Drake asked, amused at how easily she had dismantled his theory.

Again she shrugged. 'Hard to say. It would have to be some kind of man-portable device, probably heat-seeking since it struck the engine pod. Maybe a Russian SA-18 or even a Chinese FN6. The SA-18 wouldn't be too hard to get hold of if you have cash and friends in the right places. Russians aren't exactly shy about selling weapons under the table.' She reached up to flick a lock of dark hair out of her eyes. 'I want to have a look inside.'

Taking a breath, Drake followed her, having to pick his way carefully past the blackened remains of what had once been a door-mounted minigun. The formidable six-barrelled weapon was still pointing skywards, though its breech mechanism and ammunition feed had been blasted apart when the rounds inside cooked off.

Inside the burned-out compartment, the smell of melted plastic and other chemicals was overpowering. Even now, the stench lingered in the air, stinging his nose and making his eyes water. Wherever he stood, his boots left greasy prints on the soot-covered steel deck.

McKnight pointed to a blasted-out section of metal plating around the rotor shaft. 'Check this out. The explosion travelled down through the shaft and ruptured the bulkhead here. We think one of the passengers was in front of the bulkhead when it gave way. There were bits of him all over the cabin.'

The bodies, or what was left of them, had of course been removed for repatriation back to the States, but for a moment Drake fancied he could smell something beneath the burned plastic and charred metal – the sickening stench of scorched human flesh.

McKnight pointed to a couple of areas where the deck had warped and deformed from the extreme heat. 'Look. It was hot enough to soften the airframe.'

'So the fuel tanks ruptured at some point after the chopper crash-landed,' Drake reasoned. 'It couldn't have happened too quickly, otherwise they never would have had time to kidnap Mitchell.'

'It wasn't aviation fuel that did this,' McKnight said, deep in thought as she looked around. 'The burning is too localised. You can see it.' She pointed to the areas of warped decking. 'There were two or three ignition points.'

Struck by an idea, she hurried back outside to the metal briefcase that served as her portable forensics lab. Selecting a chemical swab held inside a clear plastic tube, she ducked back inside the chopper, knelt down beside one of the areas of melted decking and carefully drew the swab across it.

Replacing it in the tube, she watched it intently. It took only a few moments for the swab to turn bright purple.

'Interesting,' she said quietly.

Drake leaned closer, intrigued by what she'd found. 'Care to explain?'

Her vivid hazel eyes focused on him. 'Barium nitrate. The cabin's coated with it.'

'Okay,' he agreed, sounding vague. 'What does that mean?'

'Barium nitrate is one of the key elements of incendiary grenades. Combine it with thermite and it produces a hotter flame that burns longer and has a lower ignition point. It's our standard anti-materiel weapon.'

Incendiary grenades had been in use by most armies since the Second World War. They had even been employed to disable German coastal artillery during the Normandy landings, their intense heat fusing the breech mechanism into a solid mass of metal.

But why would insurgents have used it? Thermite grenades were specialised pieces of equipment, and not easy to come by. Anyway, destroying an aircraft that had already been rendered immobile was nonsensical – it was no threat. It would have made more sense to strip it of valuable equipment and weapons.

The answer was as obvious as it was baffling. 'They were trying to cover their tracks,' he said. 'They didn't want us to know what they were doing.'

Glancing around, he spotted something on the forward bulkhead. He had seen it not long after entering, but hadn't consciously acknowledged it amidst the chaos of the chopper wreck. Only now did he examine it more closely.

It was a small circular hole about half an inch in diameter. Reaching out, he touched it gently with his gloved hand. The metal had deformed inwards, giving way beneath the impact of a high-speed projectile.

'Small arms fire,' he said. 'They were shooting in here.'

McKnight was by his side within moments, leaning forward to examine the damage. Her arm brushed against his, and instinctively he moved aside to allow her better access. His body remembered the brief contact though.

'Looks like a 7.62mm round to me,' she said after running her finger around it. 'Fired from a high angle judging by the entry point.'

Drake's mind assembled the facts and reached its inevitable conclusion. 'An execution. One round, right between the eyes. Which means at least some of the crew survived the crash, but our friends executed them.'

'And yet they kept Mitchell alive,' she added. 'That makes no sense. More hostages would have meant more leverage.'

Drake shook his head. Too many aspects of this attack weren't adding up, and his instincts told him there was more going on here than he was seeing.

'There's more to this than just a random attack,' he decided. 'If the people who did this had access to guided missiles, they could have taken out one of the military transports coming in to land at Bagram. Instead they chose this specific chopper. They shot it down, killed everyone on board and took one man hostage. One man.' He glanced up at his female companion. 'They knew Mitchell was aboard. They did this all to get their hands on him.'

She stared back at him, both puzzled and intrigued. 'Why? What's so valuable about Mitchell?'

'Good question. I'd say it's time we found out.'

Rising up from the deck, Drake ducked out of the chopper, relieved to be away from that charred, claustrophobic space where men had died.

Keegan, who had been surveying the area around the crash site, came jogging over as they emerged. 'I swept the area for tracks.' He shook his head, confirming what they already suspected. 'Between the army search-and-rescue team, the forensics guys and our buddies from Horizon, there must be close to fifty different trails. It's a dead end – pardon the choice of words.' He gestured to the chopper wreck. 'Find anything?'

'Nothing good,' Drake replied, peeling off the filthy surgical gloves. 'This wasn't some random attack. Mitchell was their target. They wanted him, and him alone.'

'Why?'

'Good question. But we won't find the answer here. I'm going back to Bagram, check in on Frost. Maybe she can tell us more.'

'I want to stay here and look around a little more,' McKnight decided.

Drake glanced at her. 'For what?'

'Well, it's certainly not for the charming company,' she assured him, nodding towards the Horizon team. 'I want to find the launch site. It might give me a better idea of what kind of missile they used.' She pointed to a low ridge about 400 yards away, covered with tangled scrub and wind-scoured boulders. 'That's where I would have been. Plenty of cover, and right on the chopper's flight line.'

Drake paused, considering her suggestion. It was a good idea, but he felt apprehensive about leaving her out here.

Vermaak might have been less than cooperative, but he'd been right about one thing – this was a dangerous neck of the woods, and they were a long way from support if they got caught in an ambush.

Stop this, he thought, giving himself a mental slap. McKnight was quite capable of looking after herself, and she had two heavy support vehicles and at least half a dozen armed men to watch her back.

'Fine,' he agreed at last. 'Do what you have to, but don't take any chances.'

'I'll stay and watch your back,' Keegan added. 'If the launch site isn't too messed up, I might even find a trail or two.'

Drake wasn't about to argue. Keegan was a good man to have around in a tight situation, and might well prove useful out here.

'Mind if I borrow your jeep?' Drake asked, feeling self-conscious about having to ask McKnight for a ride.

'Only if you hand it back the way you found it.' McKnight tossed him the keys. 'We'll hitch a ride back with the Horizon team when they pull out.'

'Nice one. I'll meet you back at Bagram.' With that, he turned and hurried towards the Explorer. 'Call in if you find anything.'

'Okay, Ryan.'

'If there are any question marks on safety, you pull out,' he called back over his shoulder. 'Understood?'

'Would you go, already?' she said impatiently.

Drake could feel his face colouring from more than just the heat.

'You're on my team which makes you my responsibility. You die, I have to fill out the paperwork,' he said, trying to sound nonchalant. He unlocked the big 4x4 and pulled the door open. 'And I hate paperwork.'

With that, he pulled himself up into the driver's seat and cranked it back to fit his height. As he did so, he couldn't help looking at his reflection in the mirror.

'Arsehole,' he mumbled.

Throwing it into gear, he stamped on the accelerator a little too hard, prompting the big vehicle to lurch forward, kicking up dust and stones.

Chapter 9

'What do you have to report?' Kourash asked, holding the encrypted cellphone tight against his ear as he strode down the crowded city street, walking with a slight limp that he had laboriously taught himself to disguise over the years.

Another thing he had to thank Ryan Drake for.

His fake beard, webbing and combat fatigues were gone now, replaced by a slightly worn grey business suit and open shirt that hung loose on his spare frame.

The days of hiding in mountain caves where US reconnaissance drones could track them down were long gone. True concealment came from anonymity, and here he was about as anonymous as it was possible to be.

With his greying hair cut short and neat, his face clean-shaven and his wallet filled with fake identity papers, he looked little different from the thousands of other men out walking the streets of central Kabul. Just some businessman on his way to a meeting or his favourite restaurant. Nothing worth remembering.

The only thing that marked him out as different was his eyes. Or rather, what lay behind them. They were the eyes of a man who had seen death and suffering, who had caused both by his own hand, who had discarded concepts like mercy and compassion long ago.

Walking the streets of Kabul was an exercise in

self-control for him. Always he had to fight the anger and contempt that welled up inside him. These people wandering past him, so oblivious to his true nature, were the same people who had blindly allowed the Taliban to take over the country. They were the same people who allowed the Americans to rule over them, like a flock of mindless sheep.

The Americans who had used men like Kourash to fight their dirty war against the Soviets and then turned their back when the fighting was done.

He hated what Afghanistan had become. And he hated the weak and selfish men who had allowed it to happen.

'Drake just left the site, heading back towards Bagram,' reported Mehrak, the spotter that Kourash had stationed to observe the activity at the Black Hawk crash site. He was an expert at scouting and concealment, and Kourash had every faith in his ability to stay hidden while he went about his task.

'What about the others?' Kourash asked. There had been two other people in that jeep alongside Drake.

'The rest of his team are still here, surveying the area. They seem to be looking for something.'

That gave him pause for thought. These people were trained investigators who were accustomed to looking beyond the obvious. If they were to find something they shouldn't, it could be damaging; not just for Kourash but also for the man he worked with.

The man to whom he owed his freedom, and indeed his life.

'They can't be allowed to find anything,' Kourash interrupted, by now acutely aware of how delicate his situation was. He had taken a calculated risk to make all of this happen; a risk which he had not informed his associates of.

His statement was met by a moment of silence. 'What are your orders?'

Kourash hesitated, weighing up his decision. Drake was the only one he wanted to see dead; he had no particular enmity for those who worked with him. Still, if they were a threat then they had to be eliminated.

And losing one's comrades was a heavy burden for a man to bear, he knew.

'Take them out.'

For Mehrak, that was all he needed to hear. 'It will be done.'

With that, the line went dead.

After a bumpy cross-country drive, Drake soon picked up the road that McKnight had turned off to reach the crash site. Potholed and winding it might have been, but it was a road and that was good enough for him.

With her earlier advice about IEDs still fresh in his mind, he turned right at the next junction, taking a different route from the outward leg.

He was in uncharted territory now, with only the vehicle's dash-mounted GPS to guide him back to Bagram. Around him lay an open landscape of dusty scrubland interspersed with mud-walled farm compounds, fields and irrigation ditches. This was the rural, backwater world of Afghanistan, where the concept of mechanised farming was as far removed from daily life as shopping malls and Internet access.

Still, even here the reminders of wars past and present were impossible to escape. Drake slowed a little as he passed the rusting hulks of two ancient heavy battle tanks, their gun barrels still elevated as if to engage a long-forgotten enemy.

They were Soviet T-55s. Relics of another time and

another war, now serving as a makeshift climbing frame for a dozen or so local kids. Pausing in their game, they stood in silence, staring at the Explorer as it rumbled past.

Drake watched the ancient war machines in his rear-view mirror as they faded away into the distance; silent reminders of a forgotten conflict from another age. But he caught himself wondering if future generations driving this road would pass the rusting hulls of M1 Abrams tanks.

With that cheerful thought fresh in his mind, he dug out his cellphone and put a call in to Frost. As usual, her greeting was direct and to the point. 'Yeah?'

'It's me. I just left the crash site.'

'Great. I hope you've been having fun out there while I've been stuck in this shit stain of an office.'

Frost might have been a technician by trade, but she was a field operative through and through. She hated being left out of things.

'Well, you were right about one thing. Mitchell was deliberately targeted,' Drake said, hoping his admission would brighten her outlook. 'Kourash was willing to go to a lot of effort to get his hands on him, and I need to know why. Tell me you've got something.'

Reaching into the centre console, he pulled out a bottle of water and popped the lid. Already he was parched and he'd only been outside a matter of minutes.

'Well, I could but I'd be lying,' she admitted. 'I turned over his office. Nothing. His filing cabinets were empty – damn things have probably never been used.'

Drake could feel his heart sinking as he gulped down some water. 'Anything on his computer?'

'Nothing so far. I'll need more time to trawl through the drive, but according to his email history he sends off a progress report to Langley once a week. It seems he was setting up a bunch of safe houses across the country – the kind of places where they could stage operations or meet with informants. The rest of it is just internal admin stuff, nothing important. In fact, there's not much email traffic at all. If I didn't know better – and I don't – I'd say he's been slacking off lately.'

He frowned, taking another mouthful. 'So we've got an office that's hardly used, and a computer he only does the bare minimum of work on. His job was nothing special, and yet Kourash was willing to shoot down a chopper to get to him. What does that tell you, Keira?'

It didn't take her long to put the pieces together. 'Mitchell was working on something else. Something that made him a threat.'

'The question is, what?'

The GPS was telling him to take a left. Braking sharply, he turned onto another nondescript road that wound its way through the dusty landscape.

'Stay on it,' he instructed. 'I'm on my way back now. Drake out.'

Swerving to avoid a deep pothole that looked as if it would make mincemeat out of his tyres, Drake glanced at his watch. It was 11:57. Halfway through their first day, and he had far more questions than answers.

'If I'm right, it should be around here somewhere,' McKnight said as she picked her way carefully through the dry bushes and loose rocks scattered across the hillside. Her eyes were glued to the ground, searching for any sign of recent human activity.

It was just past noon and scorching hot, the dry dusty air stinging her lungs with each breath. A fine sheen of sweat coated her brow. She wiped it away with her forearm, staying focused on her task. She had served two tours with the army in Iraq, plus six months in and around Afghanistan with the Agency. She knew all about working in hot, uncomfortable conditions.

Only when she saw movement in her peripheral vision did she stop to glance around. One of their Horizon minders was moving along the ridge to take up a lookout position further ahead. He was armed with a Barrett M107 sniper rifle. Known as the 'light fifty', it was a massive .50-calibre weapon originally designed for taking out armoured vehicles.

'Please tell your man to stay back,' she called out, directing her request to Vermaak. The South African was perched on a low sloping boulder a short distance away, smoking a cigarette. Behind him sat the imposing bulk of one of the armoured jeeps, the long muzzle of its automatic cannon tracking back and forth.

Vermaak's head swung slowly in her direction, his eyes hidden behind a pair of sunglasses. For several seconds he said nothing, as if deciding whether she was worthy of his time.

'He's there for your protection,' he replied at last.

'He's also contaminating the site. If he walks all across this ridge, I'll have no idea if I've found his footprints or someone else's. Understand?'

Another long pause. She saw a muscle in his jaw clench, saw his powerful shoulders tighten. He held the cigarette to his lips and took another draw, long and thoughtful.

The man with the Barrett .50-calibre had stopped in his tracks and was looking expectantly towards his commander, awaiting orders.

'All right. Come back to the truck, Hale,' Vermaak ordered, beckoning him to return. His voice was practically dripping with disgust. 'Leave the lady to do her job.'

'Thank you,' McKnight said, hoping to pacify him.

Vermaak didn't bother to look at her when he replied. 'Just so you know, *Ms* McKnight, we're totally exposed out here. Every second we stay increases the danger to my men, and to you. Understand?'

She understood very well. He resented being here, and he resented taking orders from a woman even more.

'We'll finish up just as soon as we can,' she replied without emotion, and went back to her work.

'Ever get the feeling we're not welcome here?' Keegan asked quietly, grinning as he picked his way along beside her.

'This is Afghanistan. We're not welcome anywhere.'

'I hear you,' he agreed. As she went back to searching the ground, he added, 'Just so we're clear, what exactly are we looking for here? Burned ground from the back-blast?'

'Hardly,' she said without looking up. 'If the missile's engine was powerful enough to burn the ground when it fired, what do you think it would do to the poor guy holding the launcher?'

Keegan snorted in amusement. 'Point taken. My question stands, though.'

'Well, I doubt our friends would be stupid enough to leave the launcher itself lying around,' she said. 'But if they were up here, they should have left signs. Tracks, footprints, maybe a concealed firing position they'd prepared. They might even have used a vehicle to get here. Even the smaller shoulder-launched SAMs are five or six feet long and weigh a good thirty pounds. Not the kind of thing you'd want to be seen carrying around. If we do find tyre tracks, we might be able to figure out what kind of vehicle they belong to.'

'You know your stuff,' he remarked, impressed.

'I should. I've had plenty of practice.'

'How'd you get involved in all this, if you don't mind my asking?'

She paused just for a moment, thinking about it. 'I used to be US Army, working for the EOD teams.'

EOD stood for Explosive Ordnance Disposal; specialised teams brought in to defuse unexploded bombs, mines and booby traps. Theirs was one of the most hazardous tasks of all, as they often had to operate in combat zones while they went about the dangerous job of rendering high-explosive devices safe.

'I did a couple of tours in Iraq, then got sent back Stateside to work as an instructor. I applied for a third tour but they kept stalling me.' She grinned at the memory. 'It was pretty obvious they didn't want a woman coming home in a body bag. Or several body bags in my case. But as it happened, the Agency found out about me and offered me a job.'

'Plenty of work for you out here, huh?'

At this, her grin faded a little. 'You bet your ass there is.'

They were both silent for a time as they slowly picked their way forwards. The breeze sighed around them, stirring tiny particles of dust, while the sun beat down mercilessly from a cloudless sky.

Their time here was running short. More than once they saw Vermaak glancing at his watch.

'Mind if I ask you something?' McKnight said, breaking the silence.

'Shoot.' Seeing her look, he grinned. 'Bad choice of words, huh?'

She ignored his attempt at humour.

'What's this business between Drake and Franklin? I assume we're talking about *the* Dan Franklin. As in, the guy who runs Special Activities.'

'The one and only,' he acknowledged. 'They've got a history together, those two.'

'What kind of history?'

'The bad kind.' The old sniper sighed and lowered himself down on his haunches, staring off into the distance with a thoughtful expression on his craggy face. 'Believe me, you're better off not knowing.'

'And if I thought otherwise?' she prompted.

'Then you'd have to ask Ryan yourself.'

She was about to say something, but decided against it. Something had caught her eye. Something she'd been looking for since their arrival.

'At last,' McKnight breathed, dropping to her knees.

The sandy ground in front of her was marked by a pair of boot prints. They were faint and indistinct, the slow progress of the wind gradually wearing them away, but were still intact enough for her to discern a general size and outline. They seemed to be heading downhill.

Keegan approached from her left, his steps slow and careful so as not to walk right over other tracks. 'Looks like a big guy,' he said after studying the boot prints. 'Maybe two hundred and forty pounds.'

'Thirty pounds of which could have been the missile and its launcher,' McKnight reminded him.

'Oh, yeah,' he agreed. 'Still, look at the stride length, the weight distribution. This guy must have been well over six feet.' He pointed to another print further down the slope; this one on the lee side of a low rock and therefore better protected from the wind. 'Looks like he was wearing military-patterned boots. I don't recognise the tread, though.'

McKnight glanced at him, impressed by his insight. 'You see a lot.'

He shrugged. 'My daddy taught me how to hunt and track when I was a kid. Kinda stuck with me. Humans aren't that different from deer or coyotes – they're just dumber.'

She opened her mouth to say something, but suddenly she saw Keegan's eyes dart to some indistinct point over her right shoulder. Then without warning the older man launched himself forward, grabbed her roughly around the waist and threw her to the ground. She landed hard, a rock jabbing painfully into her ribs as his weight settled on top of her.

A moment later, the ground behind her exploded with a dull thud as something impacted with tremendous force, throwing up pieces of broken stone and chunks of dry earth that coated her in a fine spray.

For a moment McKnight's mind was frozen in shock, unable to process what had just happened. Only when the rolling crack of a gunshot reached them a few seconds later did she suddenly snap back into awareness.

'Sniper!' Keegan yelled, lying flat on the ground beside her.

Her heart hammering in her chest, McKnight stared at the foot-wide crater where the high-velocity round had struck, impacting like a miniature artillery shell. She realised with a strange sense of detachment that it would have been her own body sporting such damage if Keegan hadn't shoved her out of the way.

Vermaak and the other Horizon operatives who had accompanied them up to the ridge wasted no time throwing themselves behind cover. Within seconds they had vanished from sight.

'All units, we have incoming sniper fire from the south-east,' the South African said, speaking low and urgent into his radio. 'Anyone got eyes on target?'

'I counted three seconds before we heard the shot,' Keegan called out, his voice now calm and controlled. He knew better than to panic in a situation like this. 'He's gotta be at least a thousand yards out.'

McKnight's face and clothes were covered in dusty sand. It was in her eyes, dry and gritty, making them stream with water. Wiping them as best she could, McKnight raised her head a little to look out over the empty plains beyond, but Keegan was quick to push her back down.

'Might want to keep that down till we get a fix on him,' he warned. 'This guy's got talent.'

She glanced at him. 'How did you—'

Her sentence was abruptly cut off by the thundering boom of weapons fire. The M2 heavy machine gun mounted atop the nearest armoured personnel carrier had turned south-east and opened up on full automatic, its 2-foot-long muzzle flash reflecting off the windshield below.

The noise was unbelievable, the concussive impact of each round sending little tremors through the rock around them. Spent shell casings clattered off the vehicle's armour belt to land sizzling on the sand.

Further down the slope, the second vehicle added its firepower to the barrage, spraying tracer rounds in a seemingly random fashion. Clutching her ears, McKnight could do nothing but wait until it was over.

At last the firing ceased, the echoes dying down, though her ears were ringing. The air reeked of burned cordite, and a faint haze of smoke hung over their surroundings.

Keegan reached out and touched her arm.

'You all right?' he asked, having to raise his voice to be heard. Even then it sounded thin and distant.

McKnight nodded, unsure what to say.

'You all done up there?' Keegan called out. 'What was the point of that, except to waste ammo?'

'Suppressing fire,' Vermaak replied from somewhere behind the armoured vehicle. He sounded more irritated than panicked. 'Come to us, man. We're pulling out of here.'

The older man considered it for a moment, then shook his head. 'I don't think so. This guy's good. He would have scored a hit with his first shot from a thousand yards out, and believe me, there ain't many snipers who can do that.' He reached up and ran a hand through his dishevelled hair, pushing sweat-soaked strands out of his face. 'He's out there right now, just waiting for one of your boys to make a run for the truck. Soon as that happens, you're gonna be picking pieces of them off your windshield.'

The South African was quiet for several moments. 'What do you suggest?'

'Call in air support,' McKnight said. 'They could find him on infrared.'

'Forget it. It'd take too long to get here.' Keegan chewed his lip for a moment, weighing up his options. There weren't many.

At last he nodded as if to confirm the decision to himself. 'Where's the guy with the Barrett light fifty?'

'Up here,' came the reply. 'The name's Hale.'

'Okay, Hale. If we draw the son of a bitch out, think you can take the shot?'

The answer wasn't long in coming. 'Fuck that. I ain't getting my head shot off for this shit.'

'You want something done right . . .' Keegan said under his breath, distinctly unimpressed by his counterpart's dedication. Clearly he hadn't joined up to be a hero.

Still, bitching about it wasn't going to get them out of here. There was only one choice if they wanted to take that sniper out.

'Okay. Sit tight. I'm heading your way.' He turned to the woman lying flat on the ground beside him. 'Stay down until the coast is clear, Sam. I don't think he's got line of sight on you.'

'Great. What about you?'

He flashed a grin. 'I'll be fine.'

With that, he turned and started to crawl up the slope, slithering along the dusty ground like a snake, moving only a few inches at a time. Keegan was no stranger to counter-sniping work, and knew how best to frustrate and impede his opponent.

If he was right, his friend out there on the plains would have relocated after the first shot so as not to give away his position. Now he would be set up in his second firing point, sweeping his sights across the ridge, eagerly looking for another target.

It was hard to tell what the man was armed with. Considering most of the weapons and equipment used in Afghanistan were of Russian origin, Keegan suspected it was a Dragunov; a heavy sniper rifle developed by the Soviets back in the 1960s. They'd been killing people all over the world for the past fifty years, with great success. Like the AK-47, they weren't exactly refined, but they did the job. Their 7.62mm steel-jacketed projectiles were powerful enough to defeat almost any body armour.

A very dangerous weapon in the right hands.

As he moved, he began to hum a familiar tune under his breath. It was something he always did to keep his mind calm and focused. 'Ninety-nine bottles of beer on the wall, ninety-nine bottles of beer . . .'

The sniper had chosen his timing and location well. It was the hottest part of the day, when heat and inactivity started to erode awareness. No doubt he'd hoped to take out a couple of the personnel on the ridge, then slip away before an effective response could be organised. This was going to be a tricky one. Not only would Keegan be silhouetted against the sky, but he'd be looking for a needle in a haystack.

'Ninety-one bottles of beer on the wall . . .'

He crept forward an inch at a time, trying to keep rocks and bushes between him and the sniper, and also to avoid disturbing any of the dry vegetation. His friend down there would be looking for unnatural movements in the scrub.

Keegan could feel the sweat trickling down his face, stinging his eyes as a combination of heat and exertion took their toll. His shirt clung to his back, his hair plastered to his forehead. He ignored it all, just concentrated on maintaining his progress.

'Eighty-three bottles of beer . . .'

He was getting closer. He could see the squat bulk of the armoured personnel carrier up ahead. Hale would be close to it, just off to the left judging by where his voice had come from.

Eager to reach his destination, he picked up the pace.

Not much further now.

'Seventy bottles of beer . . .'

He felt as much as heard the faint whizz of the incoming projectile. After passing through 1,000 yards of dry dusty air, even high-powered rounds lose a lot of their kinetic energy, often making them subsonic.

Instinctively he flattened himself against the ground just as the bullet slammed into a rock beside him, blasting it apart in a shower of tiny fragments that peppered him like buckshot. A couple of seconds later, the sharp crack of the gunshot finally reached them.

In response, the heavy machine gun atop the armoured personnel carrier started up again, spitting out a long burst of automatic fire in the general direction of the shot.

'God damn, cut it out!' Keegan yelled when the last echoes of the barrage had faded away. 'You gonna shoot up the entire horizon?'

'John, are you okay?' McKnight called to him. She couldn't see him from her position and wasn't going to risk getting up to look.

Something wet was trickling down his cheek. Thinking it was just sweat, he wiped at it with his hand, only to find his fingers stained red with blood. The rock fragments must have cut him.

'Yeah, I'm good,' he replied, unsettled by his close call. 'But this guy's starting to piss me off.'

'This is taking too fucking long,' Vermaak growled. 'He's probably calling his mates to bring reinforcements right now. You want to sit here and wait for more snipers to show up?'

Keegan gritted his teeth. He was running out of time. He glanced up towards the crest of the ridge, estimating the distance at a dozen yards or so. A man at full sprint could cover that in just a few seconds.

A few seconds.

The moment he broke cover, the sniper would see the movement. It would take him a second or so to bring his weapon to bear, line up the shot, then another precious moment to put first pressure on the trigger, relax his body, exhale and fire. Travelling supersonic, the round would take at least another second to cover the 1,000 yards between the rifle and its target.

In total, he guessed he had between two and four seconds to sprint up the hill and find cover. That was a pretty big margin for error, but there were just too many factors that he couldn't compensate for. A lot of it would come down to the basic skill and shooting style of the sniper himself. He had already proven himself an excellent marksman, foiled only by luck and good observation. Whether or not he had good reactions would likely mean the difference between life and death.

Reaching down his shirt, Keegan found the charms hanging from the simple leather necklace he wore: a dice, a crucifix and a wedding ring. He gently touched the pointed spars of the crucifix, sending out a silent prayer to anyone who might be inclined to listen. After sending so many people His way ahead of schedule, Keegan was under no illusions that he was in God's good books, but he hoped the Almighty was in a forgiving mood today.

'Screw it,' he said, scrambling to his feet and taking off at full sprint, fuelled by fear and adrenalin.

The clock in his head was running.

One second. The sniper would have seen the movement, and would be bringing the big cumbersome rifle to bear on his target.

The dry dusty air seared his lungs with every breath, the muscles in his legs ached each time they bunched and released. The ground was rough and uneven beneath his boots, always threatening to give way beneath him. He paid no attention to any of it. He ran with every ounce of speed and energy he could summon.

Two seconds. The sniper would have a sight picture now, would have lined up his shot and adjusted his aim to account for wind speed, range and air temperature. His finger would tighten on the trigger until it resisted, his body would relax, and he would apply that fraction more pressure needed to fire.

A wide boulder blocked Keegan's path. No time to skirt around it. Gathering himself up, he leapt over the obstruction, landing awkwardly but managing to stay on his feet. Twenty years ago he would have made such a jump with ease, a tiny part of his mind reflected. Now, pushing fifty, he barely cleared the obstacle.

Three seconds. The sniper had opened fire. The 7.62mm projectile would have left the barrel at something close to 800 metres per second. At this very moment it would be hurtling towards him faster than the speed of sound, 9.8 grams of high-velocity metal eager to blast its way through his soft, fragile body.

He was there. Cresting the ridge at last, Keegan threw himself on the ground, heedless of sharp rocks that tore at his clothes and skin. His heart was beating so hard and fast he could feel it thumping in his ears.

But it was still beating, and that was all that mattered. He was alive.

A moment later, he heard a faint whizz as the shot zipped by overhead. Unlike the other two, there was no dull thump as it impacted the hillside. This one had cleared the ridge altogether, and would carry on for another 1,000 yards or so before it exhausted its kinetic energy and fell harmlessly back to earth.

Glancing towards the armoured personnel carrier, he saw Vermaak glaring at him, his eyes holding a mixture of annoyance and grudging respect. 'You got a death wish or something, man?'

Keegan laughed, an instinctive response to the pressure he'd been under. 'Midlife crisis. Now where's that fifty?'

'Right here,' the operative named Hale said, crawling over with the bulky sniper rifle cradled in his arms.

Keegan hefted the weapon and brought it around in front of him, flipping the folded bipod legs down so it was properly positioned. This done, he checked the telescopic sights, made sure a round was chambered and that the feed mechanism wasn't fouled with dirt. As far as he could tell, the weapon was good to go.

He reckoned the wind speed at not more than a couple of knots, blowing almost directly away from him. The air was warm and thin; they were nearly 1,500 metres above sea level in this part of the world. In short, these were perfect sniping conditions, and he had an excellent weapon to work with.

Now all he needed was a target.

'Vermaak, I need one of your boys to stand up for a few seconds.'

At this, the stocky South African actually laughed. 'You want to use my men as bait? Forget it. We're not here for target practice.'

'I need to draw the sniper out. He ain't gonna move until he has a target to shoot at. All I need is a couple of seconds.'

Vermaak pondered it for a moment. 'Then I tell you what, my friend. Any man here who wants to volunteer to be your bait is free to do it now. I won't stop him.' He raised his voice so everyone nearby could hear. 'Anyone?'

Silence prevailed, broken only by the faint sigh of the wind.

Vermaak shrugged. 'The people have spoken, Mr Keegan.'

Then, suddenly, a lone voice called out. 'I'll do it.'

It was McKnight, still lying behind cover further down the slope. Keegan couldn't see her from where he was, but he remembered exactly where she was waiting.

The veteran sniper chewed his lip, reluctant to put her in harm's way. He was, after all, here to protect her.

'You sure you want to do this, Sam?' he called out.

'You mean, do I want to stand up and get shot at by a mad Taliban sniper? Not really, but since no "men" are willing to volunteer, we don't have much choice, do we?'

Keegan glanced at Vermaak for a moment, but said nothing to that. Instead he gripped the heavy sniper rifle tight and flicked the fire selector from safe to semi-automatic.

'Okay. On my mark, I want you to get up and start running up the slope towards us. Run for no more than three seconds, then hit the deck. I'll take care of the rest. Understand?'

'Unfortunately I do.' There was a slight waver in her voice now. She hesitated before speaking again. 'Tell me you're good at this.'

'I'm better than our boy out there. Believe that,' he promised her, fervently hoping it was true.

'Good enough.'

Pushing strands of sweat-soaked hair out of his eyes, Keegan took a deep breath, trying to still his racing heart. 'On my mark, Sam. Three, two, one . . . go!'

He heard the scuffle of boots on gravel as the woman rose to her feet and took off at a run.

One second. The sniper would have seen the movement. He was bringing the weapon to bear.

Hefting the bulky, heavy rifle up to his shoulder, Keegan rose up into a crouch, immediately training his scope on the open plains beyond their ridge.

He had seen and recognised the telltale muzzle flash when the Dragunov first fired, alerting him that a round was incoming. That was the reason he'd been able to push McKnight to the ground, saving her life. It had been luck as much as anything.

Now her life was once again in his hands, and it was going to take more than luck to save it. He swept the weapon left, finding the area where he'd first seen the muzzle flash. Seeing it now through the scope, it looked as though the sniper had been crouched against the bank of a dried-up river bed. A perfect place to fire from. Plenty of cover, and a natural depression allowing him to move unseen.

Two seconds. The sniper would have found a sight picture of McKnight. His finger would be tightening on the trigger right now, taking first pressure.

The sniper would have relocated after each shot to avoid counter-sniping. The river bed ran from north to south at right angles to the ridge, following the line of the broad valley through which it had once flowed. The sniper could have gone in either direction. Which way? Left or right? North or south? He had a fifty-fifty chance, and less than a second to make his decision.

He chose right, on the basis that most people were right-handed and had a tendency to favour their good side when changing direction.

His sight picture became a blur of movement as he adjusted his aim, frantically searching for a target. The weapon was a leaden weight in his arms, burning his muscles with the strain of holding it level. The sun was shining straight in his eyes, casting long shadows, blinding him.

No target.

Three seconds. The sniper would have his target, his

body would be relaxed, his aim true, his weapon ready. The perfect shot.

Suddenly Keegan's weapon stopped moving as his eyes at last found what they had been looking for.

Between two rocks, partially hidden by shadow, he saw a shape that didn't belong. Something that didn't conform to the reassuring randomness of nature. Something man-made. The long eager barrel of a Dragunov. And just behind, its owner.

Keegan's grip tightened. His heartbeat slowed as years of training and experience took over. He was working by instinct and intuition now as he turned the weapon a fraction left to compensate for a shifting wind.

He exhaled, allowing the tension to leave his body, then pulled the trigger.

The recoil of a single 50-calibre round slammed the weapon back into his shoulder with bruising force, almost knocking him off balance. The blast from the muzzle caused a shockwave to spread across the ground in front of him, raising tiny clouds of dust. Unlike the sharp crack of most weapons, the Barrett's report was dull, heavy and ponderous, sounding more like an artillery piece than an infantry weapon.

With his ears ringing, he worked to steady the weapon, to catch another glimpse of his target.

It took him a second or so to line up his sights. Just enough time for the bullet to travel the 1,000 yards to its target.

Designed as it was to blast straight through the engine blocks of enemy vehicles, the heavy-calibre projectile made short work of a human skull. Keegan saw the sudden plume of red mist behind his target, saw the shadowy figure crumple and disappear from view, saw the long barrel of the Dragunov tilt skywards as its owner lost his grip on the weapon.

'Good kill,' he announced, taking a breath for the first time in several seconds.

'Well, fuck me,' Vermaak said, impressed by his shooting. 'Not a bad shot.'

'It's all in the reflexes, son,' Keegan replied, engaging the safety on the Barrett and laying the weapon down, grateful to be free of its cumbersome weight. Wiping the sweat from his brow, he rose up slowly and waited a few anxious seconds. He was quite certain he'd scored a fatal hit, but it never hurt to be sure.

When nothing happened, he at last allowed himself to relax a little.

'How you doing down there, Sam?' he called out.

Further down the slope, McKnight was lying in a shallow depression. Obeying his instructions, she had thrown herself to the ground after running for a few heart-stopping seconds, certain that every step would be her last, certain she would feel the crushing impact as a bullet tore through her body.

It had never happened. She was alive. She was tired, dirty, cut and bruised, but she was very much alive.

'I'm good,' she called out, making to stand up.

As she did so, she noticed something lying half-hidden in a bush to her right. Something that gleamed in the harsh sunlight. Something metallic.

Curious, she reached out and picked it up.

The object in her hand was cylindrical in shape, a little smaller than a soda can, with a nozzle at one end and some kind of base plate at the other. Its purpose was instantly familiar, though it took her conscious mind a moment to identify its origin.

Then, in a flash, the pieces fell into place and she understood.

'You can get up now,' Keegan called, mistaking her hesitation for fear. 'Our friend out there is history.'

McKnight knew she didn't have time to ponder the full implications of her find. That would have to come later. Stuffing the object into the pack she'd been using to carry her forensics gear, she rose to her feet and managed to summon up a smile for the man who might well have saved her life.

'Like you said, you were better than him.'

'This is very touching, but I think it's time we got out of here,' Vermaak interjected before hitting the transmit button on his short-range radio. 'Unit Two, the sniper's taken care of. Are your charges set?'

'That's affirm,' the unit crackled in response.

'Good. Blow it. We're pulling out.'

McKnight's eyes opened wide. 'No! Wait.'

But it was too late. The sudden flash followed by a concussive boom loud enough to rattle the windows on the nearby armoured personnel carrier told her they had just set off the demolition charges inside the wrecked chopper. Whatever secrets it might have held had just been obliterated.

She rounded on the South African, her hazel eyes smouldering with anger. 'You just blew up a crime scene, you asshole. We could have found out more from that wreck.'

Vermaak, however, was unmoved by her recrimin-ations as he lit up a cigarette. 'We've wasted enough time here, *Ms* McKnight.' Turning away, he raised his voice to address the rest of his team. 'All right, guys. Pack everything up. We're leaving.'

'What about the sniper?' Keegan asked.

'What about him?'

'He might have intel on him. Documents, cellphones . . . something that might tell us who he was working for. We can't just leave him out here, for Christ's sake.'

Vermaak took a long draw on his cigarette. 'We won't. We'll radio ISAF to send a team out. We're here for security, not intelligence gathering. Our job's done.'

His gaze switched to McKnight as the vehicle's big diesel engine roared into life. 'Now, either you come with us, or you can find your own way home, Ms McKnight. Which will it be?'

Chapter 10

Many of the Agency's operations in Afghanistan were coordinated from a compound inside the larger military facility of Bagram Air Base. It was to all intents and purposes a base within a base, housed inside its own security perimeter constructed of Bremer walls – 12- foot-high sections of steel-reinforced concrete.

After passing through the security checkpoint, during which he was dismounted and the Explorer thoroughly searched by sniffer dogs and armed guards, Drake was permitted to drive 50 yards to a nearby parking lot.

A man, presumably from the Agency's staff, was waiting for him.

Whoever he was, nature hadn't been kind to him: 5 foot 8, skinny, with bristly red hair and a lined, careworn face that made him seem a lot older than his fifty-odd years, he didn't win any points for appearance. The sweat-stained shirt and faded jeans he was wearing didn't do him any favours either.

His eyes were hidden behind a pair of aviator sunglasses. 'You're Drake, I assume?' he said by way of greeting.

Clearly the man wasn't one for pleasantries. 'That's right.'

'My name's Crawford. I'm your official liaison out here.'

'Pleased to meet you,' Drake said, extending a hand.

The older man neglected to shake it. 'Don't be. I'm a section leader in a CIA field unit, which officially makes me a pain in the ass for guys like you.'

Drake frowned. He had no interest in getting into some kind of turf war with this man, and didn't understand why he was being so confrontational. 'I don't think you understand why I'm here. One of your men has been taken hostage –'

'I know all about Hal Mitchell,' Crawford interrupted. 'The loss of a man like him is a tragedy, but I've got hundreds more men and women like him to worry about. They're my priority now. Langley sends a Shepherd team out to find Mitchell – that's great, I hope you do. And I'll cooperate with you as long as you respect our operational security. But if you jeopardise our ongoing operations or put my personnel at risk, I will not hesitate to make it my life's work to destroy yours. Clear?'

Drake understood where Crawford was coming from now. There were still a lot of men like him in the Agency; guys who had been out in the field a little too long, who had become a little too hardened to the realities of their profession. They weren't necessarily bad people, but as Crawford himself had said, they could be a pain in the arse to deal with.

'Clear.' It was obvious Crawford would accept no other answer.

'Outstanding. Now that we know where we stand, come with me.' With that, he turned and started walking towards a two-storey grey concrete office block near the centre of the compound.

Drake had little choice but to follow him.

'One of your teammates has already set up shop here,' Crawford explained. 'Quite a little firecracker. She didn't take that speech as well as you did.'

Drake wasn't surprised. 'I need to speak to her.'

True to his instructions, Frost had appropriated a small conference room within the building's labyrinth of corridors. Low-ceilinged, windowless and lit by fluorescent strip lights, the small meeting space had an oppressive, claustrophobic feel to it.

The young woman was seated at the modest table. Her laptop, several folders and countless sheets of paper were strewn across its surface.

She looked up only briefly, giving him a none-too-welcoming look. Clearly she was far from pleased at being lumbered with such a tedious job.

'Find anything on Mitchell's computer?' Drake asked, helping himself to coffee from an urn in the corner.

'Yeah, Jack Shit. You heard of him?'

'We've met a few times.' He took a sip of the coffee. It tasted bitter and nasty, but that didn't stop him downing a mouthful. He looked at Crawford, who had come in behind him and closed the door. 'I assume Mitchell wasn't based anywhere else? He didn't have any other offices to work from?'

'If he did, he never told anyone about it.'

That was all Drake needed to hear. For the time being at least, Mitchell was a dead end. 'Then we focus on Kourash,' he decided. 'What do you know about him?'

Crawford folded his arms. 'Anwari? Nasty piece of work. He and his group have been linked to at least a dozen attacks in the past six months. Car bombings, sniper attacks, ambushes, you name it. This is the first time they've shot down an aircraft, though.'

'I'll need everything you have on the previous attacks. Targets, locations, forensics reports, everything. Provided that's okay with you?' he added with a hint of sarcasm.

'I can have someone bring that up.' He certainly

107

wasn't going to do it himself. 'What are you expecting to find?'

'A pattern. Mitchell's chopper wasn't a random hit, so maybe the others weren't either. If we can figure out his intentions we might know what he's planning.'

'Now why didn't we think of that?' Crawford snorted. 'We've been on his trail for months, Drake. He's a ghost.'

'No. He's a gambler,' Drake corrected him. 'I know how he operates. He doesn't just want to hear a news report about his latest attack – he wants to see it with his own eyes. I'd bet my life he was there when they shot down that chopper, and wherever his next attack comes, he'll be around.'

While he was undoubtedly a cunning and tenacious guerrilla fighter, Kourash's weakness had been his vanity. Lingering near the sites of bombings and ambushes, believing himself safe behind disguises and false identities, he would watch his carefully laid plans unfold like some eighteenth-century general surveying the battlefield.

'And you know all of this . . . how?' Crawford was watching him closely now.

Drake fixed him with a hard look. 'Because I captured him five years ago.'

The field agent said nothing to that. Doubtless he was now pondering the same question Drake had been asking himself since this thing began – why didn't he kill him when he'd had the chance?

'This is all great, but Mitchell will probably be dead by the time Anwari makes another attack. We need to find him first,' Frost reminded them.

Drake nodded, realising he was losing perspective. 'I've been thinking about that hostage tape. The yellow stains on the wall behind Mitchell,' he said, recalling the cracked brickwork with what looked like mould growing on it. 'They looked like sulphur deposits. My guess is they're holding him in some kind of industrial area – maybe a chemical plant or a factory. That's our starting point. We need a list of all abandoned facilities in Afghanistan.'

'That could be a hell of a long list,' Crawford remarked. Afghanistan's fledgling industrial base had been largely destroyed after the Soviets pulled out. There were abandoned factories and plants dotted all over the country.

'Assuming they're not moving him from place to place,' Frost added.

Drake shrugged. 'It's a start. Worst-case scenario, we eliminate some of the places he *isn't* hiding. In the meantime I suggest we—'

He paused, interrupted by the buzzing of the cellphone in his pocket. It was Keegan. Maybe he and McKnight had had some luck after all.

'John, how's it going?'

'Could be better,' the older man remarked. 'We had ourselves some trouble out at the crash site.'

Drake felt a knot of apprehension tighten in his stomach. 'What kind of trouble?'

'We were hit at the crash site. Got a little tricky but we're okay,' the sniper assured him, much to his relief. 'We're at the base hospital right now.'

That was all he needed to hear. 'We're on our way.'

Chapter 11

The Heathe N. Craig Joint Theater Hospital, named after a staff sergeant killed trying to rescue injured comrades two years earlier, was a fifty-bed medical facility located on the west side of Bagram Air Base. It was the first port of call for many casualties brought in from the front line.

The smell of medical disinfectant as he hurried in through the main entrance stirred deep feelings of foreboding in Drake, despite Keegan's assurance that neither he nor McKnight was seriously hurt.

A quick consultation with the corporal on duty at the front desk told him that both his teammates were in treatment room 3. Drake was there in under a minute, with Frost right behind as he threw open the door and strode into the room.

Keegan and McKnight were both there. Their clothes were torn and dirty, and both were nursing various cuts and bruises, though they seemed to have escaped major injury.

'Are you all right?'

Keegan, with a couple of tape stitches holding together a facial laceration, flashed a defiant grin. 'Never better, buddy.'

McKnight was less jubilant. She had pulled up her T-shirt to expose an ugly bruise just below her ribcage, the discoloured skin cut and grazed. A female medic was busy applying a sterilised dressing.

Drake couldn't help feeling a sudden pang of guilt. He had left them out there in the field while he returned to the safety of Bagram, and this was the result. 'You're hurt.'

'Very astute, Ryan,' she remarked with a wry smile. 'But it's nothing. Just cuts and bruises.'

Unconvinced, Drake glanced at the medic for confirmation.

'We've patched her up, sir. She'll be fine,' the woman said.

That at least seemed to satisfy him. 'Can we have the room, please?'

The conversation they were about to have wasn't the kind he wanted to be overheard. Finishing up with the dressing, the medic packed away her gear and left the room.

'What happened out there?' Drake asked as soon as the door closed.

'We had a close encounter with a sniper,' was McKnight's simple reply. 'Fortunately John took him out first.' She glanced at the older man with gratitude in her eyes. 'Even then, Vermaak and the Horizon team pulled out. They blew the crash site before we could stop them.'

'It was like fuckin' Hiroshima, man,' Keegan added. 'They used enough C4 to sink a battleship. There's nothing left.'

Drake's heart sank. He was relieved beyond words that his two team members had returned more or less unharmed, but there was no escaping the fact that they had just lost a major avenue of investigation.

'What about the sniper? Where did he come from?'

'No idea,' Keegan admitted.

'Didn't you find anything on him?'

The older man threw up his hands in a gesture of helplessness. 'Never got the chance. Vermaak was so anxious to clear out of there, they left the body behind. Wasn't in their job description, apparently,' he added with a look of disgust.

'We just heard from an army patrol sent in to retrieve the body,' McKnight added. 'There was no sign of it.'

Drake couldn't believe what he was hearing. First the Horizon team tried to stop them accessing the crash site altogether, then they acted as if they owned the place, and to top it all off they had destroyed a crime scene and left a dead enemy combatant unrecovered. Their actions might well have sunk the entire investigation.

Seeing those thoughts reflected in his eyes, McKnight grabbed her rucksack, lying discarded on a nearby bed. 'It's not all bad news. In fact, I'd say we might just have lucked out.'

'How so?'

Reaching into the pack, she lifted out a small metal object and tossed it across the room. Instinctively Drake caught it and held it up to the light to take a closer look.

It was metal, cylindrical in shape, and relatively heavy for its size. The outlet nozzle at one end suggested it was an engine of some kind, and the smell of propellant confirmed this theory. He had no idea what purpose it served though.

'I found this at the launch site, just after Keegan took the sniper down. In fact, if that guy hadn't attacked us, I might never have found it at all,' McKnight explained. 'You know what it is?'

'I have a feeling you're about to tell me.'

'It's an ejector motor,' she said, looking like

112

an archaeologist who had just uncovered a priceless artefact. 'When you fire a surface-to-air missile from a shoulder launcher, a little disposable rocket like this pushes the missile clear of the tube. Once it's a safe distance away, the missile's own engine ignites and off it goes. The ejector motor just falls away when it's served its purpose.'

Taking his eyes off the rocket motor, he looked up at the woman who had recovered it. 'Can you work out what kind of weapon this came from?'

'I can tell you right now,' she said. 'It's an FIM-92 Stinger.'

Stunned silence greeted her words as the implications sank in.

Mitchell's chopper had been shot down by an American missile.

'How sure are you?' Drake asked. He doubted she would have made such a claim if there was any doubt in her mind, but he had to know.

'I've seen these things a dozen times before, and I've studied their technical drawings more times than I can count,' she assured him. 'I know what to look for, and I'd bet my life that it came from a Stinger. I'll need to check on the serial numbers to work out what batch it's from, but there's no doubt in my mind.'

'That doesn't make any sense,' Keegan said, frowning. 'Where the hell would these assholes have got their hands on a Stinger?'

Frost looked at the older man in exasperation. 'From *us*. Don't you get it? We sent hundreds of these things here twenty years ago.'

It was an open secret nowadays that the Agency had channelled billions of dollars' worth of weapons and equipment to the Mujahideen during the Soviet invasion.

At first it was Russian-made weapons bought from Czechoslovakia, Poland, Romania, and even corrupt Red Army logistics officers in Afghanistan itself. But as the war escalated, the assistance became more and more overt.

Soon state-of-the-art anti-aircraft missiles like the Stinger were flooding the country, and shooting down Russian gunships and fighter-bombers with deadly efficiency. Much as in Vietnam twenty years earlier, the weapons of one superpower were being used by proxy to fight a war against the other.

'The Agency supplied weapons like these to the Afghan rebels back in the eighties. When the war ended, we tried to buy them back.' Drake glanced at McKnight with a raised eyebrow. 'It seems we missed a few.'

The Mujahideen, though united against a common enemy in the Soviets, had never been a coherent group. Ethnic and tribal feuding had been rife even during the invasion, and when they no longer had a common cause to fight for, those simmering tensions erupted in full-scale civil war.

With the country descending into anarchy, the weapons supplied by the CIA were scattered amongst the various warring tribes, changing hands so quickly they soon became impossible to track down. The West had created a monster, and could do nothing but watch as it consumed the very country it was supposed to liberate.

Keegan was quick to see the implications. 'Christ, if news like this got out—'

'It would be a public-relations disaster,' McKnight finished for him. 'American troops shot down by American-made weapons. The media would be all over it.'

'I say let them,' Frost decided, disgusted by what she'd heard. 'The assholes who gave them the weapons deserve to be punished.'

'You're missing the bigger picture,' McKnight cut in. 'ISAF, NATO, and especially the White House want to get the hell out of Afghanistan. Bush doesn't want to go down in history as the guy who led us into a second Vietnam. But if news got out that the insurgents had surface-to-air missiles, any chance of leaving Afghanistan goes up in smoke.'

Drake let out a breath, his mind racing. 'No wonder the army were so keen to write this off as an RPG strike.'

'It might explain why Horizon were so uncooperative out at the crash site,' McKnight added. 'Maybe they were under orders to keep this thing quiet.'

Drake said nothing for several moments as he worked through everything he'd just heard. A whole lot of possibilities had just opened up in front of them, none of which were good. What the hell had they stumbled into here?

And in all of it, there was one question that kept nagging at him. What did Kourash really want with Mitchell?

Somehow he was the key to all this. Whatever secrets the man held had been worth shooting down a chopper for. Drake didn't understand how or why yet, but he intended to find out.

'All right, we need to get moving on this,' he decided. He looked up at McKnight. 'Sam, did you tell anyone else about this?'

She shook her head. 'No one. And I don't think they saw me pick it up.'

'Good.' He tossed the device back to her. 'Find out everything you can on the Stinger. I want to know where and when it was built, where it was shipped, and how the hell it ended up here.'

'I'll do my best,' she promised. 'What about you?'

'I'm going to have a word with our friends at Horizon.'

Chapter 12

Once again Drake was forced to borrow McKnight's Ford Explorer. Horizon weren't based at Bagram as he'd expected, but instead operated from their own independent compound on the outskirts of Kabul. The message was clear – they needed no one for protection.

He had called ahead to request a meeting with the most senior Horizon executive available, using a combination of persuasion and veiled threats to cut through the red tape. The call had concluded with a very unhappy Horizon operator assuring them that a 'member of staff' would be on hand to answer his questions when he arrived.

After clearing the base's heavily fortified security gate, Drake found himself heading south on Highway 76, the main artery that ran between Bagram and Kabul.

He made good progress initially, but was obliged to slow down on the outskirts of the city. Most of the locals had stopped what they were doing for *Asr*, the Islamic prayer offered during mid-afternoon, but now they were back on the roads in force, and there was no avoiding the resultant traffic jams.

Grossly overloaded vans and pickup trucks chugged along beside him on the main drag. Nobody gave way. The chokingly hot air was thick with dust, exhaust fumes and horn blasts.

The situation wasn't helped by the military checkpoints that had been set up at most major road junctions, all of them staffed by Afghan National Police (ANP). This was another new experience for Drake – the last time he'd been in Afghanistan, local law enforcement had been non-existent.

They were a strange-looking bunch. Apart from their flat-peaked caps and dusty grey military tunics, there was almost no unity or cohesion in their gear, uniforms or weapons. Some wore body armour, while some went without. Some had webbing, while others were forced to jam extra magazines into their pockets. Two of them were armed with AKs, and another was packing an old Smith & Wesson Model 39 pistol; the kind worn by US generals back in the 1960s.

Most unusual of all was the soldier with an RPG-7 slung idly over one shoulder as if it were a golf club or a garden rake. Somehow Drake found it hard to imagine police officers back in DC armed with anti-tank rockets.

He'd heard a lot about these guys over the years, most of it less than complimentary. Drug abuse, corruption and desertion were endemic amongst the ANP, with many of their personnel simply melting away during a firefight. Some were even in the pay of the insurgents. Taliban fighters captured at great cost were able to buy their release for as little as 100 dollars.

It took another twenty minutes of driving, queuing and braking to negotiate a tortuous route through Kabul's crowded streets. He was beginning to wish he had circled around the outskirts to approach his destination from the south, but by that point there was little he could do except press on.

And finally, he saw what he was looking for – a big three-storey concrete building dominating the afternoon sky. From his position it was hard to gauge the structure's size and dimensions, but it seemed to consist of a central building with wings stretching out on either side.

It wasn't a new structure; that much was certain. Its imposing grey walls were scarred and pitted by cannon fire and shrapnel impacts, the deeper shell holes showing evidence of recent repair. This building had survived the civil war and years of Taliban rule, if only through sheer strength and resilience.

The entire compound was encircled by a concrete wall at least 12 feet high, topped with razor wire. Guard towers had been placed at intervals along the wall, and even from this distance Drake could make out the long barrels of 50-calibre machine guns trained on the road beyond.

Drake slowed to a stop at the main gate. As far as he could tell, this was the only way in or out of the compound.

The guard post was manned by three Horizon security men, all decked out in full combat gear and armed with M4A1s. With two of his companions keeping a wary eye on Drake, the operative in charge of the post strode towards their vehicle. He was in his early forties, black, with a noticeable shrapnel scar on his left cheek. Clearly he had seen his share of action already.

'Identification, sir,' he said, holding out a gloved hand.

Drake duly obliged. 'I was told I'd be met by one of your representatives,' he explained as the checkpoint controller studied his documents. 'They should be expecting me.'

He was still uneasy about showing his identification to non-Agency personnel. Shepherd teams were by nature clandestine groups, and not inclined to give out any information that could compromise operational security. Nor were they required to when dealing with other Department of Defence organisations.

They didn't have to present passports or other official documents to get into or out of countries like Afghanistan. They had only to identify themselves to a ranking officer briefed in advance of their arrival, and they would be waved through without any mention being made. Their luggage and equipment could not be searched, nor could they be detained or interfered with. If the shit hit the fan they could even show up on the doorstep of the US embassy and be granted access, no questions asked.

All of this was made possible by their official mandate, issued by the Director of National Intelligence himself. It was, in effect, a blank cheque investing them with a great deal of authority. However, their powers weren't infinite. Shepherd teams were expected to conduct themselves diplomatically, to show respect to ranking officials, and most importantly to keep a low profile.

Drake was braced for another round of bartering and intimidation, but to his surprise the man handed his papers back after a few moments.

'Go on through, sir. Park in one of the bays off to your right,' he said, indicating the open tarmac area beyond the security gate. 'Someone will be there to escort you inside.'

Drake nodded. 'No problem.'

The open space beyond the gate was easily 50 yards wide and twice as long, serving as a combination of marshalling area and vehicle maintenance centre. Off to the left, at least a dozen Horizon operatives were gearing up to go out on patrol, going through the countless last-minute checks that any group of soldiers went through before an op. Drake knew the feeling well.

Five RG-33 armoured personnel carriers similar to the ones at the crash site were lined up near the main building, with a similar number parked inside a single-storey concrete structure that resembled an armoured aircraft hangar. Mechanics and armourers were busily working to make them ready for action once more, checking engines and loading up weapons.

War, it seemed, had become big business. And business was booming.

Mindful of his instructions, Drake turned off to the right, parked the Explorer near the perimeter wall and killed the engine.

The hot breeze hit him the moment he stepped out, carrying with it a heady combination of smells, from both the compound and the city beyond it. Petrol fumes from the nearby drag, oil from the maintenance area, gun grease from countless weapons, the stench of rotting garbage from uncollected waste bins and ditches used as improvised landfill, not to mention the scents of cooking meat from the kebab shops that lined the streets.

He glanced up at the rhythmic thumping of rotor blades overhead, and watched the dark form of a Black Hawk chopper swinging in a wide arc off to the north. Perhaps it was acting in support of the Horizon operation that seemed to be kicking off, or perhaps it was on some other errand entirely. One could never tell in the organised chaos that was Afghanistan.

Unbeknownst to him, someone had approached while his attention was focused on the chopper; the thump of the rotors and the general hubbub in the assembly area drowning out the sound of his footsteps.

Only when he spoke up did Drake become aware of his presence.

'Well, fuck me,' a gruff Scottish voice remarked. 'Isn't this a turn-up for the books?'

Startled, Drake whirled around to face the new arrival, and felt his heart leap in shock. 'I don't believe it.'

The man standing before him was tall, maybe an inch or so taller than Drake himself, and with the square-shouldered, well-made physique of a natural athlete. His dark hair, greying at the sides, was cut short and side-parted, while his tanned skin was telling evidence of a lengthy deployment out here.

His face might have been called handsome, but there was a hardness, a severity to his expression that stopped some way short of that. His pale blue eyes were fixed on Drake. They were soldier's eyes if ever he had seen them – sharp and eager, assessing everything and missing nothing.

He was wearing desert military fatigues, though Drake couldn't make out any obvious rank or unit insignia. Like his fellow Horizon operatives, he maintained a facade of anonymity.

Only Drake knew him for who he was.

'Ryan Drake,' he said, his voice low and menacing, perfectly matching his fearsome glare. 'Talk about a bad fucking penny.'

Drake stood his ground, not flinching for a moment. 'You should know, Cunningham.'

Suddenly the scowl vanished, replaced by a beaming grin as Cunningham threw his arms around Drake and hugged him like the long-lost friend he was.

'Jesus, it's good to see you again, mate.'

'You too,' Drake said, hardly believing what he was seeing.

Matthew (Matt) Cunningham had been a sergeant in 22nd SAS Regiment when Drake first met him nearly ten years ago. Tough, seasoned, fearless, but uncompromisingly fair and even-handed, he was the sort of NCO that any soldier would be happy to serve under.

And serve under him Drake had. One of the unwritten rules for new inductees into the SAS was that they should pick a more senior and experienced trooper, follow him, do what he did and learn from him. Cunningham had been Drake's choice. He'd been a mentor during his time with the Regiment; a teacher and a guide.

And more than that, Drake had come to regard the man as a friend.

But friends came and went all the time in the military as people switched deployments, priorities changed and task forces were reshuffled. Following Drake's departure from the Regiment, the two men had gone their separate ways and lost touch.

It was nothing personal – it was just the way such things panned out.

Cunningham released his grip so he could look at Drake properly. 'How long has it been, anyway? Six years?'

'Seven,' Drake corrected him.

'Jesus, you're right,' Cunningham realised. 'Enough to make you feel old, aye?'

'I wouldn't know,' he lied.

'Tell it to the mirror, son.' He looked Drake up and down, comparing the man before him with the one from his memory. 'I almost didn't believe it when I heard you were coming here. I thought it must have been a different Ryan Drake – had to come down and see it with my own eyes.'

Drake glanced around, taking in their surroundings once more. 'So you're working for Horizon now?'

It was phrased as a question, though it was plainly unnecessary.

'Aye, got out of the Regiment three years ago. They wanted to transfer me to a desk job, so I gave them the finger and fucked off.' Cunningham shook his head. 'Never fancied shining a seat with my arse, know what I mean?'

Drake knew all too well. He disliked the reports and the paperwork and the meetings that went along with his job as much as the next man, but he at least recognised their necessity. Cunningham was of another sort. He was a soldier through and through, as if it was bred into his DNA. He could no more change his profession than he could change the colour of his eyes.

Still, one could only play that game for so long. Most SAS operatives quietly retired from front-line service by their late thirties, either because of declining fitness or a desire to start a family. Some moved into training and administrative roles, some took jobs on Civvy Street, but the majority drifted into the private security sector.

It seemed Cunningham was one of the latter.

'Anyway, what about yourself?' he asked, changing the subject. 'Working for the Yanks now, are you?'

'More or less,' he admitted, feeling somehow embarrassed about it. The Matt Cunningham he remembered would have ribbed him mercilessly for becoming a 'spook'.

To his surprise, however, the older man nodded approval. 'Got yourself a decent gig there. One thing they're not short of is money.' He flashed a wry grin. 'You did better than me, anyway.'

Drake wasn't so sure about that. If Cunningham knew about the debacle last year and his now tenuous position within the Agency, he might have revised his opinion. 'Mostly I put that down to my boyish good looks,' he said, forcing a grin.

'Must be doing something right, at least. The Old Man doesn't agree to meet just anyone.' He gestured towards the main building he'd just come from. A door was standing open, bright light spilling out onto the tarmac outside. 'Come on, I'll take you up to his office.'

On entering the old building, Drake quickly discovered that its outward appearance of a battered, scarred, decaying relic of a previous regime was nothing but a facade. Based on what he'd seen outside, he had expected dingy corridors, cheap strip lighting and bare crumbling concrete.

Instead the interior was modern, clean and spacious, reminding him more of a newly constructed office block than a military facility. Numerous internal walls had been knocked down to make way for glass-fronted conference rooms and state-of-the-art communications centres. There was even carpet underfoot.

'Nice place,' Drake remarked.

'Aye, it puts Hereford into perspective, eh?' Cunningham said, stopping beside an elevator at the end of the corridor.

The SAS were experts at accomplishing a lot with very few resources, and this outlook was reflected both in their headquarters at RAF Hereford, and in their rigorous training process known as Selection.

Drake would never forget the ordeal known as the Long Drag; a 64-km forced night march through the Brecon Beacons in February, hauling a 70-pound pack through wind and snow, with nothing but a compass and an outdated map to navigate by.

Pressing the call button, Cunningham added, 'Used to be a Soviet prison. The kind of place people got disappeared, know what I mean?'

The elevator doors slid open with a crisp ping. Drake

almost expected soothing music to be playing within.

Exiting at the top floor, they strode down a short length of corridor, with Cunningham leading the way. He stopped when he reached a big set of double doors, reached out and knocked.

It was several seconds before the reply came, during which Drake began to wonder if they'd missed him somehow.

'Yeah!' a gruff voice finally called out.

Cunningham glanced at his companion. 'Quicker than usual. Must be in a good mood today.'

That didn't bode well for his chances, Drake thought as his friend swung the door open and led him inside.

The room beyond reminded him of a luxury hotel suite as much as an office. There were coffee tables, leather sofas and even a small drinks bar set in one corner. The wall opposite was lined with several bookshelves crammed with thick volumes, most of which were concerned with military history and philosophy.

Big floor-to-ceiling windows – made from bulletproof glass, no doubt – provided excellent views of the assembly yard below and the chaotic urban sprawl of Kabul beyond its walls.

It took Drake a moment to realise that this place reminded him so much of a hotel suite because, for its occupant, this room more than likely *was* home.

The man himself was seated behind a wide steel-and-glass monstrosity of a desk, much of its surface covered with computer monitors, cables and hard drives. Clearly he was hard at work, and it was several seconds before he even glanced up from his screen.

When he did, Drake found himself confronted by a set of piercing grey eyes, powerful and intense despite their lack of colour.

Unlike the operatives Drake had seen in the assembly area outside, he wasn't wearing a shred of military clothing. Instead he was dressed in jeans and a plain white shirt open at the collar, the sleeves rolled back to reveal muscular forearms. A light brown sports jacket was slung over the back of his chair.

'So you're the joker who's driving my switchboard operators crazy,' he said. He spoke with an American accent, his voice low and authoritative in a way that only comes with age and experience.

Finishing up what he was doing, he pushed his chair back and rose up from behind the desk. He looked as old as his voice suggested, easily in his sixties, his hair silvery white and thinning a little on top. His face was lined and careworn, etched with the memories of a long life spent making hard decisions.

Despite his age, he stood straight and walked with the vigorous, purposeful stride of someone accustomed to getting places quickly and efficiently. There was little evidence of thickening around the midriff, and his shoulders were still broad and square. For a moment Drake almost felt like a young squaddie again, about to receive a kicking from a senior officer.

He smiled, perhaps amused that he still had the ability to intimidate men thirty years younger than himself, and held out a hand to Drake. 'The name's Richard Carpenter. I'm head of our operation out here in Afghanistan.'

'Ryan Drake,' he replied, shaking hands.

He couldn't help but glance over Carpenter's shoulder at the trio of glass display cases set against the wall. Each was filled with an assortment of weaponry from all ages of warfare, from swords and knives to muskets, revolvers and automatics, all polished and gleaming.

Seeing his interest, Carpenter raised a greying brow. 'You like my little collection?'

'It's very impressive.' He'd never really understood the appeal of military memorabilia, but even he could see that the contents of those cases were likely worth more than most people made in a lifetime.

'It's become a hobby of mine,' Carpenter said with entirely false modesty. Turning aside, he gestured to a long basket-hilted sword. 'French cavalry sabre, used at Austerlitz and Waterloo.' Then he nodded to a heavy six-shooter pistol that looked like it had come straight out of a Spaghetti Western. 'Colt Army Model 1860, used at Gettysburg.'

Smiling, he glanced at Drake. 'This might be of interest to you, Mr Drake,' he said, sliding open the last display case and carefully lifting out an ancient flintlock pistol. 'British officer's pistol, taken at the Battle of Yorktown.' He laid it down on the desk, the heavy weapon giving off an audible thump as it rested on the glass surface. 'I believe the British surrendered not long afterward.'

He was smiling, but Drake detected a faintly challenging look in his eyes.

As if sensing the tension, Cunningham cleared his throat. 'I believe they had other wars to fight, sir,' he said, perhaps hoping to lighten the mood.

The old man's smile broadened as he glanced at Cunningham. 'Of course. There are always other wars to fight,' he said, then turned his attention back to Drake. 'So what can I do for you, Mr Drake? I assume you didn't come here to discuss military history.'

Indeed not. Drake was interested in far more recent events. 'I'm investigating the Black Hawk that got shot down two days ago.'

Carpenter's expression turned more serious. 'A shitty business,' he remarked.

Walking over to the bar, he opened a crystal decanter. Even from several yards away, Drake could smell the peaty aroma of malt whisky as Carpenter poured himself a glass.

'Drink?' he asked.

Drake could have murdered a whisky, but now wasn't the time. He shook his head.

'Always on the clock, huh?' Carpenter grinned and swallowed a mouthful. 'One of the perks of running this company – I get to make my own hours.'

Rounding the desk, Carpenter settled himself in his chair, threw his feet up and took another sip. Clearly he wasn't a man to stand on ceremony.

'So how do I fit into all this?' he asked at length.

'One of your security teams was covering the crash site today,' Drake began.

'That's right.'

'They pulled out against orders and destroyed the site before we'd finished gathering evidence.'

The old man stared at him for a long moment. 'Yes?'

'I'd like an explanation, sir.'

Carpenter took another sip as he surveyed Drake, sizing him up. 'According to Colonel Vermaak's report, the site came under fire from an insurgent sniper.'

'That sniper was killed before your men pulled out,' Drake reminded him. 'They withdrew for no good reason.'

'You're aware, I'm sure, that snipers often work in pairs?' Carpenter countered, his tone making it plain that he wasn't at all sure Drake knew such things. 'Taking out one is no guarantee of safety.'

'My people didn't report any incoming fire after the

sniper was taken out. That would suggest he was acting alone,' Drake reasoned. 'On that subject, Colonel Vermaak and his men didn't bother to recover the sniper's body.'

'That wasn't their job. They were there for security, not to act as a strike team.' He tilted his glass, allowing light from the afternoon sun to filter through the honey-coloured contents. 'We have a very narrow remit in this country, I'm afraid. We have to be careful we don't exceed it.'

Drake frowned. 'But I assume they understand the concept of gathering intel. That sniper might have had documents, phones, maps . . . all kinds of things on him. He might even have helped us find the people who shot down the chopper. Now, because of your men, we've got nothing to go on.'

A slow smile had begun to form on Carpenter's craggy old face. Whether it was a smile of amusement, derision or grudging respect, Drake couldn't say.

'You know, despite what you might think, we take our responsibilities here seriously. We're not a bunch of thugs with guns – we're professional soldiers, here to do the jobs the US military can't or won't do for themselves, and a lot of people hate us for it. That's our reward for risking our lives every goddamn day, so you'll pardon me if I don't welcome people inviting themselves into my facility to question how we go about it.'

Drake was in no mood to be preached to. If Carpenter expected to sign up another member of the Horizon appreciation society, he was in for a disappointment.

'It's my job to question everything, sir. And with all due respect, I didn't come here to debate the morality of your operation in Afghanistan.'

Setting his glass down on the table, Carpenter leaned forward, fixing Drake with his hawk-like stare. 'Then why did you come here, Mr Drake? What are you looking to find, huh? Some kind of conspiracy? A cover-up? A mercenary group trying to take over the country? Believe me, I've heard it all in my time. PMCs are the new boogeymen, just like the CIA was twenty years ago. No one trusts us, no one likes us, but everyone needs us. Funny, isn't it?'

'All I came here for is the truth,' Drake said, meeting his accusing stare evenly. 'And believe me, I'm good at finding it. If Vermaak was acting under orders we weren't briefed on, it would be better for everyone if you told us now.'

If he was hoping to intimidate the old man, it didn't work. 'Colonel Vermaak's team were there to provide security. Their orders were to police the site, prepare it for demolition and avoid unnecessary risk – that's all. As far as judgement calls go, they had the final word on security. If Vermaak decided it was too dangerous to stay, then I support his decision.'

'Then maybe we need to speak to the colonel ourselves,' Drake suggested.

Again, Carpenter's gaze didn't waver. 'Be my guest. He's out on front-line operations for the next two days, but I'll be happy to set up a meeting just as soon as he gets back. In the meantime, Mr Cunningham here will act as your liaison with Horizon,' he said, gesturing to his subordinate. 'I believe the two of you know each other already?'

'We do,' Drake confirmed.

'You need anything from me or my company, you go to him in the first instance. Good enough?'

There wasn't much he could say to that. 'Good enough.'

'All right. Now, unless there's anything else, I have a lot of work to get through today.' Carpenter downed the last of his drink and turned his attention back to his computers. 'Cunningham, please see to it that Mr Drake gets back to his vehicle.'

'Yes, sir,' Cunningham replied.

The interview, such as it was, was over.

'I'll be in touch,' Drake said, turning to leave.

'I'll look forward to it,' Carpenter called after him. 'Oh, and one more thing, Mr Drake.'

Drake halted and turned to look at him.

'We're both on the same side here. You find the guys who shot down that chopper, you let me know,' Carpenter said, his gaze as intense as ever. 'Then we'll have that drink.'

Saying nothing, Drake turned away once more and walked out, leaving the old man alone in his office.

'Well, that was . . . interesting,' Cunningham remarked as the two men walked back across the vehicle marshalling area to McKnight's Explorer.

'Is he always like that?' Drake couldn't help asking.

'The Old Man? Aye, you bet he is. Carpenter's an old-school arse kicker. You have to be in a game like this.'

Drake flashed a wry smile. 'I doubt I've made his Christmas card list.'

'Come on, Ryan. You pushed him, and he pushed back. How did you think he'd react when some arsehole marches in and starts throwing his weight around?'

Drake shrugged. 'I didn't come here to make friends. I came to get answers.'

'Bollocks,' his friend retorted. He knew Drake better than that. 'You wanted to see his reaction, didn't you? You wanted to push him, see what he'd do.'

Drake only hoped his intentions hadn't been as obvious

to Carpenter. 'I wanted to know what kind of man I was dealing with.'

'Aye? And what kind of man is that?'

Given the company he was in, Drake thought it best not to voice his most immediate thoughts. Cunningham, however, knew him well enough to guess what he was thinking.

'You don't trust him. As far as you're concerned he's a mercenary, a war profiteer.' He gave his friend a side-long glance. 'Why do you think companies like Horizon are in Afghanistan, mate?'

Drake shrugged. 'Security. That's their mandate.'

'Ryan, for a spook, you're pretty fucking naive.'

'Really?' For a moment, a flash of irritation showed in Drake's vivid green eyes. 'For a start, I'm not a spook.'

'But you *are* missing the big picture. ISAF should have left Afghanistan years ago. We weren't set up to fight this kind of war, to be police instead of soldiers. Too many guys are getting sent out here and too many are coming home in coffins.

'America will have a new President this time next year, and you can bet your arse the first question they'll ask is when we're pulling out of Afghanistan. So when we leave – and we *will* leave – who'll take over? The ANP?'

Drake thought about the sloppy, unmotivated group of men calling themselves police officers that he'd encountered on the way here. The moment a serious contact started, he'd be willing to bet that half of them would drop their weapons and flee. The other half would likely be killed.

'We leave those arseholes to stand on their own, and you can bet the Taliban will be back in power within the year,' Cunningham went on. 'If we can't stay, and the Afghans can't hold their own, PMCs are about the only option we have left.'

'So you're fine with guys like Vermaak being a law unto themselves?' Drake asked with more heat than he'd intended.

'None of us are angels, son. You know that as well as I do,' he remarked with a pointed glance at Drake. 'But as hard as this is to believe, most of these guys are honest soldiers just doing their job. Some are saving for retirement, some are doing it because they believe in the cause, and some just don't have anywhere else to go.'

'And which are you, Matt?'

For a moment, an unspoken tension hung in the air between the two men. They stood facing each other in that wide open expanse of concrete as music blared from distant loudspeakers and the thump of helicopter rotors echoed around them.

Cunningham relaxed, his gaze softening. The world carried on around them as if nothing had happened. 'A bit of all three, I suppose.'

'I'm sorry,' Drake said at last, realising he'd been giving his friend a hard time for no real reason. 'It wasn't fair of me to ask that.'

The older man smiled. 'No problem, mate. If I was the sensitive type, I wouldnae be here.'

Drake glanced at his watch. It was 5:57 p.m. In an hour or so it would be dark.

'Listen, I'd better get going,' he said, thinking about all the things that he still had to do once he got back to Bagram.

'No rest for the wicked, aye?' Cunningham asked.

'Remember what you were saying about me landing a cushy number with the Agency? Forget it, mate. Stick with Horizon,' he advised, hitting his key fob to unlock the Explorer.

'I'll let you know if there's any openings here,' his old friend replied as Drake pulled open the driver's door. 'I could always use somebody to shine my boots.'

'Well, since we're not in the Regiment and you're not my sergeant any more, piss off.'

'Been waiting a long time to say that, eh?' Cunningham asked, snorting in amusement. 'Seriously though, stay in touch, mate.'

Drake grinned as he fired up the engine. 'Hey, you're my liaison officer, remember?'

With that, he slammed his door shut, threw the Explorer into gear and drove off, leaving his old friend behind.

Chapter 13

Hoping to avoid the heavy traffic congestion that had characterised central Kabul, Drake took a circular route that veered off to the west before looping back northwards. And as he drove, he couldn't help taking in his surroundings.

Kabul had been around for more than three thousand years, and each architectural era had left its mark on the ancient city. Graceful archways, shuttered windows, courtyards, domes, cupolas and ornate fountains stood side by side with 1970s high-density office and apartment blocks. Satellite dishes crowded the evening sky next to minaret towers.

And everywhere there were construction sites, workers and heavy equipment clearing away rubble to make way for new developments. Trucks laden with building materials roared by on the main drag, heedless of anything that stood in their path, while a group of children were picking at the garbage beside the road, searching for anything of value.

In the distance he spotted the grandstand and floodlight towers of Ghazi Football Stadium, built by the King of Afghanistan in the 1920s in honour of their victory over the British. Quite why they would choose to celebrate the defeat of their hated enemies by playing a sport invented by them was lost on him, but each to their own.

Anyway, the stadium had seen plenty of action over the years, especially under the Taliban when thousands would pack the terraces to watch criminals being stoned to death.

His thoughts returned to his earlier confrontation with Carpenter, once again pondering the man's motives. It was of course possible that he was just distrustful of Drake because he wasn't American, or because he worked out of Langley. Or both. But Drake sensed a deeper motivation. The man was hiding something, but what?

Had he already been told that the chopper had been shot down by a Stinger, and ordered to cover it up? It wasn't impossible. After all, he'd said himself that Horizon were here to do the jobs the military couldn't.

Still, whatever Carpenter was up to, he could see little connection to Mitchell's abduction, or why his captors had gone to such lengths to get him. It also didn't explain what Mitchell had really been doing out here.

He still had far too many questions, and too few answers.

Drake's thoughts were drawn back to the present as the traffic up ahead ground to a halt, accompanied by beeping horns and shouted curses. Frowning, Drake strained to see what was wrong, but a van with a heavily laden trailer blocked his line of sight.

'Shit, this is all I need,' he grumbled, killing the engine and removing the keys.

He opened the glovebox, quickly finding what he was looking for: a Beretta 92FS handgun. Like most Agency vehicles, the Explorer came stocked with several weapons in case of a contact, from pistols to sub-machine guns.

Checking the safety, he tucked the weapon down the front of his jeans and pulled his shirt down, then unlocked his door and stepped out onto the pavement.

As he'd suspected, it was a breakdown: an ancient Volvo estate about six cars ahead of him was billowing steam from beneath the bonnet while the overweight driver tried to force it open, scalding his hands in the process. With oncoming vehicles refusing to slow down to help clear the blockage, traffic was rapidly backing up.

'Great,' Drake said under his breath, wondering how long he'd be stuck here.

He was just turning away when suddenly he collided with someone heading in the opposite direction, apparently unaware of his presence. He heard a startled intake of breath and a muttered curse in Pashtun as the stranger tripped and stumbled, having to grip his sleeve to keep from falling.

Straight away he went for his gun, instinct and training combining to put him instantly on guard. He was in the Wazir Akbar Khan district – a comparatively safe neighbourhood where many countries had seen fit to establish their embassy buildings, but even here kidnappings and attacks on Westerners weren't unknown.

Drake looked down, only to be met by a wall of fabric and a narrow grille where eyes should have been. His new friend was a woman dressed in the traditional *chadri* – a loose robe designed to keep the entire body hidden. Their use had been demanded by law under Taliban rule, but they were gradually being discarded by all but the most conservative families now. Clearly this one didn't come from a progressive household.

No wonder the poor woman had bumped into him. She probably couldn't see more than a narrow slit of the world around her.

'I'm sorry,' Drake said, helping her back up. His grip on the Beretta relaxed.

138

To his surprise, his efforts at apology received only a few gruff words in return, and he suspected they weren't complimentary. Pushing his hands away, the woman turned and hobbled off as fast as she could on arthritic old joints, her back bowed by age.

Drake watched her go, saying nothing. To anyone watching he appeared unmoved by the incident. Privately, however, his mind was racing. Something had happened when the old woman had pushed him away; an expert piece of legerdemain that nobody else had seen, but which couldn't possibly have been an accident. He'd felt something pressed into his hand when she pushed him away, something thin and square. A folded piece of paper.

He didn't open or even acknowledge it in plain view. If the woman's intent had been to covertly pass him some sort of message, he wouldn't undo her efforts by letting others see him open it. Instead he kept his fist closed around it and retreated into the Explorer to unfold the little piece of paper.

On it was scrawled a short message in English, written in a strong, flowing hand:

Tamim Bazaar. There is an old tea house on the north square. Meet me on the second floor. Come alone, Ryan.

Drake felt his heartbeat shift up a gear as the words sank in. Clearly his mysterious new friend was not what she appeared. In fact, stooped and hidden beneath that concealing *chadri*, there was no telling if she even *was* a woman. Secret messages, clandestine meetings . . . who was this person, and what did he or she want with him?

The tea house mentioned in the note wasn't familiar to him, but he'd heard of the bazaar in which it could be found. It was close, just a few hundred yards to the north, in fact. He could be there within minutes.

His first instinct was that it was a trap intended to lure him to some out-of-sight location where he would be exposed and vulnerable. He didn't discount the possibility, but he doubted this was a simple abduction attempt. Only a handful of people in Afghanistan knew his name, and nearly all of them were trusted military or Agency operatives.

No, this was something else. And if he wanted to find out what, he had little choice but to follow the instructions on the note.

The traffic up ahead was starting to move. Several good Samaritans – or impatient motorists pissed off by the delay – had combined forces to push the crippled Volvo off the road, allowing vehicles to squeeze past.

With no further excuse for lingering here, it was decision time.

'I must be mad,' he said under his breath, easing the Explorer forward and taking the next junction that led north.

It didn't take him long to find what he was looking for. Even if he hadn't been familiar with the layout, the thronging pedestrian traffic and smell of spices and cooking meat would have announced the presence of Tamim Bazaar as effectively as any signpost.

Occupying several narrow streets and courtyards, it was a sprawling conglomeration of kebab shops, farmers' stalls and retailers of every kind. In ancient times outdoor markets like this would have sold silks, spices and livestock, but these days television sets, digital watches and pirated DVDs were more in vogue.

Like Kabul itself, it was a curious mix of the ancient and the modern, all thrown together in choking heat and shouting confusion. The combined smell of grilling meat, engine fumes, goat shit, tobacco smoke and unwashed bodies was almost overpowering.

Parking the Explorer in plain view of an ANP checkpoint, Drake locked up the vehicle and made his way along the street, glancing at a few of the stalls but moving on before the owners took too much notice of him. He knew from his experience of markets back home that getting away from such people was like trying to remove barnacles from the hull of a ship.

Anyway, there were plenty of other Westerners here waiting to part with their cash, probably from one of the many American companies that had opened branches in Kabul lately; all looking for traditional Afghan souvenirs to take home to the family. Most were accompanied by heavily built minders who looked more like bodybuilders than bodyguards.

The bazaar opened out at last when his street joined several others that had converged on a large square, much to Drake's relief. Sure enough, a two-storey building occupied the east corner of the square – squat, old and weathered, with a flat roof supporting an ancient satellite dish. At ground level, Drake spotted a faded sign, written both in Pashtun and English, for the tea house mentioned in the note.

The place looked closed up, as if it had gone out of business. There were only a couple of windows out front, and they were shielded by wrought-iron bars for security. Heavy wooden shutters had been pulled closed, blocking his view of the interior. The front door was also shut, though a quick check of the handle told him it was unlocked.

Pausing a moment, he gripped the weapon beneath his shirt, pulled the door open and slipped inside.

The room beyond was low-ceilinged and dimly lit,

with a dozen old tables and chairs dotted around, their wood stained almost black with decades of spilled drinks and smoke. There was a small bar area at the back, though nobody was manning it. Another door led to a rear work area, probably a kitchen, while a flight of steps ascended to the second floor. The smell of dried tea leaves and tobacco was pervasive; probably soaked into the very fabric of the place.

Now that he was off the street, he drew the Beretta from his jeans. A military variant of the popular police officer's sidearm known as an M9, it was a 9mm, fifteen-round semi-automatic pistol. Though lacking a little in stopping power, they were otherwise excellent weapons, tried and tested all over the world.

Disengaging the safety, he held the weapon low and advanced into the room. Hollywood always shows the hero moving with his arms bent, weapon pointing up at the ceiling, and while it might look impressive, in reality it would just make it easier for an assailant to grab the weapon or knock it aside. Keeping it below waist height makes it much more difficult to take out of the game.

His eyes scanned the shadows, looking for any sign of movement. His other senses strained to detect any sounds of breathing, any scents that didn't belong. There were none. He appeared to be alone down here.

He headed for the stairs and crept up them, keeping his feet away from the centre of each step where the boards would be weakest. Still, it was impossible to eliminate all noise, and the ancient wood groaned several times under his weight as he ascended.

Reaching the top, he found himself in a short corridor, with a door standing open at the end of it.

This was it. Whoever his new friend was, they were

likely waiting for him in that room. Waiting to help him, or waiting to kill him, he didn't know.

'Fuck it,' he said under his breath, and advanced through the doorway.

His eyes took in his surroundings in an instant. A snapshot, a flash that his brain immediately processed and analysed.

The room seemed to occupy most, if not all, of the building's upper floor. Whether it had been living accommodation at one point, he couldn't tell. There seemed to be no utilities up here. But whatever purpose it had once served, the place was clearly being used as a storeroom now.

Wooden chairs and tables similar to the ones in the bar below were stacked in various places, along with sagging cardboard boxes, rusty machinery that could have belonged to anything, and a couple of threadbare floral couches that looked as though they'd been supporting the world's most obese man for the past few decades. The floor was nothing more than bare boards, warped with age and marked by a variety of stains. Some looked like dried blood.

This room was at least better illuminated than the bar below. The wooden shutters were closed, but they too had warped and shrunk with age, allowing bright shafts of evening sunlight to stream through.

Drake took another step forward, gripping the weapon tight.

His eyes were everywhere, seeking a target, seeking movement, seeking anything. The room was quiet and still, with only the background noise of the city outside, and the muted thump of his boots on the floorboards within.

Where the hell was his contact? If they wanted him here, why keep him waiting like this?

'You're getting sloppy, Ryan,' a voice announced from behind.

Drake twisted around, bringing the weapon to bear. His heart was racing, his pulse pounding, his mind focused on threat assessment and target acquisition, ready to make the countless decisions and calculations necessary to decide whether or not to fire.

But the moment he locked eyes with the figure who emerged from the shadows, it all fell apart. The decisions, the calculations, the assessments and judgements, all of them vanished from his mind as shock and disbelief swept them away.

'Anya.'

The weapon lowered seemingly of its own volition as he stared at the woman standing just a few paces away, comparing her with the memory etched for ever into his mind.

The same pale blonde hair. The same finely sculpted, almost noble features. The same wry smile and the same intense icy blue eyes. It was her. It was Anya.

But a different Anya from the one he had known. She had changed in the year they had been apart. Her hair was cut short now, her skin tanned from long exposure to the sun, her once thin and malnourished body filled out and healthy. The close-fitting black T-shirt she wore revealed the contours of her athletic physique, her bare arms betraying the taut, sinewy muscles of hard-won physical strength.

All things considered, she looked much improved since their last encounter.

'Hello, Ryan,' she remarked, taking in his appearance. He sensed she was entertaining similar thoughts, though he doubted he compared as favourably. 'How have you been?'

The question was posed as awkwardly as it was phrased. Anya had never been big on small talk, and the past year had clearly done little to change that.

'You mean since you shot me in the stomach and left me to bleed to death in the middle of the desert? I'm tip-top, thanks.'

Anya had been a wanted woman when they'd parted ways – wanted by the Russians, wanted by the Agency, wanted by Cain. Knowing that Drake would have taken the fall for allowing her to escape, she had done the unthinkable and shot the man who had twice saved her life. It had been enough to convince the Agency that he was still playing for the right team.

By almost killing him, she had probably saved his life.

But if she was expecting gratitude, she would be waiting a long time. He had been willing to follow her, willing to risk everything for her, and she'd left him behind. Left him to go back to his old life, to linger on alone, to live with a sword hanging over his head for the past year. That was something he wasn't ready to forgive.

The wry smile faded. 'I did what I could for you. You are still alive.'

'I'll be sure to send you the medical bill.' He tucked the Beretta down the back of his jeans, more or less sure it wouldn't be needed for now, and looked at her again. 'I assume you caused that breakdown back on the road?'

The breakdown that had stopped traffic and blocked Drake's path, forcing him to exit his vehicle to investigate. Then it had been a simple matter of approaching while he was distracted, and the rest practically took care of itself.

She shrugged. 'A few dollars to have a local taxi driver pretend to break down. That was all it took.'

145

'Why? You knew where I was. You could have found me before now.'

His question was implicit – if you knew where to find me, why did you leave me alone for more than a year?

He could almost feel her impatience. 'Of course I could have found you. But what then? Unless you are more stupid than you look, you will know you are being watched closely by the Agency.'

She was right, of course. Much as he hated to admit it. Keeping friends close and enemies closer had never been more relevant where Cain was concerned.

'Believe me, I'm very aware of that fact,' Drake said, flashing an accusing glare at her. She said nothing, as he knew she would. Whatever she had come here for, it hadn't been to bicker and squabble with him.

'So why now?' he asked, adopting a calmer tone. 'What are you doing out here?'

Sighing, she settled herself on one of the wooden chairs that looked in less danger of collapse than its comrades. 'You may want to take a seat,' she suggested, gesturing to an empty chair opposite.

'I'll stand.'

'Suit yourself.' She shrugged, dismissing the issue. His personal comfort was not a concern of hers. 'I'm here because I have questions, Drake.'

'What sort of questions?'

'I was in a Russian prison when we first met. I assure you, I did not end up there by being reckless or stupid. The Russian FSB intercepted me on my way to Iraq five years ago.' She looked him hard in the eye. 'It seems logical that someone I trusted betrayed me to them. When we parted ways last year, I intended to find out who and why. The trail led me as far as Afghanistan, then I

146

hit a dead end,' she said, unwilling to elaborate. 'That was when I learned you were here.'

'What do you mean, you *learned*?' It wasn't as if his arrival had been printed in the local newspapers.

'I have been keeping tabs on you,' she explained, as if it were obvious.

'Why?'

'Because you are a source within the Agency, and you are a link to Cain.' She hesitated, finding it difficult to express herself. 'And . . . because I wanted to know you were all right.'

Very compassionate, he thought, resisting the urge to touch the scar on his stomach. First she shot him in the gut, then she kept careful tabs on him to ensure he was safe – talk about mixed messages.

The look in his eyes gave his thoughts away to Anya as clearly as if he'd spoken them out loud. She seemed to withdraw a little then, relinquishing whatever tentative effort she had made to reach out to him.

'You still didn't answer my question,' he pressed. She was stalling, and that only made him more determined to reach the truth. 'Why contact me now?'

Anya leaned back in the rickety old chair, her arms folded across her chest, thin strips of orange light from outside playing across her face as her icy eyes surveyed him. 'Two days ago a Black Hawk helicopter was shot down not far from here. Less than twenty-four hours later, you and your team arrive. Given your . . . profession, it seems likely these two things are connected.'

She said nothing further, just sat there watching him, waiting for him to confirm or deny her theory.

Drake looked away, saying nothing, content to let her sweat for a while. He felt like a poker player sizing up his opponent, trying to see how far they were willing to go.

'If you want to sulk like a spoiled child, do it in your own time,' Anya said, rising from her chair as if to leave. 'But do not waste mine.'

'One of the men on that chopper was a CIA operative,' Drake said, unwilling to see her walk away. He'd bluffed, and she'd just called it.

Slowly she sat back down, keeping her eyes on him. 'Go on,' she prompted.

With a sigh, he took a seat on the chair opposite her. 'He's being held hostage by an Afghan insurgent group. If we don't close down one of our biggest detention centres and release all the prisoners within three days, they'll execute him and shoot down more aircraft.'

The woman appeared unmoved by this revelation. 'I assume the Agency will not give in to these demands?'

Drake shook his head. It was a ludicrous demand to have made in the first place; no one man's life was worth releasing hundreds of terrorists and insurgent leaders. 'They can't. You know that as well as I do,' he said. 'Our only option is to find him before the deadline. That's why we're here.'

'Why you?'

He chewed his lip for a moment, as reluctant to get into this discussion with Anya as he had been with Frost. 'Because I captured the leader of the group five years ago.'

'I see,' she said thoughtfully, taking careful note of the change in his posture, the tension in his shoulders. 'You could have killed him, but you spared his life, yes?'

Drake said nothing to that, which told her everything she needed to know.

'It is not the things we do that we regret, but the things we *don't* do—'

'Are you finished?' Drake snapped, immediately regretting it.

Anya surveyed him in silence, her gaze cool and assessing. She was sparring with him, pushing him, trying to elicit a reaction. Why, he didn't know. But she had succeeded, and that only raised his ire further.

'I've answered your questions,' he said, forcing calm into his voice. 'Quid pro quo, Anya.'

'What do you want?'

Drake leaned forward in his chair, locking eyes with her. 'Tell me what you know about Stinger missiles.'

That question caught her off guard. He could see the surprise in her eyes, even if her face appeared impassive. It seemed suddenly as if her mind had jumped up a gear, evaluating, considering, analysing new possibilities.

'We brought many into Afghanistan during the Soviet occupation,' she answered at last. 'I helped smuggle some of them over the border from Pakistan.'

Drake still found it hard to believe; she could only have been in her twenties at the time. How had someone so young become caught up in all that?

Still, those were questions for another day.

'Could one of those Stingers have shot down a Black Hawk?'

Anya was silent for a few moments, considering his question. 'No,' she decided at last. 'Not after two decades. The Stinger's battery coolant units would not survive more than a couple of years without skilled maintenance, and replacements would be impossible.'

'And if I told you we have hard evidence it *was* shot down by a Stinger?'

At this, the woman shrugged. 'I can't argue with facts.

But if a Stinger shot down that chopper, I would bet my life it was a new weapon.'

Drake frowned, perplexed by her revelation. The only theory that seemed to fit the available facts had just been shredded. Was it possible she was wrong? He supposed even Anya wasn't infallible, and yet she seemed adamant about it.

He was missing something – he knew that much. Some vital piece of the puzzle remained hidden. The problem was, he had no idea where to look for it.

He glanced at her again, struck by another thought. 'There's more to this, isn't there? You wouldn't have taken a chance like this just to catch up with an old "friend". What do you really want?'

For a moment he thought he saw a faint smile, as if she were amused that he had finally caught on to something that should have been blindingly obvious.

'You're right. Even if it took you a while,' she added. 'I came here to warn you.'

'Warn me?'

'You recently visited the headquarters of Horizon Defence. I saw your vehicle drive into the compound,' she explained. 'I imagine you spoke to a man named Carpenter while you were there.'

At the very mention of his name, she seemed to tense up, the muscles in her shoulders tightening, her hands curling into fists.

'And if I did?'

She leaned forward again, her eyes locked with his. 'I suggest you be on your guard around him. He is not a man to be trusted.'

That went without saying. Drake hadn't exactly warmed to the man during their brief meeting earlier. Still, it didn't explain what her beef with him was.

'How do you know him?'

For a moment, her eyes seemed to lose focus as her mind flashed back to another time, another place, replaying old memories.

'He was once my . . . teacher,' she said, her voice soft, quiet, tinged with old pain. 'When I first joined the Agency.'

Drake frowned. 'I thought Cain was your instructor?'

As he understood it, Cain had been Anya's mentor. He had spotted her potential, inducted her into the Agency, trained her and prepared her for the clandestine operations she would one day take part in.

Cain had eventually become her handler and, Drake suspected, something more. But whatever relationship they had once shared, it had long since turned sour.

To his surprise, she chuckled at this notion. 'Cain might have brought me in, but he was no field agent. For the work I was to do, they needed someone with more . . . unique skills. Carpenter was that man. He taught me everything I needed to know – taught me how to survive, how to fight, how to kill. He taught me how to do all of those things, and feel no emotion about it. He made me into . . . a soldier.' There was a bitter undertone in her voice when she added, 'I have a lot to thank him for.'

No wonder Carpenter hadn't responded well to his probing questions, Drake thought. If this was a man who had moulded Anya into the operative she had become, then he wasn't someone to be fucked with.

'So what's the problem?'

'I made the mistake of underestimating him,' she admitted. 'It did not end well for me.'

And then, just like that, she blinked. The memories vanished, the barriers went back up, and her eyes focused on Drake once more.

'I told you I was in this country looking for answers. Well, Carpenter is my best chance. He knows more about me than anyone left alive, except Cain. I intend to find out just how much he knows.'

And then at last the truth dawned on Drake. 'So that's why you really made contact. You need my help.'

Anya said nothing, though the uncomfortable look in her eyes told him everything he needed to know.

'You can say it, you know. It won't kill you.'

Again he saw that disapproving look. She was tiring of this game. 'I am an outsider now, Drake. There is only so much I can do alone. You, on the other hand, have the resources of the Agency to call on.'

It wasn't exactly an admission of weakness, but it was as close as she was ever likely to get.

'So what are you suggesting here? Collaboration?'

'Cooperation,' she replied. 'Keep me in the loop with your investigation, especially anything concerning Carpenter.'

Drake eyed her dubiously. 'Cooperation is a two-way street. If you want my help, you'll have to do better than that.'

Anya said nothing. The silence stretched out, broken only by the drone of car engines outside. He wasn't giving her anything this time – he wanted a concession.

'All right,' she conceded. Rising from her chair, she fished a cellphone from her pocket and tossed it to Drake. 'Take this.'

He turned it over in his hand. It was a cheap pre-paid model with an old-fashioned LCD screen. The sort of thing that had been all the rage ten years ago.

'You're really spoiling me, Anya,' he remarked with a raised eyebrow.

His attempt at humour wasn't acknowledged. 'It is pre-paid and anonymous, which means the Agency can't listen in.' She handed him a piece of paper with a number handwritten on it. 'You can reach me on this number. Memorise it, then destroy it. And don't use real names or keywords. Understand?'

'I do,' he said, already committing her number to memory.

Her precautions might have seemed excessive, but Drake knew as well as anyone the power and resources that the Agency could bring to bear. Any email, message or phone conversation featuring the words *'Mitchell'*, *'Kourash'*, *'missile'* and so on would be automatically flagged up and passed on to expert analysts for further investigation. Anya wanted to stay very much off their radar.

'Good.' With that, she retrieved the *chadri* she had evidently cast aside on entering the building. 'You know where Bibi Mahru Hill is?'

Drake nodded. Of course he did. It was hard to miss.

'I will meet you there at eighteen hundred hours, two days from now. I will be by the swimming pool.'

'I'll be there,' he assured her.

'And make sure you come alone,' she warned. 'If you bring company or I think you have been followed, I won't be there and you will never see me again.'

He didn't doubt she meant what she said. That, more than anything else, served to quash any thoughts he had of going against her wishes.

On the verge of leaving, she halted in the doorway and turned around.

'Oh, and one more thing, Drake.'

He was braced for another stern warning. 'Yeah?'

For the briefest of moments, she allowed the armour

to slip aside. The look in her eyes softened, and he saw a faint, tentative smile.

'It was good to see you again.'

A moment later, her face was hidden behind the fabric mask as she pulled the uncomfortable garment over her head. She was an old woman again, bent and arthritic, hobbling down the stairs on tired legs and aching joints.

He heard the door open and close down below, leaving him alone.

Chapter 14

Unknown to either Anya or Drake, their meeting had not gone unnoticed.

Standing on the flat roof of a building on the far side of the square and armed with a pair of high-powered binoculars, Kourash watched the old woman hobble across the square, his brows drawn together in a frown.

The *chadri* made her impossible to identify. Who was this strange new arrival?

He had been keeping Drake under observation since the man had left Horizon headquarters, curious to see what he did next. His curiosity had intensified when Drake had left his vehicle and struck out alone.

Kourash had witnessed the seemingly chance encounter with the old woman, had watched the fleeting look of surprise on Drake's face when he realised she had pressed something into his hand. Most passers-by had been oblivious to the brief exchange, but Kourash knew such tricks well.

The woman, whoever she was, appeared to be some kind of source who had made contact with Drake. After conducting their rendezvous in an old tea house at the edge of the square, they seemed to have gone their separate ways.

Picking up his encrypted cellphone, he quickly dialled

a number from memory. Two of his men were waiting in the square below.

It rang once before it was answered. The recipient said nothing, merely waited for him to speak.

'The woman is leaving the tea house,' Kourash began.

'I see her.' The voice that replied was a breathless whisper; the result of a shrapnel wound to the throat during a Soviet air strike two decades earlier. The owner of the voice was Ashraf – a lean, tough little Hazara man who Kourash had known since they were children.

A reliable man. Whatever he lacked in size and strength, he made up for in experience, ruthless aggression and the ability to think on his feet.

Standing next to him would be another man, named Faraj. Big, square-shouldered and imposing, he was the muscle to back up Ashraf's brains. He didn't talk much, because he didn't have to. He was there to get things done, not to share his opinions. He followed orders without question, and certainly without remorse.

'Your orders?' Ashraf asked.

Kourash paused for a moment, considering his options. He could keep her under observation and see what she did, but tailing people was always problematic. They ran the risk of losing her or exposing themselves. Considering the sleight of hand she had performed earlier, he had to assume she was an operative with a certain awareness of her surroundings.

Another man from his background might have dismissed the threat she posed simply because of her gender, but Kourash was not such a man.

He had known strong women in his time, and knew they were not to be underestimated.

Mina, the woman who had followed him through the long years of war and hardship that had marked so much of their relationship. The woman who had never been afraid to argue, to voice her own opinion, to show him when he was wrong. The woman who had once permitted him a glimpse of true happiness. She had taught him that there was strength and courage to be found even in the gentler sex.

But Mina was gone now, like everything else he had once cared about. He pushed her memory away, angry at himself for such sentimentality, and forced his thoughts back to the present situation.

He was by now all too aware of the danger posed by Drake and his team. His attempt to have the man's two teammates killed at the crash site had resulted only in the death of one of his own operatives. True, it had at least forced Horizon to pull out and destroy what remained of the chopper, but he recognised that such an attack would have provoked suspicion as well.

He was playing a dangerous game, and on some level he sensed he was starting to lose control of certain elements. To allow this to continue would be to invite disaster. Swift, decisive action was needed now.

He was in the midst of these contemplations when loud, echoing voices began to carry across the evening air. It was the local mosques calling the faithful to *Maghrib*, the fourth Islamic prayer, offered at sunset.

Having never known true faith, he had no need of such prayers. Still, it provided just the opening he'd been looking for. The streets would be quiet soon as the population of Kabul settled down to make their offering to Allah.

'Bring her in. Alive.'

Whatever she knew, he would get it out of her. And once he had what he needed from her, he would turn his attention to Drake.

'It will be done,' Ashraf promised.

The line clicked off. Pocketing the phone, Kourash raised his binoculars once more and trained them on the square below.

Ashraf and Faraj were already moving, crossing the square in the casual, unhurried manner of two men out for an evening stroll.

Without saying a word, Faraj peeled off right and headed for the van he'd parked a short distance away, while Ashraf carried on in pursuit of the woman. A sensible move. Big as he was, Faraj could attract attention, whereas Ashraf was small and inconspicuous.

The two men had worked together long enough to appreciate each other's strengths, and use them to their fullest. Kourash was willing to bet that only the briefest of exchanges had been required for them to formulate their plan.

He smiled as he trained the binoculars on the woman hobbling away from the square, disappearing down a side street within moments.

I'll see you soon, my friend, Kourash thought. Then we will talk.

Chapter 15

Anya's thoughts lingered on her encounter with Drake as she made her way down the narrow side streets of central Kabul, playing the part of the crippled old woman just as she had done twenty years earlier. The *chadri* was uncomfortable, claustrophobic and sharply limited her peripheral vision, but there were few better ways of concealing her identity.

Even in post-Taliban Kabul there were still enough women, particularly the older generation, clad in such garments to make the disguise viable.

Seeing Drake again had left her with mixed feelings, and she found her thoughts drifting inexorably back to their meeting. When they had parted ways last year, she had expressed her hope that they would never meet again, and she had meant it. Drake was a good man who she didn't want to become entangled in the murky world she existed in.

And yet standing face to face with him, seeing the subtle changes that another year of life had brought about, had stirred long-buried memories and emotions within her. The sense of closeness, of kinship, of being connected to another human being and knowing they felt the same way.

It had been a long time since she had allowed herself to feel anything like that. Drake had made her feel it last year during their brief, tumultuous time together, had brought her back from the cold, lonely world of pain and brutal survival that had been all she'd known since her imprisonment.

She sensed it happening again now.

Almost without realising it, she allowed her pace to quicken a little, for her back to straighten up. She was far enough away from the bazaar that no one who had been there could still see her.

A short distance behind, Ashraf was watching her intently, observing the gradual changes coming over the crippled old woman before him. The bent old back seemed to straighten out, the hunched shoulders squared, the hobbling gait became a steady, confident walk.

This was no old woman. He had suspected as much anyway, but it was always satisfying when his instincts were confirmed.

Reaching into his jacket pocket, he felt the cold steel of a Makarov pistol. He didn't intend to shoot her, but the weapon would be useful for intimidation. And if he was lucky, he could get close and use it to land a quick, sharp blow on the back of her neck. Just hard enough to put her down, to subdue her and make her easy to bundle into the van that would be waiting just yards away.

Faraj was standing by in the vehicle less than a block away, the engine idling, his foot poised on the accelerator. That was how they always conducted such takedowns.

Ashraf glanced around. They were on a quiet residential street, virtually deserted with everyone at evening prayers. Long shadows stretched across the ground as the sun dipped below the horizon. It was a perfect place to lift their new friend.

Reaching into his other pocket, he found his cellphone. A simple text message had already been composed, the recipient's name inputted. All that was required was his command to send it.

Now.

Human intuition is perhaps the most overlooked and least understood of all our mental faculties. Blinding in its potential and infinite in its subtlety, it is a trait born from millions of years of hard-won survival and evolution. And yet, it often has to break through a lifetime of conditioning and rational thought to make itself known.

That same primal ability to see without seeing, to *feel* changes in the world around us, had once helped Anya's distant ancestors sense when a hidden predator was stalking them. For them, living on a knife edge of survival in a cold, untamed wilderness, it had been just another tool to help keep them alive. Unfathomable, but tacitly acknowledged.

That intuition had faded almost beyond all knowledge for many people, but for her, it was still very much alive. Over the years, as she was forced to rely on every tool at her disposal to stay alive, her rational mind had learned to trust what her subconscious already knew.

She couldn't say when exactly she became aware of the man following her, only that as she approached a junction in the road up ahead, the sense of being watched crossed some invisible boundary within her mind to become more than just a background item of minor interest. Now it was a potential threat.

Straight away she began to consciously analyse her situation, drawing in what little information she could glean to decide on how to respond. She couldn't see the person following her, but it was almost certainly a man

161

in this part of the world. If he was behind her, she couldn't turn to look at him without making her intentions obvious, and in any case the narrow slit through which she was able to view the world sharply limited her field of vision.

Instead she tried to use her other senses to better identify this potential threat, straining to hear his footsteps above the rustle of fabric and the drone of car engines nearby. Almost without being aware of it, she changed her stance and walking style to reduce the noise of her own steps, allowing her to focus in on her pursuer.

There were no pavements on this street, and even the road was nothing but bare earth compacted down by the passage of countless vehicles. The ground underfoot was a mixture of loose rocks, dust, mud and discarded, half-buried trash. Few could travel far on it without making any sound.

Her new friend was not such a man.

There! She heard it, faint but unmistakable. The click of shoes on the rocky ground. Shoes, not boots or trainers.

She concentrated on the sound of his footsteps, trying to discern something from them. He was walking at a steady, ground-covering pace. Not running, but not dawdling either. She suspected he was keeping pace with her, perhaps 30 yards back. Close enough to keep an eye on her, but distant enough to stay out of her awareness.

Or so he thought.

She heard a faint electronic bleep, probably a cellphone, coming from his direction. And at that moment, she sensed a quickening of pace, his steps coming closer together, each footfall landing with authority as he moved in on her.

There could be no doubt in her mind now. He was coming for her.

Ashraf felt his heartbeat increase as he moved in on his target, gripping the pistol tight in his pocket. He had conducted many such lifts in the past, and always felt a rush of excitement with each new experience. Sometimes his target fought back, sometimes they meekly surrendered. Occasionally they tried to talk their way out of it, while others simply stood there, frozen with shock, unable to comprehend how their world had changed so suddenly.

But one thing remained constant. He was always successful.

The rumble of an engine at high revs told him Faraj was approaching the junction in the van. The noise of the vehicle would alert his target, would capture their attention. He or she (he wasn't ruling anything out at this stage) would be focused on the incoming van, seeing that as a possible threat, never knowing that the real danger was coming from behind.

Headlight beams spilled across the road, and a few seconds later the white panel van shot around the corner from behind a crumbling sandstone wall, tyres clawing at the ground. Faraj turned the wheel hard left, steering the van straight for the target, headlights on full power.

This was it. With several quick strides, Ashraf covered the last few yards to his target, drawing out his pistol just as the van screeched to a halt beside them. Even though he too was dazzled by the beams, he knew Faraj would already be climbing out of the driver's door, ready to assist him if the target put up a fight.

Ashraf smiled. Somehow he didn't think that would be necessary.

Jerking the weapon from his pocket with practised ease, he raised it up, ready to bring it down on the back of his opponent's neck.

Then something inexplicable happened.

His target spun around to face him, as if his approach had been expected all along. He caught a sudden whirl of fabric, then a flash of something bright and metallic, and suddenly his hand went numb as something bit into his wrist. The Makarov fell from his grasp as warm blood began to flow down his arm.

Shocked as he was, it took him a moment to realise that a blade, wielded with expert precision and merciless force, had severed the nerves and tendons in his wrist.

Anya was no longer concerned with the small wiry man who had tried to take her down. She had disarmed him with her first strike, noting in passing that he had been armed with a Makarov PM, a simple eight-round automatic ideal for jobs where concealment was more important than accuracy or firepower.

Either he had intended to threaten her into submission, or to use it as a crude club to knock her unconscious. Neither option would have served him well, but personally she had never seen much logic in using a projectile weapon for hand-to-hand combat.

Still, he was more or less out of the fight now. He wouldn't be using that hand again without reconstructive surgery, and she thought it unlikely he had another weapon on him. Judging by his sharp intake of breath, the first waves of pain had just reached his brain. Soon he would either try to flee, or take her on one-handed.

Again, neither option would end well for him.

The driver of the van was still a concern, however,

and one that had to be dealt with quickly, while she still had the initiative.

Grabbing at the face mask of her *chadri*, she yanked the cumbersome garment off and hurled it aside, glad to be free of its claustrophobic embrace. She could move and fight properly now, and though she was armed only with a fixed-bladed knife, she felt it was more than suitable for the task at hand.

The takedown man had elected to fight her, either hoping to distract her until his companion could get into the fight, or because he wanted revenge for his injury. He swung a hard, snappy left hook that she was obliged to dodge, though it provided her with the perfect opportunity to catch his arm while it was overextended and twist it backwards.

He tried to turn with the motion, but she was faster than him, and within a few moments, she had the arm locked behind his back. She heard the ragged growl deep in his throat as he tried to throw her off, but straight away she knew it wouldn't succeed. He wasn't nearly strong enough to break such a hold, and though she considered herself far from physically powerful, she had the advantage of leverage.

Now that she was facing the van again, she was afforded her first glimpse of the driver as he lumbered into view, the vehicle visibly springing upward on its suspension as his weight departed. Even in the glare of the headlights it was obvious he was a big man, tall and broad, his frame bulked out with solid muscle.

He was holding something in his right hand. Something long and curved at one end. A crowbar.

Anya had never enjoyed taking on big men like this. Trying to punch or kick upward reduced her effectiveness, and a couple of good hits in return would be enough to take her out of the fight. She preferred to ambush them from behind, but failing that, she would have to get creative.

She had wasted enough time on the takedown man. Exerting more pressure on his left arm, she drew back her right and struck a sharp blow with her elbow, targeting the overtaxed shoulder joint. There was a dull crunch as it gave way, followed by a howl of pain from her would-be abductor.

By now certain he was out of the game, Anya shoved him aside and turned her attention to the giant of a driver, quickly assessing the threat.

He was 6 foot 5 in height, 250 pounds, maybe forty years old. He held the crowbar as though he'd been using such things his entire life, his brute strength allowing him to easily wield such a heavy weapon.

His eyes flicked to the knife in her hand, no doubt weighing up his chances of getting stabbed. She was only a woman, in a country where women were kept cowed and weak, and his experience would tell him she was easy prey. But he had seen what she had just done to his companion, and now a hint of doubt would be creeping into his mind.

He would swing first, using his superior reach and strength to take her out quickly, wanting to stop her before she could use that knife. She knew that if he did manage to connect with that crowbar, such a blow would shatter bones like dry twigs.

She saw the tightening in his muscle-slabbed shoulder, the changing angle of his arm as the great body readied itself for the crushing strike.

He was smart enough to use a backhanded strike. Swinging the bar like a baseball bat would take precious time to draw his arm back, to build the momentum he needed. Time she could easily use to close the distance.

166

Still, this was her only chance.

Gathering herself up, she rushed straight for him just as he brought the weapon around with vicious force.

But instead of trying to block it, she ducked beneath the deadly strike, the heavy bar scything through the air mere inches above her head.

The knife leapt out, plunging into the back of his right leg, piercing the fabric of his jeans, his skin, the muscle beneath and finally severing his Achilles tendon. He tried to turn to face his adversary again, using the momentum of his fruitless swing to aid him, but found that his leg was no longer able to support his weight. He fell to his knees, blood staining his jeans.

Whirling around, Anya closed in and delivered a hard kick to his groin. Hardly an honourable tactic, but fights like this weren't about honour – they were about survival.

With a look of complete shock, the giant buckled over and fell into a muddy, fetid drainage ditch running along the side of the road.

Anya leapt on him before he could collect his wits, grabbed a handful of thick curly hair and yanked his head back hard to expose his throat.

The idea that a single quick slice is enough to cut a man's throat is pure fantasy. The reality for Anya had proven more difficult, dangerous and far more unpleasant.

Utilising the knife as a crude saw, she went to work with grim efficiency. The blade bit into the skin with the first slice, but it wasn't until the return stroke that she heard the gurgling hiss as his windpipe was opened.

Two more powerful saw-like thrusts cut right through the windpipe and severed the arteries in his neck, releasing a pumping spurt of blood. Her work done, Anya released her grip and stepped back to avoid the worst of the spray. She observed the results with cold, emotionless eyes.

The giant flailed and convulsed before her, his blood mixing with the mud around him, soaking his clothes, while his hands scrabbled at his throat as if they could repair the damage. There was no screaming. He was incapable of making such sounds now. All he could muster was a sickening gurgle that came not from his mouth, but from the ragged hole in his neck.

She saw the wild, panicked look in his eyes. It was the look of a hunted animal. It was a look she had seen in many men who were about to die.

And die he did. He lasted another twenty seconds or so before loss of blood and oxygen took their inevitable toll. His struggles grew weaker, his movements less meaningful, until at last he slumped forward, face down, one hand pawing aimlessly at the mud until that too stopped moving.

For a couple of seconds Anya did nothing, just stood there breathing deeply, allowing her heart rate to return to normal and her thoughts to clear. The time for swift, aggressive action was over. She needed to be calm and logical now.

The van's engine was still running, the exhaust belching steam and grey smoke. Nearby, the takedown man was groaning, trying to raise himself from the ground on two crippled arms without success.

This had been no casual mugging, it had been an organised attempt to lift her. But organised by whom? Who even knew she was in the country, apart from Drake?

She needed answers, which was why she had kept one of her would-be attackers alive. For now, at least.

Sheathing the bloodied knife, she strode over to the

injured man and kicked him in the ribs, sending him sprawling on his back. Unfazed, she knelt down beside him and quickly rifled through his pockets.

There was some money, mostly in Afghanis but with a few American dollars mixed in. No wallet, credit cards or ID, which didn't surprise her. Men like him went into such jobs sterile and untraceable.

In his inside jacket pocket she found a cellphone, which she shoved in her trousers. She would take a closer look at it when she had more time, but right now the priority was getting off this street. Even in a neighbourhood like this, such a confrontation would arouse attention, and the last thing she needed was for the ANP to show up.

'You American whore,' the man hissed, his voice strangely breathless and lacking in tone. It wasn't until she saw the jagged scar on the right side of his throat that she realised why. It was no surgical scar, but a traumatic shrapnel wound that had partially destroyed his larynx, for ever altering his voice.

He had spoken in Pashto, one of the two dominant languages in Afghanistan. Still, Anya said nothing in response. She would do her talking soon enough, and she would make sure he did his.

Leaving him for a moment, she walked over to retrieve the gun he had dropped during their brief fight. Making sure the safety was engaged, she changed her grip on the weapon slightly. It was less effective for shooting, but much better for what she had in mind.

She still didn't approve of using guns in this way, but since there was nothing else to hand, she would have to make do.

The man stared at the weapon, fear in his eyes now. He looked as the giant had done in his final moments – like a hunted animal, cornered, about to die.

Still saying nothing, Anya swung the weapon hard and delivered a heavy blow to his left temple. Enough to put him down for a time, but not enough to kill him.

No sooner had he slumped sideways than she produced a couple of plastic cable ties from one of her pockets and used them to bind his hands behind his back. With one shoulder dislocated and the other hand crippled, she doubted he was capable of harming her, but there was no need to take the risk.

Straining under the weight, she managed to hoist the unconscious man up and half-carried, half-dragged him over to the van. He smelled of tobacco and cheap cologne, neither of which could disguise the underlying odour of stale sweat.

He wasn't heavy, but the human body is an awkward shape for carrying alone, especially when it isn't cooperating, and she was perspiring by the time she reached the vehicle.

The panel door on the side was unlocked. A final heave was enough to get the unconscious man up over the edge, after which she released her grip and allowed him to fall onto the bare steel floor.

She left the giant where he was. He was far too heavy to move, and she already had what she needed.

Slamming the door shut once more, she settled herself in the driver's seat, glanced at the dashboard to familiarise herself with the make and model, then pushed the reluctant stick into first gear and drove off at a steady pace.

Chapter 16

Drake was feeling tired and strung out by the time he made it back to the Agency compound at Bagram. The journey north from Kabul had passed without event or mishap, despite his being stopped several times at ANP checkpoints for a game of twenty questions.

Much as he hated to admit it, he was running on empty. It must have been at least 48 hours since he'd had anything approaching a decent sleep, and his body was starting to remind him of that fact with increasing urgency.

Still, there was no thought of resting yet. His mind was buzzing after the day's events, not to mention the fact that they were a day closer to Kourash's deadline and no closer to finding Mitchell.

What he really wanted was a quiet room in which to think over everything he'd seen and heard, and as he approached the conference room that served as their base of operations, part of him hoped his teammates would have turned in for the night.

No such luck. All three of them were waiting for him as he pushed the door open, and none of them looked happy.

'Jesus, Ryan, where the hell have you been?' Frost demanded. 'What happened at Horizon?'

'Breckenridge wants to tear you a new asshole,' Keegan

added at the same time. 'He's been chewing my damn ear off demanding updates—'

'We tried calling you,' McKnight chipped in. 'I've had some results back on the Stinger—'

'All right, all right. One at a time,' Drake said, making a beeline for the coffee urn. It looked as if it had been switched off a while ago, but still had a cupful of sludge at the bottom.

He looked at Frost first, reasoning that her question was easiest to tackle. 'I turned my phone off for a reason – I didn't want to be disturbed. And no, I didn't get anything useful out of Horizon. They're giving me the big fuck-off.'

Frost eyed him in silence for several seconds. Knowing how volatile her temper could be, there was a good chance she might tell him to ram it.

Still, even she knew when to back down. Pouting, she retreated to the other side of the conference table and sat down, throwing her feet up on the surface as if in a show of rebellion.

Just then, Drake's cellphone started ringing. He had only powered it up five minutes ago, and on checking the caller ID he was unsurprised to note it was Breckenridge. No doubt the man was wondering why Drake hadn't submitted an end-of-day report.

'Deal with that,' Drake said, tossing the phone to Keegan. He had no patience to take such a call tonight.

'What am I – your secretary?' the sniper asked, holding the cellphone as if it were a ticking bomb. However, one look from Drake was enough to dissuade him from further protests. 'What do you want me to tell him?'

'Tell him to fuck off and let me do my job,' Drake snapped, gulping down his tepid, bitter-tasting coffee.

'Hey, George,' Keegan began, switching immediately

to a quiet, efficient tone. 'Ryan's tied up right now, but I'll have him call you back just as soon as he can . . .'

While he attempted to placate Drake's superior, McKnight moved closer and lowered her voice. 'So Horizon were hiding something?'

Drake nodded. 'I spoke to their CEO – some bloke named Carpenter. I don't know what he's up to, but he's keeping something under wraps. Maybe your theory about the Stinger was right after all?'

'No such luck,' she said, shaking her head. 'I got the report back from Langley about an hour ago. According to them, the ejector motor I found belongs to one of the Block-E Stinger variants. They weren't introduced until the late nineties.'

Drake said nothing. At a stroke, Anya's theory had been proven right, and their own working hypothesis had vanished. The question that now surfaced in his mind was what exactly Horizon had been trying to protect, if not a link to a dirty war two decades earlier.

McKnight was quick to pick up on his lack of surprise. 'Why do I feel like I'm telling you something you already know?'

'I had my doubts about our theory,' he said, unwilling to elaborate. 'So if this weapon wasn't brought in by the Agency back in the eighties, how did it end up here?'

McKnight paused a moment, looking as though she might well press her earlier point before deciding against it. Instead she moved over to the conference table to consult the dossier she had printed off.

'According to the report, our missile was manufactured by Raytheon Systems two years ago. It was delivered to the US Army a few months later, where it stayed in the Hawthorne Army Depot for the next year or so. Then, two months ago, it was shipped.'

'Where?'

'Here,' was the simple answer. 'Or rather, it was delivered here at Bagram, then ferried out in a supply convoy to Firebase Salerno near the eastern border. As far as we know, it should still be in the armoury out there.'

'Clearly it isn't,' Drake pointed out.

'Clearly.' He saw a flicker of a smile. 'But that's where the paper trail goes cold, I'm afraid.'

For Drake, the answer seemed logical. 'Then that's where we pick it up. Can you get in touch with the CO out there, find out what he knows about it?'

She shook her head. 'These are difficult questions we'll be asking, Ryan. In my experience, it's best to ask them face to face.'

'Are you volunteering?'

McKnight flashed a grin. 'Any excuse to get out of the office,' she quipped, though her playful look soon turned more serious. 'First thing in the morning I'll see about hitching a ride out there.'

'All right. Stay on it.' Satisfied that he could do no more with McKnight, Drake turned his attention to Frost.

The young woman had settled herself on one of the chairs lining the conference table, not looking altogether pleased by his quick dismissal of her earlier question. In fact, she reminded him of a sullen teenager.

'Keira, I need your help.'

'Funny how that works, huh?' she replied without looking at him.

'I'm serious. I need you to do some research for me.'

That piqued her interest at least. When Drake said research, what he really meant was covert snooping. Both of them knew and acknowledged it without explicitly saying it.

'On what, exactly?' she asked, sitting up.

'On Horizon. I want to know everything you can find on it. When it was formed, who owns it, what they do and what their capabilities are. And I especially want to know about Richard Carpenter, the man who runs the show. I want to know his background, his experience, his training, his favourite ice-cream flavour. Make it happen.'

The young woman cocked a dark eyebrow. 'I see. Any reason?'

'I'm curious.'

'That's not much of an answer, Ryan.'

'I don't have much to go on. Yet,' he replied. 'Horizon and Carpenter. Everything you can find. Got it?'

'Yeah. I've got it,' she replied in a tone devoid of emotion.

Drake wanted to apologise for being so hard on her earlier, but he couldn't summon the words. Anyway, he sensed she didn't need to hear it. Frost was many things, but sensitive wasn't one of them.

Leaving her to get on with it, Drake turned his attention to Keegan, who was closing down his phone after what had clearly been a fraught phone call.

'How did things go with Breckenridge?'

'Safe to say I won't be making the Christmas card list,' the older man replied, tossing Drake's phone back to him.

'Join the club,' Drake said, flashing a weak smile. 'Listen, Sam's following up on the Stinger and Keira's looking into Horizon. Meanwhile, our priority is Kourash. First thing tomorrow, you and I are heading into Kabul.'

'Sounds like fun,' Keegan grinned. 'What are you expecting to find?'

'Clues,' was his simple response. 'He's around here somewhere. He'd want to be close so he can watch us fumble around trying to find Mitchell. He wants to prove how superior he is. What better place to operate from than Kabul, right under our noses?'

'You sure you're not tempting fate, putting yourself out in the open like that?' McKnight asked. 'If you've got a history with him, chances are he'll remember you.'

For a moment, she saw a glimmer of something in his eyes that sent a chill through her. They weren't the eyes of a Shepherd team leader sent to rescue a man from his captors. They were the eyes of a man with only one objective – to kill.

'I'm counting on it,' he said.

Chapter 17

Pulling the van into an ancient farm compound that looked as though it hadn't been inhabited in her lifetime, Anya killed the engine and switched the lights off, allowing the cool darkness to envelop her.

As a child she had been deathly afraid of the dark. She could still remember the fear that had charged through her veins when she lay cowering in her bed in the middle of the night, convinced that horrific unseen monsters hovered all around her. Power cuts had been a common occurrence in Lithuania during her early years, and more than once she had let out a shriek of fright when the dim electric lights went out, plunging the house suddenly into darkness.

How things changed.

Now she was perfectly at home in the dark. It was a friend, an ally, a tool that she had often used to her advantage. Lack of light heightened her already keen senses, affording her an unusually complete picture of the world around her. Twenty years ago, Red Army soldiers had learned to fear the darkness because it brought *her*.

Reaching into her pocket, she fished out the phone she had confiscated earlier. A quick glance was enough to tell her it wasn't a standard commercial model. It was thicker, heavier, designed for rough handling. She had seen enough of them in her time to recognise a crypto phone.

Designed to prevent electronic eavesdropping or tracking, crypto phones used a simple but effective key-exchange algorithm to encrypt their transmissions. Such a system only worked between phones using the same encryption mode, with the same session key, which was why they were so popular between small groups of covert operatives.

If she needed further evidence that her attackers were more than petty criminals, this was surely it. Powering the unit up, she found herself confronted with a six-digit password screen. She tried a few obvious possibilities like 000000 or 012345, but her attempts were firmly rebuffed.

She would need the access code if she wanted to uncover whatever secrets lay on that phone.

The takedown man was stirring in the back. She had checked her force when she struck him with the butt of the pistol, wanting only to incapacitate him. Now it seemed he was starting to come around.

She picked up the Makarov from the passenger seat and pulled the slide back just far enough to see the faint brass gleam of a round in the chamber. After checking the safety once again, she pulled her door open and stepped outside.

They were a good 5 or 6 miles east of Kabul, parked up in a former agricultural area that had turned to waste-land after the irrigation system had been destroyed. The orange glow of electric lights hovered over the distant city, reminding her of another time, long ago, when she had sat on a wind-blown hill surveying that same capital, wondering if it would ever see peace.

Dismissing such memories, she rounded the vehicle,

tucking the weapon down the back of her trousers as she did so. She didn't imagine she would need it to defend herself, but force of habit wouldn't allow her to leave a weapon unsecured.

Hauling open the sliding door, she leaned in, switched on the internal light and surveyed her prisoner. The jolting movement of their passage over rough roads must have pushed him up against one corner of the vehicle. He was a mess, his clothes stained with blood and dirt, his thinning hair damp with sweat, his lean pinched face tight with pain.

His eyes flickered open at the sound of the door sliding on its rollers, and suddenly went wide when they fastened on her. No doubt the hazy memories of his failed takedown had resurfaced, and it was now dawning on him just what kind of situation he was in.

Clambering inside, she pulled the door shut behind her. She didn't think there were any people nearby, but she didn't want the light to draw curious onlookers.

She stared at the older man for several seconds, saying nothing, just allowing the tension and fear to build within him. It was almost palpable. He had seen what she was capable of, and knew she had him at her mercy. He was afraid, and he had good reason to be.

'You tried to abduct me tonight,' she said at last, speaking in Pashto since she knew he understood the language. 'Why?'

He said nothing to this, though she saw something else in his eyes besides fear now. Hatred, anger, impotent rage. She was only a woman, and she had hurt him worse than he'd ever been hurt before.

'I killed your friend,' she added. 'I cut his throat like slaughtering an animal, watched him bleed to death before my eyes. It took a while, of course.'

The simmering anger flared up inside him, yet still he said nothing. It must have taken a great effort of will to keep silent.

'Why did you try to abduct me?'

His dark eyes glimmered, filled with hatred, but he did not speak.

Anya had suspected as much. She was going to have to persuade him.

She understood the utility of torture, had studied the psychology and methodology behind it in depth as part of her training, but she had never enjoyed it. Of course, that didn't mean she wasn't good at it. As with all aspects of her profession, she had absorbed a wealth of knowledge and experience on this particular topic, and been obliged to put it into practice many times.

She thought to use her knife. Knives were good because they allowed far more control than firearms, but he had already lost blood from the slash wound on his arm and she didn't want to risk him passing out again, or even dying.

No, she needed something else.

Glancing around, she caught sight of something that she had noted absently when she first dumped him in the van – a toolbox, fixed against the sidewall with bungee cords. Either her two attackers had stolen the van from a tradesman of some kind, or they liked to be prepared for breakdowns.

Regardless, she undid the metal hinges holding the lid down and flipped it open. It didn't take her long to find what she needed.

Anya had few memories of the man who had been her grandfather. He had suffered a series of strokes when she was still a young girl, leaving him crippled and embittered for the final year of his life. But in his prime, she recalled him as a tall, imposing man, gruff and blunt and practical, his hands huge and square and immensely powerful to her young eyes.

A carpenter by trade, he had imparted to her one piece of advice she would never forget – there were few problems in life that couldn't be solved with a good hammer.

How right he'd been, she reflected as she lifted the battered claw hammer from the toolbox, testing the weight and getting a feel for it. It was a sturdy implement, easily 3 or 4 pounds of tempered steel, with a black rubber hand guard for better grip.

Armed with the tool she needed to solve this particular problem, she turned her attention back to her captive.

'I will only ask you politely once more,' she warned. 'Why did you try to abduct me?'

No response.

Without hesitation, Anya raised the hammer up, took aim and brought it down hard and fast on his right knee. She considered herself only mediocre in the art of carpentry, but she'd never had trouble driving a nail into a piece of wood, and her aim hadn't failed her today.

She heard a muted pop, and felt a slight yielding through the hammer as his kneecap gave way beneath the blow. She didn't think she had broken the patella itself, since it was basically a solid piece of bone, but she had certainly torn the ligaments holding it in place, and probably driven it deep into the joint between his femur and tibia bones.

A good strike. Her grandfather would have approved.

A heartbeat later, the van was filled with the man's howls of pain as a million nerve endings lit up, announcing the terrible damage that had just been inflicted on his knee.

Anya waited in silence until his screaming died down,

her face a mask of cold detachment. She might as well have been listening to a weather report, such was the lack of emotion his cries elicited.

'You forced me to be impolite,' she said at last, holding up the hammer for emphasis. 'That was your choice.'

'You'll die screaming for this, you bitch,' he said, hissing the words out through gritted teeth. This time he had spoken in Dari, and she sensed from his fluency that this was the language he had been raised with.

Good, they were making progress.

'We all die, my friend,' she replied in the same language, noting with a certain satisfaction the look of shock her words elicited.

On first arriving in Afghanistan twenty years ago, she had soon discovered to her dismay that the Mujahideen, coming as they did from countless different tribes, regions and ethnic groups, spoke a bewildering array of different languages and dialects. To communicate, she had been forced to painstakingly master each of them in turn. She was far from fluent in them all, but could at least carry on a basic conversation in most.

The knowledge had, fortunately, stayed with her over the years.

'You have a choice now,' she explained, speaking slowly and patiently.

Some interrogators chose to scream and yell at their subjects, but not her. She was always cold, logical, controlled. As she had learned a long time ago, that was far more frightening.

'I am going to ask you questions, and every time you refuse to answer, I will hurt you. The longer you make me wait, the more I will make it hurt. If you lie to me, I will know, and I will treat it as refusal to answer. It is that simple.' She leaned in a little closer. 'Now, why did you try to attack me?'

He was weighing up his chances of holding out against her. She could see it in his eyes – the calculation, the indecision, the fear. She stared right back at him, unafraid, a soldier without conscience or remorse.

'I was ordered to do it,' he said at last, practically spitting the words out.

'Ordered by who?'

'By Kourash.'

'Why?'

'He . . . wanted to know who you were. He saw you meet with the CIA man. He ordered us to . . . bring you in.'

That revelation did nothing to improve her mood. She had thought her meeting with Drake had been secure. Now she knew otherwise. Drake was a marked man, not only by the Agency but apparently also by Kourash.

She was beginning to question her wisdom in making contact with him again. Had she left him alone, she might have remained safe in anonymity. But now Kourash knew of her existence.

She had been a potential threat already. But after killing two of his men, she had undoubtedly become an enemy.

'Why is Kourash interested in this man?'

He glared at her, his eyes burning like coals. 'He will find you,' he hissed. 'He will find you just like he finds everyone. Any harm you do to me, he will revisit on you ten times over. You will beg for death before he is finished.'

The empty threats of a cornered man, she knew. They were of no concern to her. Still, they warranted a response.

His left hand was resting on the steel deck. Taking

183

aim, she struck a quick, sharp blow with the hammer. There was a crunch as the first knuckle of his middle finger shattered under the impact of several pounds of unyielding steel.

'Answer my question,' she said when his cries of pain had died down.

He must have bitten his tongue when she struck him. Spitting bloody phlegm on the floor, he at last responded. 'He visited the crash site. Kourash knew he had been sent to . . . find the men who shot down the helicopter. He was a threat to us.'

That made sense, she supposed. It was logical that this Kourash, whoever he was, would keep tabs on potential threats.

'And why did you shoot down that helicopter?' she asked. That was what Drake had been sent here to find out, after all.

He shook his head. 'That is not my concern. We are told only what we need to know.'

Again, she detected no hint of deception in him. He was a foot soldier, there to act as hired muscle. There was no sense in giving men like him information that could compromise an overall operation.

Instead she decided to try a different approach. Reaching into her pocket, Anya held up the crypto phone. 'This is your cellphone. What is the access code?'

'Fuck you, whore.' That one was delivered in English.

If he had been hoping to stir her to anger, he was mistaken. She had a far more effective retort in mind. Raising the hammer again, she calmly took aim at his other knee.

'Wait!'

She paused, keeping the hammer ready, and glanced up at his face. There was a look of desperation in his eyes now. He was breathing hard between clenched teeth, pain threatening to overwhelm him. It seemed he was at the limits of his tolerance.

Everyone had a limit – she knew that much from personal experience. All it took to find it was a little perseverance.

'No more,' he said, shaking his head. 'No more . . .'

'The code,' she prompted.

Closing his eyes, he recited the code, speaking slowly and deliberately. 'One, five, five, three, one, six.'

Anya regarded him dubiously. 'For your sake, I hope you are not lying.'

The takedown man sighed and shook his head again, broken and defeated. 'The code is correct. I promise you that.'

Lowering the hammer, Anya turned her attention back to the phone and inputted the numbers. The unit gave a single bleep, then went blank.

Straight away she knew what he'd done. A duress code, designed to wipe the phone's memory and render it useless.

Looking at him again, Anya saw a crooked smile on his face. He would die, and he knew it, but he had at least scored a minor victory.

'You asked for a code, I gave you one. Now the phone is useless to you.' He closed his eyes again, steeling himself for what was coming. 'You can do what you want to me. I have nothing more to give you.'

He was right about that.

She used the hammer one more time, then opened the sliding door and jumped lightly down onto the dusty ground, returning to the driver's cab.

A quick check of the fuel gauge told her the tank was just over half full. More than enough to do the job. She caught a glimpse of her reflection in the rear-view mirror and noticed a splash of the takedown man's blood on her cheek, wiping it away without a second thought.

It took her a moment or two to find the cigarette lighter built into the cheap plastic dashboard – having not smoked in nearly twenty years, it wasn't in her nature to look for such things out of habit.

Pushing it in, she opened the glovebox and found a tattered cleaning rag amongst the mess of receipts, manuals and other assorted junk that had been jammed inside. She suspected it was used to clear condensation from the window, but tonight she had a different purpose in mind.

The cigarette lighter popped out about thirty seconds later, by which time she had removed the van's fuel cap and jammed the rag into the opening. Making a mental note of the van's licence plate, she retrieved the glowing red lighter and held it against the rag, blowing gently on it until she had coaxed a small flame into life.

There was nothing more she needed to do. Fire and fuel would handle the rest. Leaving the doomed vehicle, she turned away and strode off into the night, already composing a text message to warn Drake against a similar attack.

She had covered about 50 yards before the desert lit up vicious orange around her, followed by a deep concussive boom as the van's fuel tank ignited. Even from this distance she could feel the heat from the raging inferno.

She didn't look back.

Chapter 18

Drake was alone in the 8-by-10 brick cubicle that served as his room. With a simple steel-framed bed pushed up against one whitewashed wall and a cheap writing desk next to it, it was hardly a luxury suite. Still, it was a roof over his head and a bed beneath it.

He knew he needed both things at that moment. It was late. He should have been asleep hours ago, but after everything that had happened today he felt keyed up and restless, filled with energy he couldn't expend.

His laptop was powered up and displaying a still image of Kourash lifted from Mitchell's hostage video. The audio-visual technicians at Langley had done what they could to enhance and clean up the grainy image, even producing a couple of composite renderings of Kourash's face sporting various combinations of hair-style, beard and moustache to account for attempted disguises.

None of them would be much use to the ISAF and ANP troopers charged with looking for him. In his fifties, with a gaunt, weather-beaten face, heavy brows and a high, deeply lined forehead, Kourash could blend in anywhere in Afghanistan.

But Drake would know him if he saw him. That much he was certain of.

'Where are you?' Drake said under his breath as he

took a drink from his glass of whisky; the potent, smoky taste was by now quite familiar to him.

Knowing how difficult alcohol was to come by on bases like this, he had had the foresight to bring a bottle of Talisker along, hidden within his pack. Being a Shepherd operative had its advantages – their bags couldn't be searched at customs, meaning it was easy to smuggle in minor items of contraband like this.

He felt guilty for drinking on the job, but he also knew he needed it. His thoughts were racing, chaotic, endlessly replaying everything he'd seen and heard today.

He took another pull, allowing the potent spirit to light a small blaze in his stomach as he stared at the picture, boring into those dark eyes that were so filled with anger and hatred. Images of the twisted, scorched Black Hawk flashed through his mind, and for a moment he could have sworn he detected something in the air besides the peaty aroma of whisky.

The scent of charred plastic and burned human flesh.

Questions. All he seemed to have were questions, and no answers.

And yet the answers he desperately sought were near. He sensed it; his instincts told him he was missing something. Something fundamental. Something he had seen and yet hadn't seen.

He frowned at the unfamiliar bleep of a text message tone, realising a moment later that it was Anya's phone. He felt a surge of anticipation and immediately rebuked himself for it as he fished the phone from his pocket.

However, his excitement quickly changed to concern as he read her message.

Two of Karl's friends found me. You were followed. Suggest you watch yourself.

Naturally the message was coded to conceal identities, and thus avoid arousing the suspicion of any CIA signals technician who happened to intercept it. Karl was her word for Kourash, just as Christopher or Cameron might double up for Carpenter. Still, the meaning was clear. Two of Kourash's men had tried to ambush her, and she blamed him for it.

Knowing Anya, he didn't doubt she would have responded to this with lethal aggression, but her revelation brought with it a pang of guilt and anger. She had taken a risk by making contact again and already he had fucked up. Burning with self-recrimination, he composed his own coded reply.

Made it back without trouble. Why did they come after you?

She hadn't said it explicitly, but in her message he sensed a certain concern. She wasn't texting just to report the encounter; she wanted to know if he too had been attacked, and if he was all right. None of which made him feel any better.

His grim thoughts were interrupted by a knock at the door.

'Who is it?' he called, irked by the distraction.

'It's Keira. Open up.'

Setting his glass on the sorry excuse for a desk, Drake rose from the bed and unlocked the door to find Frost standing before him. She was clutching several sheets of paper, and judging by her wide-eyed appearance she had been working and gulping down coffee rather than resting as he'd told her to.

'You ordered dirt on Horizon, I've got it,' she said, holding up the printed sheets with a triumphant grin. Drake spotted at least a dozen notes scrawled across them in her chaotic handwriting. 'Mind if I come in?'

Without waiting for a response, she slipped past him and into the room.

He noticed her eyes linger for a moment on the almost-empty glass of whisky, though she said nothing about it. Even she knew when to hold her tongue.

'Don't you ever sleep?' Drake couldn't help asking, impressed by her dedication but concerned about what it would mean for her performance tomorrow.

'Not if I can avoid it,' she admitted. 'Anyway, I could ask the same of you, but you'd just get all moody on me. So why don't we skip that and get down to business?'

He took a seat at the small desk. 'All right, what did you find on Horizon?'

Frost settled herself on the bed and glanced at her haphazard dossier.

'They're major players in the PMC scene,' she began. 'As far as I can tell, they've only been around since 2004 but already they've established themselves as one of the big boys out here. They recruit operatives from all over the world, with a heavy emphasis on Special Forces.'

'Why?' Drake asked.

'They don't operate like a normal PMC. Companies like Blackwater handle low-level protection details out here, like guarding roadblocks or watching over politicians we can afford to lose. Horizon are organised more like a front-line infantry regiment, or maybe a Special Forces unit. These guys are set up for full-on combat ops. In fact, they've already been used for house raids, snatch and grabs, and assaults against Taliban strongholds, all with an excellent success rate. They've got the manpower, the resources and expertise to run just about any operation they need to, fully independent of ISAF.'

'Like a private army,' Drake mused, unsettled by her revelation.

'Pretty much,' Frost agreed. 'But an army that isn't governed by the normal rules of engagement.'

'What do you mean?'

'Well, for a start they're able to hire characters like your friend Vermaak with no questions asked,' Frost explained, for some reason looking like a kid who had just found the hidden cookie jar. 'I did some digging on the guy when Sam told me what happened at the crash site.'

Flicking through her heavily annotated dossier, she found the page she was looking for and began to read.

'Piet Vermaak, born in Pretoria in 1961. Joined South African Defence Force in 1980 before moving to Special Forces Brigade in 1984. He was heavily involved in the Border War for the next few years, even led his own covert strike team until he was discharged, apparently for executing prisoners. After that, there's almost no official record of him for the next decade. He went dark, probably working the freelance mercenary circuit. Then a few years ago he pops up again, this time working for Horizon. Now he's one of their most senior ground commanders.' She glanced up from her report. 'In short, the guy's bad news. He shoots first and asks questions later.'

Drake didn't need Frost to tell him that Vermaak wasn't a man to be trusted, but this put a whole new slant on his actions at the crash site.

However, there was one name she hadn't mentioned yet.

'What about Carpenter?'

At this, the young woman grinned conspiratorially. 'I've saved the best for last,' she said, flicking to the final page in her dossier. 'Richard Carpenter. Enlisted US Army 1963, aged twenty-one. Served two tours in Vietnam before joining a task force of the 327th Infantry Regiment, better known as Tiger Force.'

That was enough to get Drake's attention. Tiger Force had been a special composite unit formed to wage guerrilla warfare against the Viet Cong, employing many of the same methods and tactics as their enemy. Unfortunately the unit became rather too good at their job, eventually descending into brutality and mindless killing. Countless rumours had circulated about them over the years, from torturing civilians, to rape, murder and mutilation.

'The unit was disbanded in '69. They were rumoured to be involved in all kinds of weird shit, like wearing necklaces made from human ears,' she said with a disdainful curl of her lip. 'Anyway, our friend Carpenter was apparently cleared of any wrongdoing. He carried on working in various Special Forces outfits, then got promoted to colonel in 1980. But it's not until '84 that things get interesting.'

Drake frowned. 'How so?'

'Because nothing happened. His service record just stops. There's no mention of any deployments, any operations, any transfers. Nothing. It's like a black hole in his life, from '84 up to '89. Then, around the time of the First Gulf War, it just starts up again like nothing happened.' She laid down her folder and looked at Drake across the table. 'Read between the lines on this one, I'd say he was involved in some kind of black op – something so dirty that they expunged the whole thing from his record.'

'I want to know what he was up to,' Drake said.

In some part of his mind he knew he was allowing himself to become distracted, that he was allowing his encounter with Anya to intrude on his investigation, but he didn't care. He wanted to know her history with Carpenter. He wanted to know why she was really here.

'Hey, I can't find what isn't there.' She hesitated, having seen something in his expression that went deeper than mere professional interest. 'Anyway, why the focus on Carpenter all of a sudden? Even if he is hiding something, who cares what he was up to twenty years ago?'

Drake glanced away. He could say nothing further on the subject without revealing his meeting with Anya last night, and that was one road he was unwilling to go down.

'It's just a hunch,' he lied. 'Something about the guy doesn't add up.'

Frost eyed Drake hard. 'You know, if I was the cynical type, I'd say you know something you're not telling us.'

'Then I should be grateful you're not the cynical type, Keira,' he said, returning her gaze. 'What are the chances of you accessing Horizon's computer network?'

Her brows rose at this. 'You mean hacking in?'

'I didn't hear anyone say the word "hacking", did you?'

Their remit as special investigators granted them a certain amount of latitude in matters of covert intelligence gathering, but hacking into the computer system of a major DoD contractor was crossing the line.

She weighed up the matter for a moment or two. 'Dicey,' she concluded. 'I can try, but I'd guess they'd have some pretty serious firewalls in place.'

Drake rubbed his jaw, wondering whether it was worth the risk. 'All right. See if you can scope it out. If it looks too dangerous, forget it.'

'No problem.' The young woman rose from the bed, heading for the door.

'Oh, and Keira,' he called after her. 'Get some sleep first. That's an order.'

She looked over her shoulder at him. 'Yeah? What about you?'

He shrugged. 'That's my problem.'

As soon as she was gone, Drake threw himself back into his work. The whisky lay untouched now – he had no desire for it and was angry at himself for his weakness. Anya had almost been killed tonight while he'd been sitting here getting drunk.

For the next few hours he remained hunched over the computer fruitlessly trawling through photographs of other attacks staged by Kourash's group, reading intelligence reports, crime scene files and analysis until the words blurred and began to seep into one another.

He checked Anya's phone over and over, searching for a text message that never arrived, then angrily turned his thoughts back to his work. The images and memories were still bombarding him, but with less cohesion and purpose now; one scene blending into the next as the consciousness governing them began to fade.

He looked at his watch – 04:13.

He replayed his encounter with Vermaak, with Carpenter, with Cunningham, and most of all with Anya. He saw the woman smiling at him from the shadows of that room above the tea house, then a moment later saw her as she had appeared a year earlier, suddenly raising a weapon and putting a round in his stomach.

And yet, again and again his thoughts drifted back to Mitchell, to his hostage tape. Over and over he saw the man's eyes flicking open and shut with unnatural regularity.

He was missing something, he realised then. Something his subconscious mind was trying to tell him. Something he had seen without really *seeing*.

And at last, an idea struck him.

Once more he accessed Mitchell's hostage tape and hit the play button, immediately finding himself looking at the same dingy room with a battered Mitchell secured to a chair in the centre of the frame. He was staring right at the camera, his eyes wide with fear as his masked captor came into view.

Kourash was soon busy launching into his tirade against Western imperialism, growing more animated as he got into full swing. Mitchell, however, continued to stare into the camera, his eyes flickering in a seemingly random fashion. A cut over his left eye was apparently troubling him.

Or was it?

Frowning, Drake leaned in, looking closer at the bound captive. He was still blinking, but there was something unusual about the eye movements. Sometimes they would flicker rapidly, other times they would close for nearly a second at a time.

'What the fuck . . . ?'

There was purpose in the seemingly random gestures, he realised. Mitchell, bound and gagged as he was, was trying to communicate using the only means still available to him – his eyes.

Blink, close, blink. Dot, dash, dot . . .

'I'll be damned.'

It was Morse code, he realised now. Mitchell had been talking in Morse code. Drake was far from an expert in such an antiquated form of communication, but he recognised enough of the letter patterns to understand the intent behind them.

If only it hadn't taken so damned long. It had been there this whole time and nobody saw it, Drake included.

He had seen without truly seeing.

Hastily reaching for a notebook and pen, Drake moved the pointer back to the start of the video and hit play again.

Part Three

Retaliation

In 1979, the Soviet 40th Army crosses the border into Afghanistan. Despite their securing major cities, Mujahideen fighters wage a vicious guerrilla campaign against the Red Army, leading to an eventual withdrawal in February 1989.

The Soviet Union will formally dissolve two years later.

Total Casualties:
14,000 Soviet soldiers killed and 54,000 wounded
18,000 Afghan government soldiers killed
90,000 Mujahideen fighters killed (estimate)
Up to 2 million Afghan civilians killed and 3 million wounded

Chapter 19

CIA Training Facility 'Camp Peary', Virginia,
3 November 1985

Twenty-six, twenty-seven, twenty-eight . . .

Forcing her burning, aching muscles to obey, Anya heaved her body up from the muddy ground, only to lower it back down again, going through the same motion again and again without rest, without relief.

Freezing rain hammered the back of her head to run in rivulets down her face and into her eyes. Limp strands of dirty blonde hair hung down around her, soaking into the mud every time she lowered herself to start another press-up. The full equipment pack she was wearing felt like a boulder pressing down inexorably upon her, crushing the life out of her.

All night long they had been at it. Running, marching, fighting, and finally this grim, unrelenting test of endurance.

She was falling behind. The dozen other men in her unit were pulling ahead of her, their movements still fast, efficient, mechanical, as if all concept of pain and weakness was foreign to them. All strong, fit, capable men in their prime.

Next to them she was nothing. And every day, with every march, every drill, every test of strength and endurance, she was made to feel it.

Thirty-four, thirty-five, thirty-six . . .

'You ladies aren't getting tired, are you?' a deep, powerful voice called out.

'Sir, no, sir!' they replied in unison. A dozen men shouting out together, proclaiming their collective strength and defiance and support of each other.

A dozen men and one woman, her voice virtually drowned out.

'Good. Because what we have here is a lesson – endurance. One of many qualities it's my sorry duty to instil in you worthless sacks of shit,' the voice went on. 'What's the first promise you made when you joined this unit?'

Again the reply came at once, twelve men and one woman crying out, 'I will endure when all others fail!'

Forty-one, forty-two, forty-three . . .

Every movement was agony. Her lungs heaved, her heart pounded, her vision swam as exhaustion clawed at her.

'Again!'

'I will endure when all others fail!'

Anya barely had the strength to cry out, could barely find breath in her lungs to make the sound. Every nerve ending in her body was on fire. Every muscle screamed at her to stop.

Forty-four, forty-five . . .

'Again!'

'I will endure when all others fail!'

This time no woman's voice cried out. This time she could summon up no words. It was all she could do to raise herself up again on trembling arms.

Through her blurred vision she saw a pair of boots splash through the mud towards her, coming to a halt so he could kneel down in front of her.

Carpenter.

She didn't look at him. She could already picture the

expression on his lean, chiselled, terrifying face. It was the same mixture of disdain and simmering resentment he'd given her the first time they'd been introduced six weeks earlier.

'What's wrong, Recruit Thirteen? Did you forget your promise?'

There were no names here. They hadn't earned the right to their own names yet. She was merely Recruit 13. Lucky 13.

Forty-six . . .

'Sir . . . no . . . sir!' *she managed to gasp.*

'Then why the fuck didn't you sound off? Are you disrespecting me?'

She couldn't speak, couldn't escape the pain and exhaustion that consumed her, burned away all rational thoughts like an inferno the rain was powerless to stop.

'Why are you slowing down, Recruit Thirteen?' *Carpenter yelled, his face so close that she could feel his warm breath on her cheek.* 'All I asked for was fifty push-ups. Fifty! Can't you even give me that?'

Forty-seven . . .

'Are you tired? Are you hurting?' *he taunted.* 'Pain and weakness are nothing. Nothing! They're beating you because you don't have what it takes to overcome them. How can you be a soldier if you can't endure?'

Muscles trembling, chest heaving, she tried with desperate strength to push her body up again. The pack pressed down on her. The rain hammered her skull. Blood surged in her ears, and stars and strange lights flitted across her eyes.

With an exhausted, defeated sob, she collapsed in the mud, utterly spent.

Satisfied that she was beaten, Carpenter rose to his feet, staring down at her without a hint of compassion or remorse.

201

Saying nothing, he turned and walked away, leaving her shaking and crying in the mud.

Central Hotel, Kabul, 11 August 2008

Turning off the water feed, Anya let out a breath and stood leaning against the wall of the shower cubicle with her eyes closed, wisps of steam curling around her. Hot water, much like electricity, was still something of a temperamental luxury in Kabul, but one that she was very grateful for.

After spending four years in a freezing Russian prison, the mere notion of hot running water under her control would always seem like a luxury.

Taking another deep breath, she opened her eyes, stepped out and grabbed a towel from the rail to dry her hair. Naked and dripping water, she walked through to the main living area.

With cheap carpets, a hard lumpy bed and air conditioning that didn't work properly, the room was certainly nothing impressive, but it was more than enough to meet her needs. She didn't sleep on the bed anyway. And unlike the more expensive and prestigious Kabul Serena Hotel, this place was low-key and inexpensive – ideal for her cover as a freelance writer trying to discover the 'real Afghanistan'.

There were plenty such people here these days.

If she ever did get around to writing a book about her experiences in this country, it would be rather more illuminating than most of the tomes penned by self-professed experts.

She had travelled here under a Norwegian identity. She tended to pick Scandinavian nationalities for her aliases, partly because it fitted with her physical appearance – tall, blonde-haired, blue-eyed – but mostly because it seemed to make international travel easier. Countries like Finland, Norway and Sweden were seen by most immigration officials as neutral and inoffensive, with generally affluent populations who didn't meddle in crime or terrorism.

Like most things based on human psychology, it was irrational, but it worked.

She tossed the towel on the bed and, seeing herself in the mirror, turned to regard her reflection.

Her body had filled out a little in the past year, partly due to better diet but mostly as a result of the intense training regime she had put herself through. After escaping Iraq last year and recovering from the various injuries she'd sustained, she had determined to claw back as much of her former strength and fitness as possible.

Daily 5-mile runs, weight training, stretching and sparring had been easy enough in her twenties, but maintaining such a demanding regime at forty-three years old had been rather more difficult.

Still, the results spoke for themselves.

With a firm, flat stomach, long slender legs, toned arms and shoulders well defined with hard, compact musculature, Anya appeared little different now from ten years earlier. The impression was heightened by her short haircut, which she had told herself was purely for reasons of practicality.

But deep down she wondered if she was somehow trying to erase the past decade.

Dismissing such thoughts, she took a gulp of water and sat down at the table to access her laptop (another benefit of her cover as a writer). It had been humming away on standby and took only a few seconds to boot back up.

Logging into her email account, she found only one new entry – there was no title, and the sender was listed simply as Loki.

She was comfortable enough with modern technology when obliged to use it, but Anya had little knowledge or experience in the confusing world of computer hacking. For that, she was forced to rely on others.

She had been introduced to Loki through a mutual acquaintance, and although they had never met in person or exchanged real names, she knew two things about her enigmatic contact – Loki was English, and he had never let Anya down when it came to information retrieval.

She opened the message, hoping against hope that good news was waiting for her.

Have run a check on the number *plate you sent. A* Volkswagen *van, reported stolen in Kandahar a week ago. No police follow-up.*

Also tried reconstituting the phone's memory – it's knackered. *The duress code wiped it completely. If the memory had still been intact I might have broken the encryption scheme, but I doubt it. It was very sophisticated, much more than normal commercial models. My guess is military or* intelligence agency.

Sorry I don't have better news.

L.

Anya chewed her lip, suppressing a surge of disappointment. She hadn't expected much when she connected the crypto phone to her laptop and allowed Loki to remotely access it (something she never would have done with another person), but there was always a chance it might have borne fruit.

Not this time.

By now she was questioning the wisdom of her decision to kill the two men who had tried to abduct her. If she had spent more time and effort on the takedown man, there was a chance she might have broken him. A slim chance perhaps, but a chance nonetheless.

It had seemed logical to kill him at the time, but now she wasn't so sure.

She had been on the receiving end of physical torture more times than she cared to remember. And although she understood its necessity on an intellectual level, to her dying day she would never forgive those who had inflicted it on her.

She would ponder that in more depth later. For now, she turned her thoughts to what little information Loki's email had imparted.

Crypto phones, though expensive, weren't difficult to obtain. Anyone with the cash could buy one. But phones with sophisticated military-grade encryption were another matter entirely.

Clearly the men who had tried to abduct her were part of something more than just another Islamic extremist group. If they had access to Stinger missiles and sophisticated communications equipment, they were something very different indeed.

It was lucky for her that last night's takedown had been hastily formulated and executed with only two men. No doubt she had been a target of opportunity rather than a planned objective.

However, they had Drake under surveillance. No one had followed her to the meeting – she was certain of that. Therefore they must have been trailing Drake, following his movements.

From her understanding of the Shepherd teams, she

knew their operatives were protected by a fog of secrecy. Only a select few knew their true identities and purpose, yet apparently Kourash had been able to penetrate that veil.

On the one hand she felt a certain relief that Kourash and his group seemed to have no knowledge of who she was or why she was here, yet on another she felt concern, disappointment and even a degree of anger towards Drake for not realising he was being tailed.

That was partly why she hadn't replied to his text message. He had confirmed he was safe, and that was enough for now. She would be certain to question him on the matter next time they met face to face, though.

Anya leaned back in her chair and took another sip of water. She had warned him of the danger, and for now at least there was little more she could do.

Drake would have to look out for himself.

Chapter 20

The day dawned hazy and vague over Bagram, the sun visible only as a brighter disc through thick dust clouds off to the east. Its red-hued rays set the nearby mountains ablaze, tinged the sky orange and cast long indistinct shadows across the runways. The temperature, which had dipped close to freezing overnight, began to climb inexorably with the rising sun.

As the local mosques called the faithful to *Fajr*, the first of Islam's daily prayers, soldiers rose from their bunks and cots to start another day.

Drake, however, had no need of the daily Reveille to wake him. He had been wide awake since his revelation the night before, and had been working laboriously to identify and decipher the message in Mitchell's grainy, low-resolution hostage tape.

By the time he shoved his way into the conference room for his morning briefing, he was haggard and bleary-eyed but triumphantly clutching his laptop in one hand and a sheet of paper covered with handwritten notes in the other.

McKnight wasn't there, having already departed to continue her search for the missing Stinger. However, Frost and Keegan were waiting for him.

207

The young woman wasted no time in voicing her thoughts.

'Jesus, Ryan. You look like shit.'

Drake wasted no time responding to her insult, even if it was partially true. He was too buoyed by his discovery. Setting his laptop down on the table, he looked up at his two team members. 'I know where Mitchell is.'

Keegan glanced at his comrade, looking like a dubious spectator about to witness a magician's trick. 'This ought to be good.'

'You were right, Keira. There was more to that hostage tape than we realised.' Opening his laptop, he powered it up and set Mitchell's video to play once again, leaving the volume muted. He had no interest in Kourash's venomous words now. 'Focus on Mitchell. Look at his eyes.'

They did as he asked, both watching the screen intently. Keegan spotted it first, accustomed as he was to searching for the subtle visual clues that would give away an enemy's position.

'He's signalling,' the old sniper remarked.

Drake nodded. 'He's using his eyes to send us a message. It's Morse code.' Finally he laid his sheet of paper down on the table and turned it around for them to see.

On it he had scrawled a series of dots and dashes as he'd picked them up from the video, some crossed out and amended as more information had emerged with repeated viewings.

But beneath it all, written in bold capital letters, were two words: HOUSE FOUR.

'House four?' Frost repeated, looking at Drake quizzically. 'What the hell is that supposed to mean?'

Drake smiled. It had seemed cryptic to him when he'd first deciphered it. Only by putting it in the context of

Mitchell's purpose in Afghanistan had he at last been able to make sense of it.

'Mitchell was here to help build an intelligence network. You said yourself, his official job was to establish a series of safe houses throughout the country. Safe . . . *houses*.'

Frost's eyes lit up. 'Son of a bitch . . .'

For once, Drake felt as though he was starting to gain ground on Kourash. He was finding his feet with this investigation at last. And now, perhaps, he had found a way out.

'What better place to keep the man hostage than in one of our own safe houses?' he asked. 'It's secure, it's anonymous to passers-by, and it's the last place *we'd* ever think to look.'

Keegan, however, didn't seem quite so eager to buy into his theory. 'That'd be a hell of a risk to take. There must be a hundred easier places to stash him.'

'Easier, but not as impressive,' Drake said, refusing to be deflated. 'Kourash doesn't just want to beat us. He wants to rub our noses in it, prove how superior he is, just like before. His arrogance and vanity are his biggest enemies.'

Frost shrugged. 'Good enough for me,' she decided, already reaching out to pack away her gear.

'You stay here,' Drake ordered, giving her a significant look. 'I want you to get started on what we discussed last night.'

Even if he was right about Mitchell, Anya's comments about Carpenter still weighed heavily on his mind. He sensed there was more going on than Horizon were willing to admit, more than one aspect to this investigation, and he intended to resolve them all before he was finished.

'But—'

'No arguments,' he cut in, turning his attention to Keegan. 'John, you're with me. We need to find Crawford and put together an assault team.'

Keegan's gaze flicked to Frost, no doubt pondering the meaning of Drake's instructions to her. 'Something I should know about?'

'Best that you don't,' Drake advised. The fewer people who knew his intention to probe Horizon's computer network, the better. 'Kourash and Mitchell are all we need to focus on right now. Let's get them.'

Both men were within his grasp. He could feel it. And now that he was closing in, nothing was going to get in his way.

Chapter 21

A small crowd had gathered to watch as the body was heaved up onto a waiting stretcher and wheeled over to a nearby ambulance; no easy task considering the size and weight of the victim.

In most cities, the discovery of a brutal murder in the middle of a street would have elicited shock and outrage from local residents, but here the assembled faces reflected only weary resignation. Kabul had seen more than its share of death over the years, and those experiences had profoundly changed its inhabitants.

Kourash had seen enough. Turning on his heel, he strode quickly away from the scene. His face might have displayed the same casual disinterest as the others, but his eyes blazed with wrath.

Two good men dead in one night – Faraj found lying in a muddy ditch with his throat cut, while Ashraf, or what was left of him, had been discovered in the smouldering remains of the van several miles east of Kabul.

Two good, capable men wasted. And to make matters worse, their mysterious killer was still out there somewhere.

His grim musings were cut short by the buzz of his cellphone. Kourash knew who it was, and flinched inwardly as he imagined the conversation he was about to have.

Punching in the access code, he retreated into an arched doorway and held the phone to his ear. 'Yes.'

'You disobeyed my instructions,' the voice on the other end said without preamble. Even over the phone line, Kourash could hear the veiled menace, the barely contained anger in that voice. 'Your job was to kill Mitchell and put an end to his work. I presume you have an explanation for this?'

'Mitchell is taken care of,' Kourash assured him.

'Then why are Drake and his team still here?' his benefactor demanded. 'Could it be the ransom demand you made?'

He allowed that question to hang in the air for a moment, and Kourash made no attempt to answer it. Any response he gave would be futile anyway.

'Did you really think I wouldn't find out? You're allowing your pride to get the better of you. You're jeopardising everything we've worked for. That puts me in a difficult position.'

Kourash's grip on the phone tightened. 'This is not about pride.'

He had known the Americans would never give in to his demands to close down Parwan Detention Facility and release all those prisoners. He'd known even before he recorded that video, and in any case he had no interest in seeing ignorant fanatics go free, but that wasn't his objective. His objective was to attract attention.

'I don't care what this is about,' the voice growled. 'This has to stop – now, today. Have I made myself clear?'

Kourash bit his lip, incensed by the fact that he was being talked down to. As if he were a disobedient child in need of reprimand.

Still, there was no denying that his benefactor was

right about one thing – this had gone far enough. It was time to put an end to Drake and his investigation.

'You have made yourself very clear, as always,' he said. 'I will handle it myself.'

With no further comment from the other end, the line went dead.

Forward Operating Base Salerno, Khost Province

Samantha McKnight braced herself as the UH-1 Huey, a veteran aircraft dating back to the days of Vietnam, touched down hard on the flat expanse of sun-baked earth that served as a landing pad. Dust and sand kicked up by the rotor downwash blasted her exposed skin like buckshot, forcing her to turn her head aside until it subsided.

As the dust storm died down, she unbuckled her safety harness and exited the chopper through the open crew door, glad to be on solid ground after the hour-long flight out here. It seemed every pilot in the US Army was now paranoid about surface-to-air missile attacks, and her own had been no exception, flying high and fast with the engines pushed to maximum.

As the dust from her arrival settled, she surveyed her surroundings with a quick, efficient glance.

Salerno was a Forward Operating Base (FOB); a Coalition outpost in the remote, mountainous border region of Khost Province. It was laid out like most other firebases she'd seen: watchtowers and machine-gun nests around the perimeter, mortar pits further back, and rows of tents, semi-permanent huts and a few larger command and control buildings in the centre.

All of it was protected by lines of Hesco bastions – steel

gabions filled with sand and rubble to create cheap and readily assembled fortifications. They were pretty good at stopping tank shells and ground-level shrapnel, but they offered no protection against artillery and mortar strikes.

In the distance, snow-capped mountain peaks towered over the firebase, some reaching to over 3,000 metres. McKnight couldn't help noticing that a cluster of emplaced Howitzer field guns were trained on those mountains, ready to provide counter-battery fire if the base came under attack.

Turning her attention to the matter at hand, she singled out a passing soldier – a short, stocky man in his mid-twenties who looked as if he spent his days pumping iron in the base gym – and approached him for directions.

'Hey, pal, where's your AWO?'

AWO stood for Ammunition Warrant Officer; the man responsible for maintaining the base's weapons and munitions. If anyone could help them track down their missing Stinger, it was him.

The soldier pointed a thickly muscled arm off to his left. 'The armoury's over that way, ma'am. Second building in. You can't miss it.'

Indeed she couldn't. As with any military base, the armoury was the most secure and heavily protected building anywhere in the complex. The reason was obvious – they usually contained enough ordnance to flatten a small town.

In this case, the only entrance to the armoured bunker was guarded by two military policemen, neither of whom was feeling very cooperative. It took no small amount of badge-waving on McKnight's part, but at last she was permitted to enter.

Passing through the steel blast doors, she found herself in a cool, clean, climate-controlled world that might as well have been on another planet, such was the contrast with the scorching heat outside.

A couple of low-level Ordnance Corps personnel were on duty there, going through inventories and typing up reports. Neither of them was the person McKnight wanted to speak to.

'What's this all about?' a gruff, fleshy voice demanded.

The base's AWO ambled into the room from an adjacent office, his voluminous gut seeming to arrive a few seconds before he did. He was a big man, both tall and broad, his wide face accentuated by his greying flat-top hairstyle. Apparently fitness tests weren't mandatory in his line of work.

'This isn't an open house,' he added, his dark gaze taking in the three new arrivals. The name tag on his shirt said 'Olson'. 'And I don't appreciate anyone forcing their way in here.'

'I understand that, sir,' McKnight replied, trying to sound more apologetic than she felt. 'But this is an urgent matter.'

Olson's eyes fixed on her. 'And you are?'

'Samantha McKnight, CIA. I need to ask you a few questions.'

Whatever element of derision or disdain had tainted Olson's attitude towards her, it vanished in an instant. He gestured to the door he had just squeezed through. 'You'd better come with me.'

The AWO's small windowless office was as neat and precise as the rest of the building. Whatever his short-comings in terms of fitness, he was clearly an exacting man when it came to organising his surroundings.

Closing the door, Olson turned to face her, his ruddy

face now visibly drained of colour. 'Let me guess. You're here to ask questions about Stinger missiles.'

She frowned, perplexed by his revelation. 'How did you know that?'

'Because you're the second agent this week to come here.'

Chapter 22

Drake was in the passenger seat of a US Army Humvee, being jolted and jostled around as the vehicle roared down the main highway towards Kabul. A second vehicle, part of the same convoy, tailed them about 20 yards back. Four armed agents were packed into it.

After they'd reported their findings to Crawford, it had taken mere minutes to call up a list of all safe houses established by Mitchell. Whatever else the man had been doing out here, he had been diligent in his official role.

The first safe house was located in Jalalabad near the border with Pakistan, with two more in Kandahar, the country's second largest city. The fourth, however, house 4, was in Kabul.

'It was only bought a month ago,' Crawford explained, one hand on the wheel, the other on the gear stick as he manoeuvred the big vehicle around a slow-moving cattle truck. He was driving with a heavy foot, pushing the engine hard. 'According to Mitchell's last report, it was still being prepped for activation.'

Which made it even better as a hiding place, Drake thought. No one was going to turn up inconveniently and see something they shouldn't.

'What do you mean, bought?' Keegan asked, having to shout from the back seat to be heard over the roar of the engine.

'How do you think we get our hands on these places?' Crawford called back over his shoulder. 'We buy them. Our guys pose as businessmen, property developers or whatever, they make an offer and buy them. Then they get to work installing all the hardware they'll need.'

Safe houses came in all shapes and sizes. Some were nothing more than one-bedroom apartments which served only as a place to sleep, while others were virtual fortresses equipped with everything from secure communications suites to panic rooms and high-tech alarm systems.

By the sounds of things, this place belonged in the latter category.

'How long till we get there?' Drake asked, unable to mask his impatience.

Crawford spared him a sideways glance. 'About another ten minutes.'

Drake was about to reply, but the buzz of his cellphone caught his attention. As he'd hoped, it was McKnight.

'Sam, how's it going?'

'Well, my theory was correct,' she began. 'The Stinger never made it out here. I've just spoken to the base AWO, and compared the delivery manifest from Bagram with the one out here. We're short by one launcher and three missiles. I even did a visual check of their arsenal to confirm it. Somehow they vanished on the way out here.'

Which meant Kourash had the capacity to shoot down two more aircraft, Drake thought. 'Any ideas?'

'It seems logical that Anwari's group had help,' McKnight said, speaking quieter as if she was afraid of being overheard. 'Weapon systems like this don't just fall off the backs of trucks. This was an inside job.'

Drake was inclined to agree. It was an unpleasant fact to face up to, but an unavoidable one.

'It could have been the AWO,' he suggested. 'He could have forged the transfer documents and helped smuggle the weapon out.'

'I wouldn't rule it out,' she agreed. 'But it would have been easier to offload the Stinger before it got here and hand him a fake manifest. If we want answers, my guess is we'll find them in the supply convoy that brought it here.'

'Agreed,' he said. 'Stay on it, let me know what you turn up.'

'Will do. I'll be off comms for the next hour or so until I get back to Bagram.' She paused for a moment, weighing up how much to share over the phone. 'Listen, there's something else you should know.'

Drake braced himself as their Humvee swerved and roared past a Toyota pickup, receiving an angry horn blast in return.

'Yeah?'

'I'm not the first person out here asking about Stingers,' she announced. 'Mitchell was here, just a few days ago.'

That was enough to shatter whatever sense of distraction he might have felt. Drake's eyes opened wider as the realisation sank in that a big piece of the puzzle had just landed right in his lap. 'He was following the same trail as us.'

'It looks that way. He came requesting a copy of the delivery manifest, then he boarded a chopper bound for Bagram. He never made it back.'

'Shit . . .' Drake gripped the phone tighter. It couldn't have been coincidence that Mitchell's chopper had been shot down as he returned from that meeting. 'I want to know about that convoy. Throw everything you have at it.'

'You know I will.' Hearing the roar of wind and engines

219

in the background, she added, 'By the way, where are you?'

'En route to Kabul. We have a lead on Mitchell's location.' He didn't have time to go into his discovery of the hidden message – that could wait until later. 'We're following it up now.'

'All right. For all our sakes, I hope you find him. Watch your back out there, Ryan.'

'I always do,' he promised. 'Drake out.'

Shoving the phone in his pocket, he surreptitiously removed the one given to him by Anya and composed a brief text message. She still hadn't replied to his previous message, but he felt obligated to honour their agreement.

May have a lead on Mike. Checking it out now.

After hitting send, he quickly hid the phone again. He didn't want his companions seeing it and asking questions. But he was willing to risk it for her.

And maybe, just maybe, he would soon have some good news.

Chapter 23

Situated on a hillside on the southern outskirts of Kabul, the villa provided an impressive view over the sprawling city. It had been built during the Soviet occupation, and used as the personal residence of some senior figure or other in the puppet government that had tried to run the country before it all fell apart.

Now it belonged to Kourash, one of several properties he owned across the country – bases from which he could operate. A monument to his former enemies, steeped in luxury and excess, and it was all his.

Downstairs in the building's lower floor, a dozen of his men worked and planned and coordinated, using secure satellite phones and encrypted computers to relay their orders and receive reports. This was the nerve centre of his operation; the place from which he planned and directed the attacks that had made him one of the most feared insurgents in the whole country.

The days of hiding in dank caves were far behind them.

But as he sat alone in the wide living area with its panoramic view of the city, none of it mattered to him. He exhaled slowly, willing his mind to calm. And as they so often did at times like this, his thoughts drifted towards Mina.

He had no pictures of her, nothing to keep her image

constant in his mind. And in truth he was starting to forget what she had looked like, the image of her slowly dissolving with each passing year. Instead he saw little flashes, moments in time that had somehow imprinted themselves in his memory.

He remembered the way her eyes had flashed with anger when they argued, the feel of her hair the first time they made love, the sound of her laughter in those rare moments when they had known happiness.

All of it was gone now. Mina had been as courageous and loyal to him as any soldier, staying by his side throughout the long years of conflict, enduring every hardship and danger without complaint. But in the end it had all been for nothing. She was gone, taken from him. And the man responsible had yet to be punished.

His pursuit of vengeance had endangered his operation, had put his very life at stake. But it would be worth it, he told himself. It would all be worth it.

All his life, Kourash had had to fight for everything. Respect, power, influence, even survival. And his long years of struggle had taught him one thing – that a man stood or fell by what he could take from life.

Well, he intended to take one more thing today. He intended to take the life of Ryan Drake.

'This is it,' Crawford warned as they approached a gated house directly ahead. 'Gear up.'

Much like the others in what seemed to be a fairly affluent neighbourhood, it was a detached two-storey structure set within a walled garden. They couldn't see much of the ground floor from their current position, but judging by the design of the upper storey, the place had probably been built in the late fifties or early sixties. This wasn't one of the ancient sandstone dwellings in the heart of the city, but a modern and spacious home that had likely once belonged to a wealthy family.

Drake didn't pause to wonder what had become of the original owners as he drew his Sig Sauer P226 automatic from its holster, pulling back the slide far enough to see the gleaming brass round in the chamber.

He was all business now. All extraneous thoughts and doubts had vanished. All that mattered was what happened in the next sixty seconds.

Jamming on the brakes at the last moment, Crawford brought them screeching to a halt in front of the main gate.

Drake was out and hurrying towards it before the vehicle had even come to a halt. The weapon was held tight in his hands as he sprinted for the wall just to the right of the gate, leaning out far enough to survey the ground beyond.

The gardens surrounding the house had probably once been as impressive and well maintained as the building itself – all expertly manicured lawns, sculpted shrubs and spotless flower beds. But such things required maintenance and attention, and clearly this place had received little over the last decade or so.

The once vibrant lawn was reduced to bare earth and a few stubborn patches of coarse brown grass. Weeds grew through cracks in the driveway, while the skeletal remains of a row of trees stood against one wall.

There were no cars in the driveway. No sign of any activity, in fact. The windows on the main building were covered by wooden shutters, blocking any view of what was happening inside.

Drake heard movement at his side, and glanced over as Keegan and Crawford backed up beside him, weapons

223

out and ready. Neither man displayed fear or hesitation. They both looked focused, resolute, prepared.

The gates were secured by a heavy padlock for which they had no key; however, the solution came in the form of a pair of bolt cutters wielded by one of the agents from the second Humvee. A single hard yank was enough to cut through the steel bolt.

As soon as the shackle fell away, Drake was moving again, with Crawford and Keegan close behind. Pushing his way through the rusty gates, he advanced across the courtyard to the front door while the agents behind spread out to take up flanking positions. These men were armed with MP5 sub-machine guns, ready to lay down heavy suppressing fire if it was called for. Two more circled around to the rear of the building in case the occupants tried to make a break for it.

Drake's radio earpiece crackled. The whole team were wearing the discreet devices. 'Back entrance, all clear. No movement.'

'Copy that,' Crawford replied. 'Stand by.'

Whatever key was required for the front door, they had been unable to locate it before leaving Bagram and there wasn't time to pick the lock. However, Crawford had a simpler, if rather inelegant, answer to this problem.

He looked at Drake, receiving a nod confirming he was ready. 'Breaching.'

Raising the Benelli M3 shotgun he'd brought specifically for breaching doors, he took aim at the lock and fired a single shot. The boom of the weapon discharge was followed an instant later by the crunch of splintering wood as the lock was blasted apart by the solid metal slug.

A single hard kick from Crawford was enough to send the smoking remains of the door flying inwards.

Drake went in first, his weapon up and sweeping the gloomy interior of the dwelling. Keegan was right behind him, with Crawford bringing up the rear. Drake heard the distinctive click as he worked the shotgun's pump action, feeding another round into the breech, though he paid it little attention as his eyes swept the darkness before him.

The cavernous room stretching before them must have been an impressive reception area back in the day. Roughly L-shaped, it occupied two floors, with a staircase off to the left leading to the house's upper storey, and an alcove to the right that Drake guessed had once been either a sitting or dining area. There was no furniture now to support either theory.

Indeed, there appeared to be no furniture anywhere – no couches, tables, chairs or cabinets – nor were there fixtures or fittings of any kind. Even the light switches were nothing but rough holes in the plasterboard walls with multicoloured electrical wires trailing out.

No sound or movement greeted them. The house was as quiet as a grave.

Reaching out, Crawford switched on the flashlight mounted beneath the barrel of his shotgun, allowing the beam to pan slowly from left to right. Bare brick and plasterboard walls reflected back at them. The air reeked of burned cordite from the breaching round, though beneath it Drake detected an undertone of dust and age.

There was nothing to suggest that anyone lived here, or had even visited this place recently.

He could feel Crawford's eyes on him. Suspicious, dubious. The tentative faith he had shown slowly evaporating.

'Clear,' he heard the man mutter. 'Unit Two. Anything round back?'

'Negative, sir.'

'Check the other rooms,' Drake said, advancing deeper into the house, unwilling to concede defeat yet. 'Move.'

Only later would he realise he had been both wrong and right at the same time.

Chapter 24

Alone in the conference room that served as their base of operations, Frost sat hunched over her laptop, chin resting on her hands as she surveyed the report from the program she had dispatched to covertly probe Horizon's firewall. So far the results were not encouraging.

With her headphones plugged in, she was oblivious to the world around her – all her attention was focused on the screen. She was just reaching for her cup of coffee when the door burst open and a young man rushed in, startling her and causing hot black liquid to spill across the table.

'Goddamn it!' she snapped, levelling an angry glare at the man who she vaguely recognised as Gibson, one of the intelligence analysts on Crawford's staff. 'Doesn't anyone in this fucking place know how to knock?'

'I'm sorry, ma'am,' he panted, his face flushed as if he had run up several flights of stairs. 'But we have a problem.'

Frost was busy trying to extract a couple of sodden sheets of paper from the black slick in front of her. 'What is it?'

'Mitchell's captors are broadcasting again. It's going out live across the Internet right now.'

Abandoning her efforts, Frost turned to look at him. 'Show me.'

With Gibson providing the appropriate Web address, it took mere seconds for her to navigate to the video stream in question and bring it up on her laptop.

Displayed in grainy low resolution was Mitchell, still bound and gagged on a chair in the centre of the shot. Beside him stood Kourash Anwari, dressed in the same frayed, cobbled-together combat uniform he had worn in the previous video.

He was clearly in the middle of some tirade or other.

'. . . the fate you saw fit to condemn this country to when you abandoned it twenty years ago.' His voice was a throaty rasp as he spoke. 'Millions of Afghans fought and died here, soaked the ground red with their blood, and when the war was over you turned your back on their sacrifice. You found it convenient to forget us. Well, today we will remind you of your sins.'

'This is going out live?' Frost asked, wanting to be sure.

Gibson nodded, transfixed by what he was seeing. He had seen other videos like this and knew all too well their gory climax, yet he couldn't look away.

Frost had other ideas. She had been waiting for just such an opportunity. The first hostage tape had been a recording, emailed to them from an anonymous address. Impossible to trace.

Not so this time.

Ignoring the hostage video, she selected a program called *RootHack1.1* and double-clicked on it. After copying over the URL of the video, she clicked a button marked *Trace*.

'. . . we gave you a chance to negotiate with us, to deal as honourable men,' Anwari went on, his voice echoing through the room. 'Instead you choose to do nothing, to ignore us as if we mean nothing. You insult us. Well, you will pay the price for this insult. The time for nego-tiation is over. If you do not meet our demands within half an hour, this man's life will end and his blood will be on your hands . . .'

Gibson glanced at Frost's laptop and frowned at the unfamiliar program, curious at what she was doing. 'What is that?'

'A little tool myself and a few others put together in our spare time,' she said as the powerful hacking soft-ware went to work. 'I call it a heat seeker. It'll identify the ISP these guys are using, then slip a nasty little Trojan into their servers that'll commandeer their routing proto-cols and use them to trace the data stream back to its source.'

'Is that even legal?' Gibson asked. He was staring intently at the screen, trying to make sense of the complex diagnostic tool.

She looked up at him with a mixture of sympathy and amusement. 'Half the things we do every day are illegal. I wouldn't worry too much about this.'

He frowned, not sure what to say to that. 'How long will it take?' he asked instead.

'Assuming they aren't using hard-core encryption, shouldn't take more than a few . . .' She turned her atten-tion back to the program and frowned when its search abruptly ceased. 'Shit.'

'What? Did it fail?'

Frost shook her head, already reaching for her cell-phone. 'Far from it. I think we've just found them.'

Chapter 25

'Well, thanks for that, Drake,' Crawford said, leaning against the west wall of the building's wide reception area while he gulped down some bottled water. 'Thanks for taking us on a wild goose chase across Kabul, and burning a safe house before we'd even put it to use. We owe you one.'

Drake said nothing as he sat at the foot of the staircase, his earlier rush of excitement and confidence long since vanished.

Crawford was right. Their mission here had been a waste of time. There was no sign of Mitchell, no sign of Kourash or anyone else for that matter. The lower floor of the building was essentially empty, there was no basement, and upstairs they had found only stacks of plasterboard sheeting, timber, nails and screws. Building materials that would likely never be used.

He had been wrong. At that moment he didn't understand how or why, but clearly he had misinterpreted whatever message Mitchell had tried to impart. He thought he had seen the truth, but wondered now if he had seen only what he wanted to see.

There are none so blind as those who think they can see, his father had once said, putting his own unique spin on that well-known phrase. Drake had never given it much thought until now.

'Maybe Mitchell was talking about some other house or building,' Keegan ventured without much optimism. 'Jesus, you'd think if he wanted to tell us where he was, he could have been less goddamn cryptic.'

Behind him, one of the agents from the second Humvee was disabling the silent alarm that had been tripped when they made entry. Drake absently noted the keypad combination as he punched it in.

917214.

For some reason numbers always seemed to stick in his mind. It had been a useful skill for memorising phone numbers.

He thought once more about the message Mitchell had managed to impart, turning it over in his mind as if it were a puzzle to be examined from different angles.

HOUSE FOUR.

At the time he had assumed the brevity of his message was simply due to the circumstances he was sending it in. Time had been short, and to have attempted anything longer might have aroused suspicion amongst his captors.

But perhaps there was another intention behind it. What was he not seeing?

Before he could ponder it further, his phone started buzzing in his pocket. It was Frost.

'Yeah, Keira?' he began wearily.

'We're in trouble. Anwari is broadcasting another hostage tape. He's giving us thirty minutes to meet his demands or he'll execute Mitchell.'

'What?' Instantly Drake's heartbeat stepped up a gear. 'His deadline is three days away.'

'Search me. Maybe the fucker's getting impatient,' she replied. 'But we've managed to trace the broadcast to a

231

small town called Jarmatoy, just south of Kabul. As near as we can figure, he's being held in an old cement plant on the edge of town.'

He couldn't believe it. He felt like a drowning man who has just been thrown a lifeline. 'Good work, Keira.' He had never meant it more than at that moment. 'I'm putting you on speaker.'

He looked up at Crawford. 'Kourash is in a town called Jarmatoy. How far is that?'

To his credit, Crawford wasted no time questioning how they had come by this information. 'About thirty klicks south of here.'

'We need to be there now.' Drake was already on his feet

'I suggest you don't hang around,' Frost said. 'You've got twenty-eight minutes.'

They had to cover 38 kilometres in 28 minutes, in unpredictable traffic and road conditions. This was going to be tight.

'We're on it,' he assured her as he hurried out through the front door towards the two Humvees that had now been brought into the weed-strewn courtyard. 'Do we have any surveillance on the target area?'

'We're working on it.'

Operations like this were normally planned out hours, days or even weeks in advance. They might have air assets, real-time satellite coverage, ground reinforcements and almost any weapons under the sun at their disposal. In this case they could call upon half a dozen operatives, a small cache of arms and perhaps the element of surprise.

The only problem with surprise was that it didn't last long.

'Okay, do what you can. We're en route now.'

232

Crawford had already clambered into the driver's seat, and fired up the engine as Drake approached.

'Understood.' Frost's voice was barely audible over the rumble of the engine. 'Oh, and Ryan?'

'Yeah?'

There was a pause. No more than a second, but long enough. 'Be careful. Out.'

Chapter 26

Drake's mind was racing as fast as the Humvee as they sped down the rough potholed road to a town he hadn't even heard of until twenty minutes ago, trying to beat the clock and save the man who just might hold the answers he needed.

But only if they reached him in time.

His earlier disappointment at failing to find anything at the safe house had been pushed to one side now as he tried to focus on the task at hand.

Air assets were scrambling from Bagram to reinforce them, but it would take more time than they had to reach the target area. For the time being at least, they were on their own.

His thoughts turned inexorably to the motives behind his adversary's change of plan. Why had he suddenly brought forward the time of Mitchell's execution? Was he growing impatient, or was he afraid of something? Was he somehow aware of the progress they had been making, and moving to forestall further discoveries?

Everything they had seen so far pointed to a plan; a series of phased, mutually supportive actions building towards a desired result.

Had he changed his plan, or had this been his intention all along?

'How long?' he called out.

Crawford didn't take his eyes off the road. 'A lot longer than if you shut the fuck up and let me drive,' he replied tersely. He was feeling the pressure just as much as they were.

Drake's phone was ringing. Amidst the background noise, he felt rather than heard it. It was Frost calling with another update.

'Ryan, you need to hurry,' the young woman implored him. 'Anwari is broadcasting again.'

Frost could do nothing except watch and wait. She ached to be out there with her companions instead of stuck in this dusty conference room, knowing they were about to put their lives on the line. When Drake returned to Bagram, she fully intended to kick his ass for leaving her behind.

On the video feed in front of her, Anwari was spitting venom once more, delivering his final hate-filled speech before he executed his captive.

'We have given you every opportunity to negotiate, yet still you ignore us. We gave you a chance to save this man's life, but you refused to take it.'

Frost watched as he reached into his camouflage jacket and drew out a pistol. The same one he had used to shoot Mitchell in the leg.

'If this is the only language you understand, then so be it.'

'Hurry, Ryan,' Frost whispered.

'This is it,' Crawford said as the Humvee roared up the side of a low hill. 'Twenty seconds!'

Drake tensed, readying himself, gripping the M4 carbine he had armed himself with from the vehicle's weapons bin. A side arm might have been adequate for a house raid, but for possible urban combat like this he wanted something with greater range and firepower.

With only seven operatives against an unknown number of hostiles, their chances of success were far from guaranteed. Still, they were all highly trained professionals, and between them they were capable of causing a lot of trouble.

Perhaps, just perhaps, it might be enough.

Keegan reached into his shirt, plucked out the necklace he wore for luck and kissed the crucifix dangling from the end. Superstitious to his core, he performed the same ritual before every operation.

Maybe there was something in it – he'd never been killed yet.

Sensing Drake's eye on him, he turned and flashed a grin.

'If you tell me this is just like old times, I'll have to shoot you,' Drake warned.

The grin broadened. 'Wouldn't dream of it, buddy.'

'Ten seconds!' Crawford called out as they crested the hill. Ahead and below stood their target.

The cement works, another relic of the Soviet attempts to turn Afghanistan into a modern Socialist republic, was a bombed-out ruin of a place. Two of the three big concrete storage silos had been blasted open, their steel shells peeled back like orange skins, with the support gantries and walkways lying broken and twisted in giant heaps of rusted metal.

Nearby, the main kiln stood as a sad wind-scoured shell, its machinery long dead and rusted solid. Off to the right, beyond the sole remaining silo, was the cement mill, where the coarse aggregate had once been ground down into fine powder. Various other buildings, offices and warehouses, clustered in around the cement processing facility, all long since abandoned.

They were hurtling towards what had once been a delivery yard near the entrance to the cement works, still moving with frightening speed. Drake braced himself, ready for the sudden deceleration that would tell him it was time.

A moment later, it came. Turning the wheel hard right, Crawford stamped down on the brakes, bringing the Humvee skidding to a halt amidst a cloud of dust and sand.

'Go! Go!' Drake yelled, throwing his door open and jumping down onto the dusty ground.

Keeping low, he sprinted about a dozen yards to the collapsed remains of a brick outbuilding and ducked down behind it, the weapon at his shoulder. The first rule of disembarking into a hot landing zone was to get away from the vehicle and find cover as soon as possible. The open ground around the Humvee was a killing zone.

A scuffling on the sand followed by the muted thump of flesh meeting concrete told him Keegan and Crawford were beside him. With both Humvees shut down, the only sound was the sigh of the wind and the tick of their cooling engines. All around was ominously quiet and still.

'You see anything?' Crawford asked, scanning the buildings around them.

'Nothing,' Keegan replied, then leaned in closer to Drake. 'What's the plan?'

Popping his phone's Bluetooth headset in his ear, Drake enabled the device and dialled Frost's number.

She answered straight away. 'Ryan, we have a Predator drone orbiting the area. We see you.'

'Good. Any activity around us?'

'Nothing. The place is quiet.'

Drake frowned, wondering if Kourash had known of their approach, or whether he was trying to lead them into an ambush. Still, they were here now. There was little choice but to see it through.

'Do you have a fix on the signal?'

'On your two o'clock, forty yards.'

Following her description, he spotted their most likely candidate. It was the only large building in that area. 'It's got to be the cement mill.'

'That'd be my guess.'

Taking a deep breath, Drake nodded to himself. 'All right, we're going for it. I'll stay on comms. Call out any targets if you see them.'

'Roger that. Watch your back.'

He intended to. Turning to his companions, Drake pointed towards the cement mill. 'That's our target. We'll move in a five-metre spread. John, you take the left. Crawford, you go right. Everyone else on me. Understand?'

He was met by half a dozen nods, which was just as well. There was no time to plan anything more sophisticated.

Drake paused for a second to focus his mind on the task ahead. He never allowed himself to wait longer than that. Dwelling too long on the situation would lead to hesitation, indecision and all too often, death.

'All right. Move.'

Bringing up the M4 to his shoulder, he rose up from behind cover and started forwards at a steady run. Sprinting was a bad idea because it was impossible to fire accurately at full tilt.

Keegan and Crawford followed a few paces behind, spreading outwards to take positions on either flank, while the four other agents moved behind Drake in a loose column. Drake and the men behind him were far enough apart that a single burst couldn't wipe them out, but close enough that they could support each other in a firefight.

At any moment, he expected a storm of gunshots to erupt around them, chewing up the ground until they found soft human flesh. All of them were wearing Kevlar vests, but Drake wouldn't rate their chances of stopping anything bigger than a 9mm round. An AK-47 could make short work of them.

And yet, to his amazement, nothing happened. The entire group crossed the open space without mishap, converging on the entrance to the cement mill.

A truck-sized set of rusted double doors stood half open, allowing them a glimpse of the shadowy interior of the building. Backed up against the door on one side, Drake glanced over at his companions.

He held up his hand with three fingers extended, and Keegan nodded understanding. Three, two, one.

Gripping the M4, he rounded the door and advanced inside, with Keegan and Crawford right behind him and the other operatives following close behind.

The cavernous interior of the building was dominated by a massive cylindrical metal drum that ran from one end of the structure to the other. Gantries and walkways lined the walls around it, with heavy machinery at one end that had once allowed it to rotate.

It must have been an impressive place when it was operational, but now it was a scrapyard; another rusting monument to a failed invasion.

One end of the cylinder had been blasted apart by explosives, shredding the outer shell and crumpling it like a beer can. The destruction had also detached it from its support cradle can so that it was lying tilted on its axis. The floor was covered with decades of wind-blown sand that had found its way in here and, with nowhere else to go, had slowly piled up, probably a couple of feet deep.

Drake hesitated, catching the scent of something in the air. Stale, rotten, decaying. It was an odour that so often accompanied war and conflict, that hung in the air for days and weeks after the battle had passed – the smell of decomposing human flesh.

'Secure the area. Crawford and Keegan, on me,' he said quietly, advancing towards the ruined machinery that largely screened the far end of the room from view. The long barrel of the M4 stood out in front of him, ready and eager for a target.

The smell was growing stronger as they approached. Drake wrinkled his nose, doing his best to breathe through his mouth. His heart was hammering, his pulse pounding in his ears.

He slowed for a moment beside part of the ancient drum mechanism, huge and rusted.

This was it.

'Go!' he hissed.

The fetid smell of decay hit them like a wave, almost knocking them back with its power. Doing his best to ignore the choking stench, Drake scanned the darkened area behind the winch assembly. Straight away his eyes fastened on the source of the smell.

'Know that this man's blood is on your hands.'

Drawing back the hammer on his weapon, Anwari held it against Mitchell's head, turned away to avoid the inevitable blood splash and pulled the trigger.

Even if it was only viewed via a video link, the crack of a single round discharging in a confined space, accompanied by the sight of Mitchell's skull being blasted apart in a cloud of blood, brain and bone was enough to make it shockingly real.

In an instant the light went out of his eyes. His head was jerked sideways by the force of the impact, then he slumped forward, unmoving, blood still leaking from the devastating exit wound.

Frost looked away from the screen, her heart sinking. They had failed.

'He's dead, Ryan,' she said, her voice now devoid of emotion as she spoke into her phone. 'We were too late.'

'I know,' Drake replied. 'Way too late.'

Chapter 27

Mitchell was sitting slumped forward in the same chair he'd been executed in. That must have been a couple of days ago judging by the state of his corpse, now hideously bloated by heat and decomposition.

Flies buzzed and swarmed around the gory splatter of blood and brains on the sandy ground, as well as the gaping hole in the side of his head. It was a horrific sight matched only by the repulsive smell of corruption.

Keegan coughed and retched, turning away for a moment to steady himself. He was no stranger to death, but the body's reaction to such things was physical as well as emotional. When it hit, it hit hard.

You failed, a voice in Drake's head echoed, filled with recrimination. You failed before you even left Langley. He was dead this whole time. You came all this way, risked your whole team for a dead man.

Drake immediately cut that voice out, shut it off so he could concentrate on matters at hand. Blame could come later. Right now there was still a chance they could find clues that would lead them to the men who did this.

'The sons of bitches must have recorded the video days ago,' Keegan said, his voice muffled by the rag he'd tied around his face to ward off the stench. He moved closer to inspect the body.

'Don't touch him,' Drake ordered. 'Let forensics deal with it.'

Keegan hesitated a moment, but nodded.

'They planned to execute him right from the start,' Crawford said, though he kept his distance from Mitchell's body. 'The hostage tape, the ransom demands . . . It was all a bluff. Mitchell was already dead.'

'They knew we'd never meet their demands,' Keegan reasoned. 'Maybe they were trying to make it look like they'd given us a fair chance.'

Crawford shook his head. 'Then why bring forward his execution? The deadline was three days away.'

Just then, Drake's Bluetooth headset came to life. 'Ryan, what's your situation out there?' Frost asked.

There was no emotion in her voice, as if all the life had been sucked out of her. She had cut away from those feelings, detached herself from what she had witnessed. It was the only way to deal with it.

'We've found Mitchell. He's dead,' was his simple reply. 'They executed him days ago and cleared out of here.'

'No sign of anyone?'

'None. They must have set the transmission on a timer, or maybe used a remote trigger.' He surveyed the room once more. 'You'd better get a forensics team out here.'

'Understood.' She hesitated. 'And . . . Ryan?'

'Yeah?'

'I'm sorry. About Mitchell.'

Drake sighed. 'Yeah. Me too.'

With that, he ended the call and removed his headset. He had nothing more to say. Debriefings would come soon enough, but for now he just felt empty.

'The Ordnance Disposal guys are sweeping the area for mines as we speak. Forensics can finish up once they're done, but I doubt they'll find anything.' Drake spoke into his phone, watching as Mitchell's body was wheeled out of the ruined cement plant. To his relief, it was bagged and sealed up.

A Black Hawk chopper had arrived about ten minutes after their own dramatic entry, complete with a squad of US Army Rangers ready to secure the scene. Drake had left them to it, instead deciding to deliver the bad news to Breckenridge back at Langley. McKnight and Frost were also on the line, dialling in from the conference room at Bagram.

'Christ, what a screw-up,' Drake heard Breckenridge say.

'Fucking asshole,' Frost muttered, perhaps thinking she was out of range of the speakerphone. He doubted she cared whether Breckenridge heard her or not.

'Mitchell was dead before Ryan and his team even got here,' McKnight said, rising to Drake's defence in a more constructive manner. 'It seems killing him was their plan all along. There was nothing anyone could have done.'

Her words were cold comfort to Drake at that moment. This wasn't like running a marathon or climbing a mountain – there were no accolades for effort, no consolations for trying and failing. In the back of his mind, he couldn't shake the notion that they had let Mitchell down.

Breckenridge cleared his throat. Not because he needed to, but because he wanted to draw attention to himself before speaking.

'That's as may be,' he allowed grudgingly. 'The official debriefing will establish the facts. In the meantime, I suggest you pack things up and get yourselves on the next flight home. You can submit your report once you're back at Langley.'

'No,' Drake said right away.

'Excuse me?'

'Kourash is still out there.'

'Your point?'

'That's not acceptable to me.'

'Not acceptable?' Breckenridge repeated, an edge of anger in his voice now. Mild insolence was one thing, but outright insubordination was something else entirely. 'The CIA doesn't operate based on what you find "acceptable", Drake. You take orders just like the rest of us. Anyway, what you're suggesting is outside your remit. You're a rescue team, not assassins, and certainly not vigilantes. If you want to turn this into some kind of revenge trip, forget it.'

Typical bureaucrat, Drake thought bitterly. Always viewing the world like it was a spreadsheet, everything fitting neatly into niches and roles and responsibilities.

'This isn't about revenge,' Drake said, practically forcing the words out. 'It's about saving lives. Kourash has at least two more Stingers he can use. What's to stop him shooting down another chopper next week?'

'Dealing with potential threats to US personnel is a job for our Afghan field office,' Breckenridge pointed out. 'You were brought in to recover our man, and you didn't do it. The operation is over. What part of that don't you understand?'

Drake could hold his frustration in check no longer.

'For fuck's sake, this isn't some hypothetical scenario we're dealing with!' he snapped. 'I'm telling you there's more going on than just a random insurgent attack. And if you'd ever taken your fat arse out of the office you'd know that when your team leaders tell you something, you should fucking listen.'

But listening wasn't on Breckenridge's agenda. Not after an outburst like that.

245

'Consider yourself relieved, Drake,' he said straight away. He was on autopilot now, barking orders with cold efficiency. 'McKnight, you're acting team leader now. I want that team on the next flight home, with Drake in tow. Is this in any way unclear?'

There was a pause. A second or two while McKnight decided what to say, whether to obey orders from a superior officer or tell him to go fuck himself. Drake felt for her. She should never have been put in a situation like that.

'No, sir. You've made yourself very clear,' she said at last, failing to keep an edge of hostility out of her voice.

'Good. Then get it done,' Breckenridge concluded. 'And Drake, when you get back, you and I are going to have a talk about insubordination.'

With that, the line went dead.

Another moment or two of stunned silence before McKnight spoke up. 'Ryan, I don't know what to say to you right now . . .'

'There's nothing to say, Sam,' he assured her, his voice quiet now. 'I'm coming back to Bagram.'

As far as his superior was concerned, it was over.

But not for him.

Chapter 28

Half an hour later Drake again found himself in Kabul's southern outskirts as their Humvee made its way back to Bagram at an unhurried pace. With no leads to pursue and no pressing time constraints, he was content to take his time and brood on his thoughts.

Crawford had for once relinquished control of the vehicle, leaving Drake behind the wheel. It was a very different experience from McKnight's Ford Explorer. Now he felt every jolt and shudder as the heavy vehicle fought its way through potholes and sudden dips.

Nobody was saying much, which suited him just fine. All three men were feeling tired and dejected after the death of Mitchell, and Drake was increasingly aware that they might have outstayed their welcome here.

Drake hadn't texted Anya about their failure yet. He had already been forced to admit it more times than he wanted to, and would save that particular task for a more opportune moment once they were back at Bagram.

'This is bullshit, man,' Keegan decided, his battered baseball cap pulled down low to shield his eyes from the afternoon sun. 'Breckenridge can't just pull the plug on us. He's got no right.'

'Unfortunately he does,' Drake replied. As far as the letter of the law was concerned, at least. 'He's our boss.'

'He's a pencil-pushing REMF, that's what he is.'

Drake glanced at him in the rear-view mirror, surprised at the vehemence in the normally laid-back operative. 'You getting mutinous on me, mate?'

Keegan's eyes met his and he flashed a faint grin. 'I'm too old to give a shit about insubordination. Anyway, I happen to agree with you – there's more going on here than a simple kidnapping. If they'd executed Mitchell days ago, why go to all the trouble of releasing that hostage tape? Why make demands that would never be met? Doesn't make any goddamn sense.'

Drake would have smiled back, but instead was forced to turn his attention back to the road ahead. Traffic had come to an abrupt halt on the approach to a bridge up ahead.

A crumbling concrete edifice that spanned a muddy drainage canal in a single ungainly leap, it had clearly suffered from decades of abuse and neglect. In places the stonework had broken away to reveal rusted steel reinforcing rods beneath.

However, the bridge itself wasn't the problem – it was the truck blocking the northbound lane that had brought traffic to a standstill. Horns sounded and angry shouts were exchanged, but nothing much was happening. It was hot, and it seemed nobody could be bothered to sort out the mess.

There were three or four other cars between Drake and the truck, but his high driving position allowed him a clear line of sight. Removing his sunglasses, he peered through the heat haze and engine fumes at the offending truck.

It was a Tata 407, an Indian-made utility vehicle painted in the colours of the Afghan National Army. But in all other respects it was a decrepit-looking vehicle, sagging on its rear axles and hastily repaired in places with what looked like amateur spot-welds. Its flatbed cargo area was covered by a worn and patched tarpaulin.

'What a hell of a place to break down,' Keegan groaned.

Crawford surveyed the scene with the kind of long-suffering resignation of a man well acquainted with such delays. 'Happens all the time with the ANA. Half their gear is older than I am. Give it about two minutes until some asshole shunts him off the road.'

But Drake wasn't hearing him. He leaned forward, struck by a sudden feeling of unease. What were the chances that the truck would come to a halt right in the middle of such a bottleneck? And why was the driver making no effort to get it moving?

Suddenly he was reminded of his encounter with Anya the previous day, and her use of a fake breakdown to bring him to a halt so she could make contact.

'This isn't right,' he said, reaching for the gear stick to put them in reverse.

'Huh?' Keegan leaned forward, alerted by the tone of his voice. 'What's up?'

No sooner had he spoken than the truck's rear tarpaulin parted, revealing the long, eager barrel of a Russian KPV heavy machine gun. Drake recognised the distinctive weapon in an instant. Normally used for shooting down low-flying aircraft, it was now swinging around to bear down on them.

'Jesus Christ!' Crawford gasped.

Drake reacted on instinct. Throwing the Humvee into gear, he popped the clutch and jammed the accelerator to the floor. Tyres skidding on the rough tarmac and throwing up clouds of dust and burned rubber, the Humvee lurched forward, straight towards the truck and the weapon mounted inside.

'What the fuck are you doing?' Crawford shouted. 'You're heading right for him!'

Drake ignored him. The KPV had an effective range of over 3,000 metres; to have attempted to retreat down a busy road would have been worse than futile. His only option, as far as he could judge in the half-second it took to make his decision, was to try to exploit the weapon's heavy, cumbersome size.

Throwing the wheel hard over, he swung the Humvee left, narrowly avoiding a collision with a small hatchback in front before stomping on the gas again.

And at virtually the same moment, the truck gunner opened fire.

The rhythmic thud of the auto-cannon's discharge sounded more like the rumble of thunder than the crack of any kind of conventional weapon. The muzzle flare illuminated the truck and the surrounding road like lightning as round after round was expelled, spent shell casings clattering onto the ground.

Their erratic movement proved to be their saving grace, as the first volley missed them by mere feet, instead striking a taxicab that was unlucky enough to be turning the wrong way.

The effect on the civilian vehicle was catastrophic. Steel and glass gave way without resistance, high-explosive shells tearing through the unprotected car to thud into the ground behind it. In a matter of seconds, it had been reduced to a shattered nightmare of twisted metal and mangled human bodies.

'He's tracking us!' Keegan called out, staring at the long barrel of the heavy machine gun as its operator struggled to haul it around.

They were now careening down a narrow side road that paralleled the canal. With water on his right and rows of shops and houses on his left, there was nothing for Drake to do but punch it and try to escape the weapon's firing arc.

Keeping his foot on the floor, he yanked the wheel left to avoid a faded red Nissan that had jammed on its brakes. The screech of metal on metal told him he'd clipped the vehicle, but he didn't care. Finding cover was his only concern.

They would not be so lucky a second time. The truck gunner had at last manhandled the 14.5mm cannon around, and now let loose with another burst.

Drake was forced to duck as the left quarter-panel beside him disintegrated in a spray of metal and smoke, leaving a gaping hole the size of a football. Above him the reinforced glass windshield exploded inwards, showering the vehicle's interior with broken fragments.

'Get down!' he screamed, unable to do anything but keep his foot planted on the gas. The engine roared and the vehicle bumped and skidded onwards. Rounds thumped into the buildings above and behind them as the gunner tried to keep pace with their desperate escape attempt, though he clearly had no concern for civilian casualties, keeping the trigger depressed on full automatic.

Drake knew it would happen sooner or later. On a busy road in the middle of the afternoon, one could only drive blind so far before colliding with something.

Suddenly he was thrown forward in his seat as the Humvee slammed into an old Toyota saloon whose driver had been too slow to react. The scream and crunch of deforming metal was almost drowned out by the roar of the Humvee's engine and the screech of its tyres as it tried to power them through, partially crumpling the unfortunate Toyota beneath it and breaking the forward axle in the process.

With Drake no longer able to exert any meaningful control, the stricken Humvee slewed off the road and down the concrete embankment into the canal, rolling over onto its roof before finally coming to rest amidst a cloud of dust, smoke and steam from the shattered engine.

Kourash picked up his phone the instant it started ringing. The call was coming from Pendar, the leader of the strike team he had allocated to destroy Drake's Humvee and everyone in it.

'Is it done?' he asked.

Situated on the roof of a building about 500 metres from the ambush point, he had both heard and seen the destruction the heavy weapon had dealt out. At least one civilian car had been obliterated and several shop-fronts damaged by stray fire, but he felt little concern for such things. They were casualties of war, and this country had seen more than its share of war.

'The Humvee crashed into the canal,' came the reply. 'We hit it hard.'

That was not the question he had asked, Kourash thought with a flash of anger. He had seen it for himself. Rather than try to retreat away from the weapon, the Humvee had launched itself forward in what had seemed a suicidal charge before swinging left at the last moment, disrupting the gunner's aim. He had watched it hurtle down the road before a burst of fire at last found it.

'Is Drake dead?' he asked, leaving a slight pause between each word and the next.

'We think so.'

Kourash closed his eyes for a moment. He hadn't come

all this way, hadn't risked everything, to let Drake slip away now. If he was alive, he was surely trapped in the wreckage. Trapped and helpless, just waiting to be finished off.

'Move in and confirm he's dead.'

'We are exposed here,' Pendar warned, an edge of anxiety in his voice now. 'If the ANP arrive . . .'

Kourash gritted his teeth, threatening to break one of the fillings in his molars. They would never get another chance like this.

'We must finish him *now*,' he hissed, clenching his fist and feeling the two stumps of his missing fingers. 'Move in. Kill any survivors. That is an order.'

'It will be done.'

Drake's mind drifted back from the verge of unconsciousness, alerted by distant shouts and panicked screams.

With great effort he forced his eyes open, and found that the world was upside down. Beyond the shattered windshield, he could see the muddy garbage-strewn channel of the canal, the line of houses stretching out on either side, and the ugly concrete bridge in the distance. Beneath him, the endless blue sky stretched out, the hot sun beating down through a haze of smoke and dust. Dry wind-blown grit whipped in through the broken windows, peppering his face and eyes.

The vehicle must have come to rest on its roof. Still strapped into his seat, he was inverted. How fucking stupid he must look, some part of his mind reflected.

He wasn't sure if he was hurt or not. He wasn't in much pain, but everything felt hazy and disconnected, his reactions deadened as if he was intoxicated. He was vaguely aware of something warm and wet dripping across his face.

'Ryan, you alive?' he heard Keegan ask.

Managing to twist around in his seat, he saw the old sniper crouched on what had once been the roof, shaking his head to clear it. His face was cut and grazed, but he didn't look seriously injured.

'Still in it, mate,' he replied, unlatching his seat belt and tumbling head first onto the broken roof of the Humvee. 'Shit. Can you see anything outside?'

'Not much,' Keegan said, peering out through the rear window. 'That was a goddamned ANA truck taking shots at us.'

Drake shook his head, slivers of broken glass falling from his hair. 'It wasn't the ANA. That was Kourash.'

Keegan's eyes lit up as the truth dawned on him. 'The son of a bitch set a trap.'

'And we walked right into it,' Drake replied, furious with himself for not seeing it coming. It all made sense now; why Kourash had broadcast that execution video, why he had allowed the signal to be traced back to its source.

He had done it to lure Drake in, to get him to a place where he could be tracked. No doubt they had been following the Humvee since it left the abandoned cement plant, just waiting for the perfect place to spring their trap.

Wincing in pain, he looked over at Crawford. The man was hanging in his seat, still secured by his belt. An angry bruise was forming down one side of his face.

'I can smell gas,' Keegan hissed. 'We need to get out of here, buddy.'

Drake nodded. 'I hear you. Crawford, can you—'

He was interrupted by a loud bang that reverberated through the interior. It was the sound of a high-velocity round ricocheting off the Humvee's armour, and it was soon followed by two more. The crackle of automatic gunfire echoed from outside.

'Shit. We're taking fire,' Keegan said, as if Drake hadn't realised already.

'Get out, John. I'll get Crawford.' Wasting no time, Drake unlatched the man's seat belt, causing him to pitch out of his seat and onto the roof with a resounding clang.

However, the impact seemed to have roused him. He groaned and opened his eyes, focusing blearily on Drake.

'We're getting out of here, mate. Come on.' Grabbing his arms, Drake pulled and hauled him towards the door. At the same time, Keegan scrambled out through the rear window, grabbed Drake's door and managed to lever it open, allowing him to drag the semi-conscious man out.

'Thanks,' Drake said quickly, laying Crawford against the side of the upturned vehicle. His eyes were fully open now, though he wore a puzzled look as if trying to work out how he'd ended up in an upside-down Humvee. 'Crawford, can you hear me?'

His eyes focused on Drake then, and the puzzlement quickly gave way to a look of irritation. 'Course I can hear you,' he snapped, shoving the younger man back. 'Remind me not to thank the asshole who taught you to drive. What kind of shit are we in?'

'We've got company,' Keegan warned, drawing his side arm and taking cover behind the makeshift barrier as another burst of fire split the air, several rounds hammering off the Humvee's broken chassis.

'There's your answer,' Drake said. Leaving Crawford to sort himself out, he stole a glance around the side of the Humvee. Sure enough, armed men were advancing towards them along both sides of the canal, clad in the uniform of the ANA.

255

But these were no ANA troopers. They were Kourash's men wearing the uniform of their enemies. He counted at least three on each side, all armed with AK-47 assault rifles.

Drake and his two companions could muster only three side arms. He had no idea where his carbine was, but he hadn't seen it inside the cab. Likely it had been thrown loose when they pitched over.

One of their attackers had spotted him and raised his assault rifle to fire. Ducking back behind cover, Drake heard the distinctive thump as a burst of fire scythed past him, chewing up the ground only feet away or punching holes in the Humvee's side panelling.

Drawing his Sig Sauer, he flicked the safety off, leaned out and snapped off several shots in his attacker's direction, none of which found their mark. He considered himself a reasonable marksman with a rifle, but even with the best pistol in the world the chances of hitting much beyond 50 yards was slim to say the least.

He heard the crack of Keegan's weapon beside him, joined a few seconds later by Crawford on his left. Their desperate volley of fire was enough to force their enemies to duck for cover, but only Keegan scored a hit. Drake watched as one man pitched forward and tumbled down the sloping side of the canal, leaving a smear of blood behind him. Several more shots from both himself and Keegan were enough to put him down for good.

However, the answering storm of automatic fire was enough to force all three operatives to drop down behind the Humvee. They could do nothing but press themselves against its armoured sides as rounds slammed into the ground around them or ricocheted off the crippled vehicle.

'We're screwed here,' Crawford called out above the

din, ejecting a spent magazine from his weapon. 'We have to fall back before they outflank us.'

'Fall back where?' Keegan gestured to the open ground beyond their scant cover. 'That's a kill zone right there. We move, and we're dead.'

Drake looked around in desperation. They couldn't retreat and they couldn't stand their ground. In a matter of seconds, Kourash's men would have outflanked and surrounded them. Then they could pick off the three helpless operatives at their leisure.

And in that moment, Drake knew Kourash had won.

Half a kilometre away, Kourash surveyed the firefight through a pair of high-powered binoculars. He had watched the three men scramble from the wreckage, looking desperately for a way out but finding none. He saw one of his own men fall, and the others press forward under a storm of fire to avenge their comrade's death.

Nothing motivated men more than the desire for revenge. He understood this concept best of all.

Armed only with pistols, Drake and his two companions were unable to put up more than a token resistance as Kourash's men took up firing positions on the edge of the canal. With a clear field of fire from an elevated position, they couldn't ask for anything better.

He had won, he knew in that moment. Drake might have proven himself more resourceful than he'd expected, but in the end it had made no difference. For all his cunning and resourcefulness, he was still going to die. He was going to pay for what he had done all those years ago.

And with Drake gone, he could turn his full attention to his true purpose. He would broaden his campaign of assassinations and bombings to encompass the entire country. The Taliban, the remnants of al-Qaeda, the countless warring factions and splinter groups and fanatics fighting for control of Afghanistan would all be swept away like shadows at the coming of dawn. And with the Coalition soldiers withdrawn, this country would finally know true freedom.

That was his destiny. That was the path he had started on when he left behind his abusive childhood four decades earlier. That would be his final testimony on a life used to its fullest potential.

Kourash allowed himself a faint smile of triumph as he trained his binoculars in on Drake, eager to see the man's final moments. He saw him crouched down behind the crashed Humvee, saw the hope drain from his eyes as the realisation sank in that he was going to die in a shit-filled canal.

This is where it ends for you, my friend, he thought.

But then suddenly the look on Drake's face changed to one of puzzlement, as if something unexpected had just interrupted him. Kourash frowned, wondering what the man was thinking.

His frown deepened as, to his dismay, Drake rose up from his hiding place without fear to stare at the top of the concrete embankment. Why was the man able to do such a thing? Why hadn't he been cut down by a burst of AK fire?

Still failing to understand, Kourash moved his gaze upwards, following Drake's line of sight, and felt his blood freeze.

'No . . .'

Drake couldn't understand it. One moment they had been pinned down, powerless to stop their enemies moving to outflank and pour a murderous rain of fire down on them, the next it had all fallen silent.

Glancing up to the place from which the insurgents had been pouring fire down on them, he saw one of them lying sprawled over the lip, his weapon lying several yards further down the slope, blood draining slowly down the bleached concrete.

'What in the hell just happened?' Keegan asked, rising slowly, cautiously up from his hiding place. His face was cut and grazed, smeared with blood and soot, but he had somehow managed to keep hold of his tattered baseball cap.

'No idea. But we're alive when we shouldn't be,' Drake said.

And then, just like that, four figures appeared at the top of the slope. Not insurgents, not men in fake ANA uniforms, but soldiers. Soldiers armed with M4 carbines and clad in uniforms that were not American or British.

Soldiers belonging to Horizon Defence.

'Good to see you again, mate,' Matt Cunningham said, flashing a grin at his friend. Smoke still trailed from the barrel of his carbine. 'Are we late?'

For several seconds, Kourash just sat there staring at the scene, refusing to believe what his eyes were telling him.

It couldn't be. It just couldn't.

Only moments before, his men had been poised to kill Drake and the two men unlucky enough to have been travelling with him. He had felt the rush of success, the joy of knowing he had prevailed over a hated adversary.

And then it had all fallen apart. His men were dead, Drake was alive, and it was all because of the last people on earth Kourash had expected to come to his aid.

259

Shaking, trembling with impotent rage and despair, he rose from his vantage point and turned away, unable to stomach it any longer.

Still stunned by what he had just witnessed, Drake stood in silence as Cunningham descended the steep slope towards him, apparently untroubled by the dead body he passed. He was a soldier to the core – he lived for this stuff.

Behind him, several Horizon operatives were checking the fallen insurgents, keeping their weapons ready until they were sure their enemies were dead.

'You did all this?' Drake finally managed to say.

Cunningham glanced at the crumpled, bullet-riddled remains of the Humvee. 'Aye. And not a minute too soon by the looks of things.' He looked at Drake. 'I thought I was done saving your arse when you left the Regiment.'

'You two know each other?' Crawford asked, one hand pressed against the side of his head. The skin was already discoloured and noticeably swollen.

'We served together when I was with the SAS,' Drake hurriedly explained. 'Matt was my sergeant.'

'That's beautiful.' Crawford's sarcasm was impossible to miss. 'How the hell did you guys show up so fast?'

'Believe me, it wasn't luck,' Cunningham assured him. 'We had intel that insurgents were using fake ANA uniforms to get through checkpoints, and that they would be in this area today.' He gestured to the destroyed Humvee. 'Looks like you caught the worst of it.'

'No shit,' Keegan remarked cynically. 'You could have warned us.'

At this, Cunningham shrugged. 'Warn you of what? To avoid every ANA soldier in Kabul? Aye, good luck with that.'

Drake suspected there was another reason they hadn't been notified of the danger; it would have alerted Kourash that they were onto him. Drake and the others had been the bait – bait that Kourash couldn't possibly refuse.

'This was Kourash's work,' he cut in. 'He laid a trap for us. He'll be close by. He's always around to watch his attacks.'

Cunningham nodded. 'Aye, so I heard. We have Afghan police sweeping nearby buildings as we speak. If he's here, they'll find him.' He looked Drake up and down. 'You all right, mate? We've a medic in our team . . .'

'I'm fine,' Drake lied. In the space of a couple of minutes he had gone from staring death in the face, to standing side by side with people he had regarded as enemies. Had he been wrong about them? Even more unsettling, had Anya?

He heard sirens wailing and turned his gaze towards the bridge. Afghan police had just turned up and were busy securing the area. Two officers hurried towards the burning remains of the taxi with fire extinguishers.

Cunningham gestured to the edge of the canal, where a Horizon armoured personnel carrier had pulled to a halt, its roof-mounted machine gun tracking back and forth, ready to lay down suppressing fire at a moment's notice.

'Looks like you could use a lift,' he observed with a wry smile. 'We'll get the three of you back to Bagram once we've finished up here.'

'All part of the service, huh?' Keegan remarked cynically. 'Thought you guys were in this for the pay cheque.'

'I'll be sure to send your Agency the bill,' Cunningham returned, then slapped Drake's shoulder. 'Feel better,

Ryan. You'll live to see tomorrow, and that's not bad for Afghanistan.'

With that, he turned and stalked away, already issuing instructions into his radio headset. Drake watched him go, torn between suspicion and gratitude.

If Horizon were friends instead of enemies, then what did that make Anya?

Chapter 29

'How could you have done this, you bastard?' Kourash spat, gripping the phone so tightly that the casing threatened to crack as he paced the living room of his villa. 'Six of my best men are dead. You have betrayed me!'

Never before had he spoken to his benefactor like this. The man who had arranged his escape from that hellish Coalition prison near the Pakistan border, where he was watched so closely that he couldn't even take his own life. The man who had provided him with weapons, money, equipment – the means to wage the war he had always dreamed of.

The man who had shared the same vision as himself, even if it was for different reasons.

It was a lie, he realised now. He had been betrayed. All his plans, all his schemes and years of toil and sacrifice, the great destiny he had foreseen for himself . . . All of it had been blown away like dust on the wind.

All because of this man.

'You betrayed yourself, Kourash. Don't come crying to me about it now.' Richard Carpenter's voice was as cold and ruthless as Kourash's was bitter and enraged. 'Your instructions were to kill Mitchell when we delivered him to you. Instead you decided to indulge in some pathetic revenge trip. *You* brought Drake and his team out here just so you could kill him. *You* almost fucked up everything I've been working for.'

'Remember what I have done for you, Carpenter,' Kourash hit back. 'Because of me, more than half the Taliban commanders in this region are dead. Deaths that you and your . . . company were able to take credit for. You would be nothing without me! Nothing!'

To his dismay, he heard laughter on the other end of the line. 'You really believe that, don't you? You're a pathetic piece of shit, Kourash. Just another piss-ant Bin Laden wannabe, another desperate little man who'll sell his soul to make a name for himself. I could find a hundred men just like you.'

Above the thunder of his own heartbeat, Kourash was dimly aware of a faint rhythmic thumping noise coming from outside. A helicopter, flying low through the suburbs. It was of no consequence to him. Such aircraft passed this way all the time.

'You know what this means,' Kourash said, forcing calm into his voice, forcing himself to be as cold and ruthless as his former ally. 'You are making an enemy of a man you helped to equip and finance. You have given me the tools to fight a war, and I will make it my life's work to destroy you with them.'

Six of his best men were dead to be sure, but he had other men at his disposal. More important, he had money and weapons and technology, all provided by Carpenter and Horizon to allow him to fight the war they wanted him to fight.

With all of these things, he would make Carpenter pay for today's betrayal.

'I don't think so,' Carpenter said, completely unfazed

by his threat. 'One thing you need to realise about dogs, Kourash. Always keep them on a short leash.'

Outside, the thump of rotor blades was coming closer, though Kourash barely noticed now. He had stopped pacing, was standing in the centre of the room as he listened to Carpenter's words.

'Those encrypted cellphones that you've been using so much,' Carpenter went on. 'We made sure to include a tracking device in each of them that only we could detect. We've been following your movements since day one.' He paused, no doubt savouring the moment before he played his final card. 'I have to admit, I like the place you bought for yourself.'

Just then, the roar of helicopter engines reached a crescendo, and suddenly the evening sun was obscured as a dark shape soared over the roof of the villa to descend right in front of the living-room window. Kourash watched in horror as a Bell 205 chopper emblazoned with the Horizon logo settled itself into a hover, not more than 50 yards beyond his window.

His eyes blazed with fury, but the anger was not directed at Carpenter. It was towards himself, for allowing his pride and ambition to override common sense, to fool him into thinking he had the upper hand.

One could never have the upper hand over men like Carpenter. Only now did he realise that.

'Don't feel bad, Kourash,' Carpenter said soothingly as the chopper's side door slid back, revealing a sniper armed with a long-barrelled rifle. 'You still have one more role to play. You're going to be my biggest catch yet.'

Unarmed, Kourash could do nothing but watch as the barrel tracked towards him, its owner taking his time to line up the perfect shot. He didn't try to run. It would be a futile effort. They would almost certainly have sent in ground forces to surround the house.

His last conscious act was to drop the phone, no longer wishing to hear Carpenter's gloating voice. Knowing he had reached the end at last, his anger and hatred faded away, replaced only with a vague sense of disappointment. Disappointment that he hadn't done more, that he would never be the man he had always dreamed of becoming.

And for a fleeting moment, he felt relief. He would be with Mina again. She at least would understand what he had tried to do here. She had always understood, had always accepted him.

He saw the lightning-like muzzle flash, heard the window shatter and felt something slam into his forehead. Then he saw and knew no more.

As the Horizon ground assault team stormed into Kourash's villa to execute the remainder of his men, Carpenter leaned back in his expensive leather chair, laid his phone down and took a sip of coffee.

That was one troublesome liability taken care of at least.

He wasn't sorry to see Kourash dead. He would have disposed of him before too long anyway, but circumstances had forced him to move his timetable forward. Kourash had been a fool. A useful fool at times, but a fool nonetheless. He was a man of grandiose fantasies and ambition but little intelligence.

He had played his part in Carpenter's larger plan, but his part was over.

Now only one problem remained – Ryan Drake.

Anwari had already executed Mitchell, removing Drake's official reason for being here. And when news of Anwari's death reached Drake, any desire for revenge he might have harboured would likewise evaporate.

The logical thing to do would be to pack his gear and head for home. If Drake was smart, he would leave Afghanistan and put this whole mess behind him.

If he was stupid enough to linger on here, he would die.

Chapter 30

Drake was sitting alone on the roof of the Agency building, leaning against the brick wall of the stairwell he'd just ascended. Judging by the cigarette butts and plastic coffee cups scattered around, this was a popular spot for stressed office workers to take some time out.

Tonight, though, he had the place to himself.

He took a sip of whisky as he stared at the nearby mountains outlined against the evening sky.

It was a beautiful evening, with the last of the sun's rays playing radiantly on the distant mountains, the crescent moon just visible in the deep azure sky to the east. The fitful wind had dropped away, the fierce heat of the day at last abating to a more tolerable warmth.

It was the kind of evening that normally brought calm and relaxation to him; that languid time before sunset when the world seemed to slow down.

But not tonight.

Despite attempts by the Afghan police to establish a perimeter around the ambush site, they had found no sign of Kourash. It was hardly surprising – the area was simply too large and densely populated to find one person amongst thousands. Much as it galled him, the man was still out there somewhere.

However, Cunningham had been true to his word. After policing the scene and bringing in a recovery vehicle to carry away the wrecked Humvee, he had arranged for Drake and the others to be transported back to Bagram. Their injuries, though minor, had been treated en route, and without ceremony they had been deposited back at the Agency's security checkpoint.

Job done, Horizon had departed. Drake had never felt so useless in his life.

'I had a feeling I'd find you up here.'

He didn't need to look to know it was McKnight. She had been waiting for him when he arrived back at Bagram, looking and acting much as he had done the previous day. She had meant well, but somehow her concern for his safety only served to highlight what a failure today had been.

She sat down beside him, glancing sidelong at the hip flask in his hand. 'Aren't you going to offer the lady a drink?'

Drake handed it over. 'Wouldn't have picked you as a whisky drinker, Sam.'

'My grandfather was Irish. Whisky's in our blood.' She grinned and took a gulp, then leaned back against the wall.

The sunlight played across her face and the breeze sighed past, moving a few loose strands of dark hair in front of her eyes. She made no move to brush them aside, and said nothing to Drake, content merely to share the silence.

'I'm sorry about what happened today,' she finally said. 'Mitchell, and Anwari . . .'

She trailed off, either not knowing how to finish that sentiment, or perhaps expecting a response from him. He wished he had one to give her, but nothing came to mind. They were losing. The man they had been sent to rescue was dead, and the man responsible had escaped.

Drake glanced up as a distant rumble disturbed the quiet evening air, sounding for all the world like thunder echoing off the nearby mountains, though there were no clouds in the deep blue sky. A moment later, a second boom rolled across the base, and a third.

'Artillery,' McKnight remarked, head cocked as she listened to the distant bombardment. It was a familiar sound to her by now. 'One of the firebases up in the hills, probably.'

Drake leaned his head back against the wall, the muscles in his throat tightening as he swallowed. 'Christ, doesn't it ever stop?' he asked, staring off into the distance but seeing nothing. His eyes were deep pools of sadness.

'It's war. It never stops.'

A silence fell between them then, broken only by the distant rumble of battle. Drake now understood a little of what Anya had gone through, living in a world like this for most of her adult life – a world of war without end.

'I never told you why I didn't kill Kourash, why I spared the life of a man who tried to take mine.'

He wasn't even sure why he'd said it, why he felt the need to bring it up now. All he felt certain about was that he wanted her to know the truth. He wanted her to know the kind of man he'd once been.

When she said nothing, he turned to look at her. 'I know you're wondering why I did it. Shit, everyone else is.'

'You're not the only one who's been on operations, Ryan. I know the score. Some of the things that happen out there . . .' She shrugged, feeling no need to elaborate. 'I figured you'd tell me when you were ready.'

He took another pull from the hip flask, exhaling as the whisky seared its way down his throat. He was ready.

'He wasn't trying to take my life. He was trying to take his own.'

'Why?'

His jaw clenched, his grip on the hip flask tightened, as he replayed that moment. The assault on his safe house, the deadly firefight that had broken out, the vicious room-to-room struggle that saw no quarter given on either side.

'Because I killed his wife.'

He looked at her then, his green eyes shining in the glow of the setting sun. 'We'd tracked him down to a safe house in Herat. We went in during the night, but one of their sentries spotted us just as we were making entry. After that, it was chaos. We were fighting room to room, even hand to hand, and his men weren't for surrendering – none of them. You can imagine how that sort of fight played out.'

She said nothing. There was no need. She could imagine the toll that such a battle must have exacted on those involved.

'That was when I saw her,' Drake went on. He sighed and looked down at the whisky in his hands. 'We knew Kourash had a wife. The rumour was she even had a hand in planning some of his attacks, but nobody briefed us she'd be there that night. I saw her pick up a weapon from one of the men we'd killed, saw her bring it up to fire on me. So . . . I dropped her. Just like that, no hesitation.'

In truth, he didn't regret killing her. He hadn't at the

271

time and he didn't even now. The moment she picked up that weapon, she ceased to be a civilian and became a threat. And she had known what it would mean for her. But her sacrifice had bought time for her husband to escape.

'In the confusion Kourash managed to bail out through a window. I saw him outside, heading down a back-alley away from the house, so I put one in his leg to stop him. We moved in to capture him, but he took one look at me and drew a pistol. I'll never forget the look in his eyes as he lifted it to his head.'

Reacting instinctively, Drake raised his own M4 carbine, took aim in the fraction of a second that he had to spare, and squeezed off a single shot. He'd always been an excellent shot, and today was no exception. The rifle kicked back into his shoulder as the round discharged, followed a moment later by an explosion of blood and bone as it hit its target.

The pistol fell from Anwari's grip and the man doubled over, howling in pain and clutching what was left of his hand. Blood pumped from the bloody stumps of two fingers. It was over.

'Tango down!' Drake called, letting his teammates know that this man was no longer a threat.

Breathing hard as the adrenalin in his blood started to thin, he approached Anwari and planted a kick in the centre of his chest that sent him sprawling.

Just for a moment, the two men remained frozen like that – the victor and the vanquished, both regarding each other for the first time.

This was the man responsible for the deaths of scores of innocent civilians, and several Coalition soldiers. Men like Drake himself. Brothers in arms. Husbands, fathers, sons who would never go home. Because of this man.

Rage and hatred welled up inside him.

'I know you can understand me' he said, spitting out each word. 'It's over. Your men are dead. Your wife is dead. I killed her myself.'

Drake saw anguish blossom across the man's features as pain far more intense than mere physical injury crushed him. He saw it all, and revelled in it.

'I'm not going to let you die here, you piece of shit. You don't deserve that. You're going to live for a very long time, remembering what happened here today.'

Unable to contain it any longer, Anwari gave voice to another ragged howl of pain. But this wasn't the scream of an injured man. It was the scream of a man whose last shred of hope had just been taken from him.

'It's my fault,' he finally said, bringing the grim tale to an end. 'He wanted to die, but I stopped him. Because I wanted him to live with everything he'd lost. If I'd let him pull that trigger, none of this would have happened. Mitchell . . . all the other guys in that chopper, it's all on me.'

He took another drink, not because he wanted it, but because he needed a moment or two to compose himself. It wasn't often that he really faced up to his past, to the man he'd allowed himself to become. But today he could hide from it no longer.

'I just . . . wanted you to know, Sam. I'm not the same man I was back then, but that doesn't change what happened. I took everything from Kourash, even his way out, because I wanted him to suffer. That's who I was. That's what I'd let myself become.' He exhaled, knowing there was no coming back from this. He had crossed a line, telling her things he'd never admitted to anyone before, perhaps not even himself.

273

But right then, he didn't care. It had to come out.

'If you want to walk away from all this, I understand,' he said quietly. 'I won't stop you.'

He felt a hand on his arm, and looked up to see Samantha's face close to his. So close that he could make out the tiny flecks of green in her hazel eyes.

'Ryan, I don't pretend to know what happened back then. I don't know who you were or what you did, but I know who you are now. You're a good man,' she said, squeezing his arm as if to emphasise her point. 'You can't blame yourself for the things Anwari chose to do here. Whatever your reasons, you gave him his life. The rest is on him. Don't ever forget that.' He saw just a flicker of that same smile that had caught his eye the first time he saw her picture. 'And you can forget about me walking away from this. I want answers just as much as you do. I'm staying.'

Drake said nothing more. There was no need. He had given her a chance to walk, and she had decided to stay. And he was glad of that – more than he was prepared to admit.

He turned his eyes back up towards the sky, and the mountains in the distance. For all its troubles, Afghanistan was a starkly beautiful country – a strange, hot, barren land that people had tried and failed to conquer for centuries. He thought about those abandoned Soviet tanks he had passed yesterday, thought about the children playing on the wrecked machines of war, thought about Anya and Carpenter and Horizon and Kourash, and the tangled web that bound them all together.

His attention was drawn to a Black Hawk helicopter coming in to land, its massive rotors beating the air as several troopers clustered in the crew compartment waiting to disembark.

Drake took a final drink of whisky. He didn't know where this was leading, what truth lay hidden deep beneath the surface.

But somehow he would find it.

Part Four
Retribution

In October 2001, US and British forces invade Afghanistan, ousting the Taliban from power, severely damaging Al-Qaeda and securing major cities and towns. However, armed insurgency begins almost immediately.

Despite ongoing unrest, full withdrawal of British and American troops is scheduled for 2014.

Total Casualties (as of 2012):
2,862 Coalition troops killed and 22,618 wounded
981 private military contractors killed and 12,272 wounded
Approx 10,000 Afghan security forces killed
Approx 40,000 Taliban and insurgents killed
Approx 30,000 civilians killed, unknown number wounded

Chapter 31

CIA Training Facility 'Camp Peary', Virginia,
21 November 1985

Leaning over the sink, Anya spat, leaving a smear of bloody phlegm on the white porcelain. A couple of hours of unarmed combat training had taken their toll on her body, leaving her battered and bruised, and in more pain than she cared to admit.

Lifting up her T-shirt, she saw dark discolouration down her side where Carpenter had laid into her, taking great pleasure in explaining the deficiencies in her fighting technique as he knocked her down again and again.

Anya was no stranger to fighting or the injuries that came with it. She had spent three years in a juvenile prison back in Lithuania, having to fight nearly every day just to survive. But Carpenter was no inexperienced teenager driven by anger or jealousy; he was a trained killer, a man well versed in the art of war. Whatever fighting skills she had once learned did not serve her against him.

She couldn't understand why he seemed to hate her with such vehemence. From the moment she had arrived here she had been nothing but respectful and obedient. She had jumped to every order, had fulfilled every task given to her, had done everything in her power to earn his respect. But nothing was good enough. If anything, her attempts to please him only seemed to deepen his animosity.

She appraised herself frankly in the mirror, seeing the greasy, dishevelled hair, the cut lip, the bruised face, the sunken cheeks and the hollow, staring eyes. Her fellow recruits were growing stronger with each passing day, their bodies and minds moulded and sculpted into something newer, something more dangerous. Little by little, day by day, they were becoming soldiers.

Anya by contrast was growing weaker. Her muscles burned from constant marching and running and climbing, her bones and joints ached constantly. She was only twenty years old yet she felt fifty. Sleep deprivation and constant humiliation at Carpenter's hands were slowly sapping her mental reserves too.

Little by little, day by day, she was losing.

Why are you doing this, she asked her reflection. What are you trying to prove? Why did you ever think you could do this?

'He's testing you,' a voice remarked, as if in response to her silent plea.

Whirling around, Anya found herself looking at Recruit 4. Tall, dark-haired, well built, he was one of the oldest, most capable and promising of the group. He spoke with a Belorussian or Ukrainian accent, she couldn't tell which. But like all the recruits, he was not American.

That was the whole point of their unit – deniability.

She didn't know his real name. She didn't know any of the recruit's names. They never spoke with her except to exchange necessary information, and even then it was done only grudgingly.

To them, she was a waste of time. Sooner or later they knew she would fail and instinctively they avoided her, as if that failure were a disease that could be passed on to them.

'What do you mean?' she asked, taking a step back. The last time someone had cornered her in a washroom she had been fifteen years old. She was not keen to repeat the experience.

'He is testing you, trying to make you break.'

Anya might have laughed if her mood hadn't been so bleak. 'As if I didn't know that already,' she said, her eyes flashing with anger at what she saw as patronisation. 'He hates me. What more is there to say?'

'You're missing the point. He is trying to push you over the edge.' He folded his arms, making no move to close the gap between them. 'Let him.'

Without saying another word, he turned to leave.

'What is your name?' Anya asked before she could stop herself.

She shouldn't have done that, shouldn't have opened up on a personal level. Still, the question had been enough to make him pause, and she realised she had committed herself now. 'Your real name, I mean.'

'We have no names here. Remember?' She saw a flicker of a smile. Not fierce or malicious like Carpenter, but something else. Something approaching compassionate. 'But before, my name was Luka. And yours?'

Just like her question, the answer came of its own volition. 'Anya.'

'Anya,' he repeated, as if trying the name out. He nodded, seemingly satisfied with it. 'I'll remember it.'

With that, he turned and walked out, leaving her alone.

Central Hotel, Kabul, 12 August 2008

The CNN anchor was, as always, immaculately dressed, her blonde hair expertly coiffed, her make-up flawless. It was about 10 p.m. on the East Coast of America; the end of another news day. Very little of which had been good.

'A video released through Al Jazeera earlier today

281

apparently showing the execution of a Central Intelligence Agency operative has been condemned by the White House,' she said, her expression deeply serious. 'The authenticity of the video has yet to be confirmed – however, this execution is believed to have been carried out by the same group responsible for shooting down a US military helicopter in eastern Afghanistan several days previously. With us now in the studio to discuss this is our defence expert Glen Richfield.'

The camera immediately switched to a man in his early thirties, with a pudgy, affable face and curly brown hair. By the looks of him, the closest he'd been to Afghanistan was viewing it on Google Maps.

'Glen, what are the implications of this video?'

'Well, this is the last thing either the CIA or the White House needs right now,' he began, speaking with the clear articulation of someone who had been briefed on the question well in advance. 'With President Bush approaching the end of his second term, these last few months in office are going to be crucial in our evaluation of the War on Terror and his Presidency as a whole. Any new administration that comes in next year is going to have to answer one key question – when are we bringing our troops home? And that's not to mention the financial implications—'

The screen went black as Anya hit the standby button on the remote control. She had heard enough.

She had already received the bad news from Drake's cellphone, his simple message explaining only that Mitchell was dead, and that it happened long before they got there.

Taking a deep breath, she closed her eyes for a moment and gripped the back of her chair, her hold growing stronger until the cheap wood creaked under the pressure. Mitchell was gone. A man she had known nearly twenty years was dead; another entry in the long list of people who had paid for that association with their lives.

Let it go, she said to herself. Let it go. His death would not go unpunished, she would make sure of it. Releasing her hold, she strode through to her hotel bathroom to check her appearance in the mirror.

Her short blonde hair was gone now, replaced by long brown locks that fell well past her shoulders, with a thick fringe covering her forehead.

Her steely blue eyes were also gone, hidden behind a pair of brown contact lenses that she had to fight not to rub at. Still, they served their purpose, combining with a pair of thick-framed reading glasses and the wig to considerably alter her facial appearance.

It wouldn't be enough to defeat facial recognition software, but that couldn't be helped. In any case, no one but Drake knew she was here.

At least, she hoped so. Not for the first time, she found herself debating the wisdom of making contact with him again. He was a constant danger to her, yet she had lived most of her life facing such dangers and still she lived.

Drake was a useful asset, perhaps her only remaining ally in Afghanistan. And as much as she hated to admit it, she wanted to see him again.

Leaving the bathroom, she returned to the bedroom, booted up her laptop and accessed a program called *DataKill*. Another little gift from Loki, it would thoroughly wipe everything from the hard drive, preventing even the most skilled technician from reconstituting it.

She no longer needed the computer. She wouldn't be coming back.

The few items she'd take with her were packed into

a simple canvas rucksack on the bed. An old habit – she always made sure to travel light.

As *DataKill* went to work on the laptop, she snatched up the bag and strode out of the room.

CIA compound, Bagram Air Base

Drake turned to regard his three teammates, feeling if possible even more strung out than yesterday. He had slept little, brooding over yesterday's failures and mistakes. Still, he had called the team together once more, determined to have at least one more crack at it.

'All right, you don't need me to tell you we're in trouble,' he began. 'We've lost Mitchell, we're no closer to finding Kourash, and we still don't know how Horizon fit into this. Unless we can come up with something today, it's over.'

With that none-too-optimistic appraisal, he turned his attention to Frost. 'Keira, where are we on that convoy list?'

'Up shit creek.'

That wasn't the answer he'd been looking for. 'Hit me with some optimism here.'

The young woman spread her hands in a gesture of helplessness. 'There were forty men on that convoy. The names for twenty-eight of them were blank.'

Drake was starting to get an uneasy feeling about this. 'Why?'

'Because they weren't US Army personnel – their names and ranks weren't listed. They were there, but as far as the official records go, they weren't there.'

Keegan tilted his chair back, one boot wedged against the table. 'I'll give you twenty bucks if you can tell me which outfit they belonged to.'

The answer was as obvious as it was disturbing. 'Horizon.'

'Bingo.'

Drake headed for a whiteboard fixed to the wall at the head of the table. Snatching up a pen, he began to write. He could have used a laptop linked up to a projector to make such notes, but the act of writing it down helped him think.

'So we've got a supply convoy with Horizon personnel running security, none of whom are listed on the official manifest,' Drake said, scribbling down the words *Convoy* and *Horizon*.

'They leave Bagram with four Stinger launchers, they somehow find an opportune moment to offload one of them, then they doctor the inventory and hand over three launchers at Salerno, with all the official documentation in the world to prove it,' he added, writing the word *Stinger* next to them. 'And, lo and behold, the Stinger ends up in the hands of Kourash and his terrible chums.'

He added the word *Kourash* above *Stinger*.

'And I bet if we ask Horizon for a list of their operatives on that convoy, it'll be conveniently lost,' Frost remarked cynically.

Having been involved in covert operations for several years now, she knew just how easy it was for people to forget incriminating facts, for important information to be lost, for documents to go missing. Governments did it all the time to avoid answering uncomfortable public questions.

'That's a pretty serious accusation,' McKnight warned. 'We're suggesting they willingly stole weapons from the US military.'

Drake turned away from the board to look at her. 'It's one that fits the facts at hand.'

He knew he was skating on thin ice. There was such a thing as 'cooking the proof' in situations like this – placing unreasonable weight on evidence that supported a particular theory while marginalising that which didn't. It was an easy trap to fall into, and a voice in his head warned him he was about to do just that.

The problem was, he wasn't listening.

'So could a hundred other theories,' she reminded him. 'For all we know, Anwari might have stolen it from the convoy himself.'

'Then why take only one?' he asked. 'If he had the ability to sneak in under the noses of forty armed soldiers, he could have taken all the launchers. Or he could have wiped out the convoy and taken everything in it. And who would have edited the cargo manifest?'

With no answer to that, she fell silent.

'What if it was some kind of protection racket?' Keegan suggested. 'Maybe the Stinger was a bargaining chip.'

Drake paused, struck by the possibility. Keegan's knowledge of the complex military and political situation in this country might have been limited, but his understanding of human nature wasn't. He had worked with the FBI for more than a decade before joining the Agency, and knew as well as anyone the power of extortion.

'So they give up one launcher in exchange for safe passage through enemy-held territory,' Drake said, following through on his line of thinking. 'When that same weapon gets used to shoot down a friendly chopper, Horizon realise the trail could lead back to them, so they're forced to go into arse-saving mode. They erase all evidence of the missing Stinger and try to cover the whole thing up.'

'Remember how eager they were to destroy the crash site when we got there,' Keegan said. 'They couldn't blow that thing fast enough.'

They knew we were getting closer to the truth, Drake thought. Unfortunately for them, Horizon didn't know McKnight had found a portion of the missile and used it to trace the weapon back to them.

'Jesus,' Frost said quietly. 'We've unearthed a fucking conspiracy here.'

'Let's not get ahead of ourselves,' Drake advised, trying to quell his own feelings on the matter. Much as it galled him, he owed his life to Horizon. 'Right now, all we have are theories and conjecture. That's not going to be enough to bring down a guy like Carpenter.'

Keegan regarded him curiously, struck by his inexplicable choice of culprits. 'Am I missing something here, Ryan?'

'What do you mean?' he asked, trying to maintain a neutral tone. He realised too late that he'd said more than he'd intended.

'You keep coming back to Carpenter. You had Keira run a profile on him right after you got back from your first meeting, like you expected her to dig up dirt on him. Now you're talking like he's the mastermind behind everything bad in the world.' He leaned forward in his chair. 'What do you know that you're not telling us, pal?'

All eyes in the room were now on Drake. Silently he cursed his own lack of restraint, though he knew it made no difference now. He had to give them something.

'Someone I trust warned me about him,' he answered at last.

The next question was obvious. 'Who might that be?'

'It doesn't matter now.' He glanced away. 'Right now we still need to work out out why they targeted Mitchell's chopper, and more importantly what he was working on—'

'Bullshit it doesn't matter,' Frost cut in. 'If you've been

287

meeting with a source behind our back, we need to know about it. Otherwise you can count me out.'

She wasn't going to let this go, he realised. Neither were the others, who were all looking at him expectantly. He couldn't blame them. He would have done the same thing in their position.

He sighed, tossed his pen on the desk and looked at each of his teammates in turn. Three people who had trusted him enough to come halfway around the world in search of a man none of them had ever met. Three people willing to risk their lives by following him.

Three people who deserved more than what he'd given them.

'It was Anya.'

'Oh, Christ,' Frost groaned, raising her eyes skywards.

'Shit, Ryan. I thought she was long gone,' Keegan said, his expression caught somewhere between shock and dismay.

McKnight, perplexed by their reactions, folded her arms and looked at Drake expectantly. 'Who exactly is Anya?'

'Bad news,' Frost answered before he could. 'We risked our lives to rescue her from a Russian jail, and the bitch almost got us all killed for our troubles. She's a fucking nut job—'

'That's enough,' Drake snapped with more heat than he'd intended.

Frost seemed ready to bite back, but one look at her team leader was enough to convince her otherwise. As fiery as she was, even she knew when to hold her tongue.

Calming himself, Drake glanced back at McKnight, trying to come up with a concise summary of the tumultuous events of the previous year. 'She used to be an operative with the Agency until she got captured. She ended up in a prison in Russia. We were sent in to rescue her, then it all went to shit. When it was over, she escaped and vanished.'

'And she left you to die for your troubles,' Frost added.

'Since then she's been on the run,' Drake went on, ignoring her. 'I never expected to see her again, but the other night she found me. She warned me about Carpenter, said he wasn't a man to trust.'

'How does she know him?' McKnight asked, clearly intrigued.

'She didn't say,' he admitted. 'But if you read between the lines, I assume they worked together in covert operations. Remember that black hole in Carpenter's service record in the late-eighties? You join the dots on this one.'

She frowned, deep in thought. 'And there's no chance she could have been lying to you?'

Drake paused, just for a moment, weighing up her words. He thought about Horizon, how they had saved his life yesterday. Could Anya have been wrong? Could she have misled him? Even if Carpenter himself was corrupt, the organisation he presided over might still be one of honest men.

'No,' he decided at last, going with his gut instinct. 'She wouldn't lie to me.'

'What makes you so sure?'

'She can see straight through lies,' he explained. 'She hates people who lie, so she won't do it herself. It's . . . dishonourable.'

'Aw, a killer with a heart of gold,' Frost remarked cynically. 'Christ, Ryan, listen to yourself. You're talking about a single unverified, undocumented source who might have a personal grudge against Carpenter. If we were journalists we couldn't run a fucking local newspaper article with a lead like that, and you want us to start a covert investigation?'

McKnight chewed her lip and glanced over at the whiteboard, now covered in Drake's hastily scrawled notes. In the centre of it all was a single word: *Horizon*.

'At the very least we need to bring this Anya in, find out what else she can tell us.'

'Yeah, good luck with that,' Keegan scoffed.

'That's not how things work with her,' Drake said, doing his best to explain the kind of person they were dealing with. 'You don't *bring* her anywhere, and you don't find her unless she wants to be found. If she decides to speak with you, she'll find a way to make it happen. Otherwise, forget it.'

Drake had already resolved not to mention the second meeting he was due to have with Anya tonight. Even if he could somehow convince his companions to let him do it his way, he knew someone would try to follow him. Anya trusted him – that was a trust he did not intend to betray.

'Great,' McKnight said, throwing up her hands. 'So what do we do now?'

Despite all the conflicting elements at play here, Drake kept coming back to the same conclusion.

'Horizon are the key to this,' he decided. 'They can lead us to what Carpenter wants to hide. But we have to do it from the inside.'

'How, exactly?' Keegan asked.

For this at least, Drake had an idea. 'I know a man who can help us.'

Chapter 32

'So let me get this straight,' Cunningham said, glancing up from his cup of black coffee. 'You want me to hack into my employers' computer network, give out classified information, risk the safety of men I've worked with for years, my career and my life, all based on nothing more than your unproven theory?'

Getting the man to agree to meet them in a crowded coffee house in central Kabul had been easy enough. Persuading him to do what they needed was proving less so.

'Pretty much,' Drake replied.

At this, Cunningham actually laughed in amusement. 'Ryan, if the CIA doesn't pan out for you, you can always try your hand as a stand-up.'

Frost, however, was far from amused. 'Your "employers" are a group of mercenaries who've been stealing weapons from the US military. You'll pardon me if I don't shed a tear for them.'

That was enough to wipe Cunningham's smile away. 'Put a lid on that kettle, mate. I don't like the sound it's making,' he said, regarding the young woman with a cold glare.

'Look, Matt, we wouldn't ask you to do this if we didn't have good reason,' Drake said, jumping in before a more serious confrontation erupted.

As fair and even-handed as Cunningham had been during his days in the Regiment, he also had a temper that it was not wise to provoke. Drake had only seen him lose it a couple of times in the four years he'd known him, and that had been more than enough.

'We're not out to risk lives or sabotage the company,' he went on. 'If Horizon are genuinely innocent in this, fine. If we search their network and find nothing incriminating, so be it. But we need to be sure.' Drake leaned in closer, looking his old friend in the eye. 'I think you need to be sure, too.'

Cunningham said nothing for several seconds. Never an easy man to read, it was hard to tell what was going on behind those blue-grey eyes of his.

He reached out and lifted his cup of coffee to his lips, taking a slow drink. The drone of conversation in the crowded room filled the air around them, though Drake was oblivious to it.

'If I'm caught doing this, I'm fucked,' Cunningham said at last. 'You know that.'

'You won't be. It's a simple process, and I'm assured it's untraceable.'

The older man chewed his lip. 'So what's involved?'

Drake let out a breath and glanced at Frost. 'Keira . . .'

'You need to find a logged-in machine that has hard-line access to the Horizon network,' the young woman said, launching into her briefing with gusto. Reaching into her pocket, she laid a USB memory stick on the notched, stained table in front of her. 'When you're ready, plug this in, and when the prompt appears on-screen, hit enter to confirm. Wait about ten seconds for the software to download, then remove the stick and destroy it. That's it – the program will do the rest.'

Cunningham eyed her dubiously. Like Drake, he was

no computer expert, but neither was he a fool. 'Aye? What'll it do, exactly?'

'It'll open up a back door in the Horizon firewall that only I can access,' she explained. 'Nobody else will be able to exploit it, and in all other respects the system will still be secure. It's even self-deleting, so once I'm finished, it'll erase all trace of what I've done. Like it never happened.'

'Just like that, eh?'

Drake couldn't decide if he saw respect or contempt in Cunningham's steely gaze, though he suspected the latter.

Either way, Frost didn't seem concerned, instead meeting his gaze with a challenging stare of her own. 'Just like that. Think you can handle it?'

'We'll see, won't we?' he replied, reaching for the stick.

He had just closed his fingers around it when Frost reached out and gripped his wrist. 'Remember, hard-line access only. It won't work any other way.'

'I know.'

'And on-site security is your problem,' she added. 'So don't do something stupid like trying to install it right in front of a surveillance camera.'

Cunningham had heard enough. Exerting his considerable strength, he yanked his wrist from her grip and pocketed the memory stick.

'I'm going to pretend I didn't hear that last part,' he said. Draining the remainder of his coffee, he turned to Drake. 'I'll text you when it's done.'

'Thanks, mate. I appreciate this.' Despite his assurances of anonymity, he knew the risk his friend was taking by agreeing to this.

'Just do one thing for me, Ryan.'

'What's that?'

'No matter how this pans out, not all of us are guilty just because of who we work for.' Unfolding a pair of sunglasses hanging from his shirt, he slipped them on. 'Keep that in mind, aye?'

'I will,' Drake promised.

Saying nothing further, Cunningham turned and strode away, soon lost amidst the thronging crowds on the street outside.

'You think he'll do it?' Frost asked, watching him go.

Drake took a drink of the bottled water he'd ordered. 'He's never let me down before. I don't think he'll start now.'

He glanced at his watch. It was 1:47 p.m.

In a few hours, he would have to leave his companions to make his meeting with Anya. That was one meeting he didn't intend to miss.

Chapter 33

'So let's make sure we're clear on this. During the entire two-hundred-mile journey from Bagram to Salerno, you don't remember anything unusual happening at all?' McKnight asked dubiously.

On the other side of the interview table, Corporal Evan Cortez sat slumped in his chair, his burly forearms folded across his chest, his dark eyes glowering. 'No, ma'am.'

'No unscheduled stops? No breakdowns? No forced detours?'

'Not that I recall.'

'That's hardly definitive, Corporal,' McKnight said, trying hard to hold her impatience in check.

They had rounded up as many US Army personnel from that convoy as they could find in the time available. Four were out running other convoy routes, one was sick with dysentery and another had returned Stateside on compassionate leave, which left them with six men to interview.

And so far, none of them had been able to offer up any proof of wrongdoing on Horizon's part. In fact, none of them seemed able to recall anything of value.

The young man shrugged, beginning to get pissed off with the endless questions that seemed to be leading nowhere. 'I don't know what you want me to say, ma'am.

I haul dozens of these convoys every month, and after a while they all become kinda similar, know what I mean?'

'Okay, that'll be all, Corporal,' Keegan decided, having been observing the interview from one corner of the room. 'We're done here.'

Cortez nodded to the sniper in gratitude. Rising from his chair, he spared McKnight only the briefest of glances. 'Ma'am.'

There was little warmth in his dark eyes.

The investigation had stalled, and there was no getting around that. Despite their best efforts, they had been unable to find any more information on the Horizon operatives assigned to the convoy, the forensics teams had found nothing useful at Mitchell's murder scene, and interviewing witnesses had achieved nothing except to waste a couple of hours of their limited time.

They were rapidly running out of both time and options – two factors that McKnight was now acutely aware of.

She only hoped Drake was having more luck.

Located in western Kabul, the Inter-Continental Hotel was one of the few secure, well-appointed hotels in the city, and as such was usually awash with journalists and foreign businessmen. It didn't have the glitz and glamour of the more prestigious Serena Hotel, but they still took security seriously.

The building had been laid down in the late 1960s, and bore all the hallmarks of that distinctly uninspired period of architectural design. Big, square and imposing, it looked as much like a block of flats in the East End of London as a luxury hotel. It had been the only large hotel still operating in the city by the time of the 2001 invasion, and had therefore become a staging area for news crews from all over the world.

Things hadn't changed much, Drake reflected as he and Frost made their way through the automatic glass doors and into the wide lobby area, their boots squeaking on the faux marble floor. Western men and women were gathered together on chairs and couches, sharing serious-looking conversations. Notepads, laptops and cellphones were everywhere, while waiters bustled back and forth with trays of coffee and bottled water.

'You're really spoiling me, Ryan,' Frost remarked with a playful grin, taking in their plush surroundings like a kid in a sweet shop. 'How come you never do stuff like this when we're back in the States?'

'Always had you figured for a cheap date,' Drake replied as he made his way towards the elevators on the far side of the check-in desk, trying to look unobtrusive. People came and went all the time in places like this, but most journalists were alert for new faces.

He had booked them a room for the night, paying for it out of his own pocket to avoid drawing undue attention. In any case, he didn't expect they would need it for more than a few hours. From what Frost had told him, it wouldn't take her long to access Horizon's servers once Cunningham had planted her Trojan program.

All she needed was Internet access and a secure place to work from. With metal detectors and security guards at the main entrance, the Inter-Continental seemed like their best bet.

A quick elevator ride brought them to the third floor, which was in the middle of being serviced by the looks of things. A plump middle-aged woman was busy dumping the contents of her laundry cart down a chute just opposite room 322. She didn't even acknowledge them as they squeezed past.

As he'd expected from a place like this, their room was a plain, unspectacular affair. The owners must have had a real love affair with the colour green, he thought. The carpets, the bed, the chairs, the curtains, even the bedside lights were all a drab olive hue.

Still, colour schemes aside, everything looked clean and efficient. It was certainly more than enough for their needs.

Throwing open the curtains, Drake found himself confronted with a panoramic view of central Kabul. Situated on a hill overlooking the city, the Inter-Continental's rooms provided views that were impressive to say the least.

Frost wasted no time unpacking her laptop. As the unit powered up, she reached for the room service brochure and began flicking through it.

'No way,' Drake said, snatching it from her grasp. 'You're here to work, not to stuff your face on my dollar.'

She couldn't have weighed more than 110 pounds, yet the young woman had a voracious appetite that seemed to know no limits, especially when the food was free.

'Screw you,' she replied, pouting. 'Consider this my hazard pay. You know I'm breaking at least a dozen federal laws for you, right?'

Drake looked at her for a long moment, then reluctantly handed the menu back. 'Fine. But keep your mind on the job.'

That seemed to improve her mood. 'Relax. As soon as your buddy Cunningham plants the Trojan, I'll get in, find what we need and bug out. They won't even know I was there.'

Drake wished he shared her sense of confidence. He

didn't doubt her abilities, but neither was he inclined to underestimate the people they were up against.

He glanced at his watch again. Almost time.

'I have to go out for a while,' he said, drawing the curtains once more. 'My phone might be busy, so text me if you find anything.'

The young woman looked up from her laptop, frowning. 'You're leaving *now*?'

'I need to speak to Franklin,' he lied. 'It should be morning in DC by now. He can keep Breckenridge off our backs for a while. And if we do find something on Horizon, we'll need his help to bring them down.'

She didn't look convinced. 'Do you trust him?'

'I don't trust anyone,' he said, one hand on the door. 'Especially not you.'

Frost gave him the finger before resuming her work.

Chapter 34

CIA Headquarters, Langley, Virginia

It was 8:30 in the morning in Virginia, and already shaping up to be a warm humid day typical of early August. The light fog lingering over the Potomac had almost burned away, and the sun shone down from a cloudless blue sky.

Surrounded by all the trappings of power that came with the position of Deputy Director of the CIA, Marcus Cain sat with his feet up on his desk, cup of coffee in hand as he read over his daily briefing sheet.

He had been promoted to this position after the debacle in Iraq last year, successfully managing to distance himself from Special Activities Division, from Drake, and most importantly, from Anya. After more than a year without incident, it was almost possible to forget the whole thing.

Almost, but not quite.

His intercom buzzed. It was his private secretary; a brisk, efficient woman in her fifties, who had been with him for the better part of a decade and knew him about as well as anyone.

Laying his coffee aside, he hit the accept button. 'Yeah, Carol?'

'Sir, I have a call for you on line one,' she informed him, her tone calm, composed, devoid of emotion.

It could have been his dry cleaner or the President of Russia on the phone; it made no difference to her. Serving with the Agency as long as she had, Carol had learned the fundamental rule of her job – that what happened behind these walls stayed behind them for ever.

'It's Mr Carpenter, sir. He was very insistent on speaking with you.'

Cain's brows rose. He knew that name well enough. It had been some time since he'd spoken to the man, and truth be told he had no desire to do so now. But he also knew Carpenter wouldn't have contacted him without good reason.

'Put him through, Carol.'

'Yes, sir. Transferring him now.'

The line buzzed once as the call was transferred, and Cain picked up his phone to take it.

'Richard. It's been a long time,' he began. Not long enough, he didn't add.

'Yes, it has,' Carpenter agreed. His voice sounded deeper and rougher than Cain remembered. Then again, choking on the dust and grit of Afghanistan twenty-four hours a day probably did that to a man. 'I hear you're moving up in the world these days, Marcus. Congratulations. When are you planning to run for President?'

His tone was heavy on sarcasm and light on sincerity.

'I'm assuming you didn't call to discuss my career plans?' Cain said, eager to get to the point.

'What? No time to shoot the breeze with an old friend?' Carpenter taunted, chuckling to himself. 'Well, I guess a man like you doesn't have much time for friends these days.'

Cain suppressed a flash of annoyance. Carpenter had been a pain in the ass as long as he'd known him; an arrogant, self-serving opportunist willing to trample over anyone in his pursuit of glory. He had been relieved beyond words when the man finally took early retirement to start his own security firm.

'I'm still waiting for that elusive point.'

And just like that, Carpenter's jovial attitude vanished. 'You have a Shepherd team out here led by a man named Drake. He's been poking his nose in where it doesn't belong. I want him and his team gone, now.'

Cain frowned. He had been briefed on the mission to find and recover Hal Mitchell, just as he was briefed on everything concerning Ryan Drake. The man had been a thorn in his side ever since the events of the previous year. He might have been neutralised for now, but he remained a potential threat.

Cain had been happy for him to be sent to dangerous places like Afghanistan, where the chances of the issue resolving itself were infinitely greater.

'That's your problem, not mine,' he countered.

'It seems to me like Drake is everybody's problem.'

'How so?'

'Come on, Marcus. We both know what happened last year. Don't forget it was *my* company who supplied you with operatives for that job. And lost plenty of good men in the process.'

Not that good, Cain thought to himself. Despite outnumbering their opponents two to one, Carpenter's supposedly elite operatives had proven no match for the Shepherd team sent in to take them down. Cain suspected the man hadn't brought his A-list players to the game that day.

'You were compensated for your loss,' Cain reminded him. 'That's what it comes down to in the end, isn't it? Money?'

'Don't patronise me.' His tone was icy cold. 'Just because you wear expensive suits and do your killing from an air-conditioned office in DC, doesn't mean you're any less dirty than I am. We both made a deal with the devil, Marcus. Five years ago, Moscow. Ring any bells?'

That stopped him in his tracks.

'I wonder what would happen if your dirty deal with the Russians was leaked to the media? It'd be a feeding frenzy, I'd say. You'd be ruined, and you'd probably take the entire Agency down with you.'

Cain's grip on the phone tightened. 'Is that a threat?'

'A warning,' Carpenter corrected him. 'We both have things we'd rather keep private. It's in all our interests to make sure Drake is . . . handled.'

Cain could feel his heart beating faster, the blood pounding in his ears. Carpenter was right. He was an arrogant, dangerous, ruthless son of a bitch, but he was right. If the truth came out, everything he had worked towards, sacrificed and compromised for, would vanish in an instant.

Cain exhaled slowly. When this was over, Carpenter would get what was coming to him. He would make sure of that.

'I'm listening,' he said at last.

Chapter 35

Bibi Mahru Hill, Kabul

Overlooking the vast urban sprawl of the city of Kabul, and with panoramic views of the mountainous landscape that surrounded it, the sandy rounded hump of Bibi Mahru Hill had always been a popular spot for locals. Now, since the fall of the Taliban, it had become one of the city's best-known tourist sites.

The main attraction, as incongruous as it appeared in such arid surroundings, was the Olympic-sized swimming pool, complete with 10-metre-high diving boards. But like so many grand undertakings begun in this country, it had never come to fruition. The massive concrete shell had never been filled, the rusting diving boards never used for their intended purpose. It was another empty, decaying memory of the Soviet Union's failed attempt to bring Socialism to Afghanistan.

Its more sinister legacy was that it had been widely used by the Taliban to conduct executions. A 10-metre fall into an empty swimming pool had proven an ideal means of inflicting a slow, painful death on enemies of the regime.

A small crowd of locals and foreigners were milling around the edge of the pool, watching groups of kids splashing in the cloudy unfiltered water that had collected in the deep end, their shrieks of laughter echoing around the concrete enclosure. In a country that had seen three decades of war and conflict, such sounds were a rare but welcome occurrence.

Standing at the opposite end of the pool, Drake watched a group of young men posing for a picture in front of the rusted hulk of a Russian BTR-60 armoured personnel carrier, all grinning and giving Winston Churchill-style V-for-victory signs. Most of them probably hadn't even been born when the Soviets pulled out.

Making his way here hadn't been easy. Avoiding the main roads and the endless checkpoints that went with them, he had instead travelled through the city's unpatrolled maze of side streets and back alleys. He could almost sense the brooding hostility amongst many of the locals he passed along the way, though he had done his best to ignore it, simply keeping his head down and walking on.

Nonetheless, he had eventually reached the crown of Bibi Mahru Hill unmolested. He was still perspiring after the long hike uphill in 90-degree heat, but nonetheless made the rendezvous on time.

Now all he needed was Anya.

A couple of Westerners with expensive-looking cameras were taking photos of the area, probably journalists looking for a new angle on an old subject. Drake was careful to stay out of shot, more from force of habit than fear of exposure. He had made sure his route from the drop-off point had been long and winding, and had worked a couple of street markets into his journey to confound anyone who might have been tailing him.

His attention was drawn to one of the photographers who seemed to be heading in his direction. It was a woman, tall and statuesque, with long dark hair tied back in a ponytail and partly covered by a baseball cap. She was clad in the hiking boots, cargo pants and loose shirt combination that seemed to be regulation apparel for Westerners around these parts. Her eyes were hidden behind Ray-Ban sunglasses that probably cost more than most of the men by the pool made in a month.

She was looking at him. Somehow he could almost feel her eyes surveying him, watching him intently. Only one person he knew had such an effect on him.

Looking closer, he recognised the confident, self-assured walk, the lithe athletic physique and the faint, knowing smile.

'I was starting to wonder if you'd show up,' he remarked, surprised by how different Anya looked. A wig, a change of clothes and a pair of glasses could do wonders to alter one's appearance.

'I was hoping *you* would notice *me*,' she countered, as if she were chastising him. 'I have been here for the past ten minutes. You are not very observant, Ryan.'

He decided not to rise to that one. 'We need to talk,' he said, reaching out to steer her towards a more secluded area of the hilltop.

In one easy move she sidestepped him, avoiding his grasp. It was an instinctive move born from habit, but the message was clear. She went only where she chose to go.

Walking together but slightly apart, they skirted the pool and headed for the eastern side of the hill, with Anya pausing to take pictures along the way.

'Never had you pegged as an artistic type,' Drake said, impatient at the delay.

'I am here as a journalist,' was her simple reply. She had no intention of breaking cover until she was out of sight of prying eyes. 'Journalists take pictures.'

Drake said nothing further, waiting until they had descended the eastern slope a little way before turning to face her once more.

'Mitchell's dead.'

She nodded. 'I saw the news report. What happened?'

'You tell me,' he suggested.

'I don't know what you mean.'

'Bullshit. Ever since I got here you've given me nothing but bullshit,' he said, jabbing an accusing finger at her. 'I almost got killed yesterday, Anya. I'm staying in Afghanistan against direct orders, and I'm doing it all based on *your word*. I think I deserve some answers.'

'No one forced you to be here,' she reminded him. She removed her sunglasses. Her intense blue eyes were now brown, disguised by contact lenses, but what lay behind them was unchanged. 'If you are afraid to take risks, Drake, I suggest you run home and hide under the bed.'

Drake had to fight hard to suppress the first response that leapt into his mind. He didn't appreciate being patronised at the best of times, and at that moment, he was not in a forgiving mood.

'Are you finished?' he asked. 'Or do you want to waste more of my time? Because unless you give me something useful, I walk away right now.'

The older woman regarded him for several seconds in thoughtful silence, as if weighing up how much he deserved to know. 'Tell me what you have learned, and I will answer your questions.'

That was very much the Anya he knew. She conceded nothing without getting something in return. Still, she had still conceded. And if she said she would answer his questions, he knew she would.

'Horizon are hiding something,' he began. 'We tracked the Stinger that shot down Mitchell's chopper to a convoy out of Bagram. Horizon were running security. The Stinger never made it to its destination. Mitchell started asking questions about it, then . . . look what happened.'

Anya listened carefully, her expression difficult to read. 'Theories?'

'I don't believe in coincidences,' he said. 'Mitchell found something he wasn't supposed to. It seems like we're following the same trail.'

'What else?' she went on.

'Kourash never intended to release Mitchell. He was long dead when we found him. I'd guess they executed him right after they sent the first video. Kourash wasn't trying to use him as a hostage – he wanted him for something else.'

'What, exactly?'

'Me.' Drake raised his chin a little. 'Mitchell was bait. Kourash made sure he was clearly identified on the hostage tape so the Agency would send me in. I don't know how he knew I was working for them, but he did. On the first day he tried to assassinate two of my team, then yesterday he tried to kill me. He almost succeeded.'

She nodded slowly, apparently unfazed by his near-death experience.

'Look, I don't have much time,' Drake persisted. 'If you know something that can help, now's the time. Tell me how all this fits together.'

She lowered her head, and he heard a faint exhalation of breath.

'Mitchell was working for me,' she said at last, keeping her back to him.

He felt as though he had been hit by a sledgehammer. 'What?'

'I had known him for a long time, from back when I was an operative myself. He was one of the few men

308

inside the Agency that I still trusted, so I made contact with him six months ago. He was working a desk job by then. He was old, he had retired from field work and I knew he didn't want to go back, but still he agreed to help me.'

Drake was stunned. This entire thing had started with Anya, not Mitchell. He hadn't been conducting some clandestine investigation on his own initiative, he had been working for her all along.

'Why didn't you tell me?' Drake fixed her with an angry glare. 'Why didn't you trust me? For Christ's sake, my team risked their lives for him, Anya. As it is, I ought to beat the shit out of you for lying to me.'

'I did not lie to you,' she hit back, her eyes flaring. 'I already warned you about the men who tried to abduct me. As for the rest, I expected you to be able to look after yourself, but maybe I was wrong.'

She sighed and looked away, staring out across the ancient capital while her temper subsided. A warm breeze sighed across the hillside, lifting loose strands of her wig and carrying with it the distant drone of traffic.

This was going nowhere, he realised. He didn't have time to stand here trading insults with her.

'All right. What did you ask him to do?' he went on, speaking quieter and softer now.

It took her several seconds to calm down, to master the emotions that had risen up inside her. 'I wanted him to spy on Carpenter and Horizon.'

'Why Carpenter?' he asked. 'Why does it always come back to him?'

She didn't say anything, but he could see the tension in her body, could tell her breathing had quickened. She was agitated, angry, filled with nervous energy she couldn't use. Fight or flight, but there was nothing to vent her anger on, no place to run. No escape from the memories now whirling together inside her mind.

'What happened, Anya? What made you hate him so much?'

'It was a long time ago. It is not important now,' she said, her voice flat, devoid of emotion. He was beginning to realise that was her way of coping with feelings that were too strong to suppress and too dangerous to endure – she simply disconnected them as one might shut down a faulty machine.

But she wasn't a machine, and she couldn't just remove those parts of herself that she didn't want to deal with. More than most, Drake knew that. Sooner or later, it always came out.

'You came all this way to bring him down,' he said quietly. 'It *is* important. To you, and to me.'

She didn't say anything for some time, but neither did she protest. Drake made no move to press the issue. Instead he waited, knowing she would speak only when she was ready.

And then, at last, it came.

'I was in Afghanistan, twenty years ago,' she finally began. 'Working as part of a covert Special Forces unit. You would know them as Task Force Black.'

Indeed he did. It was the same unit that Anya had eventually ended up leading herself. The same unit that would be torn apart by a bitter power struggle between Anya and her protégé Dominic Munro.

'I had been with them for three years. Living together, fighting together, trusting our lives to each other. They had become more than just soldiers to me. They were . . . a family. Together we were unstoppable. Nothing could stand against us.'

Now that she had started, it was all she could do to

310

rein herself in. It was like a dam that had been holding back a river for too long. And now that it was breached, there was no stopping it.

'If the unit had become my family, then their leader was surely my father. His name was Luka; a Ukrainian, a defector like me. We were alike, he and I. We had both lost everything, been forced to start again. He protected me, gave me the strength to make it through training. He used to call me *Dochka*, the Ukrainian word for daughter.'

Her voice trembled a little at the thought of him, and she had to stop for a moment to compose herself. Her real father, the man she had known as a child, was now just a vague and indistinct memory, a shadowy figure inhabiting the half-remembered life she thought of as Before. Luka had been as much a father to her as he, perhaps more so because the experiences they had shared had tempered and intensified their relationship in ways most people would never understand.

'But things change,' she said, taking up the narrative again. 'Luka became colder, more distant as time went on. With every victory we won, every operation we completed, he seemed to wither away inside. He began arguing with Cain and Carpenter, refusing orders, breaking contact with our handlers. Finally he was relieved of command.

'Not long afterwards, we were ambushed in Afghanistan by a Soviet Spetsnaz unit. It was no chance encounter – they knew we were there because someone had told them. We had been betrayed.' She sighed and shook her head. 'It was terrible, one of the worst actions we ever fought. I volunteered to hold them off while the rest of the unit pulled out. It worked. They escaped . . . I did not.'

She closed her eyes for a moment, as if trying to banish memories she would rather have kept locked away. Drake couldn't help thinking about the scars that crisscrossed her back; the ones she had been so reluctant to talk about.

'By the time I returned to the States, I was . . . different,' she said, putting extra emphasis on that word. 'But I wanted to return to the unit. I convinced them I was ready, so they allowed me back in on one condition – that I dealt with the man who sold us out. I never could have imagined who it would be.'

Anya's hand was trembling as she held the weapon level, aimed right at Luka's chest. Never point a weapon at anyone unless you intend to use it – that was what had been drilled into her from the moment she joined the unit.

At such close range she could scarcely miss.

The older man made no attempt to defend himself. He just stood there with his hands by his sides, his craggy, expressive face resolute.

'I knew you would find me, Anya,' he said in a tone of grim satisfaction. 'I knew they would pick you.'

'Tell me what they said was a lie,' she whispered, her voice ragged with grief. She felt a warm tear trickle down her cheek. 'Tell me, and I will believe you.'

The man she'd come to know as a father said nothing.

'Why?' she pleaded. The tears were flowing freely now. There was no stopping them. 'How could you do this to us? Betray everything we worked for?'

'One day you might understand,' he said. Then, just for a moment, his expression softened, and he looked on her the way he once had, with pride and love. 'Dochka. My dochka. It's all right, don't be afraid. You're doing what you must, proving your loyalty. You were always the best of us. Remember that.'

Her finger tightened on the trigger.

The older man smiled a little, gently encouraging her, then closed his eyes and exhaled. 'I'm ready.'

Driving all thoughts of remorse and compassion from her mind for just the briefest of moments, she pulled the trigger.

'I did it. I killed him. The one man who would have done anything for me, who loved me like a daughter, and I killed him.' She let out a ragged, shuddering breath. 'I followed my orders . . . like a good soldier.'

The final admission came out as a bitter, mournful lament.

Drake had been watching her in silence the whole time, seeing the barriers and the layers of self-control slowly peeling away as she narrated her grim tale. The change that had come over her was startling. She was no longer the formidable, beautiful woman she had been only moments before. Sitting there with her head bowed, she looked tired, broken and desolate.

'But being a good soldier was not enough. I did not learn the truth until many years later,' she went on. 'When I was put in Khatyrgan prison, there was a man there. A man whose face I never saw. All I heard was his voice, speaking to me day and night. He was my tormentor. He was the man who arranged my capture.' Drake saw her fists clench as long-buried anger and hatred resurfaced. 'He told me the truth, told me what really happened in Afghanistan. It was not Luka who sold me out, it was Carpenter.'

'Why?' Drake asked, captivated by what he was hearing.

'Why does the man do anything? Money, of course.' She practically spat the word. 'He had never fully trusted Task Force Black, or me. To him, we were a liability. And anyway, the war in Afghanistan was coming to an end. We were outliving our usefulness, so he took the opportunity and sold us out to the Soviets. They were so desperate to catch us that they would have paid any price.' Drake heard a snort of derision from her. 'Carpenter never expected that I would come home. When I did, he was forced to improvise. He fabricated evidence against Luka and had Cain feed it to me, knowing I trusted him.'

She raised her head up then, as if facing up to the truth at last. 'Luka knew I had been sent to kill him. He knew Carpenter had set him up, but still he allowed me to go through with it because he knew Carpenter would have me killed if I turned against him.' He heard her sigh – in resignation, in acceptance, he couldn't tell. 'He gave his life . . . for me. The good soldier.'

Drake took a step towards her, reached out to touch her arm. 'Anya, I—'

Suddenly she twisted out of his grip and rounded on him, visibly shaking with anger. 'Stop it, Drake! I am not some frightened little girl to be comforted. I don't need your pity or your sympathy. I don't need you to hold me and tell me everything will be all right. I don't need anyone for anything. Do you understand that?'

Was she trying to convince him, or herself? She had survived as long as she had by relying on no one but herself, by refusing to allow the vulnerability that came from trusting another. But there was more to living than mere survival.

Still, Drake knew better than to try to force the issue. Anya wouldn't say or do anything she didn't want to, and trying to change that would be an exercise in futility.

He lowered his outstretched hand, saying nothing.

Anya exhaled, slowly calming herself.

'Carpenter retired from the military while I was in

prison,' she said, carrying on the conversation as if nothing had happened. 'He left the service with enough money to found Horizon. He and Cain were never friends, but his connections with the Agency allowed him to turn Horizon into a major defence contractor in just a few years.'

That explained the rapid growth and success of his company, Drake thought. A PMC owned and operated by a man with access to an almost unlimited pool of retired operatives, and the political connections to ensure they won any contract they bid for. Whatever his record as a soldier, Carpenter was clearly a shrewd businessman.

'Carpenter spends his life hiding behind walls and bulletproof glass. I could not get to him myself,' she went on. 'So I contacted Mitchell and he agreed to look into Carpenter and his company. The last time we spoke, he told me he had found something far bigger than either of us had imagined. He knew Carpenter would use his connections to stall an official investigation, so he would have to gather evidence himself. That was a week ago. A few days later . . . he was abducted and killed.'

'What kind of evidence did Mitchell have?' Drake asked, eager to know what the man had been working on.

'He did not say. He was worried about security, seeing dangers in every shadow. Even our email communications had to be done via code words.'

'So he didn't share any of it with you?'

Anya said nothing to this. She merely stood there for a few moments in thoughtful silence. Clearly she had reached the same conclusion long before he had, and was facing up to the fact that Carpenter might well have slipped beyond her grasp.

'I had hoped you could recover him alive, so he could share what he had found.' She chewed her lip, for the first time looking genuinely contrite. 'Now we may never know.'

'That's not exactly true,' he said. 'There might be another way out of this.'

She frowned. 'What do you mean?'

Anya listened while he outlined his plan to use Cunningham to bypass Horizon's computer security, and how Frost would soon be able to trawl through the company's secrets.

'It's not easy, but I've got one of the best people I know working on it,' he concluded. 'She won't let me down.'

For the first time, Anya looked genuinely impressed. He had accomplished something she could not. And maybe, just maybe, he had found a way to get what she needed.

She was silent for a few moments, clearly weighing up something in her mind. Then, reaching some unspoken decision, she nodded to herself.

'All right. If you find what you are looking for, call me.'

Then, having concluded her business, she brushed past him and started walking back up the slope.

'Hey, where are you going?'

He didn't know what was going on in her mind, but he recognised the fast, purposeful walk, the slightly raised chin, the squared shoulders, the back held ramrod straight. She had set herself on something, had abandoned any lingering doubts and decided her course of action.

'We have nothing more to say to each other, Drake,'

she called back over her shoulder. 'If you find something on Carpenter, then we will talk. Until then,
goodbye.'

Without looking back or saying another word, she
carried on her way, disappearing over the brow of the
hill. And just like that, she was gone.

Chapter 36

Frost was halfway through her second cup of coffee when her phone buzzed with an incoming text message. As she'd expected from a man like Cunningham, it was simple, concise, and told her exactly what she needed to know.

It is done.

'About goddamn time.'

Setting her cup aside, she clapped her hands together and turned her attention to the laptop, booting up the program she had created to exploit the now compromised firewall.

'Okay, you son of a bitch. Let's dance . . .'

'This had better be good,' Crawford said under his breath as he reached for his desk phone. Line 1 was illuminated to let him know there was a call waiting.

He had been pulled out of the ops room only moments before with news of a priority call from Langley waiting in his office. As if he didn't have enough to do already, now he had to get his ass chewed by some desk jockey back in DC.

He already had a sneaking suspicion it was George Breckenridge, Drake's troublesome superior, demanding to know why his team wasn't on a flight home.

'Section Leader Crawford,' he said, managing to sound more calm and efficient than he felt at that moment.

'Crawford, this is Deputy Director Marcus Cain,' a smooth, deep voice announced. 'Do I have your complete attention?'

Crawford's eyes opened wider. Shit, this wasn't good.

'Yes, Director.'

'Good. Then I suggest you listen carefully, because we have a major situation here that needs to be un-fucked right now. Make no mistake when I say I'll be holding you personally responsible if it isn't. Do you understand?'

Crawford resisted the urge to swallow. 'I do.'

'Good. This is what I need from you . . .'

The mood in the conference room was fraught with tension as McKnight and Keegan waited for word from their companions in Kabul. Drake had contacted them after the meeting with Cunningham to confirm the man had agreed to help, but beyond that they had had no further contact.

Anything could be happening, and they had no idea. Their role at that moment was to remain on station at Bagram, keeping up the illusion that they were still following leads. In reality, they had none left to pursue.

Then, without warning, the door flew open and Crawford strode in, accompanied by two security operatives.

Both were in their thirties, standing over 6 feet tall and packing well over 200 pounds of solid muscle apiece, with crew-cut hair and cold, unflinching eyes. They looked as though they had been around the block enough times to know their business, and know it well.

They were dressed in suits and shirts with open

collars, though McKnight's trained eye spotted the slight bulge beneath each of their jackets. They were armed.

'Is something wrong, Crawford?' she asked.

'You're being shut down. I'll have to ask you to hand over your computers and cellphones,' Crawford replied with a hard undertone that made it clear this wasn't a suggestion.

McKnight's eyes narrowed. 'On what grounds?'

'I can't say.'

'Bullshit you can't,' Keegan hit back. 'You ain't getting anything from us until we get some answers.'

With a single curt nod from Crawford, one of the operatives moved forward to confiscate Keegan's cellphone. Keegan was a good fifteen years older than him and at least 40 pounds lighter – no match for a young man in his prime.

Then, suddenly, Keegan grabbed his outstretched arm and twisted it with enough force to spin the man around, moving with frightening speed and the confident ease of a born fighter. A kick to the back of his leg brought him to his knees, and within moments Keegan had him at his mercy.

'Bad move, son,' he said, his voice low and menacing. 'Don't do it again.'

However, the second operative wasted no time drawing his weapon and levelling it at Keegan's head. 'Let him go,' he hissed. 'Let him go now!'

Keegan stared at Crawford. 'Christ, can't you see what's happening here? You're being played, you asshole. Someone doesn't want us to find the truth.'

'I have my orders,' Crawford replied, his expression grim. 'Let him go. Don't make this any worse than it has to be.'

'We've got nowhere to go, John,' McKnight said, hating every word. 'We can't win this one.'

More than the show of force, her calm, reasoned words were enough to cut through Keegan's instinctive reaction. Even he couldn't take on two armed agents twice his size with his bare hands.

Reluctantly he released his hold, kicking the agent away in disgust before raising his hands in surrender. Rolling his shoulder, the agent glared at him with unconcealed hatred.

'Knock yourself out, asshole,' Keegan spat.

'They're covering this whole thing up, Crawford,' McKnight said, raising her arms while one of the agents searched her. The other was busy disconnecting and packing away the laptops the team had set up. 'And you're allowing it to happen.'

Crawford said nothing to this, avoiding McKnight's angry gaze.

'Do you hear me? If you go through with this, you're no better than Carpenter or the guys who killed Mitchell. Think about that next time you look in the mirror.'

Crawford tried not to hear her scathing words, instead concentrating on following his orders to the letter. Orders that had come straight from the second-highest ranking man in the Agency.

Orders that left a sick feeling in the pit of his stomach.

With a single beep, the message Frost had been waiting for appeared on the screen.

HorizonNet access granted

'Yes!' the young woman exclaimed, clapping her hands once again.

Negotiating her way through Horizon's firewall had taken longer than she'd expected, even with the back door provided by her Trojan Horse program. They seemed to be using an access protocol she wasn't familiar with, and she'd been forced to improvise.

Still, it was done now. She was inside their network and free to roam at will.

She smiled as her fingers danced across the keyboard, bringing up their main file directory so she could begin searching for what she needed. As soon as she found anything vaguely relevant, she would copy it onto the high-capacity drive connected to her laptop.

She was just reaching for her cup of coffee when she froze, alerted by a noise outside her hotel room door. A faint hum and a click.

The sound of an electronic lock being disabled.

'Oh, shit.'

An instant later, the door flew inwards with a resounding crash and two men rushed in, huge and imposing, their eyes locked on her.

She was on her feet in an instant, survival instinct taking over. Grabbing the pot of coffee that lay beside the laptop, she snatched it up and hurled it at the nearest man, rushing in straight after it with her fists clenched.

Never let them come to you. That was her first, last and only rule when it came to fighting. Everything else was fair game.

The coffee had been sitting for some time, and was by now no longer hot enough to scald him. Still, he was forced to throw up his arm to shield himself from the pot, closing his eyes as the hot liquid sprayed over his face and clothes.

In a heartbeat, she was on him, lashing out at any vital spots she could find. She tried to strike him in the throat, knowing that a blow to the windpipe would drop him within seconds, but he saw it coming and ducked aside.

Her punch hit his meaty shoulder instead, jarring her arm.

Left with little alternative, she planted a vicious kick between his legs, and this time she found her mark. Groaning in pain, he started to buckle.

Straight away Frost turned her attention to his companion, knowing he was the real threat now. She was just looking up when she felt something impact her chest, something sharp and painful.

But this was nothing to the pain she felt an instant later when the taser discharged, thousands of volts of electricity flooding her body.

Robbed of control, she dropped to the floor, teeth clenched, her body convulsing of its own volition. The torment seemed to carry on for an eternity before at last the second man released the trigger. Either he considered her subdued, or the weapon had discharged its battery pack.

Whatever the reason, she was out of the fight, and somewhere in her pain-deadened mind she knew it.

Lying helpless on the cheap green carpet, she could do nothing but watch as the man with the taser loomed over her, a huge menacing shadow blocking out all else.

She saw a hand reaching out to her, clutching a piece of loose fabric. A hood, she realised. Her last sight was of his forearm, tanned and powerfully muscled. And marring the skin, a tattoo of a sword intersected by three lightning bolts.

Then she felt the fabric pulled down over her head, and the world went dark. Her hands were quickly bound behind her back, and then she felt material, rough and coarse like sack cloth, pulled up over her, covering her entire body as if she were being placed inside a giant bag.

She felt herself being hoisted up off the ground. She was small and light, and her captor made easy work of the task. A few seconds of jolting movement followed, then she stopped.

'Clear,' she heard a male voice hiss.

More movement, and suddenly she was being pushed into something – a narrow opening, rectangular in shape, barely large enough to accommodate even her small frame.

It took her a moment to realise it was the laundry chute opposite their room.

Then, just like that, the powerful hands released their hold and she was falling, tumbling sickeningly downward, the sides of the chute banging and jolting against her.

She winced, bracing herself for the bone-breaking impact as she finally hit the basement several floors below. She only hoped her death was quick.

Instead she felt her descent slow as the chute curved towards horizontal. With her hands bound, she could do nothing but flail helplessly as she tumbled out of the end, landing amongst what she assumed was a pile of soiled bedclothes.

Within seconds she felt herself seized up again, thrown over a man's shoulder and carried off. In the distance she heard the rumble of a vehicle engine, growing closer as her captor strode towards it.

They didn't want her dead, she realised then, an icy stab of fear twisting her stomach. Not yet at least. They had other plans for her.

Chapter 37

Drake had switched off his official cellphone prior to his meeting with Anya, removing the SIM card to prevent anyone tracing his location. He waited until he was some distance from Bibi Mahru Hill before powering it up again, and straight away found a text message from Frost.

Tried calling but phone switched off. Where are you??? Have found what we need. Meet me at room. Hurry!

Excitement surged through him. She had done it! Both Cunningham and Frost had come through for him. He was almost tempted to call Anya there and then to tell her they had Carpenter by the balls, but decided against it.

Better to review what Frost had found before making any rash decisions.

Pocketing the phone, he quickened his pace. He could see the imposing white rectangle of the Inter-Continental on a hillside about a mile away.

'That son of a bitch,' McKnight hissed, pacing the conference room like a caged animal. 'I can't believe he'd turn on us like this.'

They had been locked in there for the past hour, and though conditions were far from uncomfortable, the feeling of helplessness was oppressive. Cooped up as she was with nowhere to go and no information on what was happening with Drake and Frost, frustration was starting to get the better of her.

Keegan, however, didn't reply. The old sniper was sitting at the far end of the conference table, his eyes glued to the TV mounted on the wall. He had had it on CNN for the past ten minutes or so, partly out of boredom but also because it was their only contact with the outside world.

'Would you like a burger and a beer while you catch the scores?' McKnight asked, in no mood for dumbed-down analysis of foreign affairs and interviews with so-called experts.

To her surprise, he held up a hand to silence her. 'Pipe down a minute, huh? Something's going on.'

Frowning, she directed her gaze to the TV.

As expected, it was a busy news day. Mitchell's execution video had spread to various sites across the Internet, and like blood in the water it hadn't taken long to draw the sharks. Most of the major news networks had been running stories on it, speculating on everything from Mitchell's purpose in Afghanistan, to the perceived damage to the Agency's reputation and even the implications for the War on Terror.

Now, however, it seemed a new story had emerged. Bright yellow ticker-tape messages were scrolling across the bottom of the screen.

BREAKING NEWS: TERRORIST LEADER BELIEVED DEAD – LEADER OF RADICAL ISLAMIC TERRORIST GROUP RUMOURED TO HAVE BEEN KILLED IN AFGHANISTAN

326

Staring at the screen in disbelief, McKnight watched as the sleek brunette news anchor delivered a hastily composed report on what was clearly a breaking story.

'Once again, we're receiving unconfirmed reports from the Reuters news agency that the Islamic terrorist leader identified as Kourash Anwari has been killed in a gun battle with ISAF forces in Afghanistan. Anwari is believed to be the same man responsible for executing an American hostage live on the Internet yesterday, and for a string of attacks on Coalition forces in recent months.'

'You've got to be kidding me.'

'Shh!' Keegan hissed, not wanting to miss a thing.

'The Department of Defense has yet to make an official statement on the issue – however, there is speculation that private military contractors may have been involved in the operation . . .'

The news anchor paused, head tilted ever so slightly, her eyes unfocused as she received an update via her concealed earpiece. She was good, her commentary barely wavering despite the stream of information being fed to her, but McKnight had seen that same look in operatives enough times to recognise the signs.

Something had changed. Something she needed to know about.

'We're now being advised by our sources in Kabul that Richard Carpenter, the CEO of Horizon Defence, has called a special press conference in relation to Anwari's death, scheduled to begin in just a few minutes.'

As she began recapping the latest developments to fill time until the press conference started, Keegan at last turned away from the screen.

'Care to explain what the hell is going on here?'

McKnight said nothing, because she had no answer for him.

Chapter 38

Inter-Continental Hotel, Kabul

Eager to reach Frost and the information she had uncovered, Drake took a taxicab back to the hotel, paying the driver extra to avoid the main drags. That had been just fine with him, and Drake had received plenty of toothless smiles as they pulled into the hotel forecourt and he handed over his wad of Afghanis.

Picking his way through the busy lobby area, he headed straight for the elevator bank and hit the call button.

It seemed to take an age for the elevator to arrive. He was about to abandon it and head for the stairs when at last the doors pinged and slid open. He was certain it hadn't taken this long when they'd arrived.

Then again, he hadn't been so anxious to get to the room, he thought as he ducked inside and hit the button for the third floor.

The doors were just closing when a voice called out, 'Hey, hold that elevator, would ya?'

Drake had little desire to share the lift with anyone, but he was unable to intervene when a large, meaty arm thrust itself between the closing doors, forcing them open. A second later its owner pushed his way into the lift, struggling to manoeuvre what looked like a full-sized television camera under his arm. His shirt was damp with sweat patches after carting his heavy load around.

No wonder, Drake thought. He was perspiring enough just getting himself from place to place.

The cameraman's friend was right behind him, carrying a canvas satchel that looked to be packed with spare cables, batteries, lenses and whatever other crap the camera needed to stay running. He gave Drake an apologetic smile that looked about as genuine as the marble floor he'd just walked across as he shuffled into place beside the control panel.

'Thanks, buddy,' the cameraman said, shifting his burden a little as he pressed the button for the fourth floor. 'No way was I hauling this son of a bitch up four flights of stairs.'

'No problem,' Drake lied as the doors shuddered closed.

The elevator's progress up the shaft was slow and halting, as if it kept forgetting what it was supposed to be doing and had to stop to take stock of the situation.

Drake couldn't wait to get out. He had no particular fear of enclosed areas, but it was hot and stuffy in there, and the space taken up by his two new friends added to the feeling of entrapment.

'I swear, I'm sick of Vince riding my ass about image quality,' the cameraman remarked without turning around. 'What the hell are we supposed to do with all this dust and shit floating around? It's a miracle the cameras are even working.'

'I'll be glad to see the back of this shithole,' his friend grunted. 'The place doesn't agree with me.'

Drake frowned. Something about the inflection of his voice was familiar. It was an East Coast accent, perhaps

New York or New Jersey. He had heard a voice like that recently.

Suddenly wary, Drake surveyed the two men a little closer.

The man with the satchel was the taller and leaner of the two, with curling brown hair and a tanned, weather-beaten complexion. The cameraman was an inch or two shorter than his companion and heavyset, with dark hair receding on top.

Both were clean-shaven; surprisingly so, in fact. Their jawlines were a little lighter than the rest of their faces, as if they had recently sported heavy beard growth.

Like many journalists in this part of the world, they were both dressed in olive-coloured cargo trousers and walking boots. Satchel man sported a white T-shirt with a loose waistcoat covered with pockets and pouches – the sort of thing favoured by anglers who need to have lots of implements on hand.

And yet, looking closer, there didn't seem to be anything in any of the pouches. None of them bulged outwards as he might have expected if they were filled with technical gear.

Cameraman's loose grey shirt was stained with sweat. At first Drake had assumed that the camera's heavy weight was causing him to perspire, yet he seemed to be no stranger to heavy loads, and the hotel lobby had been kept cool by air conditioning.

Perhaps he had been running?

There was a certain smell coming from him as well. Not sweat or other bodily odours, but something else. Something rich and strong; something very familiar to a man like Drake who often worked long hours.

Coffee.

His clothes reeked of it, as if he had spilled a cup over himself.

'You mean the beer's warm and the women are ugly,' the cameraman said, snorting in amusement.

He was laughing, but when he glanced over at his companion, his eyes told a different story. They were cold, serious, focused. A look passed between the two men – fleeting and barely visible to most people, but plain as day to a man like Drake who had been trained to look for such visual cues.

At that moment, the cameraman reached down to adjust something on the big unit he was carrying, perhaps checking that nothing had come loose. As he did so, his shirtsleeve was pushed up just a little to expose a tattoo on his forearm.

A tattoo of a sword intersected by three lightning bolts.

In an instant, the pieces fell into place.

As if by unspoken, mutual consent, the two men sprang into action. The man with the satchel reached out and hit the emergency stop button, bringing the elevator shuddering to a halt.

At the same moment, the cameraman opened a port on the bulky television camera and yanked something from it; something small and plastic, with two metallic barbs protruding from the front. Its purpose served, he dropped the now useless camera and rounded on his target.

Another person might have been perplexed or even rooted to the spot by indecision in the face of such a sudden, unexpected attack, but Drake knew better. The moment he'd caught the knowing glance between the two men, he had sensed a takedown and immediately went into survival mode, his mind churning through a list of possible actions, their consequences and chances of success or failure.

How or why these men were trying to subdue him, or who they were working for, were all questions he could attend to later. In that moment when his survival hung in the balance, all that mattered was what he did.

His heart had begun to beat faster, his breathing to grow deeper as his lungs sucked in more air, adrenalin pumping through his veins investing his muscles with greater strength. The ancient instinct for fight or flight was in full swing now.

And with nowhere to retreat to, his only option was to fight.

The cameraman had removed a taser concealed within the unit, no doubt intending to use it on Drake. All he had to do was jab it into his chest, or indeed any part of his body where both prongs could make good contact, and depress the trigger. The unit would then discharge thousands of volts into him, overloading his nervous system and causing neuromuscular incapacitation, effectively dropping him.

Drake had seen such weapons before, and had even used them himself from time to time. There was no defence against their effects. No matter how strong or resilient the target might have been, they went down first time, every time.

Satchel man could wait. The taser was the biggest threat at that moment.

The world around him seemed to go into slow motion as Drake's hand shot out, seized the cameraman's arm by the wrist and yanked it forward, jabbing the weapon hard into the satchel man's right shoulder.

Before he could recover, Drake clamped down hard on his trigger finger.

There was a harsh, rapid clicking sound as the weapon discharged, followed immediately by an almost animalistic snarl of pain. In the enclosed space, Drake could smell an odd mixture of ozone and burned plastic. The satchel man went down like a dead body, the taser prongs slipping free of his flesh.

It didn't matter. He was out of the fight for the next thirty seconds or so.

His friend was another matter.

Drake still had the man's arm in a tight grip, but he needed to get the taser away from him, and fast. The best way, he knew from experience, was to take the arm out of play, and that meant breaking it.

The human arm is composed of three main bones – the humerus above the elbow, and the radius and ulna below. Thick and heavy enough to support the muscles attached to it, the humerus is difficult even for trained fighters to break.

The radius and ulna, however, are a much easier prospect. A sharp blow of sufficient force directed at the midpoint between the wrist and elbow, where the two bones are thinnest, will fracture or snap them altogether. Either result was fine with him.

Gripping his wrist with both hands, Drake forced his arm down and brought his knee up, preparing to use it as a lever on which to snap the bones of the man's forearm.

He never got the chance.

His opponent was no stranger to fighting. Sensing Drake's intentions, he swung with his left hand, catching Drake on the right side just below his ribcage. The blow felt like a sledgehammer driven into his stomach, and instinctively he began to buckle, his body trying to curl up to protect its vulnerable parts.

Locked in a desperate struggle for the taser, he was

unable to block or avoid the next blow. White light exploded through his brain as the cameraman's rock-like fist caught him flush on the jaw. Dazed, he staggered sideways, pulling his opponent with him and slamming into the wall of the cramped elevator with bruising force.

Stars were dancing across Drake's vision as he sank down on one knee, still somehow gripping the taser. Shaking his head, he glanced up at his opponent, knowing the next hit would put him down for good.

Sure enough, the cameraman was already drawing back his arm for another strike. His lips were curled in a vicious snarl, his eyes gleaming as he prepared to finish his enemy. The takedown might not have gone quite as he'd expected, but the end result would be the same.

And yet, despite his dominant position, he was standing awkwardly with his weight on his left side, his footing obstructed by the motionless form of his comrade now lying curled on the floor.

In a heartbeat, Drake had taken all of this in. Millions of tiny nerves and synapses lit up, comparing what he had seen with experiences, skills, training that had been drilled into him so many times they were as much a part of him as his instinct to breathe.

In another life, before his career in the military, he had been a boxer, and a good one at that. Most assumed it was because he was simply good at hitting people, but he knew otherwise. The fundamental skill of any fighter wasn't their ability to hit, it was their ability to avoid being hit. Dodging, weaving, ducking and blocking were vital skills he had spent years mastering, and though he had long since abandoned the sport, the hard-won ability remained imprinted on his brain.

While his opponent drew back his arm to deal the crippling blow, Drake waited. He waited until the left arm began to move forward, propelled by the combined efforts of the thick corded shoulder muscles. He waited until it had built up enough momentum to put it beyond the ability of its owner to stop, until it was past the point of no return.

And at the last moment he released his hold of the taser and ducked aside.

There was a hard metallic thump as a human hand impacted a solid wall at high speed, followed by a dull wet crunch as bones and joints snapped under the pressure.

The cameraman didn't cry out. It would take another second or so for the pain to reach his brain. All he managed was a confused grunt as his fist hit the elevator wall instead of his opponent's jaw.

Seizing his chance, Drake lowered his shoulder and launched himself off the wall, driving forwards with all the strength he could summon. He had never been much of a rugby player, but he at least understood the principles of tackling – get low and hit fast and hard.

He accomplished all three things at that moment. He felt the fleshy thump as his shoulder made contact with the cameraman's chest, and heard the grunt of pain as the air was driven from his lungs. Caught off balance, his adversary fell backward until his back crashed into the far wall with enough force to shatter the cheap wood veneer, sending shards of it tumbling to the floor.

'Fuck you!' Drake heard him scream, his voice tight with pain. Only now had he realised he'd just broken several bones in his left hand. 'Fuck you!'

An elbow struck him across the back, but it was a desperate and uncoordinated hit that lacked power, and his shoulder absorbed most of the impact.

Still, Drake wasn't about to let him have another go

335

with the taser. Rearing his head up like a bull, he caught the cameraman on the point of the chin, then leaned back as far as he could manage and butted him in the face. He was seeing stars again, but nonetheless felt the satisfying crunch as the bone and cartilage in the cameraman's nose gave way under the blow.

Drake had never had his nose broken, but he had seen the effects in others, both as a boxer and as an operative. He knew what a crippling injury it could be. At that moment, blood would be filling the cameraman's sinus cavity, choking him. His eyes would be blinded by involuntary tears.

At last Drake was in control of the fight. A kick to the back of the cameraman's leg dropped him to his knees, followed by a crushing right hook that finally put him down. The cameraman collapsed in a tangled heap, his blood pooling on the cheap grey carpet.

No sooner had he gone down than Drake heard a muted thump, and suddenly something hard and powerful slammed into his right side, spinning him around with the force of the impact.

With his back now against the wall and the first wave of pain radiating out from the gunshot wound, Drake found himself face to face with his attacker.

It was the satchel man. Incapacitated by the taser burst, he must have come round while Drake was occupied with his comrade, and had evidently recovered enough to yank something from his carry case.

An automatic pistol. Drake couldn't tell the model from this angle, but he recognised the metallic bulk of a suppressor screwed onto the barrel. Struggling to keep the bulky weapon level with hands that wouldn't quite cooperate with the instructions his brain was sending out, he was lining up the weapon for another shot.

He was a threat again. A threat that had to be dealt with.

Ignoring the pain, Drake rushed forward and slammed his boot down on the man's wrist, pinning his arm to the floor. There was another muted thud as a second round was discharged, this time burying itself in the wall.

There are times for restraint and compassion. This was not one of those times.

Keeping his opponent's arm pinned under his boot, Drake snatched the bulky television camera up from the floor. It had been dropped when the brief confrontation began and forgotten by all concerned during the frantic battle for survival.

Drake was surprised by the weight as he raised it over his head. It must have been 30 pounds or more of metal, glass, plastic and delicate internal electronics.

Hardly an efficient weapon, but with no alternative it would serve.

He saw no fear in his opponent's eyes as he brought the crude club down against him, no panic or shock or dismay. All he saw was simmering anger and disappointment. The look of a player who knows he has lost.

The impact of the camera against the satchel man's skull jarred Drake's arm and buckled the casing of the expensive device, sending fragments of shattered glass and plastic tinkling across the floor.

Dropping the heavy camera, Drake snatched up the satchel man's weapon. It was a Heckler & Koch USP Compact; a small but powerful handgun chambered with .45-calibre rounds. They were designed for Special Forces operations where both stopping power and concealment were priorities.

Its owner was no longer a threat. He was lying slumped

against the wall, his eyes staring blankly ahead, blood dripping from the deep gash on top of his head. The impact had crushed his skull, killing him more or less instantly.

Now his companion had to be dealt with. Already he was starting to come round, and Drake was in no condition to go toe to toe with him again. Staggering forward, he knelt in front of the cameraman and jammed the barrel of the pistol against his forehead.

Roused from his stupor, he stared at Drake for several seconds as if failing to comprehend what was happening.

'Who sent you?' Drake demanded, pushing the barrel harder. His finger was already tight on the trigger. 'I said, who sent you? Talk or die!'

'Fuck you,' his opponent hissed, snatching something up from the floor by his side.

A moment later, Drake felt the sting as two metal prongs were jammed into his neck. The taser, dropped during the fight. It must have come to rest within his enemy's reach.

Drake's reaction was immediate. With the gun still pressed against the cameraman's forehead, he pulled the trigger before the taser could discharge.

The round entered at high velocity, leaving a hole no larger than the projectile itself. However, the negative pressure wave created by its passage pulled most of the contents of his skull with it as it exited through the back, now slowed considerably by several inches of bone and brain matter.

As the dead man slumped sideways, leaving a wide crimson stain on the cheap wood veneer behind him, Drake collapsed against the wall of the elevator, gasping for breath, his heart hammering in his chest.

He was no stranger to killing, and felt no regret about

what he'd done. It was kill or be killed in that moment, and he had done what he had to do to stay alive.

What shocked him more was the knowledge that these men were both Horizon operatives. He had recognised the Airborne tattoo on the cameraman's forearm from the day at the crash site.

They worked for Horizon, and they had been sent here to take him down. The text message from Frost was a trap intended to lure him in. And if they had been ready to kill him, what had they done with her?

A growing pain on his right side, accompanied by a spreading, sticky warmth, reminded him that he had more immediate concerns. Pulling up his shirt and the T-shirt beneath, he exposed the light Kevlar vest he'd been wearing.

Even in Kabul he wasn't prepared to walk around unprotected, and had insisted the rest of his team do likewise while outside Bagram. The Kevlar vest wasn't strong enough to stop high-powered assault rifle rounds, but it had been enough to save his life today.

More or less. The vest might have stopped the bullet, but the force of the close-range impact had likely cracked a couple of ribs. He felt as though someone had hit his chest with a sledgehammer.

Undoing the Velcro straps holding it closed, he found himself with an area of discoloured, haemorrhaged skin about the size of his fist. By the looks of it, the round had just made it through the vest to punch a hole in his side, though it hadn't penetrated deep enough to cause any serious damage.

The bleeding was less than he'd feared. The pain was another matter.

Still, he was alive. That was the important thing right now. With no time or tools with which to treat the wound, he had no option but to strap the vest up tight and allow his shirt to fall back into place.

His priority was to find Frost and get out of here.

How he would accomplish that was more of a challenge. He was in an elevator with two blood-covered bodies, and himself bore the marks of his deadly confrontation. He couldn't expect to stroll out through the lobby uncontested.

Neither could he shoot his way out. The InterContinental was a well-protected hotel – there were security guards and Afghan police everywhere. He wouldn't make it 200 yards.

But one thing was certain; he had to do something quickly. The satchel man had pressed the emergency stop button, halting the elevator between floors. It wouldn't take long for the hotel management to work out there was a problem.

He looked up at the elevator controls. There were only four floors to choose from. A locked metal panel covered what he assumed were other buttons reserved for hotel staff only.

That was all the incentive he needed. Bringing the USP to bear, he took aim at the panel and squeezed off a round.

There was a heavy thump as the suppressor did its work, and a harsh bang as the lock disintegrated under the impact of a .45-calibre slug. Quickly shoving the weapon down the back of his trousers, Drake flipped open the panel to reveal three additional buttons.

The lowest was marked B, which he assumed meant the basement. It was a possibility, but the basement was likely to be a service area, perhaps even a kitchen. Either way, there was a good chance he would encounter hotel staff, and he was unfamiliar with the layout.

The second button was labelled INS, which he suspected was designed to put the elevator in some kind of inspection mode, probably for maintenance.

The last button was marked R, which had to mean roof access. It was far from perfect, but it seemed like his best – if only – viable option at that moment.

He pressed it. A moment later, the elevator shuddered into life as the winch went to work. He was on his way up.

Ten seconds later, the elevator doors slid open to reveal a dingy, bare brick room about 15 feet square. Metal access panels with red warning signs and electricity symbols were fixed against the far wall, the dull glow of their indicator lights providing just enough illumination to make out the shapes of toolboxes, wooden pallets and other discarded crap stacked in one corner.

The air smelled of oil and machinery and dust, reminding him for a moment of his father's old garage. He half-expected to see an E-Type Jaguar parked in the middle of the room, red paintwork gleaming in whatever light managed to filter in through cobwebbed windows.

No such vision presented itself, however, and his mind snapped back to reality an instant later. He was in the elevator winch house, which he guessed was visited only when there was a problem or when routine maintenance was required.

Off to the right, slivers of daylight strained through the tiny gaps around a steel door. Grimacing in pain, he picked up the broken camera once more and wedged it between the elevator doors to prevent them from closing.

With the elevator immobile, he turned his attention back to his attackers, quickly rifling through their pockets in search of anything useful. Unsurprisingly, neither man was carrying ID or cellphone. If they happened to get caught or killed, their employer wouldn't want anything that could be traced back to him.

However, he did find a couple of hundred dollars' worth of US currency in the cameraman's trouser pocket, which he wasn't too proud to help himself to.

This done, he picked up the fallen satchel, draping the strap over his left shoulder so that it covered the spreading bloodstain on his shirt. He clenched his teeth as the weight settled against the heavy bruising around the gunshot wound, but nonetheless managed to rise to his feet.

Armed with his meagre disguise, he exited the elevator and hurried over to the steel door that separated him from the outside world. It was locked. With no time to search for the key, he drew the silenced USP, levelled it at the lock and, turning his head away to avoid flying debris, squeezed off a round.

The high-powered slug tore through the thin, brittle sheet steel with ease, obliterating the lock.

Securing the weapon once more, Drake hauled open the door. Harsh, blinding light from the setting sun flooded his vision, almost forcing him to retreat into the cool darkness of the winch room. Shielding his eyes with one hand, he and advanced outside.

Situated as the InterContinental was on a hillside overlooking Kabul, the view from the top floor was impressive, its panoramic vista broken only by the squat bulk of the elevator winch house behind him.

But Drake had no time for sightseeing. His eyes quickly surveyed his immediate surroundings in search of a way down. It had to be at least a 50-foot drop to the ground below, removing jumping as an option unless he had a serious grudge against his own skeleton.

The roof itself was a flat open space the length of a

football pitch, liberally broken up by the weathered steel of air-conditioning outlets. In the heat of the Afghan summer, they must have been working overtime to keep the rooms cool.

However, he spotted something up ahead that might serve. A small inconspicuous structure, just white-painted breeze blocks, a flat roof and a single door leading down.

A fire escape.

Wasting no time, he sprinted across the 20 yards of open rooftop separating him from escape, doing his best to ignore the stabbing pain in his side and back.

The fire door, identical to the one sealing the winch house, was also locked, but a couple of shots from the USP were enough to take care of that.

Shoving the weapon down the back of his trousers, he descended the stairs, pulling the door shut behind him.

As he'd hoped, this was a communal stairwell for guests and staff to use. One floor down, and he saw signs directing him to rooms 401–425. Ignoring them, he continued down to the next level and eased the door open, glancing both ways.

The corridor was empty. Most of the guests, it seemed, were downstairs doing whatever journalists did at this time of day. Probably drinking.

With one hand gripping the pistol, he hurried along the corridor to room 322, with the old-fashioned laundry chute opposite. This time the housekeeping lady was nowhere to be seen.

His heart was beating wildly as he fished the key card from his pocket. Taking a deep breath, he swiped it through the reader.

There was a buzz, a click as the lock disengaged, and the light turned from red to green.

Drake had the door open in a heartbeat, weapon up

and ready, sweeping every corner of the room in search of a target.

There were none. No targets, no Frost. The room was empty. All her computer gear was gone. The only sign of a struggle was the coffee stain on the green carpet near the door.

The pain of the bullet wound was nothing to the ache of guilt and grief he now felt. He had left her here unprotected, and they had found her. He didn't know how they'd done it, but somehow Horizon had found her and taken her.

They must have traced her hacking attempt somehow.

She's gone because of you, you stupid arsehole. You should have been here. You should have been watching her back.

Drake shook his head, forcing himself to refocus. Thoughts like that could come later, and he was sure they would. For now, he had to act.

Reaching for his cellphone, he dialled McKnight's number, waiting while it rang out. To his dismay, it carried on ringing for some time until at last she picked up.

'Ryan?'

But the voice that answered wasn't Samantha's. It was male, deep and rough. It was a voice that belonged to Crawford.

'Where's Sam?' he asked.

'Ryan, listen, we've . . . got a situation here.'

'Put Sam on the line right now, Crawford.'

'You can talk to her when you come in.' There was a pause, just a brief one, but long enough for him to hear hushed voices in the background. Technicians trying to set up a phone trace. 'Where are you, Ryan?'

344

Drake had heard enough. Ending the call, he turned and snatched up the satchel once more.

He was being set up. Horizon had found out about their plan to hack their system and were retaliating, first by taking out Frost, then by having the rest of his team arrested. If Anya was right, and Carpenter and Cain were familiar with each other, then almost anyone in the Agency could be compromised.

He had to leave, now.

The idea that phone traces take thirty or even sixty seconds is another Hollywood fantasy. Sophisticated systems like the ones employed by the Agency could do the job in moments. More than likely, a strike team was already scrambling to intercept him.

Adjusting the satchel on his shoulder, he pulled the door open and hurried out into the corridor, pausing only a moment to drop the USP down the laundry chute. The weapon had been useful so far, but he would never get past security with it.

Hurrying down the corridor, he dialled another number on his cellphone. The phone was compromised now, but he had to risk it.

'Did it work?' Cunningham asked, answering the call straight away.

'Get out of there, Matt. We're burned,' Drake said, his voice low and urgent. 'They've got Frost. They tried to kill me.'

'Shit,' his friend hissed. 'You said it was foolproof. What happened?'

'I don't know.' Pushing open the stairwell door again, he took the stairs down, trying to ignore the flashes of pain that rocked him with each step. 'But two Horizon operatives just tried to take me down. Get out of there now.'

'And then what?' Cunningham demanded.

'Remember the place we met for coffee? Meet me there in an hour, and come alone. We'll talk.'

'Ryan, wai—'

Drake wasn't hearing him. He cut the call without saying anything else, pried open the plastic case and removed the battery.

Each step was growing more painful as the injury to his side made itself felt, but he forced himself onward, shoving his way through the set of double doors at the bottom and into a long corridor heading towards the lobby.

Without breaking stride, he pulled his cellphone from his pocket, ignoring the fact that it was powered down with the battery removed, and pressed it tight against his ear. Hopefully it would cover both the cut on his cheek and the fact that the phone wasn't switched on.

A group of four middle-aged men, their suits struggling to contain their voluminous beer guts, were ambling along the corridor towards him, each hauling a wheeled suitcase that they could easily have carried.

Drake waited until they were within earshot before launching into his performance.

'Well, it's just not good enough, Nigel,' he said, adopting his best public-school accent and trying to look as pissed off as he sounded. 'I was told someone would meet me at the airport, and they didn't. I was told there would be a car waiting and there wasn't. I've been in a bloody taxi round half of Kabul before I ended up in this dump. How am I supposed to submit my reports if I can't even get proper Internet access?'

The older men looked at him with a mixture of sympathy and irritation as he passed. No doubt they had been through similar shit themselves.

Drake didn't even glance at them, striding by as if he owned the place. He doubted he would win any Oscars for his performance, but playing the part of the disgruntled Englishman was enough to allay most people's suspicions. He might have been a loud, obnoxious asshole, but that was all they would remember about him. In their minds he was the kind of man one most often sought to avoid.

He went through the same act in the lobby, giving his imaginary friend Nigel an earful as he passed the tables of journalists and businessmen, most of whom didn't even look up from their coffees and laptops. They had heard self-important idiots spouting the same stuff a hundred times before, and certainly weren't impressed by it.

Even the security men at the doors wanted nothing to do with him, and he was able to breeze past without so much as a pat-down. They were there to ensure no one marched in wearing an explosive vest, not to take abuse from guests on the way out.

He kept the phone tight to his ear, carrying on a stream of complaints and abuse until the main building was at least 50 yards behind him. Then at last he dropped the act and quickened his pace, eager to put as much distance between himself and those two dead bodies as possible.

The exit from the InterContinental's plush landscaped grounds deposited Drake on the Qargha Road; a main drag running from west to east across town. However, east was one direction he certainly didn't want to go. The British embassy was scarcely half a mile distant, and like the Americans they were careful to keep a close watch on the roads and buildings around their compound.

Neither could he head west. The Kabul police training centre lay just beyond the hill on which the hotel sat.

When the two bodies were discovered, it wouldn't take the police long to spot him on CCTV footage and make the connection.

He suspected they wouldn't be sympathetic to his cause.

Instead, he headed north-west, towards a range of wind-scoured hills that rose up out of the urban clutter like a natural fortress of rock. Too steep and awkward to build on, they were more or less devoid of human habitation, which suited him just fine.

Anywhere was better than here.

Chapter 39

Richard Carpenter surveyed the packed press briefing room, standing tall and imposing behind a lectern with the Horizon company logo emblazoned on it. There was a microphone built into the stand, but several others had been hastily added by the news crews in attendance.

He was wearing a dark blue suit that looked as if it had just arrived from the tailors, his hair neatly combed, his back straight and his eyes framed by a pair of sleek reading glasses.

'Good evening,' he began, scanning the crowd with his piercing gaze before glancing down to read from a prepared statement. 'At approximately nineteen hundred hours local time last night, a team of operatives working for Horizon Defence took part in an operation to apprehend the terrorist leader Kourash Anwari. I can now confirm that this man, along with approximately a dozen armed insurgents who accompanied him, was killed in the resulting operation. There were no casualties amongst Horizon personnel. The exact details of this operation must, for obvious reasons, remain classified at this time. However, I can show you a number of pictures taken in the aftermath of the battle. Please be aware that these pictures are of a graphic nature.'

The projector screen behind Carpenter flickered into life, and a series of still images began to play, showing the interior of a house with dead bodies, weapons and computer gear strewn around. Close-up shots showed several men who had taken rounds to the head and torso, with the gory results clear to see.

Last of all, the images concentrated on Anwari himself. He was lying sprawled on his back, partly curled around a leather sofa he must have fallen over. By the looks of it, he had taken a couple of rounds to the chest. His eyes were wide and staring, seeing nothing, his expression blank.

Other shots followed, showing the dead face compared to some still images lifted from the hostage tapes, high-lighting key similarities in eye and facial structure, and also showing his hand with the missing fingers.

With the brief presentation over, the projector was powered down and attention switched back to Carpenter. 'We can confirm that this is the man responsible for the recent series of terrorist attacks against Coalition personnel, and the kidnapping and execution of the American hostage yesterday.

'We will of course be working with ISAF and the Department of Defense to guard against possible reprisal attacks in the coming days and weeks, but for now we believe that a major terrorist threat has been eliminated today, and another step taken in the road to peace in Afghanistan.

'This operation should serve as an example to everyone of what Horizon can accomplish – that we have the personnel, the expertise and the ability to neutralise high-level insurgent leaders while minimising civilian casualties. We stand ready to assist ISAF in any way necessary, and with the proper resources and mandate, I believe we can make a lasting difference to this country.'

Pausing for a moment, Carpenter removed his reading glasses and looked up at the gathered reporters.

'Our only regret is that this operation came too late to save the life of the American hostage executed yesterday.' He looked down, as if struggling to maintain his composure. 'As a former soldier myself, I know all too well how it feels to lose good people under my command. The thoughts and prayers of everyone at Horizon are with his family at this time. Thank you.'

No sooner had he finished speaking than a barrage of questions poured in from the assembled reporters.

'Does this mean you'll be expanding your operation here?'

'Are you trying to take over from the Coalition?'

'How were you able to track him down?'

Their questions were met with silence. Stepping down from the podium, Carpenter turned and walked away with solemn dignity. His every step was illuminated by countless camera flashes, but he paid them no heed.

However, there was one person in the room who wasn't eager to get his attention. With cameras flashing and voices clamouring around her, Anya watched in stony silence. She had listened to Carpenter's impassioned speech and noble sentiments with absolute disgust, knowing full well how hollow his words were.

You're a fine actor, Richard, she thought as he walked away, vanishing through a side door with a couple of Horizon officials flanking him. He had played the part of the solemn, dignified leader perfectly. A seasoned old warrior, a decorated soldier stepping into the breach once more to serve his country.

The media would be eating out of his hands.

Only she knew him for who he really was.

Chapter 40

Both McKnight and Keegan looked up when the door opened and Crawford strode into the conference room. The expression on his lean, tanned face was hard to read, but it was obvious he hadn't come with good news.

Two security agents hovered by the door, keeping their side arms to hand in case anyone made a move. After their earlier run-in with Keegan, they were taking no chances.

'What the hell is going on?' McKnight demanded, gesturing to the TV screen.

Only minutes earlier, the news anchor had switched from her recap of Anwari's death and the Horizon press conference to a breaking story about the murder of two journalists at the InterContinental hotel in central Kabul. Even CNN seemed to grasp the significance of the murders, and already theories of Taliban reprisal attacks were being thrown around.

'Does this have something to do with Ryan?'

The older man stared at the screen for several seconds. 'When does it *not* have something to do with him? Boy's been a pain in my ass since he got here.'

McKnight felt her stomach knot. 'What happened?'

'You tell me, McKnight.'

'I don't know what you mean.' She could feel her throat tightening, her heart beating faster under his intense stare.

'Bullshit you don't,' he snapped, advancing on her. 'We pulled the hotel security footage. A few hours ago Drake and Frost checked into a room together, and somehow I doubt it was for an afternoon fuck. He leaves, comes back and takes an elevator ride with two guys, neither of whom survives the trip. Then straight after he tries to put a call through to *your* cellphone.'

Reaching into his pocket, he held up her phone for emphasis, glaring at her with barely suppressed anger. 'So don't give me any more crap. People are dying because of this. I want to know what the fuck's going on, right now.'

'What about Keira?' Keegan asked, rising to his feet. The look in his eyes made it plain what he was feeling. 'What happened to her?'

'She's gone,' Crawford said coldly, watching his reaction. 'We found signs of a struggle in their room, but no Frost. And the security cameras didn't show her leaving. We're doing a floor-by-floor search of the hotel but I doubt we'll find her there. It seems that the same guys who tried to take out Drake got to her first.'

Keegan's tanned, weather-beaten face paled at this revelation. 'Oh, Christ . . .'

Crawford ignored him, concentrating his attention on McKnight. 'No more games. You want a way out of this, tell me what they were doing at that hotel. Let me help you.'

McKnight stared back at him, surprised by the conviction in his eyes. 'Why should I believe you?'

To her surprise, the hard, intense gaze softened a little. 'I've been with the Agency going on twenty years. I've seen plenty of good people get screwed over. I even made it happen once or twice myself, and I can feel it happening again.' He shook his head. 'No more. I'm too old and too ugly for another hatchet job.'

Samantha was torn. She wanted to believe him but was reluctant to say anything that could compromise Drake and Frost. And yet, the thought of sitting here doing nothing while their comrades risked their lives was more than she could stand.

'They were trying to hack into Horizon's computer network,' she said at last.

Crawford's eyes opened wider. 'Why?'

'Because we think Horizon stole the Stinger that shot down Mitchell's chopper. When we started to uncover the truth, they panicked and tried to destroy the evidence.'

'This is insane.' He gestured to the television, where footage of Horizon's press conference was playing. 'These are the guys who saved Drake's ass yesterday, and *mine*. They just took out Mitchell's killers, for Christ's sake.'

'Come on, Crawford. Can't you see what's happening here?' Keegan cut in. 'Mitchell's execution tape gets released just when we're starting to make a link between Horizon and the Stinger attack. Then the man behind the killing conveniently shows up dead and Horizon claims credit for the whole thing. Drake tries to find the truth, and suddenly we're under arrest and he's wanted for murder.'

'For good reason,' Crawford hit back. 'I saw the security footage. Drake got in that elevator with those two men. He killed them.'

'Bullshit,' Keegan said, refusing to yield. 'Ryan ain't no murderer. If he did kill those guys, he must have had good reason.'

'Then I'd love to hear it. ISAF have issued a warrant for his arrest. Local police, ANA, even the military have been ordered to take him down on sight.'

'Jesus Christ, you might as well have painted a target

on his head,' the sniper exclaimed. 'The ANA would just as soon kill him as arrest him.'

Afghan security forces had a reputation, deserved or not, for shooting first and asking questions later. If they had been ordered to take down an armed and dangerous man wanted for a double homicide, they were unlikely to take chances.

Crawford was silent, chewing his lip as he stared at the news footage.

McKnight took a step towards him. 'Tell me you don't believe us.'

The veteran agent had no answer for her.

'Then help us put a stop to this. Before it's too late.'

'Say I do believe you,' he said at last. 'What would you have me do?'

She only had one card to play, and now was the time. 'Let us bring Drake in. Someone was willing to kill to silence him – surely that's got to mean something.'

The section leader's expression was glacial as he weighed up everything he'd heard. Samantha said nothing further; she had stated her case as best she could already. To repeat herself would risk alienating him. All she could do was wait.

'All right, fuck it,' Crawford said at last. 'But if this happens, it happens my way. You work under my command, you report direct to me and no one else. If you fail, I'm not responsible for it. If you find something, then I alone decide what to do with it. Are we absolutely clear on that?'

Relief flooded through her. 'Crystal.'

If they found something on Carpenter, she would make sure it got to people who could do something with it, even if she had to turn to the news media.

He nodded. 'Good. My orders were to get you on the

next flight out of here, which leaves in . . .' Crawford glanced at his watch. 'Less than four hours. So I suggest we get to work.'

Carpenter was feeling exhilarated as his four-vehicle convoy threaded its way through Kabul's streets on the way back from his press briefing. He took a sip of Scotch, leaning back in his seat as his driver manoeuvred them through an ANP checkpoint.

Already he had taken calls from half a dozen senior military and PMC leaders congratulating him on taking down Anwari, many hinting that his expertise would be much sought after in the near future. If Horizon had been a publicly traded company, he imagined their stock would be soaring at that moment.

However, there was one phone call he hadn't received yet. And when it finally came, his good mood evaporated in an instant.

'What's the situation?' Carpenter asked, eager to hear that Drake had been successfully neutralised.

'Walker and Forrest are dead.' Vermaak's voice betrayed no emotion as he announced the deaths of two of his comrades. 'Drake killed them and got away. Local police are all over it.'

It took great effort for Carpenter to resist his first instinct, which was to slam his fist down and berate his subordinate for letting Drake slip away.

'Explain to me how this happened,' he said instead, his voice icy calm.

'It seems we underestimated Drake. The little shit's tougher than he looks.'

'And now he knows we're onto him,' Carpenter reminded him. 'You just blew our best chance at taking him down.'

Vermaak said nothing, which was a wise move on his part, Carpenter reflected. Despite his failure, Vermaak knew how much his services were worth. More than that, he knew Carpenter couldn't afford to lose his loyalty, or silence.

'Take every man you can spare,' Carpenter ordered. 'Even the security teams from our compound. Set up roving patrols around the city, alert all of our intelligence assets to be on the lookout for him, and have strike teams set up and ready to move in the moment we have a confirmed sighting. I want him dead or in our hands by this time tomorrow, no matter what the cost. Understand?'

'Perfectly.'

'Good. Then get to work.'

'And the girl?' Vermaak asked. 'What should we do with her?'

Carpenter drained the remainder of his glassful in one gulp. Drake's companion was waiting for him back at Horizon headquarters.

'I'll deal with her,' Carpenter assured him. 'You just find Drake.'

Chapter 41

Cutting off the main drag into the maze of side streets and back alleyways, Drake was careful to maintain awareness of his surroundings and the people who inhabited them. This was not a pro-Western, affluent neighbourhood, but a shitty slum area on the edge of town.

There was no logical pattern to the street layout. Each building looked as though it had been thrown up with no consideration of how it would fit into a larger whole, and certainly little regard for normal construction standards. Apartment blocks crowded in close on the narrow roads, virtually blocking out the sun, many still bearing the marks of past conflicts.

The sewage system here was either broken or non-existent judging by the smell, while garbage was disposed off in refuse piles down back alleys. The drone of buzzing flies almost matched that of the traffic grinding along on the main drags, spewing dust and exhaust fumes.

Drake could feel eyes on him everywhere. Kids playing together had stopped what they were doing to watch him, while a group of old women, as bent and gnarled as old trees, looked up from their washing as he hurried past, their dark eyes surveying him but giving nothing away.

A tall, thin young man with the scraggly beginnings

of a beard brushed past him, bumping the satchel which in turn felt like a baseball bat hammering against the tender bruising on his right side. Stifling a groan of pain, Drake pushed on without looking around.

He didn't blame the poor bastards who lived here for being hostile. When the Western world had finally arrived in Afghanistan seven years earlier, it must have seemed like the coming of dawn after two decades of darkness. Now, all these years later, old women still washed clothes by hand in muddy water, people still struggled to survive in dilapidated apartment blocks while shit floated by in the street outside.

After picking his way through the chaos of Kabul's western fringe, he at last emerged into an area of flat open ground at the foot of the barren windswept hills he'd seen from the hotel. Off to his right, a row of gas towers reared into the sky, part of some kind of storage facility, but ahead of him lay nothing but brush and rock.

He was gasping for breath and sweating profusely when he finally sat down in a shallow depression filled with wind-blown garbage, gratefully discarding the satchel.

Unbuttoning his shirt and gripping the Kevlar vest, he pulled it aside to examine his injury, wincing as the movement tore away the tentative scab that had begun to form. Fresh blood welled up and began to seep down his side.

He had to do something about it. Hot countries like this were a nightmare for infections, with even minor wounds often turning into pus-filled mounds within hours if left untreated.

Hospitals were out of the question. Hospitals asked questions, filed reports, made phone calls. If Horizon were able to ambush him at the hotel, it wouldn't be difficult to track him down there.

Instead he flipped open the satchel, searching for anything useful.

There wasn't much; this was no medical kit. In fact, it wasn't much of an equipment bag either. The main compartment had been stuffed with a couple of bottles of water to pad it out a little, with only the outer pouches holding technical gear to create the facade of a toolkit.

Removing his shirt, T-shirt and finally the Kevlar vest, he laid them aside, unscrewed one of the water bottles and took a swig, then poured some on the wound.

His bruised and torn flesh protested, but he did his best to ignore it as he rifled through the remaining pouches. Battery packs, cables and spare microphone units might have been essential tools of the trade for any film crew, but for him they were dead weight that he was happy to toss aside.

However, he paused in his search when he uncovered a plastic squeeze bottle of lens-cleaning fluid, still half full. A quick check of the ingredients confirmed his suspicion that it was essentially pure alcohol.

Bracing himself, he flipped it open and sprayed a liberal dose onto the wound.

Whatever stinging or irritation he'd expected from such an action simply hadn't prepared him for the explosion of pain that assailed him the moment the alcohol solution came in contact with the open wound.

His body went rigid, muscles locked, jaw clenched as a silent cry of pain strained to break free. For a good ten seconds he could say and do nothing as he lay crouched in that shallow depression waiting for the pain to subside.

When it finally did, he unclenched his hands and let out a breath he hadn't even realised he'd been holding.

Whatever bacteria might have found their way into the wound, he was quite certain they were well and truly dead after that.

What he needed now was something to bind it. He would have loved a suture kit and a sterile medical dressing, but in this case he was going to have to make do with a roll of grey duct tape.

After giving the wound one final wipe-down with his shirt, he tossed the bloodstained garment aside, tore off a long strip of tape and quickly pressed it against the injury before the bleeding could start again. Another couple of pieces laid on top of the first strip at right angles left him with a solid, flexible dressing that should be enough to prevent both blood loss and infection.

Removing it would not be a pleasant task, but that was a problem to be attended to later. For now, he could move and walk, and he would have to do both soon enough.

Emptying the remainder of his bottle of water on his bloodstained T-shirt, he did his best to rinse away the blood, even smearing dirt on it to disguise the telltale stain. The result was a garment that looked as if it hadn't been washed for several weeks, but that was good enough for him. If nothing else, he would blend into this neighbourhood a little better.

It was time for an honest assessment of the situation.

Whether he wanted it or not, he was on the run with few resources and nowhere to turn. Horizon were clearly out to take him down, and if he didn't find a way to put an end to this, they might well succeed. His own team had been compromised or captured, so he could expect no help from that quarter.

He tried not to think about Frost and what they might

have done with her. He had to believe they wouldn't have killed her outright, otherwise why abduct her from the room? She was alive, perhaps taken in for interrogation. They would want to know what she had found, who she had shared it with.

He had time still. Time to find her, time to save her life.

He had to believe that.

Spurred into action, he planted his feet firmly on the dusty ground and forced himself up. He was tired and hurting, but he couldn't afford to give in to either of those things now.

When Carpenter learned of the failed takedown, he would come after Drake with everything he had. His only chance was to beat him to the punch.

Somehow he had to find the evidence that Mitchell had amassed.

Chapter 42

Inter-Continental Hotel, Kabul

'Someone talk to me. What do we have so far?' Crawford said, striding across the hotel roof with Keegan and McKnight flanking him, and a couple of security agents close behind. With the elevators out of service, they had ascended via the fire escape, and all three were out of breath after the hard climb.

There were Afghan police everywhere, but the Agency had their own presence amidst the organised chaos. In this case, a tall, well-built man with greying hair named Faulkner, the leader of the security team sent to apprehend Drake.

'Both bodies are still in the elevator,' he reported, falling into step beside him. 'Both male Caucasians in their mid-forties. One died from gunshot wounds, the other had his head caved in.'

'Have we ID'd them yet?' Crawford asked.

He shook his head. 'Your guess is as good as mine, sir. This place is a goddamned zoo, and the Keystone Cops over there aren't making things any better,' he added, gesturing to several Afghan National Police officers who seemed to be arguing over who was in charge.

Still, they had at least managed to cordon off the scene.

Making their way past the ANP guards with no small amount of badge-waving, Crawford and his companions were at last able to enter the winch house.

As described, two men lay dead inside the metal box, with clear evidence of a violent confrontation. The wall panelling was broken in places, a television camera lay wrecked on the floor, and both men had certainly been killed in brutal fashion. One had died from a gunshot wound to the head, while the other seemed to have been beaten to death by a blunt, heavy object, probably the camera.

'Quite a mess,' Crawford remarked as he surveyed the elevator, unconcerned by the two dead men inside. He had witnessed many such scenes before.

McKnight picked her way through the debris and knelt down to examine the man with the gunshot wounds. He was dressed as a camera operator, but it was clear that wasn't his true profession. His body was too muscular, his face too hardened, his hands calloused and marked by small scars.

Noticing a mark on his forearm, she reached into her pocket for a pen and used it to raise his shirtsleeve a little, allowing her a better look.

The tattoo marking his tanned skin confirmed her suspicions.

'This man was military,' she said, allowing the shirt to fall back into place as she glanced up at Crawford. 'Special Forces judging by the tattoo, and I'll bet it's the same story for his friend over there. What are the chances of two guys like that sharing an elevator with a guy like Drake?'

Crawford said nothing. There was no need.

'So, they were either here to meet him or to take him down,' she concluded.

His dark eyes swept the elevator again. 'I'm guessing the latter, given how they both ended up.'

'The question is, who sent them?' Crawford chewed his lip for a moment. 'Get their prints over to the Pentagon as soon as you can. If these two were military, I want to know everything about them, especially what they were doing here.'

They were interrupted by Keegan, who was standing near the door inspecting a tray of evidence already recovered. 'Hey, come take a look at this.'

Crawford hurried over. 'What you got?'

The sniper held up a plastic evidence bag. Inside were four empty shell casings. 'Four shots were fired in there. One went into the wall – probably a negligent discharge in the struggle – one was used to blow open the access panel for the roof, and the third went in our friend's head.'

Crawford frowned. 'Your point?'

'My point is we're missing a bullet.'

McKnight saw where he was going, her eyes reflecting the pain and worry she now felt. 'Ryan took a hit.'

'That'd be my guess,' Keegan confirmed.

'If he was hit, he might have gone somewhere for treatment,' Crawford concluded. 'Faulkner, get over here.'

The big field agent was by his side within moments. He didn't say anything; just waited for instructions. It seemed he wasn't big on small talk.

'Notify all hospitals and medical clinics in the area to be on the lookout for a man matching Drake's description,' he began. 'He'll likely have a gunshot wound.'

'No problem.'

'And you'd better draw up a list of all doctors,

pharmacies and vets within the city limits. Have agents or local police check them for signs of break-ins. Move.'

As Faulkner hurried off, Keegan stepped forward to speak to Crawford. 'I want to take a look at the room, see what happened down there.'

Crawford nodded. 'Okay. Go.'

Keira Frost was hanging several inches off the ground, her bound hands looped into a metal hook fixed into the ceiling. How long she had been suspended like that, she couldn't remember, but it had to be at least an hour. The pressure on her shoulders was slowly building, pain flowing outwards from the joints in waves, yet she remained stubbornly silent.

That wasn't the only pain she felt. Bruises marked her face and body where her captors had laid into her with fists and boots, beating her into submission when she fought back. One or two had even taken a free shot when she was bound and suspended from the ceiling, unable to do anything but scream obscenities back at them.

And yet she was alive. Whatever they wanted, it wasn't to kill her. Not yet.

She could hear footsteps in the corridor outside. Moments later, the deadbolt holding her cell door closed was withdrawn and the door swung open to reveal a tall, craggy-faced man who she recognised immediately as Carpenter.

He was followed by three Horizon operatives, one of whom was carrying a bucket of water.

'Keira Frost,' he said, slowly circling her. 'You've been causing a lot of trouble for my people. I assume you know computer hacking is a crime?'

'Fuck you,' she spat, glaring at him as he circled around

in front of her again. 'Spare me the James Bond villain routine, because I ain't giving you shit.'

His response was no pithy verbal comeback, but rather a fist driven into her exposed solar plexus with a strength that belied his age, knocking the air from her lungs. Coughing and trying desperately to curl up into a ball, Frost couldn't even scream back at him.

'I think you will,' Carpenter said, then glanced at his subordinates. 'Strap her down.'

Still struggling for air, Frost was powerless to stop them as they lifted her down from the hook and laid her out on the steel-framed bed that sat off to one side. She tried to struggle free, but both men were far larger and stronger than her. In under ten seconds they had secured her hands and feet to the posts, making further movement impossible.

Carpenter stood over her with his arms folded. 'Last chance.'

Frost said nothing. Instead she arced her head back as far as her situation would allow and spat at him.

'I was hoping you'd say that,' he said, giving the man beside him a nod.

A moment later, Frost's world went dark as a towel was placed over her face, held down hard on either side so that her head was pinned against the bed, unable to move. She braced herself, knowing what was coming.

The moment the third man started to empty his bucket of water onto the towel, she felt it. She could close her mouth and hold her breath, but there was nothing to stop the water trickling down her nasal passages and into her lungs, inducing an immediate urge to gag and choke.

Straight away her heartbeat skyrocketed, her body

rebelling instinctively against the feeling that it was drowning, yet still she remained silent, holding her breath, trying to keep herself under control.

She lasted about twenty seconds before panic set in. She bucked and kicked with desperate strength, the bonds cutting into her wrists and ankles until they bled, but still she found no escape. The cloth was held down even harder, forcing her head back, and all the while the steady deluge continued.

She could hold her breath no longer. Letting out an explosive gasp, her lungs greedily tried to suck in more air only to be met with an influx of water.

Now there was no stopping it. Coughing and screaming, she thrashed wildly, pain building in her brain as her body desperately sought oxygen. She was going to die. She knew it. They would just keep on pouring the water until her struggles eased, as darkness overcame her.

She was going to die here.

Then, finally, the flow of water stopped and the cloth was withdrawn. Sucking in what little air she could, Frost coughed and choked violently, expelling a mixture of water and bile. Tears were streaming from her eyes, hidden only by the soaking she had received.

'You know it was the Spanish Inquisition who first invented this technique?' Carpenter said, watching her struggles with satisfaction. 'Old tricks are the best tricks, huh? We can just keep doing this all day long. Feel like talking now?'

At least regaining some semblance of self-control, Frost glared at him with absolute hatred. 'You piece of shit! Fuck—'

She was silenced when the cloth was placed over her head and the agony started again.

* * *

The hotel room was, as Keegan had expected, bland and impersonal, with cheap furniture and mass-produced pictures adorning the olive-green walls. Still, the decor was of no concern to him as he knelt down near the centre of the room to survey the scene.

The evidence of a struggle was plain to see. A broken coffee urn lay on the floor, pieces of shattered glass all around it. It had clearly been flung with some force, perhaps used as an improvised weapon. The sort of thing a young woman would resort to when taking on a pair of far larger and stronger assailants.

He felt a sudden pang of guilt for not insisting on accompanying her, but quickly forced it down. Guilt could come later. Action and logical thought were needed now.

Looking closer at the coffee stain, he saw other marks on the carpet nearby. Whoever had attacked her must have walked through it, leaving foot prints behind. Judging by the size and depth of the prints, he guessed a pair of size 11 boots, their owner weighing well over 200 pounds.

And for a moment he was reminded of the prints he had seen out at the crash site. Same size, same weight, same height. In fact, about the same as one of the men lying dead in the elevator on the roof.

He rose slowly to his feet, glancing back towards the door.

If Frost's attackers hadn't killed her here, which he was assuming they hadn't, then they must have found a way to get her out of the hotel. But how? The stairwells were fitted with security cameras, as was the main lobby. They couldn't have jumped from a window; someone would undoubtedly have seen them.

Carefully stepping over the coffee stains, he moved

out into the corridor beyond. A couple of Agency security operatives had accompanied him in case he had any mad ideas about running away, though both men were under orders not to impede his work, and moved aside to let him through.

They must have brought Frost out here, Keegan thought as he looked around, but where then? A man carrying an unconscious woman would have been seen by someone. They couldn't have allowed themselves to be exposed for long.

'Keira, what the hell did they do with you?'

Frowning, he looked around as if seeking inspiration.

Then, just like that, his eyes came to rest on the laundry chute opposite.

Chapter 43

CIA Training Facility 'Camp Peary', Virginia,
27 November 1985

Thirty-five, thirty-six, thirty-seven . . .

Once again Anya found herself on that same muddy training field in the middle of the night, enduring the same grim exercise regime, feeling the rain hammering down on her while Carpenter strode amongst the ranks of recruits, safely protected from rain by an oilskin cape.

'I will endure when all others fail!' he yelled, repeating the mantra that had been drilled into them from the moment they had arrived here. 'I will stand when all others retreat!'

He always chose to push them hardest when the weather was bad, and she had learned that it frequently was in Virginia at this time of year.

Thirty-nine, forty . . . Come on, almost there.

'Weakness will not be in my heart! Fear will not be in my creed!'

She had thrown herself into her training with renewed vigour over the past week, refusing to break, refusing to submit. The old fire of defiance that had kept her alive as an adolescent, fighting to survive in prison, was burning inside her again. It was a test, Luka had told her. A test that she would pass.

Ignoring the pain in her arms and shoulders, she kept going,

371

pushing herself up from the ground and lowering herself down again and again.

Forty-three, forty-four . . .

'I will show no mercy! I will never hesitate!' Carpenter halted in front of her. She could see his muddy boots through her rain-blurred eyes. 'Recruit Thirteen, what's the last promise you made to me?'

'I will never surrender, sir!' she yelled, forcing the words from her throat even when it seemed she had no breath left in her lungs.

Forty-seven . . .

She was slowing down as her body reached the limits of its endurance.

She saw him kneel down in front of her, saw his eyes watching her movements, saw the the knife he always kept sheathed at his waist. 'I can't hear you, Recruit.'

Forty-eight . . .

'I will never surrender!'

Forty-nine . . .

For a moment she faltered, her strength wavering, her resolve failing in the face of utter exhaustion.

Anya's head rose up, her eyes locking with Carpenter's, burning into them with hatred and anger and defiance. *You won't beat me, you bastard. You can't beat me because I'm stronger than you.*

With a final effort of sheer will she forced her arms to extend one last time.

Fifty.

She had done it! Relief and exhilaration surged through her veins. She had done what had been asked of her, and even he couldn't take that away.

She saw a flicker of a smile on his face as he stood up.

'Well done, Recruit,' he said. 'Now get up.'

* * *

Like many such buildings in central Kabul, the office block was still under construction, with the top two floors nothing more than big open spaces littered with building materials. Power tools, electrical wiring, air-conditioning ducts and plumbing fixtures were everywhere, the work crews having finished up for the day.

The air smelled of new plastic and sawdust.

In the midst of it all sat Anya, as motionless as a statue, her eyes glued to a pair of high-powered binoculars as she surveyed the desert landscape beyond the construction site. The sun was already dipping towards the western horizon, glowing like fire through the wind-blown dust and tingeing the high thin clouds scarlet with its dying rays.

To a casual observer she might have appeared oblivious to her surroundings, all her attention focused on what she was seeing.

The reality couldn't have been further from the truth. Though her eyes were occupied, her other senses were painfully alert, constantly relaying information to her conscious mind about even slight changes in her environment. If a human body approached, she would smell the scent of sweat or cologne in the air. The slightest echo of a footstep on the bare concrete floor would bring a swift and deadly response.

Her only weapon was an M1911 semi-automatic holstered against her left thigh. Of all the weapons she had used over the years, she had yet to find a more effective and reliable side arm than the venerable Colt .45. It had served through two world wars, through Korea and Vietnam, through the Gulf and countless other conflicts before and after. Nearly a century after its introduction, it remained a deadly weapon in the right hands.

It was hot in the half-built office. The dry dusty air irritated her throat, a faint sheen of sweat forming on her brow. Her lower back was starting to stiffen up from holding the same position so long, and even the muscles in her arms were aching from supporting the heavy binoculars.

She ignored it all. She had long since trained herself to put aside discomfort, to disregard pain and fatigue. None of those things were important. Survival was what counted.

The object of her preoccupation sat about a mile distant, protected by perimeter fences, watchtowers, bastions of brick and concrete and razor wire. It was a fortress, old and scarred by past conflicts, but tall and indomitable, able to withstand almost any attack.

The Horizon headquarters building.

For a moment her magnified gaze strayed to the building's upper floor, to the big floor-to-ceiling armoured windows that marked the boundary of Carpenter's world. Such vanity, to have insisted on such a feature. Only a man like him would have desired it, to stand behind them with the world laid out below, as remote and invincible as a god.

She wondered if he was standing there at that very moment, gazing out across the city. Even Carpenter wasn't stupid enough to permit people an insight into his private domain; the windows were mirrored, showing nothing but a volcanic sunset and distant, indistinct mountains.

In any case, her attention soon turned downward, towards the compound's main gate. She watched as the armoured barricade swung open and, in a cloud of dust and exhaust fumes, a column of four armoured vehicles rolled out, bristling with weapons and Horizon operatives. The convoy picked up pace once clear of the gate, swinging north-east to head deeper into Kabul.

It was a third such sortie in the past fifteen minutes. Whatever operation they were mounting, they looked to be throwing all of their available manpower and resources at it.

Her contemplation was interrupted when she felt something buzzing in her pocket. She didn't need to look at the phone to know who was calling. Only one man on earth knew this number.

Without taking her eyes off the target, she enabled the Bluetooth earpiece she was wearing and hit the receive-call button on the phone.

'What have you found, Ryan?' she asked, her voice calm and controlled. Whatever she was feeling inside, she had long ago learned to suppress it when communicating during operations.

'It's fucked,' the man replied bluntly. 'They were able to trace the virus back to its source. I don't know how, but they did it. Two Horizon hit men tried to take me out when I returned from our meeting.'

Anya's heartbeat stepped up a notch. There was pain in his voice. He was trying to hide it, but to her it was as plain as day. He was hurt.

She felt a momentary surge of concern but angrily pushed it away. His welfare was no one's responsibility but his own.

'What's your situation?' she asked, forcing herself to be cold and clinical.

'I'm safe for now, but Frost isn't. They got to her while I was with you.'

Again she detected pain in his voice, but of a different kind. One unrelated to physical ailments, but real all the same. The loss of the young woman had shaken him profoundly. He couldn't hide it.

She wondered for a moment if he would feel the same pain for her.

'They are mobilising their forces for a big operation,' she said, switching to something she was more comfortable talking about. 'I would guess they are searching for you.'

'They're not the only ones,' he added. 'My team's been detained. We must have got too close – Cain and Carpenter are trying to take us out.'

For a moment, Anya closed her eyes, mastering the emotions that vied for dominance within her. She couldn't allow attachment and personal feelings to get in the way, she told herself. She had to be cold, clinical, logical.

Drake had become a liability. A liability she could no longer afford.

'Go home, Drake,' she said at last.

'What?'

'I said go home.' She was doing the right thing, she knew. The only thing that would keep him alive. 'Find the nearest ISAF patrol and turn yourself in. You can do nothing more here – you would not last a day with Horizon and the Agency hunting you.'

Silence greeted her for several seconds. He was beginning to realise she was cutting him loose, abandoning him like dead weight. 'I thought we were supposed to be working together.'

Her grip on the binoculars tightened. 'We agreed to cooperate. There is a difference.'

'I can't leave. This isn't over yet.'

'It is for you.'

'And what about you?'

Anya said nothing to that. Her eyes were still on the Horizon compound.

A fortress; huge, strong, indomitable. But a fortress now lightly guarded.

Reaching into her pocket, she pulled the cellphone out, dropped it on the ground and stamped on it.

Chapter 44

'Fuck,' Drake growled, killing the phone.

Anya had pulled the plug. Now that he was no longer useful, she was cutting him loose like the dead weight he'd become. He should have seen it coming. In truth, what else had he expected? Anya was a survivor, not a charity.

And in some part of his mind he knew she was right to feel that way. He had let her down, just as he had let down Frost and the rest of his team.

No. He couldn't allow himself to entertain those thoughts. Not now. He could still make this right.

Pocketing the phone, he glanced out onto the road from the alleyway he'd taken position in. The sun was already slanting down towards the western horizon, casting long shadows across the streets and buildings of central Kabul. A little further down the busy main road lay the coffee house where he and Cunningham had sat only this morning. It felt like a lifetime ago now.

No way was he waiting there for Cunningham to show up. There was always a chance his friend would have brought someone with him, or been tailed here. Drake wasn't going to make a move until he was sure Cunningham had come alone.

He had used some of the money stolen from the cameraman to purchase a pair of sunglasses and a fake suede jacket at the nearest street market. It was hardly sophisticated, but it was enough to hide his stained T-shirt and the cut on his cheek.

He'd also helped himself to a couple of packets of painkillers. At 5 cents per packet, their quality was dubious at best, but he needed something to take the edge off. His ribs were throbbing, each breath bringing another stab of pain.

At last he spotted Cunningham hurrying towards the restaurant on the other side of the road. He watched his friend closely as he halted outside. Like Drake, he was dressed in civilian clothes, but he didn't doubt the man was armed.

He was glancing around now, looking for Drake but trying to be subtle about it. If Drake saw him make eye contact with anyone nearby, or glance upward to one of the windows overlooking the street, he would bail without a second thought.

He did no such thing. Neither could Drake see any people or cars in the immediate vicinity holding position for no good reason. There were no furtive glances, no subtle hand movements that might indicate the use of discreet radio transmitters, no men or women turning their heads slightly to speak into their collars.

Of course, it was a busy street with dozens of civilians coming and going, and therefore impossible to keep track of everyone. There was always an element of risk to meetings like this. Training and observation were useful tools, but ultimately one just had to go with gut instinct.

Fuck it, he decided, emerging from the shadows. He managed to keep the pain hidden from his face as the gunshot wound protested at the movement. Maybe those painkillers weren't such a bargain after all.

Cunningham spotted him as he was crossing the street,

though he was careful to keep his expression neutral. Saying nothing, he hurried forward and met Drake on the sidewalk.

'Not here,' he said quietly, steering Drake down a side street that was too narrow for cars to pass through.

Drake wasn't about to argue. He didn't want to be on the main drag any longer than necessary. If Horizon were after him they would almost certainly have men patrolling the city's main thoroughfares.

'Talk to me,' his friend said, low and urgent. 'What the fuck happened?'

'I don't know,' Drake admitted.

It happened fast. Clapping a hand on his shoulder, Cunningham yanked him backwards, spun him around and drove him into a breeze-block wall.

As waves of pain washed over him, Cunningham grabbed him by the jacket and leaned in close. 'You don't know?' he said through gritted teeth, his face just inches from Drake's. 'I risked everything for you, you fucking prick! "I don't know" isn't fucking good enough!'

Those painkillers still weren't doing their job, but Drake had recovered enough to bat his friend's hand away, his green eyes blazing with anger.

'Maybe I should ask you the same question, Matt,' he hit back. 'You're the one who planted the virus. How do I know you didn't fuck it up intentionally? For that matter, how do I know you haven't called your Horizon mates to come and lift me?'

This seemed to cut through Cunningham's anger. Taking a step back, he looked his friend up and down. 'Aye, we could play these games all day,' he conceded. 'But believe me, I'm in just as much shit as you, Ryan. Now tell me what happened to you.'

Quickly Drake related his arrangement with Frost at

the InterContinental, his brief departure and return, and finally his encounter with the two Horizon operatives in the elevator.

'They're both history,' he concluded. 'I had no choice.'

Cunningham swore under his breath and looked away for a moment. 'You're sure they were from Horizon, aye?'

'They were the same arseholes who tried to stop us getting to the crash site. Believe me, I'd remember them.'

His friend said nothing to that. 'So why did you run?' he asked instead. 'Why not contact your mates at Langley?'

'Because I don't *have* any friends at Langley,' Drake hit back. 'Not now. My team's been detained. Carpenter has contacts within the Agency and he'll use them to shut down the investigation from that end while he hunts for me at this end. Either way, I'm fucked.'

'From both ends, no less,' Cunningham remarked with a sardonic smile.

Drake wasn't impressed. 'Piss off. We just lost our best chance of bringing him down.'

'And what makes you think Carpenter was behind this?' he asked. 'What proof do you have?'

Drake exhaled slowly, weighing up how much to tell him. He didn't want anyone knowing about Anya unless there was no other choice, but neither could he convince Cunningham unless he gave him something.

'I met with a source,' he said at last. 'Don't ask me who. They told me Mitchell was brought in to investigate Carpenter and Horizon. Whatever Mitchell uncovered, Carpenter found out about it and ordered him killed. When we came in to look for him, Horizon tried to block our investigation every chance they got, and when we got too close, Mitchell was conveniently executed. First he takes away our reason for being here, and when we still refuse to leave, he comes after *us*. He's trying to hide some kind of arrangement with Kourash and his group.'

'Not exactly up to date on current affairs, are you?' Cunningham said. 'Carpenter and Horizon are the new golden boys in the War on Terror. They announced the death of Anwari and his mates at a special press conference. The media are all over it.'

The wound at Drake's side blazed with pain as if the bullet had just struck home for the first time. He was shocked, dumbfounded by what he'd just heard.

'Kourash is dead?' he repeated.

'Aye, and then some. I saw the pictures – they weren't taking any chances with that arsehole. He's gone for good.'

Gingerly Drake settled himself on a large rectangular block of stone which had perhaps once served as a front doorstep, wincing and clutching his side as he did so. He was tired, and the wound was hurting more than he cared to admit. Reaching into his pocket, he fished out his tab of aspirin and dry-swallowed a couple.

It didn't make any sense. If Carpenter and Horizon had struck some kind of deal with Kourash to gain safe passage through his territory, and had apparently used him to take out Mitchell, why kill him now?

'It doesn't change a thing,' Drake decided. 'Whatever he's trying to hide, he's willing to kill for it. And we're next. The only way we're getting out of this – and the only way I can get Frost back – is if we take Carpenter down.'

It was Cunningham's turn to look unimpressed. 'Aye? What are you going to do, Rambo? Charge in there, guns blazing?'

'That wasn't my first plan.'

'Then what is your plan, Ryan?' he asked, his impatience

obvious. 'Because from where I'm standing we've got jack shit. We've got no information, no resources and nobody on our side. We don't even have a fucking safe house to hole up in.'

Drake paused, jolted out of his musings by that single thought. A safe house.

A secure place where one could meet contacts, plan operations, cache weapons and equipment. Or perhaps, just perhaps, hide classified documents on a major private military company.

In a flash, Mitchell's coded message suddenly reverberated through his mind, replaying over and over like a tape recorder stuck on an endless loop.

HOUSE FOUR.

Safe house number 4.

Drake could have kicked himself at that moment. Caught up in the frantic rescue attempt, the meeting with Anya and the brutal ambush in the elevator, he had almost forgotten Mitchell's cryptic message. Now, finally, it made sense.

He *had* been trying to tell them a location, but not of himself. He'd been trying to tell them where he'd hidden his evidence.

Mitchell's official role here had been to establish a series of safe houses in and around Kabul. Whatever he wanted them to find was stashed away in safe house number 4.

'I don't believe it,' he gasped as the full magnitude of it settled on him. Why hadn't he seen it before? It had been right there the whole time. He had stood in that very house only yesterday. He just hadn't known what to look for.

Cunningham stared at him, perplexed by his reaction. 'What is it?'

Drake felt like a condemned man given a last-minute reprieve. Well, perhaps not a reprieve, but at least the chance of one. But only if he acted on it now, while there was still time.

He looked up at his friend. 'Mitchell was brought in to investigate Horizon. Before he was killed, he'd amassed evidence against them. According to my source it was much bigger than anything they'd imagined, but Mitchell was so paranoid that he wouldn't go into any details. He wouldn't even say where he'd hidden it.'

Cunningham was watching him through narrowed eyes. 'All right . . .'

Drake let out a breath. 'Until now. He left a coded message on his hostage tape. All this time we assumed he was trying to tell us where he was being held, but he wasn't. He knew he was going to die. He was trying to tell us where he'd hidden his evidence.'

HOUSE FOUR.

'Safe house number four,' Drake said. He shook his head, still unable to believe he had missed such an obvious clue. 'It was there in front of us all along.'

The look in Cunningham's eyes quickly went from doubt to suspicion, and at last, to comprehension. 'Fuck me . . .'

'We get to that safe house and find the evidence,' Drake said. 'And Carpenter goes down.'

It was a couple of miles to the safe house from where they were. An easy five-minute drive in a car. On foot they'd be lucky to make it there in under thirty minutes.

Pushing himself up from his makeshift seat, he clenched his teeth as a wave of pain radiated outwards from the bullet wound at his side, threatening to drop him. Clutching at the crumbling remains of the door frame for support, he closed his eyes and willed the pain and weakness to subside.

'You don't look so good, mate,' Cunningham said, watching his friend with a mixture of sympathy and doubt. 'Maybe you should sit this one out.'

Gritting his teeth, Drake forced himself up again. 'We're doing this together, Matt. I have to be there – I have to finish this,' he said firmly, his bright green eyes boring into the older man's. 'You understand, don't you?'

Cunningham said nothing for a moment, perhaps weighing up his chances of forcing Drake to stay behind.

'You always were a stubborn arsehole,' he said at last, clearly unhappy.

Drake nodded. His friend might not have supported him, but neither would he oppose him. For now at least, that was enough.

Chapter 45

Crawford and McKnight were in the rooftop field ops tent poring over a map of the local area when Keegan hurried in.

'I know how they got Frost out of here,' he began, breathless after his rapid climb to the roof.

Crawford looked up. 'Thrill me.'

'They knocked her out and threw her down the laundry chute.'

The field agent's eyes narrowed. 'Are you shitting me?'

'She's small. She could fit down a narrow gap like that, and the chute's curved at the base. If there was enough padding beneath it she could survive the fall. It's the only way they could get her off that floor without being seen.'

'Okay. So what then?' he asked, still sceptical.

'They had a truck waiting for her. I checked with the security guards – they had a laundry truck arrive this afternoon, earlier than usual. It left real quick with only one load, then twenty minutes later a second truck shows up. The real one.'

Crawford's eyes lit up. Clearly Keegan had been busy. 'Son of a bitch . . .'

'The loading dock's covered by a security camera,' he carried on, now in full flow. 'Assuming it works, we backtrack the footage, pull the licence plate and run a trace on it. We find that truck, we find Frost.'

Crawford was amazed by how much Keegan had deduced in such a short time, but before he could say anything, Faulkner hurried over clutching his cellphone.

'Just got a call in from the local police. They found a canvas bag matching the one carried out by Drake. They also recovered some bloodstained clothes.'

Crawford was on it right away, gesturing to a map of the city spread out across the table. 'Show me.'

'Right around here.' Faulkner indicated an area of open ground on the western fringe of the city. 'It's waste ground, mostly. Some kids found it.'

'That's less than a mile from here,' McKnight observed. 'Ryan must have been looking for someplace out of the way.'

Crawford looked up at her. 'You think he's heading for the hills?'

Aside from a small village to the west, there was a whole lot of nothing for at least 30 miles beyond that point. It was the kind of rough, mountainous terrain where a single man could disappear with ease.

'I doubt it,' Keegan cut in. 'Even if he did disappear in there, there's no place for him to go. He could be trying to throw us off the scent, maybe double-back on himself.'

Crawford nodded thoughtfully. 'Either way, we won't learn anything more here. Grab your gear, we're leaving.'

But Keegan hesitated, clearly torn between his two comrades. Drake and Frost had gone in different directions, and he could only pursue one. 'What about the truck?'

'I'll follow up the truck,' McKnight volunteered. 'You'll

be more use on site than me, especially if they need someone to pick up Ryan's trail. You concentrate on him, I'll find Keira. Go, John. I've got this.'

Waiting a moment longer, Keegan finally nodded.

Anya sat alone in the Toyota 4x4, parked near an intersection on the main road leading towards the Horizon compound, the engine idling as she waited for her opportunity.

She wasn't frightened or apprehensive – she'd been doing things like this for too long to feel such emotions now – but she did feel a certain sense of anticipation, of eagerness to get it over and done with. She had always felt the same before an operation. She could handle the danger, the prospect of injury or death, but it was the waiting that had always troubled her.

The distant, low-pitched roar of a heavy diesel engine announced that the time for waiting was almost over. Reaching into the glovebox, she lifted out a half-empty bottle of whisky and took a gulp, grimacing in distaste as it settled on her stomach. She also dabbed some on her hands and wiped them on her neck and shirt, making sure the smell of potent alcohol was strong on her.

The distant rumble was growing closer now. She couldn't see it yet, but she knew that sound belonged to an RG-31 Nyala armoured vehicle. Horizon used them extensively for ferrying their operatives around and, she assumed, for conducting patrols.

Each one had a range of about 500 miles under ideal conditions, but the stop-and-start nature of traffic in Kabul combined with frustrated drivers meant they would burn through their fuel supply quickly. Sooner or later, they would have to return to base to refuel.

Without taking her eyes off the road, she pulled her

seat belt down and locked it into place, giving it a firm tug to make sure it was anchored securely. This 4x4 carried no airbags, and the last thing she wanted was to deal herself a serious injury that would put her out of action.

She would be going into this job with no weapons of any sort. No firearms, no knives or clubs – nothing but her bare hands. But as she knew from long years of experience, those could be just as deadly as any weapon.

It was a gamble, to be sure. But one didn't live this kind of life afraid of risks.

Bright headlights spilled across the potholed road up ahead. Releasing the handbrake, Anya eased the Toyota forwards, slow at first but gathering pace. She kept her lights off, not wanting to alert the driver of the Horizon vehicle.

Seconds later, the hulking form of the RG-31 appeared around the corner, easily moving at 40 miles an hour, the driver no doubt impatient to refuel so he could get out and continue the hunt for Drake.

It was in her sights now. No turning back. Switching the headlights on, she jammed her foot down on the gas and braced herself.

'Roger that,' Sergeant Nicholas Rae, the vehicle commander, spoke into his helmet-mounted radio. 'Alpha Six is inbound for refuel. ETA, two minutes.'

He was just turning towards his second in command when suddenly the driver cried out in warning and jammed on the brakes. Bright light flooded in through the exterior windows, tyres screeched and the big vehicle slewed sideways as their driver tried to avoid whatever was bearing down on them.

Too late. The interior resounded with a loud, crunching

bang as something slammed into them, accompanied by the tinkle of broken glass and the blare of a car horn. Rae was almost thrown from his seat by the impact, saved only by his belt.

As the RG-31 lurched to a halt, he shook his head and glanced at the driver. 'What the fuck happened?'

'Something hit us. Didn't see it.'

'No shit,' Rae remarked under his breath. 'Get out there and form a perimeter. It could be an ambush.'

An immobilised vehicle like this would be an easy target.

Grabbing their weapons, the four operatives in the back piled out the rear doors, rifle barrels sweeping in all directions. There was no sign of a contact. No inbound fire as he would have expected if this was an ambush.

Rae waited several seconds before stepping outside to join them.

They had been hit by a Toyota 4x4. It must have barrelled into them from the adjacent street, hitting them just to the rear of the driver's cab.

The armour plating had deformed a little from the impact, but as far as he could tell, the vehicle's chassis remained sound and engine was still running. RG-31s were heavy, durable vehicles designed to survive a lot of punishment – low-speed collisions like this were easily shrugged off.

The same couldn't be said of the Toyota. The front end had crumpled like a beer can, steam rising from the ruined engine. The driver was slumped over the wheel, long dark hair hanging down around her face.

A woman, he realised with a flash of anger. If this was nothing more than a traffic accident, she was going to have quite a bill to pay.

'Check the driver,' he ordered.

Two of his men hurried forward, one covering his comrade while he hauled open the jammed door using sheer brute strength.

The crash of protesting metal was enough to revive the driver, and she looked up, staring in bleary-eyed shock at the weapons now pointed her way. She was Caucasian, perhaps in her late thirties or early forties, and dressed in civilian clothes.

'Don't move!' Private Shaw yelled, covering her with his M4. 'Keep your hands where I can see them.'

She barely had time to comply before Private Martinez grabbed her roughly by the shirt and hauled her out of her seat, oblivious to any injuries she might have suffered. Aside from a cut above her left eye, she seemed unhurt.

'Hey, what are you doing? Get off me!' she protested, her words slurred and her eyes unfocused as she struggled to break free of his grip. No way was it happening – Martinez was easily twice her weight. 'You almost got me killed! Look at my car, it's totalled!'

'Shaw, check her ID,' Rae commanded, ignoring the torrent of abuse.

'Christ, she's drunk as a fucking college student,' Martinez warned, having caught the reek of whisky on her breath. Even her clothes smelled of it.

Shaw, meanwhile, had been busy rifling through the items scattered across the seats and floor by the crash. 'Got a bottle of Scotch here,' he remarked, holding up a half-empty bottle.

Rae gritted his teeth. The stupid bitch must have been driving drunk through the streets of Kabul. No wonder she hadn't seen them. She probably couldn't make out the dashboard in front of her face.

At last Shaw found a wallet amongst the crap littering the footwell, and quickly flipped through its contents.

'Name's Katrina Taylor,' he said. 'American. Business card says she's a freelance writer.'

This was just getting better and better. No doubt she was another wannabe journalist looking to write that Pulitzer-winning article. Rae hated her kind almost as much as he hated the people they were fighting out here.

'I see a laptop and a bunch of papers in the back here,' Shaw went on, resuming his search.

'Any weapons?' Rae asked.

'Can't see any.'

'Leave my stuff alone! That's my property!' Taylor cried, her voice high-pitched and irritating. 'You can't pull this Gestapo crap. I'm an American, I have rights!'

Martinez had heard enough. Balling up his fist, he drove it into her stomach with enough force to double her over. He watched with satisfaction as she threw up on the rough asphalt, struggling to draw breath between heaves.

'You have the right to remain silent, so shut the fuck up.'

'Sarge, what do we do with her?' Shaw asked from the other side of the crashed Toyota, apparently oblivious to what had just happened. 'We can't leave her out here. Her car's fucked and she's too drunk to find her way home anyway.'

Rae rolled his eyes. With everything else going on tonight, this was the last thing he needed. Still, Shaw had a point. Drunk and abusive she might be, but Taylor was still an American citizen. If something happened to her, it might well be traced back to them eventually.

In the end, he made the only decision he could under the circumstances. 'Secure her and put her in the back,' he said, gesturing to the RG-31. 'We'll take her in – she can sleep this shit off in the cells. And get a tow truck to recover her vehicle.'

'Come on, puking beauty,' Martinez said, hauling the woman to her feet. 'I've got a great holding cell waiting for you.'

She was too busy coughing up the remains of that bottle of whisky to resist as he pulled her hands roughly behind her back and snapped on a pair of cuffs.

Chapter 46

Darkness had descended on the city by the time Drake and Cunningham reached their destination. Crouched down behind a trickling drainage outlet, both men stared up the stony, scrub-covered slope to the safe house.

The main gate faced south, opening out onto the main road. There was no possibility of making entry from that direction. Even if they managed to get the gate open, their presence would surely not go unnoticed.

Their best chance was to approach from the stretch of undeveloped land that seemed to wind its way along the path of what had once been a river, flanked by housing developments.

From their current position, everything looked quiet and still. There were no lights burning, no sign of habitation, and now that darkness had fallen, the residential street beyond was devoid of traffic.

'This is your show, mate,' Cunningham said, then shot a dubious glance at his companion. 'How do you want to do it?'

Drake swallowed and nodded, wiping a trickle of sweat from his brow. The trip here – a brisk half-hour walk under normal circumstances – had become a grim test of endurance for him. The injury at his side seemed to pulsate in time to his heartbeat, sending ripples of pain flowing outwards through his body. Already he felt weary and drained by the effort.

Still, they were here now. All their other problems were behind them. The only thing that mattered now was finding Mitchell's evidence.

In his mind, he imagined them making entry to the house, locating Mitchell's hidden cache of evidence and exiting without ever being seen, each stage unfolding without mishap. This was going to work. They were going to succeed.

'We'll go in that way, over the wall,' he said quietly. 'From there we'll have to pick the lock and disable the alarm.'

'Got it covered,' Cunningham assured him, then flashed a wry smile. 'Just like old times, eh?'

'Stop it. You're making me all misty-eyed.' Taking a deep breath and rallying his flagging reserves of energy, Drake clapped a hand on his friend's shoulder. 'Come on. Let's go.'

Keeping low and watching their feet on the uneven ground, they advanced uphill towards the house. It was a balmy night, with a warm and gentle breeze coming up from the south. Drake's T-shirt was already damp with sweat, brought on by a combination of exertion, stress and anticipation. He did his best to ignore all three, with varying degrees of success.

The property was surrounded by an 8-foot brick wall. There was no razor wire that they could see, but there was always a chance it was topped with broken glass. If so, they would have to hunt around for something thick and durable enough to lay over it – no easy task in a country where virtually anything of value was picked up as soon as it was discarded.

Halting next to the wall, Drake turned to his partner

in crime and nodded, indicating that he would go first. He hardly felt up to a walk across the street, never mind hauling himself over a brick wall, but there wasn't much choice.

With Cunningham providing a boost, Drake launched himself upwards, threw his hands out and managed to grab the top. To his relief the wall was topped by nothing more sinister than stone slabs, with a shallow lip on either side.

Had this place become operational as a safe house, it was likely the security would have been beefed up massively. As it was, they just might make it inside.

Using his feet for extra purchase, Drake hauled himself up and over the edge, careful to keep his weight on his good side. This done, he lay flat on the top, breathing hard, watching and waiting for any change in their surroundings. If there were floodlights linked up to motion sensors nearby, he'd soon know about it.

Several seconds passed, and nothing happened. Traffic rumbled by on the distant main drag, a dog barked somewhere off to the west, and the chirp and buzz of night insects filled the warm air. He leaned back over the wall, looked down at Cunningham and gave him the thumbs-up.

Rolling over, he allowed himself to drop down on the other side. Cunningham followed a moment later, landing almost without sound.

There were no lights on in the house itself. Everything looked quiet and undisturbed. Good.

Keeping low, they darted across the meagre remains of the garden and halted next to the front door. The lock had been replaced since Crawford had blasted it apart with a breaching gun the previous day, a large section of new wood visible on the heavy door where the broken, splintered area around the lock had also been removed.

Getting in was Cunningham's job, and he would be vulnerable while he went about it. Taking the man's weapon, a Beretta automatic, Drake turned to cover his back, scanning the shadowy courtyard and the street beyond the wrought-iron gate.

Knowing his friend was covering him, Cunningham was able to concentrate his attention on the job of making entry.

The first and most obvious thing to do was to reach out and try the door. The chances of it being unlocked were negligible, but it took only seconds to check. It wouldn't be the first time an operative had wasted precious minutes trying to pick a lock that was already open.

Still, no such luck in this case. The lock would have to be defeated.

One of the benefits of working for a private military company was having access to all kinds of technology that made it easy to get into secured buildings. Reaching into his jacket pocket, Cunningham produced what looked like a small plastic pistol with a flat metal blade instead of a gun barrel.

Known as a snap gun, the device provided a quick means of picking just about any pin tumbler style lock – a notoriously tricky business using manual tools. The metal blade was inserted into a lock like a regular key, and a single squeeze of the trigger caused the blade to strike all of the lock pins at once, sending the driver pins up into the lock and disengaging the mechanism. It was fast and effective, the only drawback being that it was quite loud. Still, it was their best chance at getting in.

Taking a deep breath, he pushed the blade into the

lower part of the lock with great care. Into the broader upper part he inserted a long flat piece of metal, known as a tension wrench. When the driver pins went up into the lock, the tension wrench would be needed to hold them in place.

A bead of sweat rolled down his brow and into his eye. He did his best to ignore it, concentrating on the task at hand.

He pulled the trigger. There was a dull *ping* followed by a click as the driver pins sprang upward. At the same moment, he pushed the tension wrench in further, feeling it slip past the tumblers.

Removing the snap gun, he turned the tension wrench 90 degrees to the left. The lock clicked once more, and that was it. They were in.

Drake let out his breath as his companion tapped him on the shoulder, indicating that the door was open.

Turning, he watched as Cunningham reached out and grasped the handle. With a single curt nod, he turned it and pushed the door open.

Without hesitation, Drake advanced inside with the Beretta up and ready.

They were in.

Chapter 47

'Some local children were out hunting for rabbits when they found it,' a small, efficient-looking ANP officer explained as he escorted Keegan and Crawford to the scene. 'It was buried in shallow ground, but a jackal or some other predator must have been attracted by the smell of blood.'

He gestured to the cordoned-off area of waste ground where the satchel still lay. Beside it, partially buried in a small depression, was a ripped and bloodstained shirt. Both were covered in dusty soil as if they had recently been excavated.

'They called it in straight away,' he added. 'My men made sure not to contaminate the scene.'

'I'm surprised the kids didn't just steal it,' Keegan remarked, having noticed several expensive camera lenses and batteries lying near the satchel. He had no children of his own, but he came from a large family and knew all too well how inquisitive children could be.

The ANP officer gave him a pained smile. 'Children in Afghanistan quickly learn not to pick up such things.'

Keegan said nothing to this. The look in the man's eyes told its own story.

'Let's take a look,' Crawford said, ducking beneath the cordon.

Eager to leave before he put his foot in it again, the

old sniper followed, using his flashlight to survey the ground for tracks.

Having been taught to track and hunt animals from a young age by his father, he considered it an art rather than a science. Some people had the innate ability to discern meaning from a bent blade of grass or a scuff mark in the dust, while others didn't, and no amount of training could change that. Fortunately, he belonged to the former category.

A couple of footprints, small and light, were undoubtedly those of the children that the ANP officer had mentioned. Sure enough, none of them came within 10 feet of the bag itself.

'Wait here,' he instructed, circling slowly around the area in a counterclockwise direction, his keen eyes scanning every inch of ground in front of him.

Crawford was smart enough to say nothing. At times like this, he knew it was far better to let people get on with their work.

'Found him,' Keegan said at last, hunkering down.

Crawford hurried over and knelt down beside him. Sure enough, a faint boot print was discernible in the dust. The size and shape confirmed it had belonged to a man, but he could tell little beyond that.

'How can you be sure?'

'I recognise the tread pattern. Plus he was carrying the bag on his left side, so his weight was on the right foot to compensate,' he explained, then pointed behind him. 'He came in this way, patched himself up and changed clothes, then left.'

'Guess we can forget about picking him up in local hospitals, huh?'

The old sniper raised an eyebrow. 'I'd say so. He made it this far under his own power.'

'Great. The question is, where's he headed now?'

For that, Keegan had no answer.

Crawford's phone started buzzing. It was McKnight.

'Go, Sam,' he said, giving Keegan some room.

'Looks like John's hunch was right,' the young woman began. 'We got a make on the laundry truck, ran the plates through the police database. It was reported stolen earlier today from a cleaning company on the south side of the city.'

Crawford chewed his lip. 'Any leads on it now?'

'We've put out an APB, but it could be anywhere by now.' He heard a sigh at her end. Like the rest of them she'd been operating virtually without sleep for two days straight, and the strain was beginning to show. 'What about you? Any sign of Ryan?'

'He was here – that's about all we know right now,' he admitted.

'I'm on my way.'

'Keegan's on it,' he assured her. 'There's nothing more you can do here.'

'I know. But I . . . I want to be there.' There was something in her voice, a certain tension and emotion that went beyond mere professional concern for a comrade. He had suspected as much.

'All right. I'll call you if the situation changes,' he promised, hanging up.

Eyes and weapons sweeping the darkness, both men said nothing for several seconds; just allowed their eyes to adjust to the weak moonlight filtering in from outside.

'Clear,' Cunningham said quietly.

'Clear,' Drake confirmed.

Lowering his weapon, he turned to the right, where a soft green glow was emanating from a plastic keypad

401

mounted on the wall. It was an ultrasonic alarm unit, and a good one at that – he recognised the make and model as one typically favoured by the Agency for its resilience.

There was no time to consult the phone or any written notes. Drake had watched an agent enter the disarm code the day before and was reasonably confident he had retained it. He just hoped his brain was still cooperating.

The alarm was already counting down, triggered the moment they opened the door. Most units of this type were on a ten-second delay, leaving him with perhaps four or five seconds to input the code before it went off.

It wouldn't make a sound if it went off. Instead it was linked up to the Agency's own security service, and would immediately put an automated call through to report the break-in. Within minutes a van full of armed security operatives would come screeching to a halt outside.

Opening the cover on the panel, he keyed in 917214, sent a silent prayer to whatever deity might have been inclined to listen, and hit enter.

The simple LED readout flashed once to acknowledge the code entry, and that was it. The alarm was down.

'Good job,' Cunningham said, gently closing the door behind him.

Drake might have looked calm, but his heart was beating overtime. It had all come down to this. Either they would find what they were looking for, and Carpenter and Horizon would fall, or they would find nothing.

He preferred not to consider that possibility.

'Let's get it done,' he said, handing the Beretta back to its owner. 'You take the ground floor. I'll go upstairs.'

Normally splitting up was a big no-no in situations like this. They were supposed to advance in pairs where they could cover each other's backs, but in this case they simply didn't have time for a room-by-room search. They had a lot of ground to cover, and little time in which to do it.

Every second they stayed here increased their chances of being caught.

Cunningham nodded, well aware of their precarious situation. He fished a small flashlight from his pocket and fired it up, allowing the weak beam to play across the floor. 'On it, mate. Call out if you see anything.'

'Good luck,' Drake said as his friend advanced deeper into the house, heading for what had once been the kitchen.

Leaving him to it, Drake went for the stairs, pushing aside the pain, intent only on finding what he needed.

Chapter 48

Confused, Anya struggled to her feet, forcing her aching muscles to comply. Her rush of elation was starting to fade now as she watched Carpenter walk a slow circle around her. The other recruits were standing in a line behind her, unmoving, seemingly oblivious to the pounding rain.

'What was the final promise you made to me?' he asked.

'I will never surrender, sir.' She was trying to get her laboured breathing under control, to slow her frantically beating heart, to stand up straight as a soldier should.

'And do you know why I chose that?'

'No, sir.' She could guess, however. They were to be a clandestine unit, sent deep behind enemy lines to sabotage, ambush and assassinate. If they were caught, they could expect no rescue. The solution was simple – no surrender.

'At the Battle of Waterloo, Napoleon's army collapsed and retreated. They were broken, in mind and body. The only ones who stood their ground, who refused to give in, were the Old Guard. The elite, the best of the best.' His keen eyes swept the ranks of men standing before him. 'When the British asked them to surrender, they replied, "La Garde meurt, elle ne se rend pas!" The Guard dies, it does not surrender! That is what

404

I expect from each and every one of you. No surrender, even in the face of death.'

Last of all his eyes rested on Anya. 'Can I expected that from you, Recruit?'

Anya was just opening her mouth to reply when suddenly Carpenter rounded on her, drew back his fist and delivered a crippling punch to the centre of her chest, knocking her sprawling in a deep pool of mud.

Shocked and winded, she could barely resist as he jumped on her, forcing his knee into her chest and crushing the air from her lungs. His fingers grasped a matted clump of her hair and yanked her head up.

'You really think you have what it takes to be in this unit?' he hissed, his face mere inches from hers. 'You ready to lay down your life before you'd surrender?'

Before she could speak, he shoved her head back, submerging it beneath the surface. Anya let out an involuntary scream as thick mud closed in around her face. She couldn't see, couldn't breathe, couldn't move. She flailed and kicked desperately, trying to free herself, but his grip was relentless. She even tried to strike him, but he easily deflected the blow.

'Now you've got a hundred-and-ninety-pound man on top of you,' she heard him say. 'He's gonna drown you unless you surrender to him. Why aren't you fighting back?'

Just when it seemed her lungs must burst, he yanked her head out of the mud. She let out her breath in a sudden explosion of air, desperately gulping in more.

'Why aren't you fighting?' he demanded. 'Because you're tired? You think war only happens when you've had a good night's sleep?'

It was insane. She had been training all night. She couldn't lift the weight of a man, couldn't fight him off. She could barely stand.

'I can't—' She was cut off when he jerked her head back again.

'You can't, huh? That all you can say?' he taunted her. *'Do you want to die, Recruit? Is that it? If you won't fight for your own pathetic life, how do you expect other people to fight for you?'*

Nobody suspects a woman.

Having spent the past two decades working in a profession populated almost exclusively by men, Anya had had quite some time to ponder the relative merits of her gender when it came to the art of killing.

And sitting there now, handcuffed and surrounded by armed operatives in the back of the RG-31 as it bumped and rolled towards the Horizon compound, she was afforded a few moments to contemplate her conclusions.

Certainly she wasn't as big or as strong as the majority of her opponents had been, forcing her instead to rely on technique, skill and experience to see her through. She couldn't intimidate others in the same way men could, her voice lacked the natural depth and authority that men possessed.

And of course, there were other inconveniences and weaknesses inherent to her gender that she had become well acquainted with during captivity.

And yet, the one truth that had eluded her for so long was that all of these things could ultimately be used to her advantage.

Women were easy to underestimate, particularly for experienced operatives like this. Strong, fit, well trained and in the prime of their lives, they feared little, particularly the female of their species. Why would they? Most of the women they had known had been mothers, sisters, girlfriends, random sexual partners.

Not soldiers. Not enemies to be feared and respected.

For so long, Anya had worked, striven, fought to overcome the limitations of her sex, never realising that those same things which she saw as weaknesses could be strengths; those limitations allowed her to excel in her chosen profession.

Nobody suspected a woman, least of all the occupants of that armoured vehicle, sitting all around her, secure in the knowledge that she was drunk, frightened, cowed and handcuffed.

The first three had been an act right from the start, further exploiting their overconfidence. And as for the last one, she was working on that.

Protruding from the clasp of her wristwatch was a little sliver of metal that had gone unnoticed by the men who escorted her aboard the armoured vehicle. But as soon as she had sat down and her hands were obscured from view, she gently teased the shard out and went to work on the cuffs.

Handcuffs, utilising simple locking mechanisms, were easy enough to pick if one knew the right way to tackle them. Anya had had plenty of opportunities to perfect the art of lock picking in her long career, and was familiar with the most popular brands.

She coughed, spitting up phlegm on the deck and moaning softly to maintain the illusion of a drunken idiot slowly waking up to the fact that she's in way over her head. She could have done without being punched in the guts, but when it happened she decided to make the best of it and promptly threw up all over the ground. Her stomach still ached from its violent contortions, but like many such discomforts, she ignored it, concentrating on her task.

She was under no illusions about her chances. Despite her experience and abilities, the prospect of being killed in her effort was ever-present. But for her, there was no question of backing down, of walking away and putting this behind her.

She had waited too long for this moment.

It wouldn't be the first time she had faced such danger, and even if she was successful today, it wouldn't be the last. She wasn't destined to see old age, to find a peaceful death at the end of a long life.

She had spent her life fighting and sacrificing for hopeless causes, serving thankless masters and killing undeserving enemies. She had wasted her life and her strength, but she still had a measure of each left to her. And with both of those things, she intended to put right her mistakes.

Starting with Carpenter.

'Come on, where the fuck are you?' Drake hissed, pacing the room in growing agitation.

He had swept the entire upper floor, moving from room to room and finding little more than bare floorboards and brick walls. The upstairs bathroom didn't even have a toilet or sink; just outlet pipes protruding from the floor and walls.

Only the room next door contained anything interesting. Presumably used as a workshop, it was dominated by a workbench covered with various power tools. Packing crates had been stacked against one wall, all empty, with the crowbar used to open them still resting on top.

He didn't doubt that Mitchell would have hidden his

evidence somewhere on the property, but he also would have needed it easily accessible for his own use. So where had he stashed it?

'You found anything down there?' he called out without much hope.

'Of course, mate,' Cunningham's sarcastic reply echoed up to him. 'I've just been having a cup of tea.'

Drake shook his head, returning to his own thoughts. He was missing something – he was sure of it.

He ran a hand through his damp hair as he continued pacing, while the wound at his side throbbed with pain. Surely he hadn't come all this way just to stumble at the final hurdle.

'Think, for Christ's sake. Think!'

Wrapped up in his own grim thoughts, he barely noticed the creak of a floorboard beneath his boot, or felt the slight give in the loose wood.

But his subconscious mind did. Attentive to things he was too busy to consider, it recognised something out of the ordinary. Something significant.

Drake stopped, frowning as the realisation hit him.

Retracing his steps, he put his weight down once again.

Creak.

Kneeling down, he ran his hands over the floorboards. They were made from rough and unfinished wood intended to be carpeted over. And yet, they had all been well laid and neatly joined by a skilled craftsman.

All except one.

His heart beating faster, Drake hurried into the other room, retrieved the crowbar and, finding the loose floorboard once more, jammed one end into the gap and levered it up.

There was a slight groan as the nail slipped free of the

joist, but otherwise the board presented little resistance. It had been lifted several times by the looks of it.

Then, in an instant, Drake stopped.

He had seen something. A tiny sliver of wire gleaming in the moonlight, trailing from the underside of the floorboard to something fixed against the joist with duct tape. Leaning in closer, Drake spotted the distinctive cylindrical outline and fuse head of a thermite incendiary grenade.

It was a trap, he realised, designed to prevent Mitchell's evidence falling into the wrong hands. If he had lifted the floorboard a few more inches, it would have pulled the pin and triggered the grenade, incinerating anything within 10 feet.

With great care, he laid the floorboard aside, making sure to keep tension out of the wire. There was just enough slack to move the board out of the way, allowing him to see what lay beneath.

Nestling in the alcove between two joists was a cardboard folder with a single handwritten word on the front – *Horizon*.

With shaking hands, Drake lifted it out and laid it down on the floor. It was heavy, containing a good hundred pages' worth of documents, many of different sizes and colours.

Undoing the bindings that held it closed, he flipped the file open at a random page. His eyes darted from line to line, page to page, impatiently devouring the information contained within. He felt like a starving man presented with a sumptuous feast, yet only allowed to sample tiny mouthfuls here and there.

The folder seemed to contain a bizarre collection of information from different sources; everything from handwritten interview notes to transcripts of phone conversations, shipping manifests, emails, spreadsheets, photographs, forensic reports and even newspaper clippings.

And over all of it, written in what he guessed was Mitchell's neat, precise handwriting, were notes of his own findings and opinions, key sections of documents underlined and circled.

As Drake read on, a picture soon began to emerge from the scattered documents, words and phrases leaping out at him with shocking clarity.

. . . Horizon colluding with insurgent groups . . .

. . . supplying them with weapons and equipment . . .

. . . proof that they engineered Anwari's escape from prison . . .

. . . suggested they planned at least three separate attacks against ISAF forces . . .

. . . using them to kill off key Taliban commanders . . .

. . . Stinger missiles from supply convoy . . .

. . . possibility of attacking Coalition aircraft . . .

'Oh, my God,' Drake breathed, awed by the scale of Mitchell's findings.

He was eager to read more, but now wasn't the right time. First they had to get this document and its contents to safety. Then he would work out how to ensure it found its way to the right people.

No way was this getting swept under the carpet. Not this time.

Snapping the folder shut, he quickly retied the bindings that held it closed, then reached into his pocket for Anya's cellphone and dialled Dan Franklin's number back at Langley. He needed someone removed from this whole situation; someone who would believe what he was saying.

Someone with enough authority to keep the Agency off his back long enough to present his findings.

He was about to put the call through when a familiar voice spoke up.

'Put it down, Ryan,' Cunningham ordered.

Drake's head snapped around. 'Matt, what—'

The words died in his throat the moment he saw his friend standing in the doorway, his weapon trained on Drake.

For an instant, the world around him seemed to stop, his surroundings fading into darkness. All he could see was his friend, his jaw set with grim resolve, eyes gleaming cold and hard in the moonlight. And clutched in his hand, the pistol.

And then, like a dam strained beyond its limits, something gave way inside his mind, unleashing a torrent of thoughts and memories. He saw Cunningham taking the memory stick from Frost; Cunningham trying to convince him to go home; Cunningham casting doubt on his suspicions about Carpenter; Cunningham urging him to let him come to the safe house alone.

Matt Cunningham: his friend, the man he trusted. The man who was going to kill him.

Just like that, the moment passed, the shock and disbelief vanished, and the world snapped back into place with painful clarity. Drake was in survival mode now, his mind racing as he sat crouched there, staring down the barrel of the weapon.

'Stand up,' Cunningham commanded.

Drake rose slowly to his feet, slipping the phone into his jacket pocket. Unable to think of anything else at that moment, he hit the call button.

Within seconds, the call had been routed through the network of transmitting stations, geostationary communications satellites, cellphone masts and hard lines to Dan Franklin's office halfway around the world.

Eager for news, the director of Special Activities Division snatched up his cellphone and hit the button to receive the call.

'Ryan, what's going on out there?'

There was no response, save for the faint rustle of fabric.

'Ryan?'

Nothing. Suddenly struck by a deep sense of foreboding, he pressed the receiver tight against his ear, straining to listen.

For several seconds, neither man said a word. Both merely stood in the pale moonlight filtering through the shuttered window, motionless, staring at each other.

'Hands behind your head,' Cunningham ordered. 'You know the drill, mate.'

There was no emotion in his voice, no hint of remorse or hesitation. He was a killer, cold and hardened and ready to act at the slightest provocation.

To attempt to take him on would be futile, Drake knew. Even an amateur could barely miss at such range, and Cunningham was an excellent marksman.

Releasing his grip on the phone, he raised his hands to show he was no threat, then interlocked them behind his head. His vivid green eyes shone in the darkness, filled with anger and hatred and betrayal.

'How much did they pay you to turn traitor?'

'Traitor?' At last he saw a flicker of emotion in his friend's eyes. 'Is that what you think I am, Ryan?'

'You work for a man who uses terrorists to murder his own people for profit. You helped stall my investigation, and you're pointing a gun at me right now,' Drake reminded him. 'So tell me, what the fuck are you?'

'Shit,' Franklin hissed.

Realising at last why Drake had called him, he reached for the phone on his desk and punched in the number for the Agency's Office of Communications. Being a senior executive, his call took priority over almost all others, and was therefore answered within moments.

'This is Director Franklin of Special Activities Division. I need a priority trace on the following number . . .'

His request was immediately relayed to the National Security Agency's monitoring station at Fort Meade, Maryland. Within a matter of seconds, the NSA's bank of Cray supercomputers – designed to break some of the most sophisticated codes on earth – had locked in on his cellphone, analysed the unsecured connection to an active device, traced it back to its source and triangulated a position to within 10 feet.

Armed with this information, Franklin made a call to the Agency's switchboard requesting to be transferred to the case officer assigned to Drake's team.

'You just don't get it, do you?' Cunningham shot back. 'This is bigger than you and me. It's bigger than Carpenter, bigger than Horizon. If you could see past your self-righteous shite, you'd realise we both want the same thing.'

Drake's eyes narrowed. 'And what's that?'

'A way out,' he said. 'This war's bleeding us dry. ISAF's spending a hundred billion a year in Afghanistan and getting fuck all in return, except body bags and cripples. We both know the Americans will order a withdrawal sooner or later. What do you think will happen then?'

Drake said nothing, just waited for him to go on.

'It'll be the same as when the fucking Soviets pulled out – history repeating itself. It'll be civil war, torture, genocide – you name it. Tens of thousands will die, and all the sacrifices we made will be for nothing. I'm going to stop that.'

'By killing the same soldiers you're supposed to be protecting?' Drake demanded, bristling with cold anger at his friend's betrayal.

'By forcing a withdrawal *now*, and replacing them with something better,' Cunningham retorted. 'The army wasn't made for this kind of war – we both know that. They can't take a shit without authorisation from the UN. Horizon on the other hand . . . they can fight this war the way it needs to be fought, for a fraction of the cost.'

Drake understood all too well. PMCs weren't compelled to report casualties, weren't duty bound to fly flag-draped coffins back home in very public admissions of their losses. And most important, they weren't subject to the same oversight as the military, weren't held accountable for their actions.

The war in Afghanistan could carry on just like before, the politicians in Washington could bask in the success of having brought their boys home, and meanwhile people would carry on fighting and dying out here. It would become a quiet, dirty little war that the average American voter no longer had to concern himself with.

And for men like Carpenter, the resulting contracts would be worth billions. War had become business, and business would be booming for years to come.

Crawford's cellphone was ringing. Leaving Keegan to hunt for Drake's trail, he flipped the phone open to take the call. 'Yeah?'

'Agent Crawford, this is Dan Franklin, director of Special Activities Division. Do I have your attention?'

Crawford's heartbeat doubled within seconds, though he gave little outward sign of it. 'Yes, sir.'

'Good. You're looking for Ryan Drake, correct?'

'That's right.'

'Well, you've found him,' Franklin announced. 'And he needs your help.'

Barely twenty seconds later, the call was over. Flipping his phone closed, Crawford hurried over to Keegan.

'We've got him,' he announced without preamble. 'Drake's cellphone just went active. NSA have locked down a location.'

Keegan's eyes opened wide in disbelief. 'Where?'

'The safe house we were at yesterday.' Without waiting for a response, he turned around. 'Faulkner, get over here!'

The big field agent was there within seconds.

'Prepare an assault team, fully armed. And get some air assets on this. I want that entire area locked down, airtight. Understand?'

'Completely, sir.'

'Good. And get in contact with McKnight, tell her where we're headed. Go now!'

'Why would Ryan do something so stupid?' Keegan asked. 'He'd have to know we'd track him down.'

Crawford's expression was as dark as the night around them. 'If what Director Franklin told me is true, that's exactly what he wants.'

'Christ, Matt, listen to yourself,' Drake implored his friend. 'You were working with the same men you're supposed to be fighting. How many people have died because of this?'

Drake saw the muscles in his throat rise and fall as Cunningham swallowed, saw a flicker of remorse in his eyes.

'It's a war. Every war means sacrifices. We had to let Anwari have a few successes to get the other insurgent groups to trust him. Once they did, they were easy for us to take down. Don't you understand? He was our fucking silver bullet. We've killed more Taliban commanders in the past few months than ISAF managed in the past three years.'

'And now he's dead,' Drake reminded him. 'He's dead because he outlived his usefulness. How long do you think it'll be before you outlive yours?'

For a moment, he saw a hint of doubt in his friend's eyes.

'It doesn't have to end like this, Matt,' Drake went on, desperately trying to capitalise on the older man's wavering resolve. 'There's enough information in that file to bring down Carpenter and everyone else involved in this. If you help me, we can make a deal. Immunity from prosecution, a Presidential pardon . . . whatever you want.'

He took a step forward, his boot brushing against the floorboard he had moved aside earlier. 'I know you, Matt. This isn't you. Don't waste everything you've done on an arsehole like Carpenter. He isn't worth it.'

For a brief, agonising second, Cunningham seemed poised to relent, to lay down his weapon and accept Drake's offer. His gaze appeared to turn inward, as if seeing his actions, so easy to justify at the time, for what they truly amounted to.

And then, in the blink of an eye, it was gone.

'Nice try, but it's a little late for that,' he said with a grim smile. 'Step back, Ryan. Away from the folder.'

Drake's heart sank. He had failed.

'No,' he said, standing his ground. 'I won't.'

In response, Cunningham thumbed back the hammer on his weapon. 'Don't test me, son. Step back.'

'Or what? You'll kill me?' Drake challenged him. 'We both know you have to do it. I've seen too much, I know too much. I'm a threat now.'

Cunningham said nothing, just stood there rooted to the spot, covering Drake with the automatic.

'Come on. What's the matter? Lost your nerve?' Drake taunted. 'You can kill innocent men, but not your own friend? Is that one sacrifice too many?'

Cunningham shook his head, his eyes hardening with cold resolve. 'It's never too many,' he said, his finger tightening on the trigger. 'I'm sorry, mate.'

That was all Drake needed to hear. Pulling his foot forward, he allowed it to catch on the edge of the floorboard, dragging it a few precious inches. There was a moment of taut resistance as the wire strained against the movement, then a barely audible *ping* as the grenade pin slipped free of its fuse.

Drake took another step forward, his hands raised as he stared into his friend's eyes, readying himself for what was about to happen.

'Yeah, so am I.'

His first impression was of a terrific orange-white flash that seemed to engulf the entire room, wiping away all sense of light and shadow. It was followed an instant later by a vicious, explosive roar like a thousand bonfires all burning at once.

Standing mere feet from the source of ignition, he felt the blast of heat immediately, searing his exposed skin and blistering the surface of his jacket.

But he paid no attention to any of these things. In the

half-second after detonation, his sole focus was Cunningham.

He saw the man's eyes close involuntarily to protect themselves from the blinding light and heat, saw him throw his arm up and back away from the inferno that was now surging upwards from beneath the floor.

This was his chance.

With a primal cry, Drake lowered his shoulder and charged, catching Cunningham across the midriff and driving him backwards through the doorway. His momentum was only halted when his opponent slammed into the wall beyond with bruising force, crumpling the plasterboard facade.

Wasting no time, Drake straightened up, drew back his arm and smacked the automatic from Cunningham's hand with a powerful backhanded strike. The weapon roared as a single round discharged from the sudden impact, only for Cunningham to lose his grip on it. Drake couldn't tell where it had landed, but it was no longer in his opponent's hand, and that was good enough for him.

Now they were even.

With his opponent disarmed, Drake went to work, lashing out with vicious, powerful strikes to his face and body. All of the anger and pain of his betrayal, held in check by sheer willpower, had at last found an outlet. In his mind, Cunningham was no longer a friend. He was an adversary, and a dangerous one at that. He had to be dealt with quickly.

A knee to the stomach doubled Cunningham over, followed by a brutal right hook to the jaw that dropped him to the floor. Drake was on top of him in an instant, pinning him down so he could pummel him again.

The air was rapidly filling with smoke and noxious

fumes from the still-burning grenade, stinging his eyes and choking his lungs with each breath. Now burning at 2,500 degrees, the thermite reaction was more than enough to ignite the wooden floorboards and joists around it.

A sudden crash from behind told him the molten thermite had just burned through the floor to drop down into whatever room lay below. Glancing around, he saw a column of flame rising from a metre-wide hole where the grenade had once been.

And lying just feet away from it was Mitchell's folder. He had to get to it before the flames consumed it. Surrounded by such heat, a paper folder would be incinerated within seconds.

But first he had to finish his enemy. Glaring at Cunningham, he drew back his right arm to deliver a blow that would put him down for good.

But his momentary hesitation had bought Cunningham a precious second or so to recover his wits. Even as Drake swung for one last strike to put him down, Cunningham's arm swept upwards and parried the blow, deflecting it enough for him to twist aside and avoid it.

Caught off balance, Drake could do nothing to defend himself as Cunningham's fist drove into his side. His friend knew his injury, knew exactly where to strike to inflict maximum damage, and didn't hesitate to exploit his advantage. There was a sickening crack as an already weakened rib gave way under the blow.

Once a boxer, Drake knew as well as anyone that a single punch could turn a fight around. Many times he had seen dominant fighters felled by weaker opponents, brought down by one lucky strike that just happened to make contact in the right place at the right moment. There was always that instant of hesitation, that fraction of a second when everything seemed to stop, when the two adversaries stood frozen in time, perfectly balanced.

That was the turning point.

He couldn't see it now, but he felt it.

The world around him seemed to grow hazy as a tidal wave of pain exploded outwards from the point of impact, driving all before it. Drake felt as though he had been struck in the side with a sledgehammer, as if his entire ribcage had been caved in, crushing and tearing his internal organs. A sudden burst of warmth told him his makeshift dressing had come away, fresh blood welling up from the reopened wound.

Managing to wedge a knee between himself and Drake, Cunningham drove it upwards with all his strength, throwing Drake backwards through the doorway to land in a sprawl on the rough floorboards beyond.

The room was well and truly ablaze now. Though the thermite had burned right through to the level below, much of the floor was now on fire, with flames licking up through gaps in the boards. Choking smoke filled the air, red and orange in the glow of the fire.

Through hazy, streaming eyes, Drake looked up as Cunningham staggered through the doorway, bloodied and bruised but defiantly on his feet. He stooped down and snatched up the crowbar Drake had discarded earlier, wielding the simple but brutally effective weapon with practised ease.

Drake could do nothing to defend himself. He had no weapons, no objects to use as a shield, nothing with which to deflect the blow.

Staring into Cunningham's eyes, Drake saw no trace of the man he had once known. A killer stood before him now; a soldier ready to finish his enemy without remorse, without hesitation.

Something was pressing into his back; something hard

and square. He had barely noticed it amidst the burning pain of his broken rib and the choking fumes that seared his lungs with every breath, but his subconscious recognised it as something significant. A small, hard, square object lying discarded on the floor . . .

In a flash, his pain-racked brain assembled the pieces and realised the truth.

Even as Cunningham raised the crowbar to strike, Drake rolled aside, reached beneath him and felt his fingers close around the butt of Cunningham's Beretta.

It must have landed there when he struck it from the older man's grasp.

With no time to aim, he brought the weapon up in Cunningham's general direction, flicked off the safety and pulled the trigger.

There was a sharp crack, and suddenly a cloud of red sprayed outwards from the man's right shoulder, spinning him around with the force of the impact. For a fleeting moment he saw utter shock reflected in his former friend's eyes.

Squinting and struggling to hold the weapon level, Drake adjusted his aim and capped off another round just as Cunningham disappeared into the smoke and haze. The bullet sailed harmlessly past him, burying itself in the wall opposite.

Get up, a voice in his mind implored him. Get up now!

Gritting his teeth against the pain that blazed as hot as the fire consuming the room around him, Drake rolled over onto his stomach and forced himself up from the ground, muscles trembling with the effort.

On his feet, if only through sheer force of will, he staggered out through the doorway with the weapon raised, rounding the frame in time to see Cunningham disappearing down the stairs clutching his arm.

'Shit!'

Turning back into the room, he pulled his T-shirt up against his mouth in a feeble attempt to keep the smoke from his lungs. It didn't do much good, and already he was coughing and gasping for air.

With water streaming from his eyes, he glanced down at the floor. Mitchell's folder was still lying where he'd left it, its edges curling in the intense heat. One side was already alight as the flames rapidly spread out to consume it.

Cunningham would have to wait. That folder was the priority.

Braving the intense heat, he rushed forward and snatched up the folder, desperately beating it against his leg to extinguish the flames. It was charred and scorched in places, but still intact.

But he wouldn't be if he stayed here much longer. Already the floor was sagging inwards and flames were licking at the walls eagerly seeking more fuel.

Clutching the documents inside his jacket, Drake turned and fled, bumping into the wall outside before staggering down the corridor. He still gripped the Beretta in case Cunningham returned to finish the job, though his ability to hit anything more than 6 feet away was dubious.

His vision growing vague and hazy, he stumbled down the stairs, almost losing his footing. Smoke was billowing out of the corridor below. Whatever room the thermite had dropped down into must also be ablaze.

There was no sign of Cunningham, but a glance at the front door showed it standing ajar. He had made a run for it, fleeing into the surrounding neighbourhood.

Driven by his own body's desperate need for oxygen, Drake dashed for the door, kicked it open and staggered outside.

He could go no further. Exhausted, he fell to his knees, still clutching the burned and crumpled folder as though his life depended on it, which it probably did.

Behind him, a tremendous crash announced the collapse of the burning upper floor. Smoke was now streaming from the first-floor windows, and though he couldn't see it from his position, he was certain flames were now licking at the roof.

With trembling, soot-smeared hands, he laid the folder down. Cunningham had come within seconds of destroying it for ever, yet here it was, safe at last.

Redemption for him, and retribution for men like Carpenter.

The screech of tyres drew his attention to the main gate, where a Ford Explorer had just skidded to a halt, its headlight beams blindingly intense. Moments later, several figures emerged from the vehicle and streamed in through the open gate, all clutching weapons.

'Ryan!' he heard a familiar voice call out.

Sure enough, Samantha McKnight came rushing towards him, her eyes flitting between the dirty, injured, haggard-looking man who bore little resemblance to the Ryan Drake she knew, the damaged folder lying beside him, and the burning house behind.

'Jesus, are you all right?' she asked, kneeling down beside him.

Despite everything, Drake managed a smile as he picked up the charred folder and held it out to her. 'Never better, Sam.'

A few hundred yards away, Cunningham backed up against the rough brick wall of a block of flats, breathing hard and bleeding from the gunshot wound to his right arm. The injury was unlikely to prove life threatening, but he could feel blood trickling down his arm, dripping from his fingertips. Pain burned through him.

Drake had gotten the better of him. Despite Cunningham's best efforts to mislead him, to stifle his investigation, to keep him safely ignorant, he had found Mitchell's evidence. He should have killed him outright instead of trying to reason with him.

Now there was no telling how far this would go. It was out of control.

He had to report in. He hated the thought of admitting failure, especially when the stakes were as high as this, but there was no choice. His employer had to know what was going on.

With his good arm, he reached for his cellphone and dialled a number from memory. It wasn't a number he'd had much occasion to call in the past, but he had committed it to memory nonetheless.

'Is Drake taken care of?' a deep, authoritative voice asked as soon as the phone was answered.

Cunningham gritted his teeth. 'No.'

There was a pause on the other end. Not a long one, but long enough to assure him his news had not been met favourably.

'What happened?' Carpenter asked, his voice cold and emotionless. He had commanded men in battle for decades, had sacrificed lives and even risked his own on occasion. He wasn't about to break down in anger now.

That would come later.

'We found the safe house. Drake evaded me.'

'And Mitchell's files?'

Cunningham sighed and looked down at the ground, hating every word he was about to say. 'He has them.'

A steady, rhythmic thumping prompted him to glance

up just as a chopper roared overhead, skimming low over the rooftops. He couldn't make out what type it was, but there could be no doubt it was heading for the safe house.

Nearby, a set of shutters flew open and an elderly man leaned out to watch the spectacle. Cunningham backed up, merging with the deeper shadows at a corner of the wall.

'The Agency are here,' he added, having to raise his voice to be heard above the din. 'They've brought in air support.'

It took Carpenter only moments to reach a decision. 'All right. Get your ass out of there. We'll talk about this later.'

'My cover's blown,' Cunningham said, knowing how feeble and pathetic he must have sounded. 'Drake knows I was working for you.'

'You don't work for me, Cunningham. Not any more,' the older man coldly informed him. 'If you're lucky you might make it through tonight alive. After that, you're on your own. Now get the fuck out of there. I'll deal with Drake.'

With nothing more to say, he hung up.

Chapter 49

'Jesus Christ,' McKnight gasped, eyes wide in disbelief as she skim-read Mitchell's report, carefully leafing through the charred pages. 'It's incredible . . .'

Beneath her, the cityscape of central Kabul flitted by at over 100 knots as their Black Hawk helicopter beat a path through the night air towards Bagram Air Base.

The chopper had touched down in the waste ground behind the burning safe house a couple of minutes after McKnight's arrival, disgorging half a dozen Agency security operatives who had quickly established a perimeter around the building.

After explaining himself and the contents of the damaged folder, Drake had been bundled aboard the chopper along with McKnight, Keegan and Crawford.

'Carpenter arranged for Kourash to escape from prison,' Drake said, shifting position to get more comfortable on the hard bench. 'He was using him this whole time, planning attacks against our people, earning the trust of Taliban commanders so he could take them out.'

In his torn, burned and filthy clothes, his face smeared with soot, he was a pathetic sight. His ribs had been bandaged and a fresh dressing applied to the bullet wound at his side, though further medical care would have to wait until they touched down.

'And Horizon took all the credit,' Crawford finished for him.

Drake nodded. 'They were trying to prove they could do the army's job. If they take over security in Afghanistan, Carpenter and his mates stand to make billions.'

'And your buddy Cunningham was in on it, too?' Keegan said, seated opposite. He could see the hurt and betrayal in Drake's eyes.

'He did his best to steer us away from the truth, made sure we failed when we tried to hack Horizon's computers.' Drake swallowed a gulp of bottled water. His throat was still parched after inhaling several lung-fuls of smoke. 'He played us all. He played me.'

'What'll happen to him?'

Drake paused. He didn't imagine his friend's future was looking good at that moment. 'If he's got any sense, he'll disappear for good. If not . . .' He shrugged, feeling no need to finish that line of thought. 'The first thing we need to do is get people to Horizon head-quarters. They took Keira. My guess is they're holding her there.'

'Unless they're done with her,' Keegan said, his face ashen.

'They wouldn't do that. Not yet,' he said, not sure who he was trying to convince. 'They would want to know how much she'd uncovered.' He leaned forward, staring Keegan in the eye. 'We'll tear that building apart if we have to, but we'll find her.'

The sniper nodded. He didn't have to say what he was thinking – Drake knew well enough the bond that had developed between them.

Instead he glanced at McKnight; the woman who had played such a big part in all of this, and who wasn't even part of his team. 'Sam?'

428

She looked up at him, tearing her eyes away from the folder. 'Yeah?'

'I never got the chance to say this before, but . . . thank you.'

'For what?'

'For all of it. You risked your life for us more than once. We wouldn't have made it this far without you. I won't forget that.'

She nodded, understanding the sentiment and his need to express it. 'Tell me something, Ryan. Are all your operations like this?'

'Pretty much,' he admitted, unable to hide a grin.

But it quickly faded as he glanced outside, catching a fleeting glimpse of something coming towards them, something that glowed bright red like a hot coal. It took him a moment to realise what it meant.

Too late.

There was a blinding white flash, and an instant later the world around Drake was engulfed in chaos. The aircraft heaved violently, throwing them sideways in their safety harnesses with bone-jarring force as a thunderous boom reverberated through the cabin.

Trailing smoke and flame, the stricken Black Hawk yawed wildly to port, swinging in a wide arc as the pilots fought for control and overcompensated in their panic. Blaring alarms mingled with frightened shouts and the scream of tearing metal as the overloaded airframe started to give way.

Snapped right off its damaged runners by the violent movement, the starboard crew door flew off like a piece of cardboard. Drake watched as the ground spun and lurched sickeningly beneath them, his view obscured a moment later by smoke from the crippled engines.

Caught with his safety harness unlatched, the aircraft's

door gunner fell, slid across the listing deck and disappeared out through the open door with a wild, terrified scream. Drake could do nothing but watch in horror, clutching the cargo straps behind him in a white-knuckle grip.

'I've lost hydraulics!' the pilot yelled. 'Can't hold it. We're going down!'

The chopper yawed to starboard so hard that Drake could see nothing beyond the door but trees and fields. They had to be listing at 40 or 50 degrees by now. For a moment he thought the chopper was going to tip right over and plough into the ground. Then, in a final desperate effort, the pilot managed to haul the dying aircraft back from the brink.

It was only a temporary reprieve. Still locked in a death spiral, the big chopper ploughed through a stand of juniper trees, its rotors scything through branches and foliage like a knife through butter. Unable to take cover, Drake threw up his arm to shield himself as glass and pieces of tree bark peppered them.

His last sight was of a big area of flat open ground stretching out beneath them. Then his world was filled with a horrible sickening roar as the aircraft ploughed into the ground. The forward bulkhead rushed towards him, there was a flash, and then he knew no more.

Vermaak smiled as the wreckage of the stricken chopper came to rest amidst a cloud of smoke and dust. The Stinger had done its work with deadly efficiency, crippling the low-flying Black Hawk's engines before the crew even had a chance to react.

It was almost too easy.

Reaching up, he pressed the transmit button on his

encrypted radio unit. 'They're down,' he reported, his voice calm and devoid of emotion.

The same couldn't be said of Carpenter.

'Move in,' he ordered, his voice edged with tension and anticipation. His future depended on what happened here tonight. 'I want confirmation those files are destroyed.'

'And if anyone's still alive?' Vermaak asked. He knew the answer before he'd even asked the question, but he needed to hear it from Carpenter himself.

'There were no survivors, understand? No survivors.'

Vermaak smiled again. Fighting and killing had become a mere matter of business for him over the years, but in this case, he just might take pleasure in putting a round through Drake's head.

'Understood.'

Drake's mind drifted on the verge of unconsciousness, random thoughts and memories coming and going as if his brain were a misfiring engine. But somewhere deep down was a voice urging him to get up.

Sensations came first. He could feel dry wind-blown grit peppering his face and eyes, mixing with the warm slickness of blood dripping down the left side of his face. The chill night air carried an odd mixture of burned plastic, cordite, oil and aviation fuel.

And in a flash, his memory of the sudden explosion, the sickening crash came flooding back. They were down, but they were alive. They had survived.

It must have been Horizon. Somehow they had tracked his chopper and shot it out of the sky, just as they had done with Mitchell.

You have to get up. Get up now.

With great effort he forced his eyes open. The crew compartment was a mess of broken equipment, shorted-out instrument panels and buckled metal.

Something fluttered past his face. A piece of paper, burned and charred along one edge. They were everywhere, he realised; scattered all across the crew compartment like litter. Mitchell's evidence folder, torn apart during the crash. He watched as another piece, caught by the fitful breeze, slid across the deck and out through the gaping hole where the crew door had been.

With his growing awareness came the first waves of pain. He felt as if he had been sealed inside an oil drum and rolled off the edge of a cliff, his body battered and thrown around the enclosed crew compartment like a rag doll. Still, experimental movement of his arms and legs told him that nothing was broken. He could still function.

The chopper was lying tilted on its port side at about a 45-degree angle. Crash-landing in open ground, it must have tipped over into some depression or down an embankment before coming to rest.

'Drake?' a weak voice called out. 'You okay? What the fuck happened?'

Looking over, he saw Crawford struggling to get up, his face tight with pain as he clutched his left arm. His harness must have come undone during the crash.

'We got hit by a missile.'

Crawford's eyes opened wider. 'Horizon.'

'They'll be coming for us. They won't take any chances.' He would have done the same thing in their position. He glanced left, seeing Samantha still strapped into the seat opposite, her eyes closed and her head lolling to the side.

'Is that arm broken?'

Crawford shook his head, flexing and tensing the limb experimentally a few times. 'Feels kinda weird, but I don't think so.'

'Good. Check on the pilots.'

As Crawford clambered through into the cockpit, struggling to keep his balance on the listing deck, Drake looked over at Keegan, who was fighting to disengage himself from his harness.

'John?'

'Yeah?'

'You all right?'

At last his harness released and he pitched sideways, slamming into the deformed airframe with a hollow clang.

'Is it a cliché to say I'm too old for this shit?' he groaned.

'Only if you're a cop.' Drake pointed to the starboard crew door, now raised up off the ground because of the helicopter's tilt. 'Get up on lookout. I'll get Sam.'

'On it, buddy.'

As Keegan clambered to reach his improvised vantage point, Drake released his own harness and unstrapped himself. Bracing his boots against what had once been the port side airframe, he stumbled through the wrecked crew compartment to reach McKnight.

A quick check of the pulse at her neck confirmed she was alive. She must have been knocked unconscious on impact.

'Sam, wake up,' he hissed.

There was no response.

'We've got company,' Keegan called from above. 'Three vehicles inbound.'

'Shit,' Drake said under his breath. 'How far?'

'Three hundred yards, maybe three-fifty.'

It was them, he knew. A Horizon strike team were

coming to finish them. Just as with Mitchell's chopper, a couple of thermite grenades tossed in through the open hatch would be enough to kill them all and incinerate whatever evidence had survived the crash.

There was no time for gentle coaxing; if they didn't get moving, they were as good as dead. Turning his attention to McKnight, he drew back his arm and slapped her hard across the face. 'Come on, Sam! Wake up!'

The blow snapped her head around, but slowly her eyes fluttered open as consciousness returned. She stared at him for a moment, struggling to focus. 'Ryan?'

'Yeah, that's right. It's Ryan.'

'What happened?' she asked, looking around at the wrecked compartment.

'We took a Stinger hit. We crash-landed. Hang onto me,' he advised, unlatching her harness. He caught her as she fell forward, but was unable to keep from groaning in pain as his broken rib protested at his exertions.

'Are you hurt?' he asked, hoping she hadn't noticed.

'I don't think so.' She was well and truly conscious now. Pushing her dishevelled hair out of her eyes, she looked at Drake again. 'They're coming to kill us, aren't they?'

The grim finality in her voice made it seem as though it had already happened.

'Two hundred yards,' Keegan called down from his makeshift lookout position. 'They're splitting up, moving to outflank us.'

Drake gripped McKnight by the shoulders, staring right into her eyes. 'We're not dying here. Not now, not after all this. I'm getting us out. Understand?'

Before she could say anything further, Crawford stumbled through from the cockpit. The look in his eyes told them everything they needed to know. 'Both pilots are history,' he confirmed, unwilling to go into more detail.

Drake nodded. He had expected as much. A high-speed impact like that would have crumpled the cockpit like cardboard.

'If it's not too much trouble, I sure could use a weapon,' Keegan called down.

Drake looked around. 'Where's the weapons bin?'

Choppers like this always kept a stash of weapons on board in case they came down in hostile territory. The problem was, he had no idea where they were on Black Hawks.

Crawford pointed to a storage locker fixed into the wall on the port side. 'There!'

Sliding down to it, Drake grabbed the release handle and pulled. It wouldn't budge. The crash must have buckled the hinges, but a couple of hard kicks were enough to dislodge it. Wrenching it open, he was met with a rack of four P90 sub-machine guns.

The P90 was a compact, lightweight weapon; two characteristics that made it ideal for use in cramped spaces like vehicle interiors. They looked futuristic and intimidating, but like most 9mm sub-machine guns they were basically useless beyond 100 metres. An AK-47 was still lethal at more than four times that range.

'John, heads up,' he called, tossing one up to him, followed by a couple of spare magazines.

'Thanks, pal,' the older man replied, then added in a more urgent tone, 'Better hurry. They're closing in.'

Sure enough, Drake could see headlight beams reflecting off the ground outside. Rather than flickering up and down as the vehicle bumped over uneven terrain, the beams were burning steadily. At least one of the vehicles had stopped while the others circled around behind their position.

'Any cover nearby?'

The sniper craned his neck around, doing his best to survey the landscape from his limited vantage point. 'We're pitched into a wadi or something. Can't tell how far it runs, but it should give pretty good—'

He was interrupted when a burst of automatic fire tore through the night air, and instinctively dropped down inside the chopper just as several high-powered rounds slammed into the airframe. Most ricocheted off the armoured skin, but one or two punched right through to bury themselves in the rotor column.

Drake recognised the distinctive bark of AK-47s. The Russian-made weapons were ubiquitous in countries like Afghanistan, which made them a perfect weapon of choice for the Horizon strike team. Anyone finding dead bodies riddled with AK rounds would assume they had been killed by insurgents.

'Shit! Sons of bitches must have snuck in behind me,' Keegan said, visibly angered at having missed their approach.

Taking a breath, he rose up from the listing deck with the P90 up at his shoulder and capped off several rounds before ducking back down again.

His short burst was met with a storm of automatic fire, heavy-calibre rounds slamming into the dirt around the hatchway, kicking up clouds of dust and broken stones.

'I think they're pissed at me.'

Quickly Drake unlatched two more weapons from the rack and thrust them at Crawford and McKnight. 'Grab as much ammunition as you can carry and get ready to move.'

'Where are we going?' McKnight asked, sliding the unusual box magazine into its groove along the top of the weapon. As soon as it was home, she racked back the priming handle to chamber the first round.

With dubious armour protection and hundreds of pounds of aviation fuel still in its tanks, the crashed chopper could easily be turned into a steel coffin by a single well-thrown grenade. Their only chance was to make a break for it.

'Anywhere but here,' Drake replied, snatching up what remained of Mitchell's evidence folder. Many of the pages had been scattered in the crash and he had no time to gather them all, but with luck there was enough left to make the difference.

'Targets, fifty yards out,' Keegan warned, flinching as another burst of fire traced its way along the top of the doorway.

'Headcount?' Drake asked, shoving the folder down the front of his shirt. This done, he forced a couple of spare magazines into his belt.

'Fuckin' lots,' was the simple reply. 'I can't hold them off.'

'Bin it, mate,' Drake advised. 'We're moving now. I'll take point, you bring up the rear. Everyone else on me. Crawford, Sam, ready?'

He was met by a pair of nods.

'All right. Move!'

Chapter 50

The reinforced windows of Carpenter's office provided panoramic views over Kabul, allowing its sole occupant gaze out across the city without fear of attack. The armoured glass would withstand anything short of an anti-tank round.

But Carpenter was oblivious to the impressive vista at that moment. He had shut himself away in his office with explicit instructions that he not be disturbed for any reason. All of his attention was focused on events several miles to the north unfolding in real time on his computer screen.

His bird's-eye view of the battle came courtesy of a small remote-controlled drone orbiting several thousand feet above the crashed chopper, its only weapon a high-resolution infrared camera mounted in the nose.

Carpenter had vectored one of these little aircraft into the ambush area to survey the crash site for survivors. Sure enough, he could see bright white blobs of colour moving around the interior of the crashed chopper; the unmistakable thermal images of human bodies. Clearly someone had survived the crash, though if Vermaak and his strike team had anything to do with it, it wouldn't be for long.

Already he could see men converging on the crash site from three separate directions, pausing occasionally to lay down covering fire while their comrades rushed forward. It was a textbook example of a fighting advance by men who were well drilled and used to working with each other.

And it was just as well, because time was running out. Even he could do nothing to hide the fact that a Coalition chopper had been shot down on the outskirts of Kabul, triggering a search-and-rescue response from all units in the vicinity. The survivors had to be eliminated quickly before any relief effort could be mounted.

Involuntarily his hands clenched into fists. His career, his company, everything he had worked to build in the past five years, and perhaps his very life, now hung in the balance.

It all depended on what happened in the next few minutes.

The RG-31 shuddered to a halt at last. The rear doors were swung open and Anya was pushed roughly outside, making sure to stumble and fall with a groan of pain as she hit the ground.

Cursing under his breath, the big Hispanic operative moved forward and lifted her bodily to her feet. She noticed with a momentary feeling of distaste that his hand found her breast as he raised her up.

Her eyes took in everything as she was escorted towards the main building. She saw a couple of other armoured jeeps parked near a maintenance area, in the process of being refuelled. Several operatives were milling around, some standing off to one side and smoking.

All were armed with M4 carbines; an excellent assault rifle that had served her well on many operations during her long career.

Over by the perimeter wall, she was relieved to see the ruined Toyota pickup truck being lowered from the winch of an armoured recovery vehicle. Its engine bay had been crumpled and deformed by the crash, rendering it inoperable, but that didn't matter now. It still had a part to play.

Normally at times like this she was able to purge her mind of all other thoughts, concentrating solely on her objective. Yet, oddly, she found herself thinking of Drake.

She felt guilty for leaving him behind, for allowing him to be drawn into this mess when it was of her making. Once again he was paying the price for her mistakes, and as hard as she tried to cut herself away from such thoughts, she couldn't get past the feeling that she owed him more than that.

She shook her head to rid herself of such doubts as she was led inside the main building.

She had been here once before, a very long time ago. It had been different then, of course. Different owners, and a different purpose. She had been different too. But even now, after all these years, this place still elicited a lingering sense of dread in her.

The holding cells would be down in the basement. That was the way it had been twenty years ago, and she didn't imagine much had changed since then. Carpenter wouldn't have troubled himself to alter such a feature of this building, especially when it served such a useful purpose.

Sure enough, after taking a left off the main corridor, she was led down a flight of stairs that she remembered all too well. They might have been given a new coat of paint since then, but what lay beneath hadn't changed.

Two guards accompanied her down; the big Hispanic

440

man named Martinez, one hand clamped around her arm, and his smaller companion Shaw.

Reaching the bottom of the stairs, she found herself facing a narrow corridor with heavy steel doors set along each side, each secured by deadbolts. She couldn't tell if any of them were occupied, but there were no other operatives around, the cells being impossible to escape from.

She almost smiled. Perfect.

Allowing herself to stumble, she pretended to lose her footing and sagged in her captor's arms; a dead weight, a useless burden.

'Get up, goddamn it,' Martinez growled, shoving her forward irritably.

Her time had come. With a single twist of her wrist, she slipped free of the handcuffs and spun around to face him, swinging the now exposed ratchet as a crude, blunt hook.

Her aim was perfect, the rough metal edge making contact in the centre of his forehead, gouging a bloody path across his right eye and down his cheek. Screaming in pain, he twisted aside, clutching his mangled face.

I will show no mercy. I will never hesitate.

Rounding on Shaw just as he swung the barrel of the M4 to bear on her, Anya grabbed the weapon's protruding foregrip and yanked it upwards, forcing it away from her. An instant later, her right hand leapt out, striking a quick, vicious blow to Shaw's exposed throat.

When it came to unarmed combat, Anya knew of few more effective ways of subduing an opponent than a hard blow to the thyroid cartilage surrounding the larynx. The intense pain and temporary inability to breathe thus produced was enough to drop even the toughest fighter, and Shaw was no different.

Coughing and gasping, eyes wide with fear, he released his grip on the weapon, staggered sideways and fell to his knees, trying to make for the stairs. It was a futile effort, and soon ended when Anya brought the butt of the M4 down on the back of his neck.

With one opponent now removed from the fight, she turned her attention to Martinez. Injured and half blinded he might have been, but he was still a threat, and threats had to be dealt with.

Keira Frost opened her eyes, startled by the agonised cry echoing from the corridor outside her cell. But no sooner had it started than it was abruptly cut off.

She swallowed, her throat dry, her skin cold and clammy. Bound on the floor as she was, she could do nothing to protect herself. She had chafed the skin around her wrists raw trying to break the plastic cuffs, to no avail. She knew from experience that they were near impossible to remove by brute force.

She had never had much fear of water until today. Even now she vividly remembered the agony of trying to draw breath that wouldn't come, the terror of knowing she was drowning, the helplessness of fighting in vain to break free.

In the end she had told them what they wanted to know, had given them every detail of her hacking attempt, the information she was trying to access, the suspicions Drake and his team harboured towards Horizon. She had told them everything, and she hated herself for it.

Where Drake was now, whether he was even still alive, she had no idea. More than likely she would never know. They would kill her once they were certain she could be of no further use.

She tensed at the sound of footsteps in the corridor outside. Footsteps, slow and deliberate, coming closer. Coming for her.

In a feeble attempt at retreating, she shuffled along the floor, backing away from the door even as the footsteps halted outside.

This was it, she knew. They had come to kill her.

She stared wide-eyed as the bolt was withdrawn and the door swung open.

But nothing could have prepared her for the sight that now confronted her.

Chapter 51

'Contact!' Drake yelled, ducking down as a volley of automatic fire sliced through the air above him. The rounds came so close to his head as they whizzed past that he could actually feel the change in air pressure. Taking a rough bearing on the muzzle flash, he fired a short automatic burst in reply.

Beside him, Keegan was capping off rounds with his own weapon, taking his time and aiming well to conserve ammunition. Empty shell casings littered the ground all around them.

Despite their grave situation, Keegan's face was a picture of calm, as it always was during contacts. Drake could have sworn he was humming a tune under his breath.

As he'd thought, the chopper had come to rest in a dried-up river, its crumpled nose buried in the dust and rocks that had once formed the stream bed. He suspected this had once been an irrigation channel, part of a larger network used to supply farms in this region. Decades of fighting had destroyed many of these delicate water systems, consigning once lush farmland to drought and abandonment.

'We're pinned down,' McKnight hissed. Sighting a target moving amongst the tangled scrub 50 yards away, she swung her weapon around and loosed a long, sustained burst. 'We've got to find cover. We're sitting ducks out here.'

'I hear you,' Drake agreed.

He glanced around, seeking anything that might provide more substantial protection.

About 100 yards further along the river bed lay the crumbling remains of a farm compound. Like most of the buildings in this region, the dwelling itself was surrounded by a high wall, either for protection from the elements or for keeping livestock penned in.

It was a gamble, but anything was better than where they were.

'That's our play,' he said, pointing to it. 'Can you make it that far?'

'Only if you hold my hand,' she quipped, flashing a wry smile.

Ignoring her remark, Drake turned to the others. 'We make for that compound over there. Two-by-two formation. John, on me. Sam, Crawford, you follow.'

'Copy that,' Keegan replied without looking around.

'That's a lot of open ground to cover,' Crawford warned him.

'It's all we've got. If we stay here, we're dead,' Drake said bluntly. Now wasn't the time for gentle persuasion.

He took a deep breath, rallying his flagging strength.

'Okay, go! Go!'

'You have got to be shitting me,' Frost gasped, staring in disbelief at the woman now standing in the doorway. Cold blue eyes stared back at her.

It was Anya. The woman she had risked her life to rescue from a Siberian prison. The woman who had threatened to kill her on the flight home, who had dislocated her shoulder during a violent confrontation in

Saudi Arabia. The woman who had shot Drake and left him to die.

She was standing mere feet away, clutching an M4 assault rifle, watching her as a predator might regard its prey. A splash of blood coated her cheek. In her shock, Frost barely registered the fact she now had dark hair, or that her eyes were a different colour.

Saying nothing, the older woman drew a knife from her belt and advanced on her, the blade gleaming in the electric lights.

Frost was breathing harder, her heart hammering in her chest as she tried to back away. She could only imagine what Anya intended to do with that blade.

Then, just like that, she spoke.

'I am not here to kill you,' she said, kneeling down beside her. 'Unless you give me a reason to.'

Frost felt the blade against the skin of her wrist, but only for a moment. With a single firm slice, the plastic cuffs came away, releasing her hands.

Wasting no time, Frost jumped to her feet and backed away, too shocked by this sudden turn of events to say anything for the next few seconds.

'W-what the fuck are *you* doing here?' she finally managed to stammer.

'I did not come here to rescue you, if that's what you mean,' Anya replied, quick to quash any such thoughts. 'But if you want to get out, follow me, stay silent and do as I say. Understand?'

Still too shocked to give any other response, Frost merely nodded.

Satisfied, Anya turned away, reached up and yanked the long brunette hairpiece free, throwing it aside to reveal a mane of short, dishevelled blonde hair. And with a little more care she drew a fingertip across each eye to remove the contact lenses she'd been wearing. She would need unimpeded vision from now on.

This done, she crept out into the corridor with the assault rifle up at her shoulder. Frost followed behind, noting the two Horizon operatives lying sprawled on the floor, one with blood pooling beneath his head.

With the M4 covering the stairs leading upwards, Anya knelt down beside one of the fallen men and patted down his pockets until she found what she was looking for: a cellphone.

'What are you doing?' Frost asked as the woman dialled a number.

'I presume you forgot what I said about keeping quiet,' Anya said without looking up. 'Just be ready to move when I give the word, and stay close to me.'

With the number inputted, she gripped the assault rifle tight and hit the button to connect the call.

In the walled marshalling area outside, Anya's rusty, battered Toyota pickup truck sat parked near the perimeter wall. With its paintwork faded to a dull, pale blue, bald tyres and an exhaust barely held together by increasingly futile spot-welds, it was an unremarkable vehicle to say the least.

Unremarkable but for its cargo.

Packed into a space between the fuel tank and the transmission was a metal box containing several pounds of Composition 4 plastic explosive. Inserted into it were several electric blasting caps wired into a battery, the firing switch controlled by a simple, commercially available cellphone.

The instant Anya's call connected, the change in voltage was enough to trigger the switch, which in turn caused electricity to surge into the blasting caps.

Five seconds after dialling the number, her improvised

bomb detonated with enough explosive force to crumple the pickup truck like a toy. The shockwave rushed outwards in all directions, reverberating against the concrete wall opposite with crushing power, while the contents of the fuel tank added to the destruction.

Up in his office, Carpenter flinched at the bright flash off to his right, followed a moment later by a shockwave that seemed to reverberate up from the very core of the building. Rising from his desk, he watched in disbelief as a section of the perimeter wall appeared to lean precariously outwards, before collapsing in a cloud of smoke and broken masonry.

Flames were roaring upwards from a ruptured fuel tank, with a pall of smoke and dust now hovering over the entire scene.

'What the fuck . . . ?' Turning his attention back to his desk, he picked up his phone and hit the quick-dial button for the building's security centre. As always, the call was answered straight away.

'Wilson here, sir,' the duty security chief began.

'Wilson, what the hell is going on out there?'

'We're working on it now, sir.'

Only a fool would try to storm the Horizon building. Even with the wall breached, every possible approach was covered with security cameras and emplaced machine guns.

Logically he knew the Horizon compound was, to all intents and purposes, impregnable, but that didn't stop his gut telling him something wasn't right.

'Take every man you can spare and form a cordon around that breach,' he ordered. 'Anyone comes within 50 yards of our wall, shoot to kill. Do you understand me?'

'Yes, sir.'

'One more thing,' he added. 'Have a chopper fuelled and standing by on the roof. I want to be airborne in ten minutes.'

He was too close to this whole affair. It was time he distanced himself, perhaps left Afghanistan permanently. And if the shit hit the fan, he had no intention of waiting here for ISAF to come and arrest him.

'Copy that, sir. Ten minutes.'

Hanging up the phone, Carpenter turned his attention back to his computer screen, and the real-time images of the battle unfolding around the ruined chopper. He could still see figures moving near the wreck even as bright blobs of tracer fire arced in around them.

Vermaak and his men were closing the noose.

Chapter 52

With Crawford and McKnight covering them, Drake and Keegan rose up and charged along the shallow depression, hunched over to present smaller targets. The ground was rough and uneven, and covered with rocks that made their footing treacherous. Hidden explosives were a constant menace, but there was no time to check for them.

Stopping after about twenty paces, both men dropped to their knees, weapons trained outwards while Crawford and McKnight sprinted past. Nothing was said, because concealment was vital to their survival.

Glancing over his shoulder, Drake saw Crawford and McKnight take up firing positions close to the compound. That was their signal to move. He looked at Keegan and gave a simple nod, pulling himself to his feet again.

They had covered about 40 yards before they were spotted. Bullets whizzed past, slamming into the ground and showering them with dirt and fragments of rock. There was no way to avoid such things; they just had to keep running and hope that luck was with them.

Sighting several muzzle flashes off to their left, Drake raised his P90, took aim and put down half a dozen shots on their position. The kick of the weapon in his shoulder was a familiar sensation, and instinctively he adjusted his aim with each shot to allow for the recoil. At least one of his shots found its mark, and he heard an agonised scream as his target went down.

'Go! Get in there!' Crawford yelled as both men rushed past and into the compound. 'You too, McKnight.'

He was about to fall back himself when something slammed into his left shoulder. It hit hard – hard enough to spin him around. Caught off balance, he fell to his knees and looked down, noting with a kind of hazy detachment the bloody hole in his shoulder.

'Shit . . .'

Keegan was first in through the door to the compound, sweeping his sub-machine gun from left to right in search of a target. The big open area, about 40 feet square, seemed to be deserted. The walls were simple mud brick, cracked and worn by long years of exposure to the elements.

There had once been a roofed dwelling set against the west wall, but it had long since collapsed, taking a portion of the outer wall with it. All that remained were piles of rubble.

'Clear,' he hissed.

Drake was next in.

'Keegan, take position . . . by that breach,' he gasped, backing up against the solid cover of the stone wall, sweating and breathing hard as McKnight hurried past.

Nobody followed her.

Drake's stomach lurched. Reaching out, he grabbed the woman by the arm. 'Where's Crawford?'

'He . . . he was right behind me.'

Rushing back to the entrance, Drake peered out into the winding, arid river bed they'd just sprinted along. In the darkness, it was hard to make out details amongst the rocks and straggling bushes.

451

Then, at last, he saw what he was looking for, and felt his blood run cold.

Encased within an armoured panic room at the core of the Horizon building, with its own independent air supply, phone lines and access strictly controlled by biometric safeguards, the security room was undoubtedly one of the safest places in Kabul, if not the entire country.

No unauthorised personnel could get in or out.

Three operatives were manning the room, their eyes glued to the bank of monitors facing them. Fully twenty surveillance cameras covered every possible approach to the compound, with intercom links to the four permanently manned guard towers and secure radio comms with any roving patrols they had set up. Even the rooftop heliport was covered.

Nonetheless, despite all these safeguards, the mood in the room was fraught with tension. Each man was well aware of the explicit orders that had come direct from Carpenter himself. No one was to come within 50 yards of their perimeter.

And Carpenter was not a man to look kindly on failure.

Glancing up at the clock, Frank Wilson, the acting head of security, hit the intercom to connect him with his roving security teams.

'All sectors, check in.'

'Sector One, all clear.'

'Sector Two, clear.'

'Sector Three, we're clear.'

As the security operative for sector 3 gave his brief report, the door behind him eased open and a figure slipped silently out into the corridor, stealing towards him with the sinewy grace of a predator born to end lives. Momentarily preoccupied with his radio, he neither saw nor heard what was coming for him.

The instant he let go of his radio, strong hands clamped over his mouth, yanking his head back with vicious force. He felt the cold steel of a blade pressed against his throat.

'Drop your weapon,' a voice whispered in his ear. It was cold and hard, yet too high-pitched to be a man. 'Drop it now or you die.'

The blade pressed in tighter, slicing the skin. Warm blood flowed down his throat and instinctively he tried to pull away from the knife, but that only caused it to press in harder.

Resistance would mean death. Even in his state of shock and fear, he realised that and released his grip on the carbine, allowing it to clatter to the floor.

'I will take my hand away now,' the voice informed him. 'If you try to call for help, you die. Cooperate and you will live.'

Definitely a woman. How the fuck could a woman have gotten the better of him like this? And how the hell had she even managed to get in here?

The gloved hand was removed from his mouth, though the knife remained firmly in place. Any attempt to cry out would result in the blade being thrust into his windpipe.

'Where is the security room?'

'What—'

Suddenly the knife switched position, moving up to his face, the tip pressing into the skin of his lower eyelid. Her other hand clamped around his jaw, preventing him from twisting his head aside.

'Let me make this simple. Each time you don't answer, I will cut part of you away.' The gleaming, wickedly sharp blade pressed deeper. 'And they will be things you will miss. Do you believe me?'

'Yes,' he said, trembling, sick with fear. He didn't doubt for a second that she would carve out both of his eyes without hesitation.

'Good. Where is the security room?'

'One floor up, main corridor, on the left.'

'What is the access method?'

'Biometric.'

'Eye scanner?'

He tried to shake his head, but immediately realised how unwise such a movement would be. 'Fingerprint.'

'Lucky for you.'

The next thing he knew, both the knife and the gloved hand were withdrawn. He started to turn, but before he could act, something struck him hard at the base of his skull. White light flashed across his vision, his legs buckled and he went down.

No sooner had he fallen than Anya hooked her hands beneath his armpits and dragged the unconscious man into the stairwell she had just emerged from.

She was obliged to put the knife to work, though not to kill him. She had kept her promise on that account. Bound to a water pipe by the handcuffs she had escaped from earlier, the unconscious guard would live, though minus the thumb and forefinger of his right hand. Those she took with her.

She didn't think he was lying about the biometric reader. But if so, she would know exactly where to find him.

Raising her M4 once more, she hurried out into the corridor with Frost close behind. Anya knelt down, picked up the weapon dropped by the security guard and handed it to her companion.

'You know how to use that, I assume?' she asked without turning around.

'I think I can manage,' Frost replied in a sour tone, pulling back the priming handle to check that a round was chambered.

With a faint smile, Anya glanced at her watch. Fifty-seven seconds until the next perimeter check.

'Good. Follow me.'

They had to hurry.

Crawford had often wondered what it would feel like to be shot. During his time in Afghanistan he'd seen casualties brought in by evac chopper or Humvee, some moaning in pain, some crying and begging for help, others quiet and peaceful as if untroubled by their injuries. But in all his years in the service, he'd never experienced it himself.

Now he had.

It didn't hurt as much as he'd expected. He could feel the tingling warmth of blood on his skin, and he sensed the force of the impact as if someone had clouted him hard across the upper arm, but the pain hadn't found him yet.

He could hear voices over near the lip of the wadi, and looked up just as three Horizon operatives appeared out of the darkness, weapons up at their shoulders.

Gritting his teeth with the effort, he raised the P90 with his good arm and opened fire. His closest target jerked as rounds slammed into him, some stopped by his body armour but others tearing through his flesh. Only when a round entered his skull just above his right eye did he fall back and collapse in a bloodied heap, while his companions threw themselves down to avoid a similar fate.

It was just as well, because Crawford had expended the last of his ammunition.

Dropping the useless weapon, he struggled to his feet and made a last desperate run for the compound. He was starting to feel the extent of his injuries now, every movement sending flashes of pain through his body. He closed his eyes, trying hard to ignore it as he struggled onward.

Almost there.

Unknown to him, he was being watched. Crouched behind a rocky outcrop on the other side of the river bed, Piet Vermaak raised his AK-47, took careful aim and loosed a single well-placed shot.

He didn't feel the impact right away, but he heard the dull wet thud as the round tore through his thigh, severing arteries and muscle. Unable to support himself, he collapsed to the ground with a groan of frustration, pain and despair.

'He's down,' Vermaak spoke into his radio. It was almost too easy. 'Move in.'

He was down, and he knew he wouldn't get up again. Judging by the size of the wound, he'd been hit by a 7.62mm AK round that had torn through his thigh muscles as it exited. Blood was pumping from the severed arteries.

Groaning in pain, he rolled over to see the remaining two Horizon operatives coming for him. Knowing he was unarmed and no longer a threat, they didn't hurry. They were waiting until they had a clear shot. They'd just seen him kill one of their comrades, and now they were out for revenge.

His concentration was waning, his vision growing hazy. With a trembling hand, he reached for the side arm holstered at his hip, knowing even as he did so that he'd

456

never make it. Even if he could find the strength to aim and fire the weapon, both men had the drop on him.

He had heard that one's life was supposed to flash before one's eyes at a time like this, but no such thing happened for him. He wasn't afraid. It had all happened too fast for that. His only thought was that he wasn't ready to die.

At that moment, the din of weapons fire cut through the air and both men went down, crumpling before his eyes under a hail of impacts.

'Clear!' he heard a voice yell. A British voice. Drake's voice.

'Got his fucking number,' Keegan said as he knelt down and ejected the spent magazine from his weapon. He had emptied the remainder of his magazine into Crawford's would-be killers.

'What took you so long?' Crawford asked, managing a pained grin as Drake knelt beside him. Wisps of smoke trailed from the barrel of his weapon.

'Had to stop for a breather.' He smiled back, but his smile vanished when he saw the extent of Crawford's injuries. 'Come on, mate. Let's get you out of here.'

The next thing Crawford knew, he was being hauled to his feet by Drake, with Keegan covering them. Pain lanced through him when he put weight on the injured leg. He stumbled, on the verge of blacking out, but Drake hauled him upright again.

'Come on, get up. You still have to kick my arse for going AWOL, remember?'

'Don't tempt me,' he replied, stifling another groan of pain.

With Drake half-dragging, half-carrying him, they staggered into the compound and collapsed against the wall, breathing hard. Crawford was pale, his face tight with pain, drawing fast, shallow breaths through clenched teeth.

Drake forced himself up, ignoring the pain of his own injuries. 'Keegan, cover the door.'

'On it, buddy.' He had already taken up position beside the doorway, though he was obliged to duck as another burst of AK fired traced its way along the wall, blasting away part of the frame.

Drake jabbed a hand towards the gap in the west wall. 'Sam, cover the breach.'

Nodding, she rose up and hurried over, keeping low to avoid stray rounds.

Drake, meanwhile, had turned his attention back to the injured man. He grabbed the torn fabric of Crawford's trousers. 'I've got to look at it.'

The shoulder wound was still leaking blood at a steady rate, but it was unlikely to be fatal in the short term. The gunshot wound to his thigh was another story. Several big arteries ran through that area, and if one of them had been severed, he'd bleed to death in minutes.

With a single jerk, he ripped the trouser leg apart, exposing the gory exit wound. A 7.62mm round doesn't leave much to chance, and this was no exception, tearing apart Crawford's quadriceps muscle on its way out. By the looks of things, it had also severed an artery. Blood was pumping out in time with his pulse.

Crawford guessed his thoughts. 'Doesn't look good, does it?'

Drake avoided his gaze. 'We have to stop the bleeding.'

Removing his belt, he wrapped it around Crawford's leg, just above the wound. 'This is going to hurt.'

'What else is new?' Taking a deep breath, he tensed up and gave a nod.

He was as ready as he could be, but he couldn't stifle

a cry of pain as Drake pulled the makeshift tourniquet tight. Painful it might have been, but it was doing its job. The bleeding began to slow as the constricted arteries tried to force more blood through.

'Son of a bitch!' he groaned, spitting on the ground. 'That was fun.'

Over by the doorway, Keegan shook his head. 'Doesn't make any goddamn sense. What are they waiting for?'

Before Drake could reply, a bright flash lit the night air, followed by a thunderous boom that seemed to shake the very ground beneath them.

'What was that?' McKnight called out, unable to see from her position.

Leaving Crawford for a moment, Drake ducked over to the doorway. Pillars of fire rose up into the night sky from the shattered wreck of the chopper, casting their baleful orange glow for hundreds of yards in all directions. Caught in thermal updraughts, pieces of burning paper fluttered up into the darkness like fireflies.

'The chopper,' Keegan replied. Crouched by the doorway, his craggy face was illuminated by the glow of burning aviation fuel. 'It's gone.'

And they were next.

Chapter 53

The mood in the security centre was fraught with tension as operatives scanned the external security cameras, looking for any sign of approaching hostiles. So far, nothing.

Wilson's radio crackled into life. 'Perimeter here, sir.'

'Go,' Wilson commanded.

As instructed, he had dispatched most of his remaining men to cover the perimeter, particularly the breach now opened in the outer wall. Several men had also hurried forward with extinguishers, braving the fire and smoke to tackle the flames that were still raging.

'It was the car we brought in,' the crackly voice reported. 'The thing went up like Hiroshima – must have been packed with explosives.'

Wilson felt a knot of fear twist his guts. One of their patrols had been involved in a smash with a civilian vehicle apparently under the control of a drunk driver. When they had requested to bring her in and keep her in holding overnight, he had agreed without much thought. It had been an inconvenience, nothing more.

He had even dispatched a truck to tow her crashed vehicle into the compound, knowing it would be stripped by looters before dawn if it was left unattended. Anyway, if they decided to press charges against her, they would need the vehicle as evidence.

Only now did he see the crash for what it was – a ploy.

Mere seconds after receiving the report, he keyed his radio. 'Martinez, what's the status of that detainee?'

There was no response, save for the crackle of static.

'Martinez, report.'

At that moment, the electronic door locks clicked open as the biometric reader outside recognised an authorised thumbprint.

Wilson spun in his chair as the armoured door slid open on its metal runners, moving with crisp precision to reveal the new arrival. And in a sudden, heart-stopping moment of absolute shock, Wilson found himself face to face with the detainee.

Taking a step inside so that the automatic door could close behind her, Anya surveyed the room and did an immediate threat assessment. Three men in charge of the building's security system, all armed with Glock 17 automatics, all staring at her in blank shock.

She expected that to last another second or so. In situations like this, there was always one who acted without thinking; always one who had to be put down.

Sure enough, the man on the furthest side of the room reached for his weapon. Without hesitation, Anya raised the M4 carbine, got a good sight picture of his head and pulled the trigger.

There was a single, loud crack, followed by a wet crunch as the back of his head disintegrated in a spray of blood and bone. He went down immediately, toppling sideways in his chair, having never even managed to draw his weapon.

She had the other two covered in a heartbeat.

These two were smarter than their companion; smart enough to know that they didn't want to meet a similar fate. Neither man moved a muscle.

She knew she should kill them both. They were enemies, whether through choice or by sheer bad luck. They had seen her face, and subduing them would take precious time.

But they were no threat to her now. It was likely they had no knowledge of or involvement in Horizon's misdeeds. For all she knew, they could have wives, children, families. People depending on them. People who would mourn their deaths.

It happened almost before she knew it.

'If either of you want to see tomorrow, lie down on the floor with your hands behind your head,' she instructed.

Neither man was inclined to argue with that; not with a high-powered assault rifle pointed at them.

As the two operatives slid off their chairs and onto the floor, Anya glanced at the bank of television monitors facing her. There were cameras covering every conceivable angle of the building, including the rooftop helicopter pad.

A Bell 205 chopper had just touched down. Its rotors were still turning, which meant the pilot expected to take off again shortly. It was here to pick someone up, and she had a feeling she knew who.

Hitting the button behind her to unlock the door, she waited a few seconds while Frost entered, clutching her own weapon in a death grip. The young woman surveyed the two captives on the ground and their dead companion on the far side of the room, saying nothing.

'Can you handle these two?' Anya asked without lowering her weapon.

She nodded. 'I've got them.'

'Good.' Lowering the carbine, Anya turned to face her. 'Disable the door lock when I leave. You'll be safe here until help arrives.'

Designed as it was to resist intruders, Frost could hold out in this room for days if need be. The armoured walls had even muffled the sound of the gunshot.

'What about you?'

Anya glanced at the image of the chopper waiting for its high-priority passenger. 'I have to pay a visit to an old friend.'

She was just reaching for the door release when the young woman spoke up again. 'Anya, look . . .' She sighed, struggling to express what she was feeling. 'For what it's worth . . . I still don't like you.'

Anya glanced at her, offering a small, barely perceptible smile. 'The feeling is mutual. Good luck, Frost.'

With that, she hit the door release button, slipped through and was gone.

'They'll be coming,' Drake said, checking the semi-transparent magazine on his P90 to see how many rounds were left. 'Everyone get ready.'

With the chopper destroyed, there was only one more loose end to tie up, and that was them. The Horizon strike team would come at them with everything they had now, wanting to finish this quickly.

Drake turned his attention to Keegan, who had clambered up a set of stone steps to a low parapet running along the top of the wall. That position afforded the sniper a far greater field of fire.

'John, how many rounds have you got?'

'Last mag,' the sniper replied without taking his eye off the weapon's sights. 'Not much to hold them off with.'

'Then make every round count.'

The old man flashed a wolfish grin. 'Always do, buddy.'

McKnight had taken up position on the other side of the compound, crouched by the collapsed pile of stones that had once been a shed or dwelling, the barrel of her weapon sweeping the darkness. Drake hurried over to her.

'What about you, Sam?' he asked, speaking low and quiet.

'One clip in the weapon, plus one spare.' She glanced at Drake and managed a weak smile. 'I guess waving a white flag's out of the question, huh?'

Drake shook his head. 'Wouldn't hold my breath.'

'Figured as much.'

Drake hesitated, about to move away. He couldn't do it. He couldn't leave her here alone to hold this position.

'Sam, get over there,' he said, pointing over to the far corner of the compound, where stood the remains of some kind of kiln or oven.

She shook her head. 'I'm not going anywhere.'

'You'll be safer there.' Unwilling to debate the matter, he grabbed her by the arm and pulled her away from the gap. Pain burned outwards from his broken rib.

'Damn it, Ryan,' she hissed, shoving him away. 'It doesn't matter where I am. If they get in here, we're all dead. So shut the hell up and get on that wall. I'll cover this position.'

Drake was about to argue, but a shout from Keegan silenced further debate.

'Movement, fifty yards. This is it.'

Drake glanced back at the woman.

'Trust me, Ryan. Go,' she implored him, eyes shining in the light of the burning chopper.

Reaching out, Drake grasped her hand tight, wishing he had time to say the things he wanted to say. But this wasn't the time, and it certainly wasn't the place. Instead he let go and took up position on the other side of the breach.

No way were those bastards getting in here. Only one side was getting out of this alive, and he would make sure it was his.

Not far away, concealed in the darkness and tangled scrub, Piet Vermaak surveyed the old farm compound with the keen, analytical gaze of a born soldier.

Like penned sheep, their enemies were all confined within those ancient walls. At least one was heavily wounded, as Vermaak himself had made sure. Dead comrades could be left behind if need be, but few could stand to abandon a wounded man. Instead he became a drain on his own side, requiring people to treat and tend him.

That left three able-bodied defenders, surrounded, with limited ammunition, standing against a dozen heavily armed operatives. Vermaak might have smiled if the situation had been different, if there wasn't so much at stake.

His radio earpiece crackled. 'We're in position. RPG's standing by.'

Time to put an end to this.

Vermaak hit his radio's transmit button. 'Fire.'

'Incoming!' Keegan cried out in warning.

Instinctively they flattened themselves against the

ground as a volley of rocket-propelled grenades arced in from several different directions, all converging on the compound they had sought shelter in. Designed for knocking out tanks, they were also ruthlessly effective against lightly armoured structures.

One sailed right overhead, its rocket motor still trailing exhaust gases, and exploded about 50 feet away. Another found its mark, however, striking the north wall of the compound and blasting a gaping hole in the ancient stonework.

Drake covered his head as chunks of masonry rained down on them, dust and smoke filling the air. Decades-old mud brick was just no match for several pounds of high explosive.

These rockets had a smaller kill radius than fragmentation rounds, but they were doing a pretty effective job of reducing the compound walls to broken rubble. Several breaches had been opened by the first salvo. More than they could cover.

Shaking his head, Drake picked himself up. Dust swirled around him, stinging his eyes and choking his throat.

'Contact! Targets, thirty yards and closing!' McKnight raised her P90 and started snapping off shots.

'How many?' Drake called, his ears ringing.

A burst of fire slammed into the wall that McKnight was crouched behind, showering her with stone fragments. 'Shit!' She pressed a hand against the fresh cut on her cheek. 'Lots, and they're not stopping.'

Drake took a deep breath, rallying whatever reserves of strength remained to him, and rose to his feet. Rushing over to the newly opened gap in the north wall, he took up position on the left side, raised his weapon up to the shoulder just as he'd done a thousand times before, and peered out.

He caught a momentary glimpse of dark figures emerging from the dry scrub barely 20 yards distant, before at least two of them opened up on him, firing in sustained automatic bursts. Ducking down, he watched as several tracer rounds zipped through the gap mere feet from his head.

He waited for a break in the fire. There was no time to ponder the risks, to analyse the situation and consider alternatives. When the chance came, he acted, leaning out with the P90 at his shoulder, and sighted his target.

Taking first pressure on the trigger, he put down a dozen rounds on semi-automatic, gritting his teeth as the weapon kicked back into his shoulder again and again. His target crumpled beneath the relentless hail of fire, and straight away he switched his attention to another, the barrel of his sub-machine gun trailing smoke as he brought it to bear.

Carpenter could do no more here. The final assault on the compound was by now well under way, bright flashes illuminating the screen as RPG rounds exploded and tracer fire was spat in different directions.

Drake was beaten. He was outnumbered, outgunned and about to be overwhelmed. It was over.

Nonetheless, Carpenter intended to be far away from here by dawn. He could hear the distinctive thump of rotor blades as his chopper settled on the rooftop helipad, signalling that it was time to leave.

Spinning around in his chair, he removed a picture from the wall behind him to reveal a safe with an electronic keypad. Inputting his access code, he heard a faint hum as the bolts were withdrawn, then grabbed the handle and pulled the door open. Within the armoured box lay bundles of money in assorted denominations – $250,000 in total.

The first rule of any military engagement was to always have an exit strategy.

After transferring the better portion of the money into his leather briefcase, he snapped the safe closed once more, grabbed his case and rose from his chair.

'Spoils of war, Richard?' a voice asked mockingly.

Startled, Carpenter spun around to face the unexpected arrival. And just like that, he froze, rooted to the spot, his eyes wide and staring in absolute, uncomprehending shock.

'What's the matter?' Anya asked, her eyes pools of ice as she stared at him down the sights of her assault rifle. 'You don't look pleased to see me.'

Drake was in his own world now, aware of nothing except the weapon in his hands and the picture down the reflex sight. It was always like that in combat. Even surrounded by comrades, you were alone, fighting your own battle, concentrating on all the things you had to do to survive and keep going.

The bolt snapped back as he squeezed off another round, but didn't move forward to draw another into the breach. He turned the weapon on its side, seeing about twenty rounds remaining in the partially transparent magazine.

Normally he would have yelled out a warning to his companions, but he resisted the urge now. Nobody could cover him.

Instead he racked back the charging handle to

manually draw the next round into the breech. With luck it was just a defective round, or dust or grit might have fouled the moving parts.

Beside him, McKnight was firing in rapid bursts, her face streaked with dust as empty shell casings pattered to the ground at her feet. Keegan added his firepower to the desperate defence, and he even heard the crack of Crawford's side arm.

Drake was just bringing the newly cleared weapon up to aim when a burst of fire impacted the wall, tracing its way along until one of the rounds hit him on the left side of the chest, spinning him around and knocking him down. He hit the ground with bruising force, sharp rocks tearing his clothes and cutting his skin.

He recovered, rolled over and struggled up to his knees. Every breath brought a fresh stab of pain. Blood pounded in his ears.

Through the thudding of his heartbeat, he heard Keegan's voice. 'Ryan! You okay?'

It's nothing. The vest stopped it. You're alive – get up and fight. Get up now!

He had been hit by a ricochet, most of its kinetic energy already drained away by the time it found him.

Reaching out, he grabbed his fallen weapon and looked up just as a figure in dark military fatigues appeared in the smouldering gap left by the RPG. Without hesitation, Drake raised the sub-machine gun and emptied the last of his ammunition into his target.

He was about to move when something landed on the ground next to him with a heavy metallic *thunk*. Glancing down, he saw the round metal body of a fragmentation grenade lying a couple of yards away.

It was an M67, the standard frag grenade of the US

Army. It was lighter than the Vietnam-era M61 it had replaced, but more dangerous, with a casualty radius of up to 20 metres. No way could he get clear in time.

M67s have a standard-delay fuse of just over four seconds. Assuming roughly a second for it to fly through the air and land, plus another second for him to react, that gave him about two seconds to play with. Many soldiers 'cooked' grenades by pulling the pin and waiting a couple of seconds before throwing, but it took a brave man to hold a live grenade for more than a second or two in the heat of battle. So he had anywhere between zero and two seconds to do something.

Either way, he had no choice but to attempt what he did next. Throwing himself forward, he snatched up the device and hurled it back through the hole in the wall, flattening himself against the ground.

Half a second later the grenade detonated with a concussive boom loud enough to leave his ears ringing, followed by an agonised scream. Drake might have avoided the grenade's lethal hail of shrapnel, but its owner hadn't.

He could do no more here. He was out of ammunition.

'John, I'm out! Fall back!' Drake cried, heading towards McKnight, who was still snapping off rounds at the west wall.

Up on the parapet, Keegan was singing quietly under his breath even as the desperate firefight raged all around him.

'Get sixteen gamblers to carry my coffin, six pretty maidens to sing me a song.'

Spotting movement off to his right, he swung the P90

around and put down three rounds, scoring two hits, one of which was almost certainly fatal. If the bastards wanted him, they would pay a heavy price.

'Take me to the valley and lay soil o'er me.'

Shots tore through the parapet to his left, blasting apart the ancient mud bricks and showering him with dust. Homing in on the weapon's distinctive muzzle flare, Keegan took careful aim and squeezed the trigger.

He managed two shots before the firing pin hit an empty breech.

'Cos I'm a young cowboy and I know I done wrong.'

He saw the flash out of the corner of his eye, and the distinctive trail of exhaust smoke as the RPG sailed in gracefully towards him.

He had done what he could. Leaping down from the parapet, he landed and flattened himself on the ground just as the RPG round impacted. With a thunderous roar, the parapet on which he'd been standing disintegrated in a cloud of dust and smoke and flame.

'John! Are you all right?' Drake cried, half deaf from explosions and gunfire.

'Ask me in the morning.' Bruised and bleeding but still whole, Keegan scrambled to his feet and started towards Drake.

No sooner had he taken a step than something thumped hard into his back, knocking the wind from his lungs. He staggered forward a few more paces, still in shock, not realising he'd been hit. His legs gave way beneath him and he fell, only to be caught by Drake.

'Come on, mate! Move!' Drake yelled in his ear, dragging him over to Crawford who was still lying propped against the outer wall.

There was no recognition in the man's eyes as Drake approached. They were glassy and staring, seeing

471

nothing. His arms hung limp by his sides, one hand still clutching his automatic.

He was gone.

Cursing himself for abandoning the critically wounded man, Drake glanced up as McKnight rushed over, throwing aside her empty P90.

'What happened?' she asked, looking down at Keegan.

'He took a round through the chest.' The grave tone of Drake's voice was more chilling than Keegan's groans of pain and ragged breathing. 'Crawford's dead.'

McKnight glanced at the agent slumped against the wall, tears in her eyes.

Drake's attention, however, was focused on those who were still living. Gently he laid his friend down and tore his shirt open to examine the injury. The AK round had passed straight through him. Frothy blood was leaking from the exit wound on his chest.

They had no medical gear with them, particularly the chest-draining kit that he so desperately needed. Each breath was filling Keegan's chest cavity with air, crushing his lungs under the pressure.

He was finished, and they both knew it.

'How am I doing?' Keegan asked, struggling to draw breath. 'No . . . no bullshit.'

Drake gripped his hand, obeying the older man's wish. He wouldn't lie to him now. 'You're lung-shot, mate. I'm sorry. There's nothing I can do.'

He saw a pained, grim smile. 'Figured as much.'

Reaching into his torn, bloodstained shirt, Keegan's trembling hand found the lucky charm necklace he always wore. It had kept him safe all this time, but it seemed even his luck had finally run out.

'It's okay, man,' he whispered. 'I'm . . . ready.'

His eyes were growing dim and unfocused. With one

472

last convulsive breath, his body shuddered and lay still, his unseeing eyes still staring at Drake.

Drake bowed his head in grief, unable to look at him. Another good man dead.

His grief was short-lived. A faint whoosh beyond the compound's shattered walls announced the launch of another RPG.

In a final desperate act, Drake reached for McKnight, trying to shield her with his body as the wall beside him erupted in a storm of smoke and masonry.

Chapter 54

For several seconds, neither of them spoke a word or moved a muscle. They both stood there on opposite sides of the room, staring at each other. It was the first time Carpenter had laid eyes on Anya in almost a decade.

She hadn't changed much in that time. Standing tall and unbowed, she seemed to possess the same subtle grace and poise that had so caught his attention the first time he had met her.

Her hair was shorter than he remembered, her skin a little more tanned from long exposure to the sun. But her eyes remained the same. Those vivid, intense, remorseless eyes were now locked with his.

Years of pent-up rage and hatred and pain burned behind them.

'I like what you have done with the place, Richard,' Anya remarked, glancing at their opulent surroundings. 'It is . . . more comfortable than the last time I was here.'

Carpenter winced inwardly. He knew exactly what she was referring to, knew there were some things she could never put behind her. And he was the cause of it.

'How did you get in?' he asked. He couldn't help it. He had to know.

She flashed a faint, knowing smile. 'With your training, Richard. You taught me everything I know, remember?'

Yes, he did remember. How could he ever forget? He

had taught her to use everything at her disposal to complete her mission, how to shut out pain and weakness and fear, how to kill without hesitation. He had helped mould her into the perfect soldier. And now here she was with a gun trained on him.

'What do you want?'

'What do I want?' she repeated, taking another step towards him. 'Twenty years of my life I sacrificed for you. I want to take back what you took from me.'

Resisting the urge to swallow, Carpenter glanced down at the briefcase lying on his desk. 'If this is about money . . .'

'It was always about money with you, Richard,' she said, glaring at him with cold fury. 'That was your problem – you were willing to give up everything and everyone for it. And believe me, you will be punished for that. But first I want you to get on your radio.'

Struggling to see through eyes clogged with blood and dust, Drake rolled over and heaved himself slowly up from the ground. Every bone and muscle in his body blazed with agony.

He coughed, trying to draw breath. Warm air laden with dust and smoke filled his lungs, choking him.

Wiping his eyes, he looked over at McKnight. She was lying half buried by rubble from the collapsed wall, her eyes closed. He couldn't tell if she was breathing or not.

With the world lurching sickeningly in and out of focus, he tried to reach out to her, tried to feel for a pulse.

'She can't hear you now, man,' a low, menacing South African voice said.

Crawford's pistol was still lying in the dead man's lap. Summoning up his waning strength, Drake snatched it up, bringing the weapon to bear on Vermaak.

It was a feeble effort, and easily blocked with a well-placed kick that sent the weapon flying out of his grasp. A second kick to the face knocked Drake sprawling, stars dancing across his vision while blood pounded in his ears.

His head lolled to the side, and through blurry eyes he saw something protruding from the ground beside him. A twisted length of metal rod, perhaps once part of the wall that had so recently been demolished.

Piet Vermaak stared down at the injured man, eyes glittering with malice and hatred. Behind him, two other Horizon operatives stood with their weapons at the ready, silhouetted by the flickering orange glow of the burning chopper.

Suddenly his eyes fastened onto the burned and crumpled folder shoved down the front of Drake's shirt. It didn't take him long to put the pieces together.

'What do we have here?' Throwing his AK-47 aside, he knelt down and snatched the folder from its hiding place, easily defeating Drake's attempts to hold on to it.

As he leafed through the pages, a smile spread over Vermaak's face. 'This is what you risked everything for, man. A few burned pieces of paper.'

But no sooner had he spoken than his radio crackled into life, Carpenter's grainy voice filtering over the airwaves. 'Strike team, what's your sit rep?'

Still smiling, Vermaak hit his transmitter. 'We have it all. Drake, and the evidence. I'm about to get rid of both.'

'Negative. Stand down,' Carpenter ordered. 'Fall back to the vehicles and get out of there.'

The smile vanished then. 'Say again? We have Drake. It's over.'

'I said stand down,' Carpenter repeated. Was his voice trembling? 'Do not touch Drake. Acknowledge my last.'

Drake wasn't listening. All his attention was focused on that shard of metal protruding from the ground. With desperate, feeble strength, he started to crawl towards it, inch by painful inch, his hands clawing at soil and rubble.

Almost there. He could almost reach it.

After a moment of indecision, Vermaak shook his head. He hadn't come this far, hadn't lost all these operatives, to turn tail and run now. Reaching up, he switched off his radio and glanced at his two companions.

'There were no survivors tonight. Understand?'

Neither man said a word. Both knew better than to argue with him.

Satisfied, he turned his attention back to Drake. But the brief hesitation had bought him a few precious seconds.

As Vermaak took a step towards him, Drake closed his fingers around the metal rod, yanked it from the ground and with a primal snarl of hatred, twisted around and plunged it into the man's thigh with all the force he could command. He felt the taut resistance of skin and flesh, felt the ragged end tear and cleave its way through thick muscle.

Growling in pain, Vermaak responded with a kick to Drake's injured ribs. Agony exploded through him and he fell backwards, pain and darkness threatening to overwhelm him.

He was finished. He coughed, blood streaking the ground beneath him. All he could see were McKnight's eyes, wide and staring.

Nearby, Vermaak yanked the rod from his leg and threw it aside. Blood flowed down his combat trousers, gleaming in the firelight, but he barely seemed to notice. He was no stranger to pain. This wasn't enough to stop him.

'Persistent little fuck, aren't you?'

Drawing his side arm, Vermaak took a step towards his helpless adversary, kicked him over and knelt down atop him, forcing a knee into his throat. He wanted the man to see his death coming.

'You should have gone home when you had the chance, Drake.'

He smiled with malicious hatred as he raised the automatic.

Suddenly, a volley of shots rang out behind him, accompanied by the dull thumps of bodies hitting the ground.

Teeth clenched in anger, Vermaak whirled to face this unexpected threat, bringing the weapon around at the same moment.

Shrouded in pain and darkness, Drake had no idea what was happening. All he could hear was gunfire. And dimly he was aware of Vermaak turning towards it.

'Ryan . . .' a weak voice called out.

Turning his head with great effort, he saw McKnight staring at him. She was alive, and with a trembling hand she had managed to push Crawford's side arm across the ground to him.

Groping out, as much from instinct as rational thought, Drake felt his fingers close around the butt of the gun. His heart was pounding, adrenalin surging through his veins. Images of Keegan, of Frost and Mitchell and Anya and Crawford, whirled through his mind as he raised the weapon up, jammed it against Vermaak's thick muscular neck and fired.

The report of the shot was muffled by human flesh.

Drake heard only a dull pop, and saw a faint cloud of red mist ejected from the other side of the man's neck.

Vermaak's body went rigid as if hit by lightning. Then, slowly, he turned to look at Drake, his eyes holding no malice or hatred now; only utter shock.

He opened his mouth as if to speak, blood dripping from one corner, but only succeeded in making a strangled, gurgling moan. Then the shock faded from his eyes, the rigid body went limp and he pitched sideways with an exhausted groan, landing in a heap.

One hand was still outstretched, trying to grasp the burned and torn folder that held the ruin of one man and the salvation of another.

Managing to prop himself up on one arm, Drake surveyed the scene. The two operatives who had accompanied Vermaak were lying in crumpled heaps with their blood staining the ground.

'I couldn't do it, Ryan,' a familiar voice said.

Drake's head snapped around.

Cunningham was standing at one of the holes blasted in the outer wall, an AK-47 in his arms. Smoke still trailed from the barrel.

'I couldn't let them kill you.' The look in his eyes was one of absolute grief and guilt as he surveyed the carnage within the compound. 'You were right. That was a sacrifice I wasn't prepared to make.'

Drake glanced down at the weapon in his hands. The slide had flown back to reveal an empty breech. He had used the last round on Vermaak.

'This doesn't change a thing,' he warned his former friend. 'It doesn't undo what you did, Matt.'

Cunningham swallowed, but nodded. 'I know. But maybe it's a start.'

He made to turn away, but hesitated, looking back over his shoulder.

'I'll see you around.'

With that, he turned and vanished like a ghost into the darkness.

Chapter 55

She could feel Carpenter increasing the pressure, could feel his hands pressing down on her with murderous strength, forcing her head beneath the surface once more. This time she knew he wouldn't release her until it was over.

And just like that, something snapped inside her. Months of pain and resentment and humiliation finally broke free of the tenuous control she had maintained all this time.

Summoning whatever strength she had left, she drove her right knee up between his legs. She was half blinded by the muddy water but her aim was true, and she felt the satisfying impact as her knee connected with his groin.

Carpenter let out a gasp of pain, and for a brief moment his grip slackened. That was her chance. Throwing another punch that connected flush with his jaw and jarred her arm, she managed to stun him long enough to shove him sideways, using her leg to kick him off her.

She was on top of him in a heartbeat, and almost before she knew what was happening she had unsheathed his knife and

481

pressed it against his throat. Now she was the one with murder in her eyes.

For a long moment they remained frozen like that, their eyes locked, rain sluicing down on them both. Carpenter was staring at her, but she didn't see the usual disdain or resentment in him now.

For the first time she saw fear, and some part of her relished it.

Just as Luka had said, Carpenter had been trying to make her snap. Well, today he had finally succeeded and this was the result. It was as if another person had taken over her. She ached to kill him, to revisit on him all the months of torment he had inflicted on her.

'I will show . . . no mercy,' she hissed, raising the knife above her head and plunging it down with all the strength she could summon, driving the blade into the muddy ground only inches from his head.

'Remember this,' she said, releasing her grip on him. 'Remember what I could have done to you.'

'I did what you asked.' Carpenter surveyed Anya across his desk. 'It's over.'

She remained unmoved by his attempt at supplication. 'No. It's not over, Richard. Not yet.'

She looked around, slowly surveying the plush office; the expensive furniture, the books, the computers, the big floor-to-ceiling windows and the expansive view beyond. Spoils of war.

'I know what you did,' she said, her voice low and quiet now. 'Twenty years ago. I know it was you who sold us out.' Seeing the look in his eyes, she smiled in satisfaction. 'You thought your dirty little secret would never come out? You ought to choose your business partners more carefully. My captors at Khatyrgan prison took great pleasure in telling me all about the deal you two struck. They even played me a recording of the conversation.

'We were loyal to you. We risked our lives for you, and you sold us out for a few extra zeros in your bank account. And when I made it home, like the coward you were, you blamed the whole thing on Luka. He was my brother in arms. He was a friend, a father, and you sent me to kill him.'

She looked at him again, and for a moment the mask slipped aside. He saw the depth of the hurt and betrayal that still lingered in her soul.

'He took it, Richard. He took the blame, for me. He let me kill him to save my life. He was a better man than you could ever be.'

He took a step towards her, hands raised. 'Anya, what happened was—'

'Don't,' she warned, raising her weapon. She regarded him with a look of utter contempt. 'You disgust me, Richard. You're a coward and a liar. You had no right to ever call yourself a soldier. In fact, the only reason you are still alive is because I want something from you – a name.'

He frowned. 'Whose name?'

'The Russian you sold me out to.'

'Anya, you don't understand. This . . . this is bigger than you or me. There was more at stake . . .'

Jerking the weapon left, she squeezed a single shot that tore into his office chair, blasting away leather padding and fragments of wood. She made a show of training the weapon on him, aiming low, not to kill but to maim. He got the message.

Sighing, he at last gave her the name she wanted.

Straight away the colour drained from her face, and she felt her heart begin to pound. He hadn't lied when he said this was bigger than both of them. What would a man like that want with her?

'Whatever they paid you, I hope it was worth it,' she said at last.

He knew what was coming, knew any attempt to placate her would be futile. Reaching for the glass of whisky on his desk, he took a long slow drink, savouring the taste. He knew it would be his last.

'You still don't get it, do you?' he said, making no effort to conceal his hatred now. 'You were expendable, Anya. People like you are always expendable.'

Anya realised now that he would never understand the depths of his crimes. He had betrayed people willing to fight and die for him; he had used them up and thrown them away when they had served his purpose. And she had allowed herself to be part of it.

Just for a moment she thought of Luka's final words to her, right before she took his life.

It's all right, don't be afraid. You're doing what you must, proving your loyalty. You were always the best of us. Remember that.

But he'd been wrong. Luka had been the best of them, not her. He had been willing to sacrifice his life, to destroy the trust and loyalty she had always felt towards him, to see his memory tarnished and his accomplishments forgotten.

And he had done all of it for her. Taking careful aim, she squeezed off another shot. The round struck Carpenter on the right side of the chest with such force that he was knocked backward, collapsing onto the thick carpet with a muted thud. He coughed, trying to draw

484

breath, but it felt like a lead weight was pressing down on his chest, crushing the life from him. Foamy blood oozed from the hole in his chest.

Anya walked forward to look at him as he tried pathetically to rise. 'The air from your punctured lung is escaping into your chest cavity. Every breath you take is killing you. But you might survive yet, if someone can get to you and insert a chest drain in time.'

In desperation, he looked up at his desk, at the phone sitting on the polished surface that could summon a dozen of his operatives into the room. Anya followed his line of sight and guessed his thoughts.

She knelt down, eyes still on him as he started to crawl towards his desk. 'You can make it, but you must hurry. You're haemorrhaging internally,' she informed him. 'Your lungs are collapsing. By my guess, you have about sixty seconds to live.'

Slowly, painfully, inch by inch, he crawled forward. He coughed, blood staining the carpet. His limbs numb as his consciousness started to fail.

'Come on, you can do better than that,' she taunted. 'If you won't fight for your own pathetic life, how do you expect others to fight for you?'

He reached out for his padded leather chair, hand flailing. He almost managed to pull himself up before his waning strength failed him and he collapsed against it with a ragged, defeated sigh.

'That's what I thought,' Anya concluded.

The old man coughed, spraying frothy blood on the carpet. His vision was growing dim as his body surrendered to the enveloping darkness.

'That was the one thing you never understood about

our work. Sooner or later, everyone is expendable.' She rose to her feet and looked down at him with a mixture of pity and contempt. 'You've just pissed yourself, Richard.'

With a final strangled gasp, he convulsed and then lay still.

Her work done, she turned and strode out of the room. She left the briefcase where it was – it was blood money and she had no interest in it.

The chopper was still waiting patiently, engines idling, when Anya pushed open the door and strode out onto the roof, assault rifle in hand.

For a few moments, the pilot merely stared her, perplexed as to what this woman was doing on the roof when he had been ordered only to pick up Carpenter.

Moving with long confident strides, she walked over to the cockpit window as if to have a word with him, then calmly raised her weapon and levelled it at his head. There was little need to explain herself. She preferred to let the gun do the talking.

Thirty seconds later she was strapped into the co-pilot's chair, keeping her new friend covered while he spun up the engines and quickly ran through his pre-flight checks.

She should have felt elated as they lifted off and the Horizon compound slowly receded beneath them, yet her mind remained troubled. She had won a victory today, but a small one. If Carpenter was right, there remained a far larger war to fight.

But she was a soldier. No matter what else they had tried to make her, she was a soldier. Fighting wars was the only thing she had ever been good at.

And she would give them a war unlike any they had ever known.

Part Five

Reconciliation

'A war begun for no wise purpose, carried on with a strange mixture of rashness and timidity, brought to a close after suffering and disaster, without much glory attached either to the government which directed, or the great body of troops which waged it. Not one benefit, political or military, was acquired with this war.'
– Reverend G.R. Gleig, British Army chaplain, speaking of Afghanistan in 1843

Chapter 56

'Well, I think that just about covers it,' Franklin said, closing the thick file that represented Drake's final report. The two men had been in a closed meeting in the Special Activities Division leader's office for the past two hours, during which Drake had done most of the talking.

Laying the folder aside, Franklin surveyed his friend across the desk.

Two weeks of rest and rehabilitation had done much to restore Drake's health, though it was clear he had taken a great deal of punishment. His ribs were mending well, and his many cuts, bruises and gashes were also much improved, but some wounds went deeper than that.

He had lost something out there; something of great value. Franklin could see it in his eyes.

'Naturally you're going to be asked to testify in front of Congress,' he warned. 'They're already kicking up a real shit storm about this.'

Much of Mitchell's evidence had been destroyed in the desperate battle outside Kabul, but what remained had been more than enough to prompt a full Congressional hearing – behind closed doors, of course. Horizon's activities worldwide had been suspended pending the results of the investigation.

Carpenter himself, however, was unable to appear before Congress. He had been found dead in his office in Kabul, killed by a single gunshot to the chest.

Frost had also been recovered from the building, remaining holed up in the impregnable security room while she waited for an Agency assault team to retrieve her. The building's formidable security systems had presented no threat after she disabled them, though she had been unable to explain what had happened to Carpenter. All security camera footage of her escape from the holding cells, as well as his death, had been conveniently lost.

'Better late than never, eh?' Drake remarked cynically.

'That's the way things work on the Hill. Fix the barn door when there are enough people around to see you do it, and let the horses take care of themselves.' Franklin sighed and rose up from behind his desk, moving stiffly as his injured back protested. 'You did a hell of a job out there, Ryan. Nobody could have asked more of you.'

Drake said nothing as he stood up. Perhaps nobody could have asked more of him, but Keegan, Crawford and Mitchell were still dead. They might not have asked for it, but they deserved more from him.

Rounding the desk, Franklin laid a hand on his shoulder. 'For what it's worth, I'm sorry about Keegan. He was a good man.'

Drake looked his friend in the eye. Whatever water had passed under the bridge for both of them, he meant what he said.

'Yeah. He was,' Drake agreed.

Franklin glanced away for a moment. 'Listen, if you need time off, take as long as you want. The same goes for Frost. You both earned it.'

Hearing Frost's name brought a pang of guilt. The young woman had learned of Keegan's death only after being retrieved from Horizon's headquarters building, and he knew it had hit her hard. She had barely spoken to him or anyone else since their return to Washington.

Drake shook his head. 'Thanks, but I've rested enough.'

The prospect of sitting alone in his house with nothing to do but brood on his mistakes didn't sit well with him. Here at least he could be useful.

Today, however, the paperwork could wait. He had something far more important to attend to.

Keira Frost sighed as she pulled the bike into her driveway and killed the engine. She had been out for most of the day, wandering the streets of DC without really seeing anything, watching the tourists gawking at landmarks, before riding down the I95 to the coast and back.

It was a route she was quite familiar with, and normally enjoyed, but not today. She felt as if all the life and energy had been sucked out of her. Nothing held her interest, nothing gave her enjoyment any longer.

Pulling off her helmet, she frowned, suddenly wary. She could hear the distinctive tap of a hammer against metal. It was coming from her garage.

Opening the storage compartment beneath the seat on her bike, she removed the Smith & Wesson .38 revolver she always kept there. Unlike automatics, revolvers could be kept loaded for long periods without any maintenance, making them ideal as backup weapons.

Checking that all six chambers were loaded, she advanced towards her garage, keeping the weapon low. The banging continued. Someone was definitely in there, and now that she was closer, she could see that the padlock on the door had been unlocked.

If someone was trying to steal her car, they were in for a disappointment. The damn thing hadn't run since the day she brought it home and dismantled the engine.

Frost backed up against the wall, taking a couple of deep breaths to get more oxygen in her bloodstream. Then, cocking the revolver, she gripped the edge of the door and hauled it open.

'What the hell?' she gasped.

Glancing up from the engine bay of her Ford Mustang, Drake held up his oil-covered hands in mock surrender.

'I know you weren't happy with your raise this year, but that's a bit extreme, don't you think?'

Frost lowered the gun, feeling faintly ridiculous with it in her bike leathers.

'Ryan, what the fuck are you doing in my garage?'

'Working.' Straightening up, Drake gestured to the car's engine bay. When she'd left this morning it had been a confusing mess of disconnected pipes, valves, wires, radiators, cylinders and countless other components she didn't understand.

But now, to her disbelief, it appeared whole and complete. The engine block had been reassembled, the cylinders all put in place, the spark plugs all connected. All the replacement parts she had bought months earlier and almost given up on ever being used were now installed, gleaming in the overhead light.

'You can't be serious,' she said, her mouth almost hanging open in shock.

He must have been working at it all day long. She'd had no idea he even knew about engines.

'My dad was mad about cars. Every weekend he'd be out in the garage taking engines apart, and making me help.' He shrugged, wiping his hands on his already filthy T-shirt. 'Believe it or not, I learned a thing or two.'

'Does it work?'

Smiling, Drake reached into his pocket and tossed her a set of keys. 'Only one way to find out, Keira.'

Hardly daring to hope, she opened the door, settled herself in the driver's seat and put the key in the ignition. The interior smelled just the same as the day she'd bought it; that curious combination of old leather, oil, dust and machinery.

Closing her eyes for a moment, she turned the key.

The starter motor whined, the engine turned over once, twice, caught and faltered for a moment, then suddenly burst into life with a deep, throaty roar that shook the entire vehicle.

'Give it some power,' Drake advised.

Hardly able to believe it, Frost pressed her foot down. The big V8 engine growled with increased power, rough and unsteady for several seconds, then gradually settling down to a smoother, more controlled roar.

When at last she shut it down and stepped out, her ears were ringing and she was beaming in delight.

'It'll probably sound like a dog for the first hundred miles or so,' he warned, arms folded. 'The engine will need some time to run in, but—'

He was interrupted when the young woman suddenly threw her arms around him and pulled him close in a fierce, heartfelt embrace. Drake fell silent and just held her. For the first time in a long time, he felt as though he had done something good.

When at last she pulled away, she wiped her eyes as if the engine smoke had irritated them. 'I know why you did this, Ryan,' she said, running her hand along the car chassis. 'Thank you.'

'It was long overdue,' he said, then gestured to the waiting car. 'So, she's all ready to drive. Where do you want to go?'

495

The young woman looked up at him. 'Same place you do.'

Located on the north wall of the CIA's Original Headquarters Building, the Memorial Wall was a simple but poignant tribute to Agency employees who had died in the line of service, each one represented by a simple star carved into the stone.

A few weeks ago there had been eighty-five stars. Now, three new ones had been added. And beneath the carved monument, framed by stainless steel and set within inch-thick glass protection, was the Book of Honour, containing as many of the names of the fallen as were allowed. Some would for ever remain unknown.

Leaning a little closer, Drake could make out the three new entries.

- *2008 – Harrison T. Mitchell*
- *2008 – David S. Crawford*
- *2008 – John J. Keegan*

'It's funny,' Frost remarked, her voice hushed and soft. 'All the time I worked with him, I never even knew he had a middle name.'

That was too much for her. Drake heard a muffled sob, and turned to see her with one hand covering her mouth, her eyes red and streaming.

She had to let it out.

He could feel his own eyes stinging as he pulled her close, holding her in silence while she gave in to it at last.

Epilogue

It was a warm, balmy evening not unlike the one when this had all started. Drake was sitting on his back doorstep with a glass of whisky in his hand, staring up at the sunset-tinged clouds without really seeing anything. The sounds of car engines, television sets, stereos and children playing were a familiar, comforting background drone.

The sounds of normal, everyday life going on around him. Around him, but not with him.

He wasn't sure whether he should have felt grief, sadness, anger or something else, but no emotions stirred in him. After everything that had happened, he just felt drained and empty.

He took another sip of whisky. He might have steered away from it lately, but today was an exception.

He almost didn't bother to look when his cellphone started ringing, but habit eventually won out. It wasn't in his nature to leave a ringing phone unanswered.

The call was from a withheld number.

Frowning, he answered it, bracing himself for a tele-marketing call.

'Yeah?'

'Ryan.'

With that single word, everything changed. Laying

down his drink, he sat up straighter, feeling his heart beating fast and urgent.

'Anya.'

'I can't stay on the line for long. They'll try to trace it.'

'What do you want?'

'To say thank you, for everything you did,' she said. 'And to say that I am sorry for what happened to your friends. It's hard to lose people you care about.'

Drake closed his eyes at the sudden pang of sadness and longing her words evoked. 'Yes, it is,' he agreed. 'I heard about Carpenter. I suppose I have you to thank for that?'

'He got what he deserved,' she confirmed. She said nothing for the next few seconds, and he began to wonder if she was still there. 'Ryan, I . . .'

She trailed off, either unwilling or unable to go on.

Drake held the phone a little closer. 'What is it?'

He heard a sigh, faint but audible nonetheless. The sigh of someone facing up to a truth they have tried not to acknowledge. 'It is hard to lose people we care about,' she repeated. 'I . . . I am glad I didn't lose you.'

Drake exhaled, raising his eyes towards the sky again. He wondered where she was at that moment, whether she was watching that same sunset.

'Will I ever see you again?'

Silence greeted him. Strained, anxious, desperate. A silence aching to be filled. An admission desperate to be made.

'Goodbye, Ryan,' she said at last.

She hadn't said it because she couldn't.

She didn't have to.

'Oh, and one more thing,' she added. 'You have a visitor.'

With that, the line went dead. And sure enough, moments later he heard a knock at the front door.

'I don't believe it.'

She had to be close. Setting his glass down, he stood up and looked around, thinking for one wild moment that he could catch up to her before she left the area, find her somehow and say the things she hadn't been able to.

And then, as soon as it came, the thought vanished. Anya wouldn't be found unless she wanted to be. That was the way it had always been with her, and always would be. And for today at least, it was enough.

He smiled a little as he looked up at the sunset-tinged clouds. He didn't know what the future held for either of them, but he sensed, somehow, that he hadn't seen the last of her.

The knocking was repeated, a little louder now. Someone was waiting for him.

Hurrying through his disorganised house, he unlatched the front door, gripped the handle and pulled it open.

It was no random visitor who had stopped by tonight.

Standing on his doorstep was Samantha McKnight.

Like him, she had been through the mill during their time in Afghanistan. The final desperate stand in that ruined compound had left her with several fractured bones and various other injuries. However, a couple of weeks of rest and recuperation had done a lot to restore her health.

She looked now much the same as when they had first met. Bright, confident and, much as it hadn't escaped his notice first time around, attractive.

They had parted company several days after the mission's end, when Drake was well enough to fly back to Langley for debriefing. Not being a member of his team, she had remained behind, though they had both agreed to look each other up the next time they were in their respective countries.

It had seemed like an empty promise at the time, but even then he had caught himself hoping it wasn't. And now here she was, standing mere feet from him.

'You're a long way from Kabul,' he observed.

'I guess I was ready for a change of scenery.' McKnight smiled – that same smile which had so caught his attention the first time they met – then glanced over his shoulder. 'Well, aren't you going to invite me in, Ryan?'

Drake smiled. There was no need to ask – they both knew the answer.

Acknowledgements

Writing 'that difficult second book' is something a lot of authors seem to approach with thinly veiled trepidation, and so it was for me when I first sat down to tackle *Sacrifice*. It took about two chapters before I realised my fears were unfounded, and I can honestly say that this novel has been an absolute joy to work on, due in large part to the people I've been lucky enough to have around me.

My thanks as always go to my editors Kate Burke and Georgina Hawtrey-Woore at Century for their help in shaping this book (and for keeping it to a tolerable length!), my copy-editor Mary Chamberlain for her tireless work in stopping me from contradicting myself, and my agent Diane Banks, who has been my guide through the complex but ever-fascinating world of publishing.

I'd also like to thank my good friend William Wilson for his insights into the murky and often baffling world of military terminology, and for recounting his experiences while on deployment in Afghanistan. His stories of the problems, challenges and humour encountered by soldiers in the field were invaluable as I tried to do justice to that troubled but starkly beautiful country, and the brave men and women serving there.

Lastly, I will always be grateful to my wife Susan, and to all my friends and family for their tremendous support and encouragement. It means more than most of them will ever know.

dead
good

*For all of you who find
a crime story irresistible.*

Discover the very best crime and thriller books on our dedicated website – hand-picked by our editorial team so you have tailored recommendations to help you choose what to read next.

We'll introduce you to our favourite authors and the brightest new talent. Read exclusive interviews and specially commissioned features on everything from the best classic crime to our top ten TV detectives, join live webchats and speak to authors directly.

Plus our monthly book competition offers you the chance to win the latest crime fiction, and there are DVD box sets and digital devices to be won too.

Sign up for our newsletter at
www.deadgoodbooks.co.uk/signup

Join the conversation on: